D0710937

IF THOUGHTS COULD KILL . . .

David stood his ground. His mind, freed from whatever grip Voss had put upon it, flexed almost exultantly.

In the core of his brain he felt a point, a tiny mass of neurons that seemed to flex and pulse, a physical presence. Though neither painful nor even unpleasant, it was something new and it rocked him. He touched two fingers of each hand to his temples as if to contain it.

The Facility man froze. His face went dark with a rush of blood that drained immediately, leaving him yellowy as the wall behind him. His eyes dilated in surprise and then terror, and spittle bubbled on his lips. He tried to scream and made a croaking sound instead. David saw blood dribbling down his face.

As suddenly as it had flared, the image was swallowed into the point and the point winked out. David lowered his hands; they trembled and his face was hot.

Be sure to ask your bookseller for the Bantam Spectra horror titles you have missed:

The Amulet by A.R. Morlan
The Horror Club by Mark Morris
Blood of the Children by Alan Rodgers
Fire by Alan Rodgers
Night by Alan Rodgers
The Demon by Jeffrey Sackett
House Haunted by Al Sarrantonio
The Well by Mike Sirota
The Light At the End by John Skipp and Craig Spector
The Scream by John Skipp and Craig Spector
The Bridge by John Skipp and Craig Spector

BRAINSTORM

STEVEN M. KRAUZER

BANTAM BOOKS
NEW YORK · TORONTO · LONDON · SYDNEY · AUCKLAND

BRAINSTORM
A Bantam Spectra Book / September 1991

SPECTRA and the portrayal of a boxed ''s''
are trademarks of Bantam Books,
a division of Bantam Doubleday Dell Publishing Group, Inc.

All rights reserved.
Copyright © 1991 by Steven M. Krauzer.
Cover art copyright © 1991 by Lisa Falkenstern.

No part of this book may be reproduced or transmitted in any
form or by any means, electronic or mechanical, including
photocopying, recording, or by any information storage and
retrieval system, without permission in writing from the publisher.
For information address: Bantam Books.

ISBN 0-553-29377-X

Published simultaneously in the United States and Canada

*Bantam Books are published by Bantam Books, a division of Bantam
Doubleday Dell Publishing Group, Inc. Its trademark, consisting of
the words ''Bantam Books'' and the portrayal of a rooster, is Reg-
istered in U.S. Patent and Trademark Office and in other countries.
Marca Registrada. Bantam Books, 666 Fifth Avenue, New York, New
York 10103.*

PRINTED IN THE UNITED STATES OF AMERICA

RAD 0 9 8 7 6 5 4 3 2 1

For Dorrit

Grateful thanks to
Kristina Karasek, M.D.,
for technical counsel
and to
Marcia Karasek
for geographical research

BOOK
ONE

CHAPTER ONE

Davidd McKay knocked twice, waited, knocked three times more. The guy who opened the door was thin, with dark, styled hair and a sharp V-shaped chin that needed shaving. He looked down at David and said, "What the hell?"

David smiled pleasantly. "I'm looking for some action."

The guy wore pleated slacks and a silk shirt with the top two buttons undone to show several gold neck chains. David was dressed in jeans and a windbreaker over an "I ♥ NY" T-shirt. "Are you Vinnie?" David said, still smiling. "The man said ask for Vinnie."

"The *man*?"

"You know." David shrugged disarmingly. "I forget his name."

Vinnie glanced up and down the hall. The room was on the twelfth floor of a place called the Jamison Arms Hotel, overlooking Seventh Avenue a few blocks north of Times Square. From behind Vinnie came the clack of wooden chips and the sounds of men's voices.

"A gag, right?" Vinnie said.

"That's not it," David said reasonably. "I'd like to get into the game."

"How old are you, kid?"

"Eleven."

Vinnie toyed with the gold band of his Rolex. "This has been cute and all, but I got to be going. . . ."

David dug into the front pocket of his jeans, pulled out his money clip, and thumbed back the corners of the top bills to show Vinnie they were hundreds.

Vinnie gaped. David made a little gesture with the clip.

"Vinnie," David said, "can we talk about this inside?"

It turned out to be a suite, the front room bland and ordinary with a sofa and a couple of chairs, a writing desk bolted to the wall, paintings of sailboats and seascapes, and a TV showing Johnny Carson doing his monologue, the sound turned off. David heard Vinnie say in the next room, "He's got the dough. . . ." and someone interrupt, "You gone nuts, Vin?"

David went to the door and saw five men around the table and Vinnie leaning over it. David settled on a fat man in an impossibly garish Hawaiian shirt, a tentlike billowing swirl of flowers and tigers and tropical birds in the most vividly primary colors.

David said, "Nice shirt."

All six stared at him. David caught hints of amusement, though the fat man removed a cigar from his mouth and frowned. David advanced into the room. "I'm not saying it's loud," David went on, deadpan, "but it *could* use a volume control." He'd heard the line on some TV sitcom earlier that evening.

The fat man's frown dissolved, and he burst into laughter, the gaudy shirt flapping like a sail in a high wind. "You're okay, kid." The fat man gestured at an empty chair. "Take a pew." He had the most money, two ten-chip stacks of blacks and a scattering of yellows and reds, two thousand and change.

As David leaned over the vacant chair and put eight hundred-dollar bills on the green felt, a middle-aged black man studied him from across the table. "Where'd you get the money, kid?"

"Newspaper route," David said, grinning to let him know it was a joke. A lot of times it deflected further questions.

Another man chuckled. "Lay off the third degree." He was younger than the others, with a crew cut and bodybuilder muscles. He watched Vinnie replace David's money with chips, said, "He's got what it takes. No one under eighteen admitted unless accompanied by cash."

David quick-counted his chips. Vinnie had held back a hundred, the standard fee for the guy who organized the game, paid for the room, supplied the refreshments, and guaranteed no trouble from the hotel or the police.

"You want a couple of phone books, kid?" the black man offered in a wiseguy way.

"That'd be good," David said politely. "Thanks."

The bodybuilder smiled at David. "Get him a pillow, Vinnie."

Vinnie went into the bedroom, and David looked around. The remaining two players were a tall rugged-faced man in a western shirt, and a guy with a bald, sweaty head that reflected the glow of the lamp hanging above the middle of the table. The only other furniture was a low armchair and a countertop with whiskey bottles, glasses, ice chest, and a covered silver bowl. A woman in a short leather skirt and matching halter top studied David from the chair. David said, "Hello," and the woman said, "How you doing?"

"What's your name, kid?" the bodybuilder asked.

David thought the woman was pretty. " 'Kid' is okay."

"You on the lam, kid?" the black man said. "You steal someone's lunch money?"

David stared at the black man, met his eyes, and

smiled slightly, until the black man got a funny look and broke the gaze. The fat man said, "I like your style, kid." He offered his hand. "Call me Mike."

David shook with him. "Pleased to meet you, Mike."

Vinnie returned with two pillows and stacked them on the chair. Atop them David was high enough to see the action and to deal when it came around to him. "Ante twenty-five?" David asked.

The black man regarded him sourly. "Kindergarten is in session, boys." He looked around the table. "Is this weird?"

"Hell no." Mike began to deal. "This is New York."

The game was five-card stud, and soon after David sat down, the table's luck began to swing from Mike to the black, whose name was Packard. The bodybuilder, Jo-Jo, managed to rake a pot every once in a while and hold about even, but the cowboy was squeezed out in three hands, and a half hour later the nervous bald guy went all-in on two high pairs and lost to Packard's three treys.

David's cards were miserable, but he had learned that luck ran in streaks, and on most deals he managed to limit his loss to his ante. Once he stayed in for four cards with a pair of aces wired, then had to drop when Packard filled a straight on the last round. Packard enjoyed taking his money, though Mike and Jo-Jo had by then accepted the idea of him at the table. David won three small pots and dropped out of a larger one, bluffing two queens as three until Mike pulled a legitimate triple sixes. After that the cards turned stone-cold once more; David folded eleven deals in a row, his stack of chips shrinking at twenty-five dollars a pop.

It was past two-thirty in the morning when Packard raked in the last of David's seven hundred.

"You play a decent game, kid, I'll give you that," the black man said. "Better luck next time."

"I've got more money." David didn't like the way he sounded: petulant, a little whiny, like a kid. He slid off the pillows. "I'll be right back."

"Let's break," Mike said, pushing his bulk from the table.

"When I'm running hot," Packard complained.

"Aw, find something to do," Jo-Jo said, waving in the direction of the pretty woman in the armchair.

David went into the bathroom and splashed cold water on his face. His reflection in the mirror was red-eyed from weariness and Mike's cigar smoke, but he felt mostly okay, considering. He shouldn't have let Packard get his goat, though, and it was dumb to tell them he was still in before giving it some thought. He considered quitting anyway; he was breaking a lot of rules if he didn't—bucking a streak, letting another player irritate him, and worst of all, risking his safe-money. The idea of going broke scared him plenty.

"So," he said to the mirror, "you better not." If the cards changed, he knew he could take Packard. *You're not after Packard,* he reminded himself. *This is about money—anyone's money.*

There were other good reasons to stick it out. It was hard enough to find a game, and even when he did, for each one he could talk his way into, there were two where he was turned away.

Also he couldn't stay in New York after this night. That was another rule: He always got out of town afterward, because just by playing he left a trail; win or lose, they'd talk about him, Vinnie and the girl and the other players, and you never knew who might hear and put him together with the story.

David doused his face with another double hand-ful of cold water. "Think like a winner," he said aloud. "And goddammit, concentrate." He grinned;

after all, he *was* a kid, and it tickled him to say a swearword.

"Doing okay, kid?" Mike poured whiskey over ice.

David shut the bathroom door behind him. "Fine, Mike."

"You want a Coke?"

"Thanks."

"What's yours, Jo-Jo?" Mike had been drinking steadily, and his voice had taken on the slightest bit of slur.

"Club soda," Jo-Jo said. He slapped his flat stomach. "My body is my temple."

David went on to the front room. Vinnie was slumped before the television watching a black-and-white movie, the sound turned up to a barely audible level. "I need some more chips, Vinnie," David said.

"Hold on a sec," Vinnie said, staring at the screen.

David recognized the picture: *The Maltese Falcon*, the scene near the beginning where Sam Spade is telling the woman that his partner has been murdered. "She's the one who killed him," David said. "You're supposed to think it's someone else, but at the end you find out it was her."

Vinnie looked up at him. "Thanks, kid," he said. "I appreciate you telling me that." He hoisted himself from the chair. "Whaddaya got?"

David dug out the money clip. "Six hundred and twenty. Make it six even."

Vinnie held out a hand palm-up. "Fork it over."

Mike was pouring David's Coke when the bedroom door opened. The woman came out smoking a cigarette and took her place in the armchair. Packard emerged a moment later, went to the counter, and took the lid off the silver bowl. "You're some piece, Francie, I will say that." Packard looked around and winked at Mike and Jo-Jo and Vinnie.

"Sorry I can't return the compliment." Francie

blew smoke in David's direction. "Kid there probably's got more horsepower than you."

Packard's dark face purpled. He turned, took a step toward her. Vinnie moved quickly between them, said, "Chill out."

Packard hesitated. David sensed he wouldn't push it.

"Finish what you were doing," Vinnie said.

Packard turned back to the counter, took a folder of cigarette papers and a baggy from the bowl. Mike brought David his Coke and sat down next to Jo-Jo. Packard began to roll a joint.

David scanned the piles. Jo-Jo was down to a hundred or so less than David's six hundred, while Mike had stayed about even. Mike continued to act friendly toward him, though David had seen drink ring changes in good fellowship before.

Packard was up over two thousand, including most of David's seven hundred, but Francie's wisecrack had made him mad again, and David expected he'd become the object of the anger. That was okay; it might turn Packard reckless. David could read Packard, he was certain he could, and all he needed now were cards worth pushing.

Packard sat down, lit the joint, and drew in hard, a half inch of the thin tip glowing and then dimming into ash. He threw his head back and closed his eyes, held the position for a half minute like he wanted them all to look at him, and finally expelled a big cloud of gray smoke toward the ceiling. He cradled the joint in the ashtray next to Mike's cigar, picked up the deck, and said, "Let's play poker, girls." He was talking to them all, but he was looking at David.

The cards began coming after the break, and David bet them hard. On two hands in a row, he raised a hundred on a low pair and drove the others out. He passed a bust, and on the next deal Mike went two black chips on four spades showing. David called the flush bluff with two kings and raked in over five hundred.

He folded five successive middling hands and watched Jo-Jo's pile go down. Packard was dealing when David caught eights against Jo-Jo's ace up-card. Mike and Packard dropped, and neither David nor Jo-Jo improved on the rest of the up-cards.

"My aces are a lock," Jo-Jo said. He counted his chips, then shoved them into the center of the table. "Three hundred—all in."

David stared at him for a good half minute. He was growing more tired, and that made even Jo-Jo harder to read. He didn't have the ace under, David *knew* he didn't—or did he merely want to believe? If he won this hand, he'd be about even on the night, and that was better than losing, but still it wasn't good enough. He had to leave town with as much money as possible. . . .

His attention was drifting. It was past five in the morning, and he was tired as any kid would be at that hour even if he had slept until noon the previous day and taken a nap after supper, but dammit, his concentration was going down the drain.

Jo-Jo peeked at his hole-card, and David stared hard at him. David drew breath and palmed three blacks, threw them in, said, "Call." He flipped his eight to show the pair. "Aces win." He waited.

Jo-Jo gazed at him neutrally, then smiled. He turned his card—a seven. "Except I don't have them," he said.

"You're good, kid," Francie said. She had come over to stand behind him.

Jo-Jo shook hands around and wished everyone luck. To David he murmured, "Take 'em, kid." Jo-Jo said good night and went out.

"Down to three." Vinnie stretched elaborately. "Call it a night?" he suggested.

"Lucky guess," Packard said to David, ignoring Vinnie.

"Jo-Jo sure had me convinced," Mike agreed, his face screwed up in half-drunken bewilderment that could have been funny.

"Getting late," Vinnie said. No one paid any attention.

"You want to try me on, kid?" Packard grinned crookedly.

Packard had smoked one joint and half of another; maybe that was what made him hard to read. But he was still showing, not so clearly but maybe clear enough, and there was no telling when David would have another chance.

"Your deal," David said to Mike.

Packard turned his nasty smile on Vinnie. "Go watch another picture," he said. Vinnie went into the other room, and they heard the TV come on again.

"Good luck, kid." Mike shuffled the cards.

"He'll need it," Packard said.

It was the smoke, David thought, the cigar's reek mixed with the sweet acrid smell of the marijuana. He felt light-headed and wondered if he could be stoned. Whatever the cause, he was fogging up, and his time was running out.

He stayed even for another half-dozen hands, winning one moderate pot and taking the antes with an obvious pair of tens in another. On Packard's next deal David almost threw in his cards. Something made him look again: He had misread one as a six, but now he saw he held a pair of nines, against Mike's jack and Packard's queen.

Mike had something small under, David thought. Packard did not check his down card.

"High man bets a hundred without looking," Packard said.

"Call," David said quickly, and threw in a black chip.

Mike folded—David had read him right, at least.

Packard grinned and dealt David a five and himself an ace. "Power bets blind again," Packard said. "Two hundred."

"A kidder," Mike said darkly, his gaze skipping from one hand to the other.

"What do you say, kid?"

Look at the card, David thought. "Call," he said.

Francie leaned forward, placed a hand on David's shoulder. Vinnie had come in from the front room and was standing behind Mike.

"Cards are coming," Packard said, and dealt David another nine. He hesitated a moment, then dropped a queen on his hand. Packard stared at the cards, his eyes glassy with the marijuana. "Pair of queens to a pair of nines," Packard said. "How do you like that, kid?" Packard reached for his chips. "Power still bets blind."

David could feel the warmth of Francie's hand through his T-shirt. He closed his eyes, drew a quick deep breath, struggled to filter the air from the rancid smoke, and thought with all his strength: *Look . . . at . . . the . . . card. . . .*

Packard bent back the corner of his hole-card— and smiled instantly. "Make that three queens," he said. "Sorry, kid, maybe I should have peeked earlier, saved you a bundle." Packard took his time counting out chips. "Five hundred."

Francie squeezed David's shoulder. David thought how nice it was to be touched, and stared at Packard, and knew he was lying, he had a five or a six or a seven down, he had to, because if he didn't, David had lost it, the money and a whole lot more. . . .

But Packard had looked at the card, hadn't he?

David counted out chips, thought for a moment about raising.

"You're getting pale, kid," Packard said. "Past your bedtime."

David tossed in five blacks. "Call. Deal 'em."

"That's what I'm doing." Packard took his time, pretending to have trouble peeling the top card off the deck—or was he finally nervous?—but that sort of thinking would get David nowhere.

Packard laid a card in front of David, took his time studying his hand. "A six," Packard announced. "No visible help—pair of nines showing."

With the nine in the hole, David was holding three of a kind. David watched Packard worry another card from the top of the deck, slip it up where only he could see it, bloom into another smile, and then slam the card faceup on the table.

"Beat a full house, kid?" Packard said.

The card was an ace: Packard was showing two pair, aces, and queens, and if his hole-card was a queen, as he'd claimed, David's three nines was a sure loser.

"How much you got left, kid?" Packard said.

David counted his chips mechanically, searching some corner of his mind for reassurance: Packard did not have the full house—*he did not*—and David's triple nines would hold.

"Eleven hundred," David said.

Packard sorted through his chips, his fingers a little clumsy. "A thousand and change." He pushed his blacks forward. "Make it a grand. Save you a hundred so you can start another paper route."

David touched at the thin welt of scar at his hairline, stared at Packard, and felt nausea well up from the pit of his stomach. He could not fight it, that and the fatigue, and did not try, but threw in ten of the eleven black chips that represented all the money he had in the world. Packard grinned at him meanly, and David met his gaze for a moment before sliding his forefinger under his down-card and flipping it over.

For what seemed like forever, Packard's grin did not change, and then, finally, it dissolved like melting wax. Packard slapped his palm hard on the tabletop and said, "Son of a bitch."

David pulled in the pot, excused himself, pushed back his chair, and stumbled into the bathroom.

A few minutes later Francie said, "Kid?"

David was leaning over the toilet, his hands propped on the seat. There was Coke-colored vomit in the bowl. The sight of it made him retch again. Francie waited until he was finished, then touched at him gently. "Shut the door, please," David said.

Francie kicked the door closed and wiped his mouth.

"You didn't get any on your shirt," Francie said. "You must have done this before."

For some reason, that struck David as hysterically funny. "Sure," he said, hardly able to choke out the words through his manic laughter. "All the time."

"Hey," Francie said softly. "I've seen men do plenty worse."

All of a sudden his laughter had become sobbing. Francie threw the towel in the corner and said, "C'mere."

David went into her arms, and she held him close, his head cradled between her breasts. She rocked on her heels and said something soft that meant nothing. After a time she put her hands on his arms, and he let her pry him away, looked up while she wiped away the tears.

"You did good," she said. "Go out there and finish up."

He managed to smile and thank her.

Vinnie looked scared when they came out of the bathroom. "You all right, kid?" Mike stopped in the act of pouring a drink and glanced at David with concern. Packard was next to him at the countertop, rolling another joint.

"He's fine," Francie said. She stood close by David's side.

"How'd you do that?" Packard said thickly.

"Pay him off," Francie said to Vinnie.

"How'd you talk your way in here in the first place?" The black man was very stoned now.

"Pay him off, Vinnie," Francie said.

Packard raised both fists and took a step toward David. Mike grabbed his arm, spun him around, and hit him once, on the point of his chin. Packard went down on the carpet, turned over on his back, and began to snore.

Mike gazed ruefully down at Packard. "I guess that eighty-sixes me in this game."

Vinnie shook his head. "He had it coming." He regarded Packard, looked back at Mike. "You move fast for a half-drunk fat man."

Vinnie turned away, counted off a sheaf of hundred-dollar bills, shoved them in David's hand. "Watch your ass, kid," he said.

The street was quiet in the lurid dawn light. Francie said, "Where do you live?" Steam rose from a manhole.

"I'm . . . I'm leaving town."

"You could crash with me for a night or two."

David shook his head. "Thanks," he said.

"You're a sweet kid," Francie said.

He hugged her again. He couldn't stop himself, and it was awful letting go. When he finally did, she pulled a pencil and a wrinkled envelope from her handbag, scrawled something.

"You call me someday," Francie said.

"Sure I will," David lied. The worst thing was

that he knew how badly he would want to, during the dark times that he was certain lay down the road.

The port-authority building was too brightly lit and smelled of disinfectant. David went past sad grizzled men in tattered clothing who lay slumped against bare walls. At the bank of coin lockers he had trouble getting the key into the slot, had to use one hand to steady the other. The light-headed feeling had mostly gone by the time he got down to the sidewalk with Francie, but now it returned, and that puzzled and troubled him. Despite his weariness he should have recovered by now, but as he extracted his blue vinyl gym bag from the locker, he realized the disorienting sensation was growing more insistent.

The clerk behind the bars of the ticket cage was reading the *National Enquirer*. David wanted to be pleasant, but when he said, "Could you help me please?" he sounded sharp and irritable.

"Keep your shirt on, sonny." The clerk tapped at the newspaper page with a bony forefinger. "Elvis was spotted twice this week. Katmandu and Wilkes-Barre, Pee-Yay."

David's disorientation waxed, like a gathering wave. "The next bus," he said.

"What about it?"

"Where does it go?"

"D.C."

"Washington is good." David slid a hundred through the slot beneath the bars.

The clerk returned a ticket and change and said, "Gate Six, three minutes. Better shake a leg."

When he stuffed the ticket and cash into the pocket of his T-shirt, his fingers were slick with sweat. As he turned away from the clerk, the revolving door across the waiting room spun, and two men entered.

David did not know the younger one, who wore a suit, a white shirt and tie, and wing-tip brown shoes, but he recognized the uniform, common to everyone the Facility sent. The other man, dressed more casually in jeans and a sport coat, was named Voss. Voss's eyes were half-closed, as if he might have been drunk or in some kind of trance.

David stared at them and concentrated, but he felt short-circuited. He pushed down rising panic as Voss's hooded eyes found him, and though David did not recognize this tightening vise that seemed to grip his brain, he knew that Voss was its source.

David shook his head violently and forced himself to move. The Facility man expected him to flee, so when David came straight at them instead, the man's surprise gave David a few extra steps. The Facility man came unglued, and his hand darted under the arm of his suit coat, but by then David was holding the gym bag with both hands wrapped around the handles and bringing it around.

Voss's mouth opened as David caught him on the side of his head. There were books in the bottom of the bag, hardback texts in history and arithmetic, and one of them must have hit Voss in the right spot, because he whirled away and went down on the false-marble floor.

Behind David someone cried out. David turned and saw the short-barreled revolver aimed in his direction. Voss flopped over on his back, twitched, and lay still, and the vise unclamped from David's mind. The Facility man waggled the gun and said, "You little shit."

A woman said, "Someone call the cops, why don't they?" The Facility man glanced down at Voss, frowned, and took a step toward David.

David stood his ground. His mind, freed from whatever grip Voss had put upon it, flexed almost exultantly.

In the core of his brain, he felt a point, a tiny mass of neurons that seemed to flex and pulse, a phys-

ical presence. Although neither painful nor even unpleasant, it was something new, and it rocked him.
He touched two fingers of each hand to his temples as
if to contain it.

From the point, image bloomed to fill his mind
and sear beyond it.

The Facility man froze. His face went dark with
a rush of blood that drained immediately, leaving him
yellowy as the wall behind him. His eyes dilated in
surprise and then terror, and spittle bubbled on his
lips. He tried to vent his terror in a scream and made
a croaking sound instead.

The man clutched at his chest, and David felt a
stab of terrible guilt. Instinctually he tried to shut
down, to rein the image and draw it back within the
point. The gun fell to the floor, and the man spun
around, bolted for the revolving door. His forehead
rammed into the edge of one of the partitions, and
when he stumbled away, David saw blood dribbling
down his face.

As suddenly as it had flared, the image was swallowed into the point, and the point winked out. David lowered his hands; they trembled, and his face
was hot.

People were between David and the gates, a semi-
circle of odd, bewildered faces. David said, "Excuse
me," pushed through.

The driver was about to shut the door as David
reached Gate Six, out of breath and on the verge of
collapse. He went shakily down the aisle and dropped
into a seat in the back near the toilet and was asleep
before the bus crossed the Hudson.

CHAPTER TWO

Linda Gaylen had anticipated her return with something like dread, but when she stepped into the vast, low-ceilinged editorial bull pen for the first time in a month and was immediately surrounded by a crowd of her colleagues, she felt a flood of affection so profound, she feared for a moment she'd break down in tears of relief and gratitude. To avert such a corny reaction, she said, "What is this, a revival meeting? Doesn't anyone have anything to write?"

"You look great, Linda," Jack Kincaid said. He worked the sports beat for the magazine.

Linda fingered a carmine stain on his Notre Dame sweatshirt. "I see O'Malley's has chili on special today."

Everyone laughed. Beyond the circle of her friends, across the expanse of cluttered desks and glowing computer screens, Linda saw Brian Dancer standing behind the window of his cubicle, smiling in her direction.

"I'm sorry about . . ." Amanda Blaine, the front-desk receptionist, waved a hand vaguely. "We were thinking about you," she finished.

"I know you were," Linda said sincerely. When she had come out of surgery, the first thing she saw was a huge Magen David made of roses, with a banner across it saying, *Mazel Tov* Shlomo on the Occasion of Your Bar Mitzvah." Attached was a note signed by everyone in the office: "Shlomo got stage fright, so the florist let us have this for half price." It was the brand of humor she expected from them, and it had made her laugh despite the pain and the emptiness of her loss. During the subsequent recovery period, not one of them had failed to visit her, bringing something fattening, a bit of office gossip, and always their genuine care.

"Back to work, peons." The ring around her parted to reveal Dancer in the flesh, all three hundred pounds of it. He wore his unvarying uniform of safari shirt and khaki slacks that might have been fashioned by Omar the Tentmaker. Dancer stabbed a stubby finger in Linda's direction. "And you," he said, "in my office, double-time. You've done enough goldbricking for one lifetime."

Dancer took her very gently by the arm, and his boyish face turned solemn. "I missed you," he said in a low voice. "I don't just mean your rapier wit, either. You okay?"

"I'm good," Linda said.

Someone cleared his throat in embarrassment at the honest sentiment, especially coming from Brian Dancer, who prided himself on a hard-boiled pose that nonetheless no one took seriously. But then Frank Alameda, the movie critic, crooked an arm to cradle an imaginary violin and began humming "Thee and Only Thee," and everyone broke up.

Dancer glanced at Frank and said, "You're fired." Frank puckered his lips and gave Dancer a raspberry. "Come on," Dancer said to Linda. "Let's powwow." He guided her across the bull pen to his office, and once inside gestured her toward the couch. It sat under a wall tessellated with awards and plaques and was swaybacked from years of Dancer's napping bulk. Linda perched on its edge to keep from sinking into the cushions.

"You sure you're ready to go back to work?" Dancer parked himself in his swivel chair.

"I am back to work." Linda took a compact Panasonic from the oversized satchel containing the tools of her trade, set the cassette recorder on the sofa beside her. "Nathan Purdy called me the other day."

"Forget Nathan Purdy," Dancer said. "I want to hear about you."

On his second try Dancer got his ankles propped on the desk. All of his weight was in his middle, his stomach and his butt anchoring bandy legs and narrow shoulders so solidly that now, leaned back in his chair with his feet up, he was in perfect equilibrium, as immovable as the Lincoln Memorial. He had joined the staff of *American Weekly* out of Columbia J-School and now at thirty-two was the youngest executive editor in the newsweekly's seventy-year history, and as good a friend as Linda had.

Now that Richard was gone . . .

She remembered that Saturday as a series of details rather than a flow of events. An elegant furnishings store in Reston and a breathtakingly intricate rug that the woman said—truthfully, Linda sensed—was a Kirman. A tomato-and-cheese sandwich and a long-necked bottle of Miller at the counter of a working-class bar outside of Martinsburg within sight of the Potomac. And Richard, fairly bubbling with happiness at their first full day together in so long with no responsibility to attend to, reminding her that it was their five-month wedding anniversary.

Richard McGillis was darkly handsome, taller by six inches than her five seven, slim with clean patrician features. He always dressed beautifully, and that day, in twill slacks and a polo shirt, he looked spruce enough to step into a spread in *GQ*. He was senior counsel to the Senate Ethics Committee and had for the previous eight weeks worked almost around the clock on the investigation into the campaign financing of a member from the Midwest. During that same period Linda seemed always a day behind on one story or another, and often it was nine at night before they saw each other.

Then, two days earlier, she had tracked down an informant who provided the documents she needed to blow the lid off a defense-procurement scam, while at virtually the same moment, Richard's senator agreed to resign. Linda wrapped her story at six the next night, a few hours before *American Weekly*'s deadline, as Richard closed down the panel's investigation and completed negotiations on disclosures and restitution with the disgraced lawmaker. Suddenly Saturday had become a surprise gift that they'd accepted with pleasure, and no more plans than an autumn drive through the countryside of northern Virginia.

She remembered Richard reaching over to tenderly pat her still-mostly-flat abdomen as they waited for the only traffic light in a little crossroads village called Bluebird, the warmth in his touch through her blouse, and the look on his face. She remembered him asking her to check the map as he turned the corner, and she remembered leaning forward to unlatch the glove compartment.

Because her head was down, she never saw the other car coming directly at them in the wrong lane. Others had to tell her what had happened after that, when she opened her eyes three days later.

A sheriff's deputy and a psychologist on staff at the hospital visited her first. The psychologist told her that Richard had died instantly, and assured her he had not suffered. The deputy explained that the driver of the other car had been convicted of drunken driving twice in the previous year, had no valid license, was speeding, and at the time of the accident had a blood-alcohol count of point-two-three, according to the autopsy performed on his mangled body.

The combined speed of the two vehicles at the moment of impact was estimated at sixty-three miles per hour, the deputy told her. The resultant force ripped their engine block from its bolts and drove it against the fire wall, impelling the steering wheel into

Richard's face, fracturing his skull, and causing massive and fatal cranial trauma. His seat belt was impotent to help him in the face of such a violent crash, though Linda's had saved her life.

Or part of her life, at least; she did not need the doctor to tell her that she'd lost her baby. She could feel the void within her and for the first time allowed herself to cry.

Because she wanted to understand the change in her body, she insisted the surgeon explain exactly what had occurred, and he obliged, kindly, sympathetically, and in detail. The collision had propelled a tool kit, a set of wrenches and screwdrivers in a vinyl folder, from the open glove compartment into her midsection. When she was brought into the emergency room fifteen minutes later, she was unresponsive, pale, clammy, tachycardic, and her blood pressure was dangerously low; the distension of her abdomen and a large hemotoma indicated internal bleeding.

A central line was put in, and she was given blood products while an exploratory laparotomy was performed. It revealed that the blow of the tool kit, a four-pound, mostly metal, missile, had caused a tear of Linda's uterine artery, the main vessel that nourished the fetus. At two months it was not viable, and it was aborted. In an emergency hysterectomy her uterus was removed and the vessels ligated.

Although she had lost a lot of blood, the surgeon told her, she would recover completely, the only reminder of her ordeal a ten-centimeter midline scar bisecting her abdomen from the pubic bone to the navel. The surgeon coughed discreetly and went on: Of course she would no longer menstruate and could never bear a child. Linda thanked him for his consideration, and for saving her life.

"I've had plenty of time to get my head straight," Linda said to Brian Dancer in his office. "I went through the denial, the guilt, and the anger, and I accept that there'll never be a time when I won't miss Richard. I'll always wonder which of us the baby would have looked like and miss feeling her in my arms."

"I'm sorry," Dancer said softly.

"So am I. But I've gotten through to acceptance, and I'm ready to carry on."

"If I can help," Dancer said, "you say, 'Jump!' and I'll ask, 'How high?'"

"That means a lot to me, Brian."

Dancer cleared his throat and gestured at the tape deck on the sofa next to Linda. "Tell me about Nathan Purdy."

Linda smiled. "He's a little weasel."

"I mean something I don't know," Dancer said.

Nathan Purdy, a civilian programmer in the Pentagon, was a social misfit and malicious troublemaker who spent his spare time risking his job and a possible prison term by hacking various government computers. On occasions over the years, he'd come to Linda with dirt, some of it worthless, much of it personal and unsavory. He seemed to have no motive beyond an obsessive loathing for humankind, including, Linda sensed, himself.

"He gave me something pretty juicy," Linda said.

"He has been known to tell a fib or two," Dancer pointed out.

"This time I believed him," Linda said. "I had a hunch."

Dancer half closed his eyes, but she knew he was listening. From the bull pen came the muted noises of ringing phones, voices raised and lowered, the machine-gun chatter of dot-matrix printers. The mosaic of sound was soothing, familiar, something to come home to.

"Nathan gave me a year's worth of memos," Linda told Dancer, "written by a Colonel Maynard Burton, the Military Intelligence and Defense Department liaison to the Department of State. They went through eyes-only channels to the chief of the DEA's Phoenix office."

"What was in 'em?"

"Times, dates, and various locations in southern Arizona."

"Why is an army spook in regular contact with a federal narc?"

"Right," Linda said briskly. "That is the question. Also most of the memos mentioned 'vehicle N-three-four-four-MP' or some similar kind of ID number. I gave it to Binary Bob."

Binary Bob Berkowich had phoned Linda a year earlier and asked to see her. He turned out to be a skinny, almost beardless, twenty-year-old MIT dropout who lived in an unprepossessing house in a pleasant neighborhood in Falls Church. In its shielded basement Linda was confronted by a hundred thousand dollars' worth of computer and communication equipment. "What exactly is it you do?" Linda had asked him. Binary Bob pushed his glasses up on the bridge of his nose, smiled, and answered, "Magic."

"I thought it was a car license," Linda said to Dancer, "but Binary Bob pinned it down as the tail number of a cargo plane belonging to Paloverde Air Transport, a charter outfit based at a private airport outside Phoenix, with a business office here in D.C. The general partner is a man named Kenneth Castile."

"How long have you been on this?"

"Couple of days." Linda stood and started to pace, into the story now. "Castile, Burton, and Paloverde go back together more than twenty years. In the late sixties Burton was in Laos working as an adviser to the Hmong, our mercenaries in the secret war. Castile was in country at the same time, flying supply drops for Air America, the CIA's proprietary airline. Paloverde Air Transport was smaller but also CIA run; its mission was ferrying spooks into and out of the Agency's base at Long Cheng, near the Plain of Jars.

In the midseventies when Congress made all the fuss about the CIA, Paloverde was sold to Castile and became, to all appearances, a private charter operation."

"You think Castile's still in the game?"

"That's what I asked him yesterday when I dropped by his office. He said no, and I believed him." Linda gestured at the tape machine. "It's on there if you want to listen, but I'll cut to the chase."

Linda felt fine; she was back in her element. "I showed Castile my cards: what I knew from the memos, plus the stuff Binary Bob came up with—records of Burton's travels over the last year, and from airline computers the same on Castile. Bob had also called up flight plans filed by Paloverde. The timing matched. The Paloverde planes were making regular flights to Mexico, Central America, and Bolivia."

"Drugs."

"That's a fair guess," Linda said. "Castile claims he doesn't know what he was carrying. He tried to sell me the idea it might have been small arms."

Dancer snorted. "Right. Burton is exporting guns *from* Latin America *to* the United States."

"But otherwise Castile was telling the truth."

"How do you know?"

Linda smiled. "I'm good."

"So are guys like Castile," Dancer pointed out.

Linda took her place on the couch. "Brian, I've been in the business fifteen years. I know people, and I've got instincts. You get so you can recognize a lie."

"You are good," Dancer admitted, "at least compared to the rest of the stumblebums who work around here. So what's next?"

"Confirm it's drugs."

"How?"

"With Castile's cooperation," Linda said. "I'll promise to keep him as clean as I can."

"You meant to all along. That's why you went to him in the first place."

"Burton's the story," Linda explained. "He's a life-long spy, and by now he's pretty far up the chain. So he uses his position to wave off the DEA from incoming Paloverde flights, probably with your basic 'top-secret intelligence mission' cock-and-bull story. That's what he told Castile, and you can't blame Castile for buying it. When a pal from the old shadow realm asks a favor, you say yes, and you don't ask questions."

Linda looked pleased. "We're in a win-win situation." She bent back one forefinger with the other. "If the scheme stops with Burton, we've got a pretty good story." She reversed the fingers. "On the other hand, what if it *is* a sanctioned operation?—an arms-for-drugs deal, a helping hand to a coke-dealing foreign national who happens to be a U.S. asset, a conduit for funding illegal covert action—then it's stop-the-presses time."

Dancer considered for five seconds, nodded. "All right, it's a go."

"Thanks, Brian."

She had the office door open when Dancer said, "Hey Gaylen."

"Yeah?"

"Do me two favors."

"Sure, boss."

"Don't spend too much of my money," Dancer said, "and for chrissake be careful."

American Weekly's editorial and advertising offices looked across the Potomac to the Washington Monument from the top ten floors of a glass-and-steel tower on Wilson Boulevard in Rosslyn. As Linda descended in the elevator through its bowels, she looked at her watch and whistled impatiently. The afternoon spent doing legwork on the phone had evaporated too quickly, and there was only a slim chance of being on time for her second appointment with Castile.

Her heels clicked on the polished floor as she went

through the lobby at a half trot, preoccupied with the best way of bucking traffic into town. Near the front door was a fountain rimmed by a marble bench where a boy was sitting, a nice-looking kid in tennis shoes, jeans, and a windbreaker over a T-shirt. He gave Linda a look that almost seemed expectant. Outside in the brisk wind of the October afternoon, Linda gazed back. The boy was watching her.

To avoid the parking problem, she decided to leave the Porsche in the underground garage, then had trouble flagging a cab; it was past four, and the rush hour was gearing up. When a taxi finally pulled over, she settled into the cushions of the back compartment with relief. She felt good, and reaffirmed in her decision to get back on the job.

From her earliest days on the high-school newspaper, doing hard-hitting exposés on such vital topics as why students preferred pizza to corn chowder, she'd known that reporting was the profession she was meant to pursue. With a B.A. in journalism from the University of Montana, she'd signed on as a spot-news reporter at the Great Falls *Tribune*. A year later she moved to *The Denver Post*, and two years after that to the *Los Angeles Times*. Her stint there climaxed five years back with a share of a Pulitzer as part of a three-reporter team. Their story detailed the involvement of most of a bank's board of directors in the laundering of money for several major depositors, all of whom happened to have intimate and verifiable ties to organized crime.

The Pulitzer brought offers from two networks and *The New York Times*. Instead she signed on with *American Weekly*, because she wanted to work with the already legendary Brian Dancer. Once again her instincts were accurate: She brought in the stories, her salary jumped, and at thirty-six she was on a fast track to the top of her profession.

The cab melded into the crush of vehicles crawling

across the Roosevelt Bridge. There was no question in her mind that work was the best way to get through the rest of her recovery period. She was physically whole again, and sure as hell done with sitting at home brooding. She thought of a line she'd read in an interview with Joseph Heller. Heller said that when he became blocked while writing *Catch-22*, he put the book aside and took to watching television with his wife. Soon after that he was back to work on the book. "I couldn't imagine what people in America did at night if they weren't writing a novel," Heller told the interviewer.

It wasn't much different for her. She was a reporter; she reported. "Journalismo, ergo sum," she said aloud, which got her a funny look from the cabbie.

The cab pulled to the curb, and Linda gave the driver a ten for the eight-thirty fare. She stood on the sidewalk a moment, glancing up at the building housing Castile's office, drew a deep breath, and murmured, "It's show time."

Kenneth Castile gestured to a chair. "Would you like some coffee, Ms. Gaylen?"

"Thank you." Linda sat.

Castile poured from a percolator on the countertop behind his desk. "What can you do for me?" he said evenly.

Linda liked his choice of words. "I think it's unfortunate you went along with Burton, but I can understand why." Linda took the proffered cup. "The fact that you were an unwitting participant is going to color the way I write about you."

Castile regarded her noncommittally. "You'll portray our involvement as innocent?"

"I'll write the truth," Linda said.

Castile's office was modest, severe, and offered a nice view of the White House. He pursed his lips. "All right. What do you want?"

"Access to your people in Phoenix and truthful answers to my questions."

Castile clasped his coffee cup in both hands and watched her over its rim. "What's to keep me from simply calling Burton and curtailing the operation?"

"You've had two days to call him," Linda returned. "You haven't, have you?"

"No," Castile said truthfully. "Why haven't I?"

Linda shrugged. "Maybe you're afraid he'll try to throw the blame to you, so you've got a vested interest in helping me get the truth out. Maybe you don't like being lied to and used. Maybe you don't want to be responsible if Burton decides to kill me to stop my story." Linda studied him. "Maybe you're a decent citizen who finds it morally repugnant that Burton is perverting his position and making a couple million while doing his part to keep up the street supply of dope."

Castile stared steadily at her for a good half minute. After that he put down his coffee and picked up the phone.

As she got halfway through the throng crowding the bar of the Old Ebbitt Grill, Linda snapped her fingers and swore under her breath. She could see the gang in the corner, gathered around a couple of tables they'd commandeered and pushed together, Frank Alameda, Jack Kincaid, Amanda Blaine, and a half-dozen other *American Weekly* staffers. Kincaid waved her over, and Linda shook her head and raised a finger to indicate she'd be there in a minute. She made her way back past noisy knots of drinkers, went outside and down five doors to the travel agency. It closed in a quarter hour, and the only person left was the middle-aged frosted-blond woman who had issued Linda a ticket to Phoenix a few minutes ago.

As Linda entered, a young boy stood up and thanked the woman. He turned and Linda recognized him, for a moment did not understand from where, and then remembered that he'd been sitting by the fountain in the *American Weekly* building lobby an hour and a half earlier. The boy went past her, smiling and nodding as one does with a stranger encountered in the absence of other people. Linda felt an odd, disconcerting confusion, and when the agent said, "I'm terribly sorry," Linda for a moment did not know what she was talking about. The door shut behind the boy.

"Your American Express," the woman explained.

"Oh yes."

"I'm always doing that," the woman said. "Leaving it in the imprinter, I mean. My boyfriend says I have a subconscious need to make people return to me." She offered the green card, which was in the magazine's name.

"What did he want?" Linda asked.

"I beg your pardon?"

"That boy. What did he want?"

The woman hesitated. "He asked for some . . . some information on Europe. For a school project."

Linda glanced at the rack of brochures against one wall. On the left was a column of brochures on various European countries. The boy had been empty-handed when he'd gone out.

The woman looked uncomfortable. "Well," she said, "I've got to close up. I've got a date tonight." She tried to smile, girl to girl, and did a bad job of it.

When Linda got back to the gang, they were downing drinks, grabbing up handfuls of peanuts, and gossiping in indiscreetly loud voices. The Grill was jammed, the bar ringed by a double row of predominantly young men and women in suits, and most of the tables already taken. Everyone seemed to know everyone else; Washington could be a small town that way. As much business was done here and in a few other favored watering holes as in the various halls of government.

Linda did her best to join in because she didn't want them to feel uncomfortable in her presence, from some perceived need to respect her loss. But her thoughts were high-centered on the boy, and the travel agent's lie. He had been asking about her; as unlikely and inexplicable as it was, Linda felt the strongest hunch that it was true. And that odd, confused sensation that had passed over her . . .

She ordered a beer and forced herself to concentrate on the rhythm of the ribbing, wisecracks, and behind-the-back digs at Brian Dancer that were the staples of these gatherings. "I hear he buys those safari suits by the gross and his closets are full of them," Kincaid said. "Any truth to that, Linda?"

Linda took a swig of her beer. "Are you suggesting that I spend a lot of time at Brian's apartment?"

"Perish the thought," Frank said.

Linda opened her mouth to reply and shut it again. Frank said, "What the hell is it?" sounding alarmed.

Linda stared past him. A group of drinkers had moved away from the bar to take a table. Through the gap they left, Linda saw at the end of the leather-padded counter the boy. He was working on the last of a cheeseburger.

As she rose and came around the table, the boy looked up at her with apparent alarm. But then his gaze softened, and as it did, Linda felt the confusion again. She stopped, had to reach out for a chair back to steady herself. The boy slid off the stool, and other customers hid his small form. When she reached the bar, he was gone.

A hand took her elbow, and Linda turned to find concern on Kincaid's stubbly face. "What is it, Linda?"

"Nothing." Over the heads of the patrons, she saw the street door open and a moment later caught a glimpse of the boy before he was swallowed up by the sidewalk crowd. "Nothing," Linda repeated, working to convince herself. What possible interest could the boy have in her?

Linda mustered up a smile for Kincaid. "Got to run," she said. "Early flight to Phoenix."

"You're sure you're okay?"

Linda turned the smile up a few watts. "I'm on a story, Jack, a good one," she said. "If that doesn't put me back on track, nothing will."

Later that night, over dinner alone in the Georgetown brownstone that remained for her possessed with Richard's spirit, she remembered the comment. She'd meant it casually, but now she realized it might be quite literally true.

The man who met her flight at Sky Harbor Airport the next morning introduced himself as Frank Wickenberg. He wore cowboy boots and a Stetson, was tall and slim with a craggy, weathered face, and reminded Linda of the Marlboro Man. He carried her bags to a pickup truck at the curb in front of the terminal and helped her into its cab in a manner that was almost courtly. Linda liked him.

When they were on the interstate heading north through the Arizona capital, he said, "I've never much cottoned to this business." He glanced at her. "What you're here about, I mean."

The city began to give way to desert, heat waves shimmery on its horizon. "The problem is," Frank said, "I don't see how I'm gonna arrange for you to get what you want without putting my own pecker in the vise. Pardon my French."

"We'll think of something," Linda said.

"It better be soon," Frank said. "Burton's man just called and ordered a charter to Oaxaca, day after tomorrow."

CHAPTER THREE

Emile Rogan took his time contemplating the line of men. Most looked too wasted to lift the whip, let alone swing it. Their scrawny carcasses consisted of little more than skin over skeleton, and the heavy tropical air was thick with their stink. The ones with open sores had their own pet herds of flies clustered about the ulcers. Some wore tattered trousers, others torn shorts, and a few were mostly naked. "*¡Opte!*" the spig said for the second time. "Choose!"

The men stood in ragged double rows facing a long, low adobe building. The ground had been trampled to barren, sunbaked dust that drifted in the thick, hot air. Scattered around the adobe was a shacktown, half a hundred low huts constructed of banana-tree leaves, packing crates, rusting plate metal, and plastic sheeting. There was no fence, but Rogan reckoned that if they didn't care whether you ran off into the jungle, running off was probably a piss-poor idea. He'd have to scam some other way out; in the week since they'd brought him, Rogan had decided that sticking around was a notion that did not much appeal.

Rogan scanned the sullen inmates. "Hard to decide," he said. Almost none of the men met his eye.

The spig smiled. He had lousy teeth. "By all means take your time," he said in Spanish.

The two prisoners who didn't turn from Rogan's gaze were distinguished mainly by not looking like they were going to drop dead before sundown. One was a dapper Greek queer named Chepolous; the other was dark and big, almost as big as Rogan, and spoke native Spanish. Rogan gestured with his cuffed hands at the big man, gave the spig back his smile, and said, "Him. I choose him."

The spig put his hand on the butt of the pistol hanging in webbing strapped around khaki shorts. "Him?" the spig repeated stupidly. "Why not someone weaker?"

"You know," Rogan said.

The spig stepped back, his eyes narrowing.

At the spig's quick movement, the five other spigs came out of their stupor and got interested, like trouble would be a welcome change of pace. They were spread out where they could watch the men, and they were hung with plenty of iron, each wearing a pistol and toting a long gun besides, two of them with Remington double barrels, the other three with Russian AKs.

Rogan contemplated the hook above him, hanging at the end of a rope threaded through a pulley bolted to the wooden roof of the building. "Let's get the show on the road," Rogan said.

The spig barked Spanish too fast for Rogan to follow. The shotgun spigs came over and covered him while the head spig yanked down the hook and pushed its point through a link of the short chain connecting the cuffs binding Rogan's wrists. The spig pointed and said, "¡Usted y usted!" Two men broke from the line and put their weight on the rope's other end.

Rogan's arms were jerked over his head. He was four inches over six feet and had weighed two hundred and sixty hard pounds a week earlier, though he imagined he'd lost some bulk since arriving. The spig snapped his fingers and waved two more men over to join the rope crew. Rogan went up on tiptoes, his knuckles knocking against the pulley. His arm sockets ached dully; they were bearing his weight plus fifty pounds of chains double bound and locked around his ankles.

"What's his name?" Rogan gestured with his chin.

The spig stepped aside. The big dark man stepped out of line and came forward, smiled at Rogan. "Camacho," he said. *"Llamo Camacho."*

"You put that beaver mag in my hootch, Señor Camacho?"

"Por supuesto, no," the big man lied.

"I'm going to kill you, Camacho," Rogan said, almost conversationally.

The spig spun Rogan around and slammed him up against the wall so his cheek scraped hard against the rough adobe. From the corner of his eye, Rogan saw Camacho move behind him, and the guttural murmurs of the men told him Camacho was picking up the whip. The whip had three rawhide thongs. Tied to the end of each was a six-inch length of barbed wire.

"Ocho," the spig said.

"Eight is good," Rogan said. Camacho laughed, and Rogan felt the first lash of the whip.

Camacho had practice. Rogan could hear the whistle of the rawhide in the air a split second before the end lengths lashed against his back, the wire barbs tearing through his skin and lodging in muscle before ripping free, and the warmth of his blood oozing down in three thick rivulets.

Camacho grunted, and the rawhide whistled, and the metal clawed into Rogan's meat again. It hurt like crazy.

The weight disappeared from the other end of the rope, and Rogan slumped to the dirt. His pants were squishy with blood, and his back felt as if the flaying had exposed all of his nerve endings. Hands reached under his arms and tried to drag him up. Rogan went limp, made himself heavy as possible.

"Help them," the spig said.

"Not me," Camacho said.

"Muy pesado," someone said close to Rogan's ear. "Deadweight." *Not dead yet,* Rogan thought.

The spig swore, and keys rattled, and the chains around Rogan's legs went away. Rogan hadn't figured on coming through the beating in quite such bad shape, but losing the chains was a step in the right direction.

This time he let them wrestle him to his feet, though he slumped groggily against the two men supporting him. Rogan opened his eyes and saw the spig to one side and Camacho facing him, the whip in his hand, the barbs greasy red with Rogan's blood. Rogan said, "You got a nice touch, Camacho."

Camacho leered at him, and Rogan straightened and shook off the men holding him, cocked his knee, and drove the flat of his foot into Camacho's crotch. Camacho's pubic bone shattered with a satisfying crunch. As Camacho screamed, Rogan swung both hands, and the hard edge of his manacles struck Camacho in the side of his skull between the jaw joint and the temple.

Camacho fell to the dirt, blood pouring from his ears and eyes and nose. Rogan stared down at him, his smile dreamy and faraway.

"Geez that felt good," Rogan said.

One of the guards shoved the muzzle of his shotgun into Rogan's gut. The head spig called, "No!" and another spig came up behind Rogan. The shotgun spig looked scared enough to fire anyway, so keeping perfectly still seemed the smart course of the moment, and that's what Rogan did while a gun butt slammed into the back of his head, and consciousness winked out like a switch had been thrown.

•　　•　　•

Someone was rubbing a lit torch over Rogan's back. He rolled over, pushed the torch away, and said, "The fuck are you doing?"

"Saving your life, maybe."

In sputtering lantern light Rogan made out Chepolous, the queer, squatting next to a paint can on a plank floor. "Why didn't they kill me?"

Chepolous shrugged. "There is no fathoming how they think. They're like us, you know. The warders."

"Faggots?" Rogan sneered.

Chepolous waved away the insult as if it were a stray insect. "Prisoners. Watching us is their sentence."

Rogan sat up and nearly bumped his head on the ceiling. It was wood slats like the floor, and less than three feet above it. The walls were the same distance apart, forming a coffinlike tunnel a couple yards long with a trapdoor at one end. "Why don't they take off?"

"The same reason as we." Chepolous dipped something gooey from the can with his hand. "In the vicinity there are several Indian villages. The natives live quite decently; they raise crops, and some have electric generators. They serve the camp as hunters."

"For meat?"

"And men," Chepolous said. "Escapees, or anyone from the outside who might stumble upon this place. The Indians are paid by the head—I mean that literally, by the way. They bring it back here, so we are reminded."

"You're gonna tell me no one's ever gotten past them?"

"Correct," Chepolous said.

"Who pays the Indians?"

"Whoever runs this place."

"Who's that?"

"Who knows? Roll over."

Rogan pointed at the goop in the Greek's hand. "What is that shit?"

"An antibiotic made from plants. Without it, in this climate, you'll most assuredly die of massive septicemia. With it, it is merely *likely* you will die."

"You a doctor?"

"I was. Roll over."

Rogan gave him a look.

"I'm not going to rape you," Chepolous said.

Rogan laughed and did as he was told. The salve burned at his back again. "How'd you buy your ticket here?" Rogan said, to take his mind off the pain.

"I killed women. I got away with it for a good while."

"Strangers?" Rogan guessed.

"Oh certainly."

"You just don't like women, right?"

"Loathe them." Chepolous dipped another handful of balm on Rogan's back. "However, in the ultimate instance I chose wrong. She belonged to someone important—a mobster, a president—"

"Same difference," Rogan interrupted. "How'd you do her?"

"Intravenous battery acid," Chepolous said.

Rogan whistled. "You're crazy," he said.

"You're not?"

Rogan grinned. "You tell me. You're the doctor."

Chepolous wiped his hands on his trousers and sat back against the wall. "Speaking of diagnoses, Camacho is dead."

"No shit," Rogan said. "I assume he was chief dick of this circle jerk."

Chepolous nodded. "Apparently he considered you a threat to his authority—"

"He had that part right."

"And wanted to demonstrate his power," Chepolous went on.

The magazine Camacho stole from the head spig

and planted in Rogan's hootch was some stupid fuck-book with pictures of spig girls showing spig beaver, ugly broads Rogan wouldn't have screwed with some-one else's prick. In these parts, though, it was appar-ently worth eight shots with barbed wire.

"Fixed his wagon," Rogan said, half to himself.

"You did it with a certain professional elan."

"I'm not here for shoplifting at K-Mart." Rogan sat up. "Incidentally, where are we?"

Chepolous shrugged. "Lately I've been leaning toward Nicaragua."

Rogan shook his head. "Southern Hemisphere."

Chepolous looked at him curiously.

"Don't they have Boy Scouts in Greece?"

Chepolous still didn't get it.

"The constellations," Rogan said. "Never mind. The point is, how do we get out?"

"We die," Chepolous said. He roused himself, took the paint can, and crawled to the trapdoor at the end of the box, rapped on it. It swung open, and a shotgun barrel poked inside. Chepolous started past it.

"Wait a minute," Rogan said.

Chepolous looked back at him.

"How long will I be in here?"

Chepolous gazed up at the low ceiling. "For-ever?" he suggested.

CHAPTER FOUR

August Breunner lay back on the double bed and loosened his shirt collar. Weariness overwhelmed him, yet sleep would not come. The American was slumped in a Leatherette chair, watching the ten o'clock news. Despite the chuffing air conditioner, the motel room was stuffy and tepid, and the bright, babbling chatter of the anchorwoman and the glare of the overhead light fixture were giving Breunner a headache. The American tamped a cigarette on his wrist. "Must you?" Breunner said.

"Must I what?" the American said, mocking Breunner's accent. He lit the cigarette and dropped the match into an overflowing ashtray. The smoke he blew out spiraled up to join the cloud hovering near the ceiling. "You don't much like me, do you, Doc?" he said, as if genuinely interested in the answer.

Breunner made a weak, meaningless gesture. He liked few Americans; those he knew were venal, manipulative, and almost cheerfully amoral. This one, whose name was Voss, was all of that and a murderer as well. He was perfectly aware that Breunner both disliked and feared him, and he took pleasure in the knowledge.

Breunner sat up, stared at the phone on the bed table. His gaze did not, of course, elicit a ring. They had received only two calls in the thirty hours they'd spent in this room, at seven that morning and again two hours ago. On both occasions it was Simic, reporting no progress and iterating his order that Breunner and Voss were to remain in place. Simic's only encouraging news was that the boy had not left Phoenix by means of any commercial transportation.

An advertisement came on, and Voss leaned forward to turn off the television. "He's not doing so hot, is he?" Voss said. "Our buddy Simic."

Breunner looked up at him, startled.

"Getting jumpy, Doc?" Voss laughed. "Don't worry, your voodoo wasn't strong enough to turn me into a mind reader. It's pretty obvious what you were thinking."

"The boy has likely gone to ground," Breunner said stiffly. "Once he surfaces, Simic's resources will find him. They have served us well thus far." Breunner wondered why he was defending a man whom he abhorred even more than Voss.

Voss snorted derisively, drew on his cigarette. Breunner and Frieda Kohl had discovered him six years earlier among a group of inmate subjects resident at Stateville Penitentiary in Joliet, Illinois. Voss was serving a life sentence for robbing a liquor store of twenty-seven dollars and then raping and murdering the clerk.

Breunner had steadfastly argued against using convicted felons, but Simic countered that prisoners could be coerced into silence and cooperation. In the preliminary experiments Voss returned results almost twice as anomalous as those of Franz Wein, the Swiss traitor who had been with the Facility for thirty-four years without developing to any utile degree. After Wein's death, they had screened over eighteen thousand people before uncovering Voss and could no longer be choosy. Breunner did not know how Simic arranged Voss's release from prison, only that he could do such things.

Given the alternative, Voss was eager to join the Facility. However, when his gift improved with training and he realized his value, he asked for money, and later women as well. Simic provided them.

In the motel room Voss stood and stretched. "I kind of miss the kid," he said. "He was turning into a half-decent poker player." He lit another cigarette, and Breunner suppressed a grimace. "How'd they trace him in the first place?"

Breunner did not wish to antagonize Voss, and besides, there was no reason to withhold the answer. Voss knew better than to commit any indiscretion; in the first place he was unlikely to be believed, and in the second he was most certain to be killed before he was able to prove his assertions. Eventually, Breunner thought, Simic would have him killed in any case.

"Simic has assets, to whom he distributed photographs and other information," Breunner explained. "Five days ago the boy was identified in New York and kept under surveillance until you could be brought in."

"This much I figured out," Voss said. "What I meant was, didn't he know they were on him?"

Breunner shook his head. "He has no ability to pluck random thoughts from a crowd of people, as you know."

Voss grinned. "But he's got other abilities. How bad did he get Anderson . . . Andrews, whatever the hell his name was? The FBI guy you sent along to make the snatch."

"What makes you think he was a federal agent?"

"His cheap suit, his bad haircut, and his swell personality," Voss said. "He okay?"

"Certainly," Breunner said smoothly.

Voss turned suddenly and aggressively, stabbed out his cigarette, thrust a forefinger at Breunner like a dagger. "Here's a hot fucking tip, Doc," he said. "Do not lie to me."

Breunner sat up on the bed, as surprised as he was frightened. The agent, whose name was Anders, had been apprehended without resistance in a New York alley three blocks from the port authority. He was presently in a private room in the psychiatric ward at Walter Reed, where with the help of sedatives he was recovering. He was a relatively sane young man, and according to the latest report Breunner had received, now accepted that his vivid vision—of a leather-faced man with knife blades instead of fingernails, bent on invading his mind and killing him in a most horrible way—was nonetheless imaginary. One of the younger nurses had pointed out that the hallucination recalled a character in a popular series of horror movies, a fact that Breunner was still working to explain.

"How did you know I was lying?" Breunner asked Voss.

"You tell me, Doc." Voss fingered the scar tissue beneath his close-cropped hair. "You're the one who cut my head open."

"You can sense untruth?" Breunner said.

"Looks like it." Voss turned, paced to the wall and back. "That's why it's just you and me this time, because they don't want to risk another of their guys getting zapped. Me to jam him, you because your pal Simic guesses that once the kid knows he's lunch meat, and he's going to run crying into your arms."

Breunner was taken aback at the perception and wondered in what other ways he might have underestimated Voss. Simic did indeed believe that an aspect of Breunner's relationship with the boy was paternal, and that under stress he might turn to Breunner for protection.

"I hope it's true, for your sake," Voss said. "Because if it isn't, and he decides he wants to zap you for the hell of it, I'm not so sure, this very moment, I won't let him. If I find out you really fucked up my mind, what'll happen won't be pretty."

"Mr. Voss," Breunner said softly.

"How'd they keep tabs on him while you were patching me up?" Voss pressed.

Voss had taken a significant blow in the confrontation at the New York bus terminal, and Breunner insisted he be placed under observation for twenty-four hours. Fortunately he had not suffered a concussion, nor were his psi powers impaired. "From the ticket agent Simic's resources learned the boy's destination," Breunner explained. "When he arrived in Washington, he was again put under observation."

"But they weren't about to move in," Voss said. "Not after what happened in New York."

Breunner nodded. "He was followed from a good distance until he boarded a flight for here."

"If Simic's guys are so hot, why didn't they keep on tailing him once he arrived?"

"They meant to," Breunner said. "The boy eluded his keeper."

"How?"

"We . . . we are not certain." In fact, an agent had spotted the boy deplaning—and fifteen minutes after the boy had left the terminal, the agent found himself in the coffee shop and, he reported, "remembered" that he was supposed to keep after him. The agent could not explain his lapse.

"Maybe Simic ought to give the kid a little more credit," Voss said broadly. "He's one hell of a lot more powerful than you thought, isn't he?"

Breunner swung his legs off the bed, moving stiffly. Voss laughed at the effort it took. "Excuse me," Breunner said, with contrived dignity. He drew himself up, went into the bathroom, and locked the door behind him.

Breunner removed his glasses, lay them carefully atop the toilet tank. He splashed water in his face, groped for a towel. In the mirror above the sink, an amorphous, wavering image watched as he dried himself. When he replaced his glasses, hooking them over one ear and then the other, the image sharpened:

Now the face was splotchy-skinned and slack, the visage of a man who looked every one of his seventy-two years, and sad and afraid and ashamed.

The despite in which he held Voss did not ameliorate his guilt at performing the operation. It was either he or Voss, so he had chosen himself, as always in his life. That life had been a confirmation of the caution that one should never wish too hard, for fear one's wish might come true. In Breunner's case everything his experimental models had predicted had proved appallingly accurate.

For nearly a year, since the early emergence of the boy's empathetic ability, Frieda Kohl, always the theoretician in their abominable partnership, had argued in favor of surgical enhancement. Breunner brought all his powers of persuasion to bear in countering her: If the surgery failed or produced unwanted side effects, forty years of work would be nullified in the flash of the surgeon's knife.

Frieda remained adamant. She was convinced that her hypothesis was accurate, and that Breunner could implement it. Her assessment of Breunner was, to his anguish, correct; his skills in the operating theater were remarkably acute, even at this late stage of his life. Here was another of the cruel jokes that characterized his existence, the great gift granted while the opportunity to use it for the commonweal was denied.

For years Breunner had accepted his moral bankruptcy, but the idea of operating on the boy proved him capable of compassion after all, and the boy had sensed his anguish. To that extent perhaps Breunner was partly to blame for his escape, though Simic would never know, thank God. Both of them—Breunner and the poor boy—had merely postponed their fates; he would be recaught, and Breunner would be forced to perform his surgical black magic. In the bathroom of the hotel room, Breunner stared miserably at his reflection but would not look away, as if this self-examination were a penance.

At least the boy's escape posed no immediate threat of exposure of the Facility. But a solution to the problem of controlling him when recaptured was required as quickly as possible, and when Frieda again pressed for surgery, this time with Voss as the subject, Breunner knew objection was pointless. She had already begun work on a new theoretical model, and she rushed it to conclusion. Its object was to give Voss the power, in the boy's presence, to render him impotent during his recapture and subsequently when back under Facility custody.

Breunner ran her computer models for himself and saw that her theory was correct, as far as it went. In her haste Frieda had neglected to explore the question of side effects. Breunner projected their probability as high, though he could predict neither form nor intensity. He said nothing. Instead, three weeks after the boy's flight, he leaned over Voss's anesthetized form and delicately but sure-handedly slid the scalpel's blade into the rubbery meat of Voss's exposed brain.

When Voss came around three days later, he was of course angry; prior to the operation he had been drugged, as Simic had no intention of soliciting his consent. Similarly Simic had calmed Voss's postoperative wrath by, Breunner assumed, bribery or threat.

As near as they could ascertain, the operation was a success; once again Breunner's abhorred brilliance was verified. So too was his projection of side effects; Voss had just demonstrated that he'd gained at least some of the boy's power of empathy. Breunner pondered on it for fully five minutes before it came to him. He brushed a hand through his thinning hair, drew a deep breath, and unlocked the bathroom door.

Voss was sitting at the room's desk, the Phoenix telephone directory opened to the yellow pages. Breunner looked over his shoulder and saw the listings for motels.

Breunner sighed, hardly gratified by this confirmation of his suspicion. "You can sense the boy," he said.

Voss stared at him. "Good guess, Doc," he said. "He can sense me too, I bet, right?"

Despite himself Breunner felt a palpitation of excitement. "Did you feel that in New York?"

"Yeah."

"From how far away?"

"A block, maybe a block and a half." Voss got out another cigarette, rolled it between his fingers. "I'm stronger than him."

"How is that?" Automatically Breunner went into professional mode, encouraging the subject but allowing him to report in his own way, the kind, nurturing doctor. . . . Breunner pushed the self-mocking notion aside, gave Voss his clinical look.

"When we came in, me and the FBI guy," Voss said, "the kid knew what was going on right away. I could tell from the way he turned, looked at us, and so on, but a moment before that he'd seemed normal, tired but not worried."

"Why didn't you tell me this earlier?"

"Because I'm not so sure I want to ever run into him again." Voss stared at the carpet. "You don't have to tell me what happened to that FBI guy. I saw his face. He was scared shitless, and the kid did it to him." Voss looked up. "I'm stronger, sure, like you told me all the time with the business with the cards, the more you use it, the more powerful it gets."

"Yes?"

"What if he's gotten stronger too? What if I can't jam him?"

Breunner frowned. "You can give it up. I don't think he'll . . . attack you if he understands you are retreating."

"Great," Voss snapped. "And then you operate again to make me even stronger, and if it isn't enough, you can do it again, you and that dried-up Kohl bitch, until my brain is Hungarian goulash."

Breunner said nothing. Voss stared up at him for a long moment. "Never mind," Voss said finally. "Let's do it. If he's still here, holed up somewhere, let's find him."

"How?"

"First things first. One hundred thousand dollars, and once we get him, I'm off the job. Simic lets me go, and I don't ever hear from you people again."

Within himself Breunner felt a leaden heaviness. "I am sure I can convince Simic to meet your terms," he said levelly.

Voss's face went dark. "You're lying again, Doc."

Breunner cursed himself for his stupidity.

"But it doesn't really matter," Voss went on in a low, hard voice, "because the moment I stop jamming him, you and Simic and the rest of your Facility creeps are in an instant world of hurt."

"Listen a moment. . . ."

"No, you listen, Doc." Voss stood so his face was no more than a foot from Breunner's. "I'm fucked. At Joliet I at least knew I'd die a natural death. I let Simic take me from the frying pan into the fire. If he doesn't kill me, maybe the kid will. You sure he can't?"

"I don't think . . ." Breunner stopped himself, told the truth. "Probably not yet. When his powers are more practiced, it is a distinct possibility."

"That's your problem. I want out. Do we have a deal?"

"To the best of my ability to guarantee it," Breunner said quickly, and not dishonestly.

Voss tapped at the page of the telephone directory. "Phoenix is like everywhere else," he said. "The hotels and motels are pretty much clustered together—Black Canyon Freeway, Apache Boulevard, the interstate, over by the college. If he's here, odds are he's in one of them; if so, I'll sense him as we drive past. Okay?"

Breunner nodded.

"We understand each other?" Voss said.

"Yes."

Voss stood. "All right," he said. "Let's go cruise the Strip."

Linda Gaylen tried to steer with her left hand and hold the paper steady with her right and did a bad job of both. Finally she pulled the rented Toyota Land Cruiser to a stop, turned on the overhead light, and re-examined the map Frank Wickenberg had drawn. She followed the route with her finger, matching it against her recollection of the last hour of driving: north on the freeway, which became I-17; off at the Rock Springs exit and north again on the paved road for one-point-six miles to the second gravel road, at the intersection with four mailboxes; west past four ranch gates, two on either side, for three miles exactly; and finally south into the desert on this climbing washboard dirt track that was so rutted it could have been a creek bed.

She was certain she had made no wrong turns, but when she checked her watch and the odometer, she saw she had only three minutes to cover the last half mile. She engaged the four-wheel drive and lurched forward, bouncing hard against the seat belt as she jolted into the ruts.

At first Frank had rejected her idea out of hand: Of course the buyer counted the packages, and of course he would know one was missing. Not if you convinced him it must have shaken loose and was lodged under one of the seats, Linda said. Frank admitted that could happen, but the buyer would want to search the plane. Not if you made him jumpy about prolonging the meet and promised delivery the next day, Linda said. Frank didn't like it, but he liked her and wanted her help, so in the end he'd agreed.

The butte loomed ahead, and Linda let out a breath of relief. Her headlights illuminated a path to the top of the table rock, perhaps thirty feet above the desert floor. She grabbed up her satchel and a five-cell flashlight and went toward the trail.

The butte's nearly level top was fifty yards across and roughly rectangular, the edges dropping in a skirt of cliff all around except for the eroded section where the trail switchbacked. As she was catching her breath from the climb, she heard the approaching drone of an engine, and a few moments later saw the plane's silhouette against the starry night. At the butte's center Linda waved the flashlight. The tail door drooped open, like the unbuttoned bottom of a toddler's nappies.

As the aircraft passed above the butte at no more than two hundred feet, a small parachute billowed. A half minute later the wooden crate thudded to the ground, the chute collapsing over it. The plane's wing lights waggled, and it disappeared into darkness.

Linda knelt and unclipped the chute from the toggle bolts screwed into the wooden slats. The crate weighed about thirty pounds, and it took an effort to wrestle it up into her arms.

She turned toward the trail, and a man's voice said, "Stay there, Doc. We don't need any heart attacks." Linda was halfway across when the man appeared at the edge of the butte.

He was stockily built, with a dark complexion and short dark hair, wore dark pants and a black leather jacket. He regarded her with a curious frown and said, "Where's the kid?"

She dropped the crate. She was in the middle of nowhere, not a soul around except whomever the man had spoken to, and she was pretty certain she was in possession of a large amount of illegal drugs. He didn't come on like a cop, but he had to be involved with Burton, as friend or enemy; either way she was in trouble.

The dark man took a couple of steps toward her

and stopped again, cocked his head as if listening for something. Linda groped for a story that might get her out of this, but she couldn't seem to think; for the moment she felt not so much panicked as fog-brained.

"It wasn't him," the man said slowly. "It was you." He advanced across the table rock.

Linda forced herself to concentrate, to coax thought from her sluggish mind. "What are you talking about?" she managed.

From behind the man and below the butte, a voice called, "Is it he?" The voice was flavored with a Germanic accent. The dark man ignored it, continued toward her. Linda backed away until she ran out of butte, her boots on the edge of the thirty-foot drop-off.

The man reached for her, and Linda swatted his hand away, drove her boot up between his legs. The man turned, and her foot glanced off his thigh. While she was still off balance, the man grabbed a fistful of her blouse, ripped. She felt the cool desert-night air on her stomach and the tops of her breasts. She slapped at his face, but he caught her arm above the elbow, twisted hard enough to bring a gasp of pain, forced her down on one knee.

The Germanic voice cried out. "You! No, stay here, please." As the dark man rode her down onto the dirt, Linda heard the scratch of feet on the gravel of the trail. The dark man's face was close to hers, and the fog in her mind was growing denser, more opaque, as if he had already penetrated her, mentally at least. . . .

A new voice said, "Let her alone, Mr. Voss."

The weight of the man went away, and her mind fog cleared. Linda scrambled away along the cliff edge on hands and knees, drew deep, ragged breaths. Before she stood, she darted her hand into her satchel, operating on instinct, and groped for the tape deck. She slid her fingertips along the keylike buttons, coughed to cover the sound as she clicked the third one down.

As she stood, she heard a low moan of astonished disbelief; the scene confronting her was so unlikely, so incomprehensible, that it was a moment before she realized the moan had come from her.

The dark man stood blank-faced, his hands loose at his sides, like a gunfighter in a western movie. Across the butte near the top of the trail, in a similar pose, was the boy—the same boy she had been certain was following her in Washington. She remembered the jarring mental discomfiture that had touched at her in the travel agency, the same sensation she'd just undergone.

"You're done running, kid." The man inclined his head toward Linda. "She's coming too, if that gets your rocks off. They'll be real interested in finding another one."

The boy glanced at her, and Linda gathered her jacket to her bare stomach. "You can sense," the boy said.

"That's right." The man's expression remained carefully blank. "I thought I was homing in on you, but actually you were on my tail, right?"

The boy nodded.

His calm seemed to shake the man a bit. "How'd you get here? You learn to drive since I saw you last?"

The one below called, "Voss! What is going on?"

"I bought a bicycle," the boy said.

Voss barked out a laugh. "You followed me on a *bicycle*?"

Linda saw the boy look at her. "Not him," he said softly. "You."

Voss recaptured his blank look. "That's sweet," he said. "Now let's get going." The man took a sideways step toward Linda, though he kept his eyes on the boy. Linda backed away.

"I told you to leave her alone, Mr. Voss," the boy said.

"You're jammed, kid," the man said, but he

stopped moving. "If you weren't, you would have zapped me already."

The boy shook his head. "I don't want to hurt you."

The man's face suddenly creased with anger. "You already have, kid." Linda watched him struggle to blanken his expression once more. "It's your fault they cut my brain, so I could jam you up. Well, now it's done, and they're going to cut you too, maybe her, and the more I think about it, the more I like not being the only freak in the carnival."

He reached under the leather jacket and came up with a short-barreled revolver, waved it in Linda's direction without looking away from the boy.

"Put it away, Mr. Voss," the boy said. "Put it away and leave."

"Fuck you, sonny," the man said, and grabbed Linda's wrist with his free hand.

Linda tried to jerk away, and to her surprise the man released his grip. She turned and saw the boy in the middle of the butte's flat top, staring intently. The man had lowered the gun, held it pointed at the ground almost as if he had forgotten about it.

"You're jammed," the man mumbled, as if trying to convince himself.

"Listen to me," the boy said reasonably, almost gently. "I've gotten stronger, just in the last few days. Even I don't know how much." Linda saw the boy look to her. "I'm afraid to know," he said.

The boy turned back to the man. "The thing is, Mr. Voss, if we go head to head—" The boy giggled nervously at whatever in-joke he'd just made. Linda realized he was afraid. "I think I'll win," the boy concluded.

"I doubt that." The man's voice was taut, as if he were straining under the burden of some physical effort.

"Don't make me prove it," the boy said.

The man hesitated, then brought up the gun once more.

The boy raised his hands to the sides of his head and stood his ground.

The man gasped, cried out, "Don't." Linda saw him thumb back the hammer. She lunged toward him.

The gun went off, but it was no longer in the man's hand. He had dropped it, the impact releasing the cocked hammer and sending a shot whining off into the night. Linda drew up short as the man cried out and clapped both palms to his head. From below, the Germanic voice cried, "Don't hurt him!"

The man stumbled away. His eyes were wide and crazed, his mouth agape, his swarthy face now pale. "Wait . . ." Linda said.

The man looked at her, screamed madly and with evident torment, and scrambled from her, his hands pressing at his skull as if he wished to crush it. He reeled to the cliff edge, and it crumbled under his heels, and he cartwheeled out of sight, his cry cut off by the thump of his body on the desert floor below.

Linda dropped to hands and knees to peer over the edge. The man lay spread-eagled on his back. His head was lodged up against a rock, and around it was an aureole of blood.

When she stood, the boy was beside her.

"I think he's dead," Linda said.

"He is," the boy said flatly.

"What did you do to him?"

"Nothing. He did it to himself. He just . . . sort of had a blowout."

Linda struggled to regain her wits. "Who are you? Why are you—"

"Keep your voice down, please."

"I want to know—"

"There isn't time."

The boy smiled and touched her arm. Linda felt herself calm.

"If the other man down there finds out you're

here," the boy said softly, "you'll be in danger. It's my fault—I led them to you." The boy frowned.

"Led them to me how?"

The boy ignored the question. "I'll take him away. Wait fifteen minutes at least before you leave. Dr. Breunner can't know about you."

If the whole mad business weren't straight out of the Twilight Zone, Linda thought, it would almost be funny. There was something about the boy she liked a lot, his concern, his earnestness as he went on thinking aloud.

"Yup," he said, satisfied. "You'll be okay and in the clear."

Linda pointed at the body lying below them. "What about him?"

"You don't want to be connected to him."

"Why not?"

The boy shook his head impatiently. The voice from beneath the other side of the butte shouted, "David, are you all right?"

"Yes," the boy called over his shoulder. To Linda: "Will you do what I said?"

"Not before I get some answers."

The boy surprised her by smiling again, and she realized his hand was still on her forearm. "I'll be all right," he said, and Linda knew it was true.

She watched him turn and cross the butte, heard him holler, "I'm coming, Dr. Breunner," before he disappeared down the trail. Linda took a few steps after him, but the boy was right, and she stayed where she was. On the thin, clear night-desert air, she heard the man say, "Hello, David. Where is Voss?"

"Hello, Dr. Breunner," the boy said. "Voss isn't coming."

"Who belongs to this vehicle, David?"

"I don't know." The boy's tone was even. "I want you to do what I say. I'll hurt you if you don't."

Linda heard a wounded gasp, and then the man said, "Do you hate me that much?"

"We're leaving," the boy said. "Get behind the wheel."

"Don't you want your bicycle?"

"Screw the bicycle." To Linda on the butte, the boy's voice sounded weary and, for the first time, child-like. A moment later a vehicle motor started up and then receded, and after a minute red taillights came into view several hundred yards down the dirt road. Linda was sorry the boy was going but knew it was the right thing; he'd be fine, and it was necessary that they part. . . .

"What the hell?" Linda said out loud. She felt as if she were surfacing from hypnosis. The thought that had just passed from her mind, as the vehicle contin-ued away from her, was insane. She had no idea what was going on; who any of them—the boy, the Ger-man, the dead man—were; and sure as hell no way of knowing whether the boy would be all right, why he thought he was at fault for this encounter, or any-thing else about the bizarre little playlet in which she had just acted without a script.

Nor had she any idea why she did as she was told and waited the full fifteen minutes. She was too drained to argue, especially with herself.

To pass the time she used her pocketknife to work open one side of the crate. Inside were ten plastic bags of white powder, each half the size of a throw pillow. After a while she gathered up the crate and her satchel and went down the trail, moving gingerly with the weight. As she drove out, the crate rattled in the back of the rig as if trying to draw her thoughts back to Castile, Burton, and her story, but the serenity that had gripped her in the moments after the boy had left was gone, replaced by a jumble of questions, to which, she suspected, she would not soon be getting answers.

CHAPTER FIVE

Rogan was doing sit-ups when the trapdoor of the box opened and the head spig stuck his head in. "¡Vamos!" the spig said.

Rogan grunted and rolled over, began to do push-ups.

"Come!" the spig ordered again.

"Keep your shirt on," Rogan said. He held his head up so he could stare at the spig in the doorway while he snapped off a quick twenty. He was showing off, sure, let the spig know that he was still full of piss and vinegar, but he also wanted to give his eyes time to get used to daylight, since during the last half month he'd spent all but the few hours comprising Chepolous's visits in pitch blackness.

Rogan finished the push-ups and looked around elaborately. "Let's see do I have everything." In one corner lay the scrawny corpse of a rat, the latest of twenty-some-odd he'd killed with his hands. Otherwise the cramped compartment was empty. Rogan crawled down to the opening, jerked a thumb over his shoulder. "Almost like a home away from home," he told the spig as he climbed out past him.

It was midday, the sun high and glary. The prison camp hadn't changed in any way Rogan could see: The ramshackle hovels around the adobe building still baked in the heat, and most of the inhabitants still looked like extras from *Night of the Living Dead*. Rogan grinned, because he had to admit they had one thing over him: After the box he smelled worse.

The spig said in English, "Come wit' me."

Rogan said, "Go fuck yourself."

"Listen to what he has to say." It was Chepolous, squatting on his haunches in the shade of the camp's main building. Rogan regarded him thoughtfully. Chepolous had been okay to him while he was in the box, enough so Rogan found himself almost trusting the little queer.

Of course, now that he was out, the hell with that. Trusting anyone was the main path to serious trouble; for example, it had brought him here.

"He wants something from you." Chepolous spoke quickly and ran his words together, so the spig couldn't follow the English. "Why not see what you can obtain in return?"

"You got any food?" Rogan said to the spig.

"Sí. You come."

"First I need a shower." Rogan gave Chepolous a grin. "You wanna watch?"

Chepolous pointed his chin in the direction of the spig. "You're pushing him," Chepolous said.

Rogan showed the grin to the spig. "He can be pushed," he said.

Rogan's shower was sun-warmed river water poured from buckets by two prisoners into a fifty-five-gallon drum with holes punched in its bottom, the whole contraption hung from a log tripod. Running his hands over his body, Rogan took stock. The cuts on his back had scarred without infecting, and his muscle tone was okay thanks to the exercise routine, but he'd lost at least fifteen pounds in as many days. Most of the time the box was swelteringly hot, and the bastards fed him only once every twenty-four hours, usually a plate of some smelly stew with plenty more beans than meat.

The water slowed to a dribble. "Keep it coming," Rogan snapped at the two prisoners perched precariously atop the tripod. "Goddammit, I can piss faster than that." The two scrambled around, and the water flow picked up again.

His daily meal was delivered by Chepolous, who stayed while Rogan ate. Rogan had to admit that the company, and the few minutes of lantern light, did help to keep a fellow from going batshit, especially since he didn't know how long he'd be in. That was something Chepolous couldn't tell him, but the Greek was a goddamned font of knowledge on other matters.

"How did they bring you here?" Chepolous asked him on the third day.

"Chopper."

"From where? How long did it take?"

"Fuck if I know—they knocked me out with dope. Horse tranquilizer, judging by the hangover." Rogan licked at his plate. "What about you?"

"They put a hood over my head. I couldn't see and could hardly hear. I lost track of time."

"Is this train of thought heading anywhere in particular?"

A guard banged open the trapdoor and ordered Chepolous out before the Greek could reply.

Rogan had the answer to his own question when Chepolous returned the next day. "You figure out where we are yet?" Rogan asked.

Chepolous smiled. "Your astute observation of the night sky started me thinking. I made some inquiries. Some of the others were awake and unblindfolded when brought here. They could tell me where they came from, how long the flight took; a few noted the direction. Of course, most were so terrified their recollections must be deemed suspect. Nonetheless—"

"So where are we?" Rogan interrupted.

"Somewhere in the upper Amazon drainage, I would say."

"What country?"

Chepolous shrugged. "Brazil, perhaps, or Bolivia or even Peru. This place is so remote from anything resembling government control that national borders have little meaning."

"What you call your no-man's-land," Rogan said.

"Aptly put," Chepolous said ironically.

Chepolous in his subsequent visits became increasingly amused at Rogan's waxing interest in the camp. "So," Chepolous said during the second week, "what is the master plan? Do we tunnel to Rio de Janeiro?"

"What do you expect I'd be thinking about in here?" Rogan barked. "Chess problems?"

Chepolous laughed politely. "And?"

"I'm working on it," Rogan growled.

The next day Rogan heard through the box's slats the unmistakable sound of a chopper. Supply run, he decided. The jungle provided water and meat, but some items would have to be brought in.

"Once a month," Chepolous confirmed. "They drop several pallets in a clearing fifty yards outside the way perimeter."

"They never land?"

"Would you?"

Rogan frowned. "All right, how about we jump the guards, and then we—"

"Starve," Chepolous finished. "The choppers won't come—there's a radio code that must be given, and it is changed periodically. The Indians will not deal with us if we cannot pay. We would be lucky if they didn't overrun us for whatever they could scavenge." Chepolous shifted on his haunches.

"Sorry, my friend. There is no way out."

Rogan snorted. "Fuck that noise," he said.

•　　•　　•

The spig wouldn't give him a knife, so Rogan broke the loaf in half and tore off some of the hot meat with his fingers, stuffed it inside the bread. "What is it?"

Chepolous straddled a wooden chair, his arms folded atop its back. "Capybara, probably."

Rogan took a large bite. "What's that?"

"A very large rodent."

"Giant rat, huh?" Rogan waved the sandwich at the spig, then took a big bite. "I got a cast-iron stomach."

The spig sat behind a desk that was a sheet of plywood on some packing crates. The office within the adobe had only one window, so the room was nearly as stuffy as the box, despite the electric fan blowing in the spig's face. Above a swaybacked iron-framed bed, the wall was covered with photos of naked women. "¿Hables español?" the spig asked.

"No," Rogan said.

"That is a prevarication, right?" Chepolous gave Rogan a wink, knowing the spig wouldn't get the word.

"Yup," Rogan said. "Why give him a break?" Actually he spoke and understood the language fairly well. "What's your name?" he said to the spig.

"Pepe Gomez," the spig said.

Rogan laughed, flecking the desk top with bits of meat and bread. "Spanish for Joe Smith," he said to Chepolous.

Chepolous took a packet of Marlboros from his pants pocket. "Hey, you been holding out," Rogan said. "Gimme one of them butts."

Chepolous lit two cigarettes and gave one to Rogan. Rogan took a long drag, then another bite of his sandwich. "Awright, Joe," he said to Gomez, "what's your pitch?"

"Camacho, the one who framed you?" Chepolous reminded him.

Rogan kept looking at Gomez. "The one I greased, you mean."

"He was con boss," Chepolous said.

"That we know. What I'm wondering is what are you?"

"The power behind the throne?" Chepolous suggested.

Rogan laughed. "He wants me to take over."

Gomez said, "*Sí.*"

"What do I do?"

"You insure no men give him trouble," Chepolous said. "But since few are capable of it, your real job is to give him no trouble yourself."

"What do I get?"

"A few privileges," Chepolous said. "Extra food. A chance to survive."

Rogan stubbed out the cigarette on the desk top. "Sure, I'll do it—until I figure out a way to wax his ass and get the hell out of here."

"Whatever you say," Chepolous sighed wearily.

"That's right," Rogan said. "I'm the boss."

CHAPTER SIX

As it turned out, there was no larger conspiracy: Maynard Burton, officer, gentleman, and drug pusher, was at the top of the operation, which was run solely for his own profit and had nothing to do with his intelligence duties. He was indicted the day *American Weekly* came out with Linda's story.

Beyond that the exposé produced a lot of smoke but little fire. Fingers were pointed at the people who were supposed to ride herd on Burton and his ilk, both houses of Congress held committee hearings, and Burton's attorneys threatened the revelation of intelligence secrets if Burton received more than a wrist slap, a ploy Linda guessed would work for Burton as it had for so many others. The DEA office in Phoenix, along with Kenneth Castile, came off as victims of an imperfect system.

The story sold a lot of magazines and brought Linda a good deal of genuine regard from her colleagues, along with a discreet job offer from the leading investigative columnist in town, who was syndicated in two hundred and fifty-seven papers. She turned him down in favor of a hefty raise from Brian Dancer. She knew she should be pleased and encouraged by the money and the esteem and could not understand why instead she felt let down, hollow, and unfulfilled.

At first she tried to blame it on postpartum blues; she'd experienced mild depression before on successfully completing a story, but this time it was more profound. Her second idea was that, with the story behind her, she once again had the emotional leisure to admit thoughts of her loss.

Walking the halls of Congress, where Richard had spent his professional time, and especially while alone in their brownstone, she found it impossible to block out his image, and that of the child she had lost. She wondered if she might have had a son, and if, when grown, he would have had the maturity, and the burdens, of the boy in Arizona. . . .

There was the third aspect of her malaise: When she was not grieving, she found her thoughts returning to the desert butte.

The morning after that eerie night, she had called the Phoenix police department. Until the actual moment when the receptionist answered, Linda had intended to cleanse herself by telling the whole story. Instead she heard herself say, "There is a dead man near a butte north of the city," and continue with the directions for finding Voss, ignoring the woman's increasingly urgent interruptions. When she hung up, Linda did not attempt to divine a rationalization for her uncharacteristic actions, beyond the irrationalization that the boy would have wished her to say no more.

Then, two weeks after the incident, on an oddly warm November evening as she was flipping over a tape of Brahms's first piano concerto, Linda remembered the cassette that she had recorded that night.

She adjusted the volume of the Brahms and went to the liquor cabinet in the corner of her spacious living room to pour herself an inch of Glenfiddich. When she curled up on the couch again, tucking her feet beneath her, she was frowning in puzzlement. She knew exactly where the tape was: in a rack of similar cassettes on a shelf in the study she used as a home work-space, rewound and marked and dated with a typed label. What she did not understand is why she had neglected to review it.

That recalcitrance prodded her into action. She stood, straightened her robe around her legs, and took the single-malt Scotch into the study. She found the tape exactly where it was supposed to be, inserted it into the deck, and drew over a yellow legal pad as it began to play.

On the paper she wrote the names Voss, then Breunner, with the word "Doctor?" in brackets before the second name. As the tape neared the end, where the boy and Breunner were talking, she added the name David; she'd forgotten having heard it mentioned. In another column headed with a question mark she wrote the words "sense," "jamming," and "blowout."

She rewound the tape and ran it again. This time she made a list of phrases, like the script of a play.

Voss: "She's coming too."
Voss: "I thought I was homing in on you."
Voss: "They cut my brain, so I could jam you up. . . . They're going to cut you too, maybe her."
David: "I've gotten stronger. . . . I don't know how much."
David: ". . . head to head . . ."
David: "You'll be in danger. . . . my fault—I led them to you."
David: (to Breunner) ". . . do what I say. I'll hurt you if you don't."

Next to the second entry, Linda added in parentheses, "but he was homing in on me." She studied the list, sucking absently on the end of the pen. Voss would have abducted her; someone might then perform a medical operation on her; the boy had some power, which he feared—as well he might, Linda thought, remembering how Voss had died. She recalled the fog in her brain when Voss appeared, and how it had lifted when the boy joined them; and then, at the end, her delusion that everything was fine and the boy perfectly safe after he left her.

She sipped at the drink and went on staring at the sheet before her, the scrawl of her notes, and slowly understood why her subconscious had protected her from the questions now gnawing at her. She was apprehensive, though not so much for the boy or even for her own freedom or physical safety. Her fear at root was one that many shared, though not often in such odd association:

Linda was scared of learning something about herself that she might very well not wish to know.

By the next morning, reporter's instincts, augmented by a certain anger at her own timidity, had taken over. As soon as she got to the office, she dialed Binary Bob's number in Virginia. When he answered, Linda said, "You want to get an ice-cream soda?"

"Sure," Binary Bob said. "Twenty minutes?"

"I'll be there," Linda said.

Binary Bob made his living, a rather good one, by selling information; he compared it to the work of a private detective, except instead of employing undercover operations, stakeouts, and bribes, he hacked computers. His typical client was a capitalist with a financial interest in the machinations of a competitor or an enemy. Although he subscribed to his own code of ethics—he would not steal trade secrets or money, unfairly frame someone, or plant data-destroying viruses—his activities were definitely outside the law. Thus the coded conversation, which meant that in twenty minutes, from a pay phone, Linda would call a second pay phone outside a Baskin-Robbins in Arlington. It was also the reason Binary Bob had contacted her in the first place and offered to perform certain researches for her on a *pro bono* basis. "I've read your stuff," he told her. "You're one of the good guys. Working for you will help keep my conscience in check."

Three hours after they made contact and Linda outlined what she was interested in, a guy in a messenger-service uniform delivered a manila envelope. In it were a dozen pages of computer printout and a note saying, "Hope this helps. Keep on punching. BB." Linda squared the pages and began to go over them.

The body found at the foot of the butte had been identified through fingerprints as one Jack Voss, according to a five-'graph item on page seven of the *Arizona Republic*. Police identified Voss as a convicted murderer from Illinois with no known relatives. The coroner listed cause of death as "accidental," and the case was closed.

The second page of the printout, apparently from some law-enforcement mainframe, gave the details of Voss's conviction, and the date six years earlier when his life sentence had been commuted at the discretion of the governor of Illinois. The parents of the victim had objected passionately, and Linda didn't blame them. She remembered her terror at his touch, and the profound conviction that he surely would have raped her had the boy not appeared.

The partial name Dr. Breunner yielded four hits: an oncologist in Seattle, a chiropractor in Bangor, an American Studies professor at Yale, and a research psychiatrist at the University of Rochester Medical School in upstate New York. Linda spent the next few hours on the phone, speaking to people in the four cities' Associated Press bureaus, of which *American Weekly* was a member. All the Dr. Breunners were long-established, well-respected, and otherwise ordinary professionals, except for the Maine chiropractor, who had died in his sleep at the age of ninety-seven three weeks earlier. By the time she'd completed her legwork, Linda was convinced none was her man; the Dr. Breunner to whom the boy had spoken had eluded completely the modern computer's omnipotent gaze, which in itself was of interest.

On the boy Binary Bob had come up with two pages listing over six dozen missing male children first-named David and meeting his general description. It was a depressing and discouraging roster, which Linda threw aside in melancholy and frustration.

Despite her skill and experience in dredging up information, she could think of no further avenues to pursue and in the days that followed was partially successful in assigning the boy to the back of her mind. Inevitably grief once more intruded; her haunts were too familiar, and at the same time alien, empty, and depressing in Richard's absence.

On the night in her apartment when it became overwhelming, she cried for the second and last time, and when she was done, she took stock of her possibilities. When she arrived at the office the next morning, she went directly to Brian Dancer's cubicle. He looked up, nodded judiciously, and said, "You look like shit."

Ignoring the crack, Linda said, "Brian, I need a change."

The waitress was about to ask questions about why he was by himself, but David wasn't in the mood to tell one of his stories, so he smiled, and the waitress hesitated. "Smells good in here," David said nicely, "and I'm plenty hungry."

"I expect you'll be wanting the turkey dinner." The waitress was a roly-poly black woman with a massive bosom swelling against her white uniform.

"All the trimmings, and there's pumpkin pie for dessert."

David gave the menu a second look. He'd been scanning the part that listed burger varieties and hadn't noticed the card paper-clipped to the top of the opposite panel, with a drawing of a gobbling turkey on one side and a blunderbuss-toting Pilgrim on the other. "You bet," David said, working to put enthusiasm into his voice. "It wouldn't be Thanksgiving without turkey dinner, would it."

"I should say not, hon." The waitress scribbled on her pad. "Milk to drink?"

"Milk'd be good."

David checked his Casio watch as the waitress toddled off: Thursday, November 22. Funny how you didn't pay much attention to holidays when you were alone and on the run.

David pushed the maudlin thought aside; he'd learned no good came from dwelling on such matters, and besides, he had other things on his mind. The New England Patriots, for one. They were playing the Cardinals on Sunday, and his first destination that morning after the bus pulled into Market Terminal was the Busch Stadium box office, where he treated himself to a forty-yard-line ticket. Saint Louis was as good as any other place to spend a long weekend, and these days he didn't have to move as often.

Not that Simic's agents weren't still tracking him. They were. His picture and description must have been distributed pretty widely, because in the three weeks since Arizona, he'd sensed people concentrating on him on six occasions in four separate cities. For now that was not a big problem. No one was going to take a chance on getting close, and that was a break in more ways than one. Truth to tell, he felt guilty about what had happened to Voss on the butte and the agent in New York, even though they'd brought it on themselves.

He'd given a lot of thought to that night a month ago in the port-authority terminal. He was aware from poker that his sensing powers had improved since leaving the Facility. In the first few games, he could perceive only whether an opponent was bluffing or not, but pretty soon he got colors, red or black; then shapes of the suits; quickly after that numbers; and then a pure, focused picture of the entire card, as clear as if he were looking through the other player's eyes.

It was the same with his transmissions, and that was the part that scared him some. He got angry and made someone else angry too, but worse. When confronting a guy who could steer him to a game, he made himself confident, so that they got the idea it was okay to tell him. But it was always just feelings, until the bus station in New York, when he'd located that shining point in his mind, and pulled from it that vision, and sent it hurtling into the mind of another. . . .

The waitress brought his milk and salad and wished him hearty eating. A good idea, David thought, and set aside recriminations about the past and fears of the future to concentrate on the now. The restaurant was a family kind of place, warm and plain, with a view of the Gateway Arch through the front window. When he'd spotted it from the bus, it reminded him of a McDonald's gone berserk on steroids. He grinned; that probably had something to do with burgers being his favorite food. While he was thinking about that, the waitress returned with a steaming plate heaped with turkey and stuffing drenched in thick rich gravy, candied sweet potatoes, and green peas. The heck with burgers, David thought, and settled in with knife and fork to do some serious damage to the abundant meal.

Reality rearrived along with dessert. It was stupid to think that the relative safety he'd been enjoying since Voss's death was anything but temporary. Sooner or later Dr. Breunner was sure to make another Voss.

Knowing that didn't make solutions come any more easily. The only one that presented itself was Linda Gaylen.

Had been Linda Gaylen, David corrected himself. He forked up a bite of his pumpkin pie and chewed reflectively. After what had happened, he could never go to her again, not without taking the chance of putting her in the Facility's clutches. Whichever way he looked at it, he did not have that right, no matter how badly he needed her. . . .

He had first sensed her a year earlier, but at the time it hadn't meant much of anything to him.

Mr. Simic and Dr. Breunner had flown him from the Facility to some military base. He knew it was near Washington because he'd recognized the monument from the air. An unmarked car drove the three of them to a building on the other side of the Potomac in Rosslyn, where in an ordinary-looking office he'd read the Zener cards for some man whom, he supposed, Mr. Simic and Dr. Breunner were trying to impress. He couldn't remember whether the other man had been impressed or not.

What he remembered was a new sensation of touching out at someone with his mind, someone not in the room but in the near vicinity. It was almost like a low-level alarm buzzing in the front part of his brain.

He was accustomed by then to the various oddities his abilities revealed, and he attached to the feeling no special significance. Although he got the idea that the person he sensed was different, in those days he assumed there were plenty like him, like his parents had been. . . .

But by the time of his near capture in New York, he knew he had assumed wrong. In the three months since he'd escaped, he'd been near probably millions of people, keeping as he did to the bigger cities, and felt no one. The person he had sensed had been different all right—different like him.

Realizing that, David felt buoyed with the first glimmer of optimism he'd felt in a long time. That person would understand—the possibilities and the dangers—and maybe would help.

After reaching Washington he had taken a bus to Rosslyn, then spent several hours of walking before he recognized the building. From there it was a matter of waiting, then of following, and finally learning from the travel-agency lady that the name of the attractive young woman was Linda Gaylen and that she was flying the next morning to Phoenix.

He had no way of being certain she would take his side, of course. She was a reporter; maybe she'd want to tell his story, or maybe she just wouldn't care to mess with something as powerful as the Facility. But that night on the butte he'd sensed that she was good and kind and would understand.

Now, as David finished his dinner, he knew it didn't matter how good and kind she might be. If he ever went to her again, the same thing would happen: He would draw them to her, and in so doing would condemn her to the same life that he lived, one of fear and fleeing.

Until they made another Voss and found him again and put him back in the Facility.

In the truck as they drove away from the butte, Dr. Breunner denied he would ever operate and pleaded with him to return, told him they needed him, but the doctor was scared and lying, and David told him to shut up.

He lied back, telling Breunner he had made Voss die. He could do the same to him, David told Breunner. Breunner went pale, and the truck swerved. After that Breunner did what he was told and answered David's questions truthfully.

David had Breunner drive to downtown Phoenix and into an underground garage across from some hotel with a taxi stand out front. There was no one in the garage at that hour. David told Breunner to open the hood and stay in the truck. When Breunner hesitated, David gave him a touch of fear. He was too angry to feel guilty about it; at that moment he hated Breunner and the Facility and everything they had taken from him.

After some fumbling with the wrong levers, the front of the truck popped open. David climbed up onto the bumper, unclipped the distributor cap, and put the rotor in his pocket, as he'd seen Burt Reynolds do in some movie. Breunner opened the door, and David told him to stay where he was, not to move for ten minutes, that David would be waiting outside the garage to make sure Breunner did as he was told. It was more movie bull, but it worked.

He took a cab to the airport and bought a ticket on the first plane out, a businessman's flight to Denver. Once the plane was in the air, he tried to sleep, but he was too wired.

From the moment Breunner began ineptly driving the truck down the awful road, David felt a gut-wrenching hopelessness. He'd been so close to her and the opportunity to explain and to beg her help, and now the moment was gone.

In the restaurant David pushed away the half-eaten wedge of pie. It wasn't fair, dammit. They'd taken his life, and now they'd taken her, and there wasn't a damn fair thing about it.

In the pictures, especially the love stories, they were always talking about broken hearts. He'd figured that was a lot of movie mush, but now he thought he knew what they meant.

CHAPTER SEVEN

"This place we are going," Breunner said.

"It's called La Nulidad," Simic said.

" 'The Nullity'?"

"Or 'The Lost.' " Simic made a dismissive gesture. "Where people send people they want to lose."

Breunner turned away and peered down at the triple canopy of jungle, broken by occasional swamp and the meander of a river. Within the helicopter it was surprisingly quiet, the noise of the rotor deadened to a dull bass tattoo by thick soundproofing. On embarking Breunner had noted that the craft's camouflage-painted exterior provided no hint of its provenance, not even an identification number. The property of someone powerful, Breunner thought; in that way he and the helicopter had much in common.

"They are all the same, these places." Frieda Kohl exhaled a cloud of smoke, stubbed out her cigarette in the armrest ashtray. She sat in a jump seat facing Breunner and Simic. "Refuse heaps."

"This one is different," Simic said. "People who go here, they're not so much locked up as *swallowed* up."

Because of the time and trouble expended before Voss was discovered, since then teams of parapsychologists working under grants administered by the Facility's cover foundation had screened inmates of all major American prisons, with no success. Thus on Voss's death they had been forced to search abroad.

In recent weeks Breunner and Kohl had visited seven institutions in five countries. It was depressing duty, and it had not produced anyone who was remotely close to being suitable.

Breunner gazed at the four men in the seats behind him. They wore uniforms without insignia and carried machine guns. To Simic, Breunner said, "Political prisoners?"

"Not the way you mean," Simic said. "Some got in bad with a dictator or backed the losing side in a coup. Some ended up on the outs with other kinds of big shots. Basically they all made the same mistake." Simic smiled. "They tried to pull a trick on the wrong mean son of a bitch."

Simic had to be in his fifties, though he looked much younger; his hard-featured, high-cheekboned face was almost unlined, his compact body slim and erect. His accent—vaguely Slavic, Breunner thought—had been faint twenty years ago and since had become almost imperceptible. He wore a khaki jumpsuit and very black sunglasses.

"The government is paid a lot of money to ignore it," Simic went on. "Like most governments they owe our people a favor."

"A warehouse," Frieda said. "Let us hope they have what we need among their stock." She was a small woman, no more than an inch or two over five feet, and given to quick birdlike gestures. Her graying hair was tied up in a tight bun, and her features seemed perpetually pinched.

The radio emitted Spanish. Through the windshield Breunner saw the larger helicopter ahead of them pull up and hover. "We're here," Simic said.

Their aircraft descended, and below them the camp grew larger, a scattering of hovels and cadaverous filthy men staring up with slack, lobotomized expressions. "My God," Breunner murmured.

Frieda glanced down with detached interest, lit

a cigarette. "Why put them here?" she asked. "Why not kill them?"

"Here is worse," Simic said.

Rogan sat on the bole of an assai palm and watched the others work. Gomez's gun boys looked more alert than usual, which was smart, Rogan thought, considering the prisoners all had machetes. They went on hacking at the jungle, their heads down. In two days they'd nearly doubled the size of the clearing.

"I don't think Gomez knows anything except that he is to extend cooperation and accommodation to whoever is coming," Chepolous said. He was lolling against the palm's trunk, his hands folded behind his head.

Rogan heard the incoming chopper. "We due for a supply drop?"

"No."

The chopper noise grew louder, and then the machine cleared the treetops. Rogan said, "Well I'll be fucked!"

Chepolous was gazing up with mystification. The chopper looked like a gigantic insect skeleton, no body except a long, thin beam with a rotor on top and a two-man bubble cockpit hanging from the front end.

"CH-fifty-four Tarhe sky-crane," Rogan said. "I haven't seen one for twenty years." Clipped to the sixty-foot length of its belly was a prefab building. "And that looks like a mobile surgical hospital," Rogan went on. "I think I'm having one of them Vietnam flashbacks you read about."

A second chopper came in under the Tarhe, a Bell passenger model. Doors opened on both sides as it descended past fifty feet, and Rogan saw gun muzzles pop out. The prisoners scattered to the perimeter of the clearing as the chopper touched down. Four soldier boys came out and covered them with M-16s. One barked an order in rapid Spanish.

"Everyone back to the camp," Gomez ordered.

Rogan regarded the choppers and the gunmen. "You know what I'm thinking?"

"Yes," Chepolous said. "Come on."

Rogan ignored him, said mostly to himself, "What goes in has gotta go out."

"You know why the procedure has failed thus far," Breunner said stubbornly.

"And I have since refined the model," Frieda flared. "It will work if we find the proper subject."

"But if we once again choose incorrectly . . ."

Simic gestured, palms up. "You can't make an omelet without breaking a few eggs."

Breunner had attempted the new enhancement three times since Frieda's modification, in prisons in Turkey, Uganda, and Cambodia. Two subjects emerged violent maniacs; the third became a catatonic, incontinent vegetable. Breunner stared at Simic. "What happened to them?"

"They were terminated."

"They were human beings," Breunner said.

"That's funny coming from you, Doctor."

Breunner slumped into a swivel chair. It was late the previous night by the time the equipment was unpacked and assembled, and he slept poorly afterward. The mobile unit comprised two rooms, with a large one-way window installed in the partition. Now they sat in the operating facility; the other room was white-walled and contained only a desk, lamp, two chairs, and the isolation unit, which looked like a carnival ticket-seller's booth except that its window was set at head level. Breunner had come to abhor the place.

Fear had stolen the life he should have had. It began in 1943 when he received his degree at the Medizinische Akademie in Düsseldorf; the next day he was assigned to Buchenwald. Refusal to perform the experiments the Führer demanded meant imprisonment or execution, so he did what he was told.

The tests involved the inoculation of prisoners with fatal diseases in an attempt to devise medications. It amounted to murder, and when the camp was liberated by the Allies, Breunner expected to be arrested and condemned. Instead he was interviewed, in German, by a civilian who revealed nothing about himself, not even his nationality. Breunner assumed from his accent he was Russian or American, and his vocabulary and phraseology marked him as a fellow physician. He wanted the results of the experiments, Breunner's and the other doctors' at the camp. Breunner turned them over and was locked up.

Two days later the man came back. "You could hang," he said.

"Yes."

"Do you want to live?"

"Yes." Breunner was twenty-six years old and terrified.

"Then you'll do as you're told," the man said.

Eventually he was put to work in research, and no one was more surprised than Breunner himself when he proved to be very good; indeed, he could say without bragging that he had been—still was—near brilliant. Nor did he go unrecognized; twenty years after he'd mortgaged his soul, he was given to Simic and the Facility.

Now he belonged to the devil.

Simic's voice was thick with menace and seemed to vibrate in the operating room. "You'll do it, Dr. Breunner." He flavored the word "doctor" with an insinuating sneer. "We can prove enough to turn your ass to green meat. It's still open season on Nazis."

Frieda seemed shaken by the threat. She turned and peered through the one-way window, lit a cigarette.

"I was not a Nazi," Breunner snapped.

"You could still die for one," Simic said in his low voice.

"This gets us nowhere," Frieda said, not looking around.

Simic let his expression soften. "She's right. We'll find an appropriate subject—"

"If there is none?" Breunner interrupted.

"Then we'll go with whoever comes closest," Simic said. "You're going to do it, Doctor."

Simic's voice turned persuasive. "Whatever else, you're a scientist. In your way you want the boy as badly as anyone."

Breunner sighed miserably and heaved himself from the chair. "Let us get it over with," he said.

The woman was maybe fifty, and about as ugly as a duck with the goiter. Still, she was the first one Rogan had seen in the better part of six months. "What say you and I get down and play the dirty dog?" he asked her.

"Do you see that mirror, Mr. Rogan?" she said. She called herself Dr. Kohl.

"Sure."

"Behind it a man with a machine gun is observing. If you touch me, he'll kill you."

"I think you're bullshitting me," Rogan said.

He expected her to argue, but she only looked at him curiously. "You are in superior physical shape to the other men here. Why is that?"

He'd limited his weight loss to the fifteen pounds that disappeared in the box, and he hadn't taken sick with any of the tropical shit the others always seemed to have. He grinned at her. "I get plenty of exercise and watch what I eat," he said.

That got him another funny look. "Gimme a smoke," he said.

She set the pack and a book of matches on the

table between them. Rogan lit up and put the pack in his shirt pocket.

"Why are you here?" When he didn't answer, she gestured with her own cigarette and added, "There will be other incentives if you cooperate."

Rogan figured they could find out on their own if they wanted. "I trusted the wrong guy," he said, "instead of my own instincts."

"Go on."

"This guy paid me a lot of money to kill this woman," Rogan said. "Check that—he *promised* me a lot of money. I didn't know why he wanted her dead, nor much care. I killed her sister instead."

"Why?"

"He set it up that way." Rogan blew out smoke. "It turned out that the sister was the one he was really after, but he figured if I knew who she was, I'd tell him to go piss up a rope."

"And who was she?"

"Main squeeze of a very powerful bad guy with a lot of contacts, worst sort of dude to fuck with. Soon as I did her, he put out the word."

"Where was this?"

"Nairobi. Anyway, before I can get of town, before I even know I've fucked up, I'm surrounded by niggers with guns. Next time I wake up, I'm in a canvas sack and my head hurts. Next time I wake up after that, I'm here."

The woman leaned forward, gave him a look. "You said you failed to trust your own instincts. Tell me about that."

Rogan shrugged. "People try to feed me a line of shit, I can usually tell. Call it a sixth sense. I had a bad feeling this time, but I needed the money, so I greased her." Rogan waved a hand. "Look what it got me."

"Have you killed many people, Mr. Rogan?"

Rogan gave her the grin. "Do gooks count?"

• • •

"They didn't do the card business with you?" Rogan asked Chepolous in Gomez's office.

"No," the Greek said. "As soon as I told them I was a physician, they terminated the interview. Perhaps I shouldn't have."

"You want a smoke?" Rogan offered the pack. "She gave me a carton."

"I'm trying to quit."

Rogan laughed and lit up. He turned the desk fan a little so it hit him in the face. Chepolous regarded him. "What did they do after the cards?"

"They gave me a test. Maybe it was my final exam."

"What sort of test?"

"There's these pairs of sentences, like 'I enjoy drawing pictures' and 'I enjoy beating my meat.' I'm supposed to pick one."

Chepolous nodded. "MMPI or a similar inventory. They draw a psychological profile from your responses."

"You mean like did I want to fuck my mother?"

"In a manner of speaking," Chepolous said. "You responded honestly?"

"Funny thing is, I did."

"Why?"

"Hunch." Rogan said. "I think they're looking to take someone back with them, some type."

"A sociopath?"

"Is that what I am?"

"I think it's safe to say," Chepolous said ironically.

"What's that mean?"

"You are unburdened by moral sense."

"That's me," Rogan said cheerfully.

"He's another Voss," Breunner said.

Simic turned the swivel chair to face him. "I thought that's what we're looking for."

"Even if the enhancement is successful, we may not be able to control him."

Simic turned to Frieda Kohl. "How did he score on the cards?"

"In the ninety-eighth percentile," she said, stubbing out a cigarette and lighting another.

"Better than any of the others on whom Dr. Breunner operated."

"Yes."

"Then we proceed." Simic stared at Breunner long enough to give him a chance to protest. When he did not, Simic stood and paced across the operating room. "If the enhancement does work on him . . ." He was thinking aloud, as if voicing success would insure it. "Like Voss he's not traceable."

Frieda nodded and consulted some notes. "After Vietnam—he was decorated three times, incidentally—he stayed in that part of the world, first Bangkok and then Manila. He became involved in various criminal enterprises, eventually contract murder. He was never caught until now. His responses lead me to believe he is able, on a rudimentary level, to sense deception."

Simic nodded judiciously. "Plus he can operate in the United States without standing out. He's at least nominally American."

"Another recommendation," Breunner said.

"He's the one, Doctor," Simic said.

"Too bad."

"Not if the enhancement works."

"I meant for us," Breunner said.

Simic stared at him angrily, then spun on his heel. "What about this Chepolous?" he said to Frieda. "The physician."

"What about him?"

"Is there any chance he might guess the nature of our work?"

"Not from anything I told him."

"Rogan seems to be his friend. What did *he* tell him?"

The question hung in the air a moment, and then Breunner said, "No . . ."

"They're disposable, Doctor," Simic snapped. "Can't you get that through your head? They are all disposable."

Breunner drew a ragged breath. "Except the boy."

"Right," Simic admitted. "Except the boy."

Chepolous threw off the thin blanket and said, "Who . . . what is it?"

"It's me."

Chepolous made out Rogan's bulk in the darkness, crouching beneath the low roof of his hootch. "What time is it?"

"Beats me," Rogan said. "I left my watch in my other pants."

Rogan's tone made Chepolous shrink back from him.

"They're taking me out of here," Rogan said.

"You've . . . you've come to say good-bye."

"Something like that."

Chepolous's eyes adjusted, and he could see Rogan's expression: happy, almost hungry.

"They say I've got to do something for them first," Rogan said.

"What?"

"Kill you."

Rogan almost liked the Greek, so he did it quickly, clamping down on his neck with both hands until he quit kicking. What little noise Chepolous made didn't attract any attention that Rogan noticed when he dragged the featherweight body from the hootch. He slung it over his shoulder and made his way a couple hundred yards out into the jungle, the farthest he'd ever ventured from camp. Rogan didn't spook easily, but when he heard movement in the brush, he left the corpse and hightailed it back double-quick.

The funny part was the next morning, when the Indians came in with Chepolous's head and claimed the bounty.

Simic held open the door of the prefab building and said, "After you, Mr. Rogan."

Rogan leered at the guy and stepped inside, saw the two guards with their guns leveled and beyond them Breunner and the Kohl woman, in gowns and surgical masks. They stood beside a table draped in a lot of green cloth, bright long-necked lamps focused on it. Rogan said, "What the fuck?" and Simic hit him on the back of the head with just the right amount of force.

It took both guards and Simic to heave Rogan up onto the operating table. Frieda Kohl peeled back Rogan's eyelid, peered at his pupil through an ophthalmoscope. "No concussion," she said.

"Of course not," Simic said with professional pride.

Frieda flicked on an electric razor and ran it over Rogan's head in long rows, as if mowing a lawn. Hair clumped to the floor.

"We must wait until he's conscious before anesthetizing him," Breunner said.

"That doesn't make a whole lot of sense," Simic said.

"Are you telling me how to perform an operation?"

"What I'm telling you," Simic said coldly, "is not to fuck up, especially not on purpose. Because if you do, Dr. Kohl here will know, and she'll tell me. Won't you?"

Breunner looked at her and saw it was the truth.

After all, she had as much to lose as he. He said nothing; there was nothing to say. Frieda went back to her work.

A few minutes after she finished, Rogan began to stir. Frieda was ready with the hypodermic and had already tied the rubber tube around Rogan's arm. She injected him in the fold of the elbow, and he went limp once more. Frieda picked up a scalpel and made several deft cuts, then peeled back a flap of skin as if opening a trapdoor.

Breunner turned on the drill, its whir filling the small room. He drew a steadying breath and bent over Rogan. The whir become a whine as the spinning steel bit into bone.

BOOK
TWO

CHAPTER EIGHT

The freckle-faced guy across the octagonal table drew a king to top his nine-ten-queen, and David sighed. No poker face was going to buy him this pot. The guy pushed two black chips to the table's middle and worked hard not to look at David. David was showing a four-straight to the jack.

"You're a lucky son of a buck, Joe Don," David said, borrowing an expression he'd heard during a game in Branson, Missouri, two days earlier. "You pulled your straight." David smiled ruefully. "Looks like I got caught bluffing." David peeked at his hole-card once more—a queen, for the smaller straight—flipped his other cards facedown atop it. "I've got to fold."

"He don't have it either, kid," one of the other players said. "You're showing a jack, and the other three have been buried."

"Only two were buried," David contradicted. "Right, Joe Don?"

Joe Don looked around the table, then showed his hole-card, the case jack. "Like you figured," Joe Don said, almost apologetically. This was a particularly pleasant bunch, though David no longer ran into any real antagonism of the sort he'd gotten from Packard in New York. Also it had become a lot easier to persuade bartenders and bellhops to tell him where to find games, and after that to talk his way in. He'd fine-tuned his ability to give a touch of good feeling, just enough to win people's confidence without them feeling any inkling that they'd been zapped. That was the word Mr. Voss had used in Arizona, and it struck David as appropriate as any other.

David chucked in his last five-dollar yellow chip as a sporting gesture, patted the table with both palms. "Thanks, gentlemen," he said. "I guess I'll call it a morning." The room was on the third floor of an elegant old hotel called Marigold's Crystal Plunge; the curtains, illuminated by the first low rays of sunrise, were linen, the old paintings on the walls were real, and the captain's chair from which David rose was solid oak. He didn't need pillows anymore; he'd grown a good two inches in the past ten weeks.

David descended flights of the flaring staircase to the high-ceilinged lobby. Men and women in terry-cloth bathrobes and plastic sandals crossed the thick carpet to doors marked Mud Bath, Main Pool, Massage. At the hotel's barred cashier's window, David handed the clerk the two hundred-dollar bills he'd decided not to risk in the game. The clerk placed the money in an envelope, which he carefully stashed in the safe. David thanked him, folded his receipt, and placed it in his shirt pocket as he wandered out onto the hotel's front porch.

He'd lost a little over four hundred since midnight, but it had nothing to do with his play nor his strength. It was just one of those nights when the cards did not come; no gambler could do anything about that. Since Arizona he'd raised his safe-money to two thousand, along with a playing stake of nearly twice that. With his skills and that much money, the odds he'd ever go bust were infinitesimal.

From the porch David looked up and down the Grand Promenade. Hot Springs, Arkansas, was smaller than the sort of town he usually chose, but it was homey, the people friendly, and because it was a resort, lots of strangers passed through. The January morning was clear and a little crisp, maybe forty-five degrees going on sixty once the sun got to cooking. He felt warm enough; he was wearing a fleece-lined leather aviator jacket he'd bought on impulse in Fayetteville. It had looked cool on the store-window dummy, and he thought it looked pretty cool on him.

He considered going up to his room and decided he wasn't tired yet, so he took a seat in one of the rockers dotting the porch. The town at this hour was quiet—"Too quiet," David murmured, smiling. It was what the scout always said to the cavalry sergeant in western pictures, right before a passel of redskins came thundering over the nearest ridge line. But then his smile faded, because he knew his recollection of the clichéd line wasn't about the town, or cowboy movies.

For over a month, since he'd treated himself to Thanksgiving dinner and the Patriots game in Saint Louis, he'd sensed no one homing in on him; that was the quiet he found ominous. As best he could puzzle out, it meant two things.

First, Mr. Simic was confident he could track down David anytime he wished.

Second, David had a strong hunch that Mr. Simic had found someone to replace Mr. Voss, someone whom Dr. Breunner and Frieda Kohl could operate on and turn into a jammer—maybe one a lot stronger than Voss. That had to be why the surveillance had stopped; they wouldn't risk any ordinary agents when all they had to do was wait until the new guy was recovered from the surgery.

Along with his sensing and his ability to give feelings, he suspected his transmission powers were increasing as well. But he couldn't think of any good way to know; he wasn't about to start zapping people at random. Still, he'd probably be forced to find out sooner or later, because once the Facility's new guy was ready, Simic would put out an all-points bulletin,

Be on the lookout for a sandy-haired kid traveling alone by bus or plane, eleven years old—

David sat straighter and looked at his watch. It was Friday, January 4, and he was no longer eleven; two days earlier he had turned twelve. It seemed weird to forget your own birthday; even while he was confined at the Facility, Dr. Breunner had made sure he got a cake and some presents. Before that, David remembered, he'd always been a little resentful that his birthday came so close after Christmas, because he had a sneaking suspicion his parents weren't so generous with the gifts as they might have been if he'd been born in, say, June. The one time he tried out the idea on his mom, she told him that she knew he was going to be a big kid and she didn't want to be toting him around in her belly during the hot, humid summer months. Then she'd ruffled his hair and said, "You weren't some kind of accident, you know," and she hugged him.

But his mom wasn't what he wanted to be thinking about just now, so he stood and went back inside, crossed the hotel lobby to the newsstand. *American Weekly* was on the eye-level shelf, next to *Time* and *Newsweek*. He bought a copy and took it into the coffee shop, where a lady in a billowy dress said in a syrupy Southern accent, "You by yourself, hon? I'll warrant the folks are still in bed," and showed him to a booth. He left the menu unopened on the table and ordered hot chocolate; he didn't feel so hungry at the moment.

He leafed through the magazine while waiting for his drink, then turned the pages a second time as he sipped the rich, sweet chocolate, licking whipped cream from his upper lip, where the other day he'd thought he noticed a downy fuzz. He figured Linda Gaylen's name would not be among the bylines; it hadn't appeared for a couple months, since the story about the army guy who was smuggling drugs. He remembered how she looked that night in Arizona, a pretty woman with soft blond hair, a neat, trim figure, about as old as his mother would be if she were alive. . . .

A voice over his shoulder said, "There you are."

The woman standing at the table wore a white uniform with a short green apron. She had appeared now and then during the poker game, serving drinks. She was in her twenties, with soft features and reddish hair that fell across her forehead. David stood up politely.

The woman glanced down at the table, empty except for the magazine and hot chocolate. "I just got off work," she said. "Aren't you hungry?" She cleared her throat. "They said you lost a lot of money."

David understood then. "I'm all right," he said. "I've got a little left." Now he did feel hungry, and anxious for company. "Would you like to join me?" he asked. "I can treat."

The woman smiled again and slid into the booth opposite him. "We'll go Dutch," she said.

David had waffles with molasses, and the woman, whose name was Sherrilyn Casey, had scrambled eggs and hominy. David had never tried grits, so Sherrilyn made him taste hers. "I think I like hash browns better," David said.

"You're a Northern boy." But she was too polite to ask prying questions of a stranger, so she told him about herself instead. She had grown up in a tiny town called Wilbur in the northeast corner of the state, on a farm where her father and mother bred mules for farm work. "A more ornery creature you never did see," she told him, and David laughed. She was divorced, with a nine-year-old daughter. As coffee arrived, she said, "My Carrie stays with her daddy on the weekends."

David nodded, though he was unsure what she was driving at. "I've got a doublewide on the South

Flat," Sherrilyn went on. "There's room, if you're looking for a place."

Now he recognized her thoughtful Southern way of offering charity without making the recipient feel small or ashamed. He started to explain that he had enough money to get by, then stopped himself. He could use the companionship of someone good, and he sensed Sherrilyn might need someone like him as well.

On Sunday they drove north in her old dented pickup truck through rolling hills forested with oak, hickory, and gum trees. In the pickup's bed was a folded blanket held down by a cooler full of pop and sandwiches. Traffic was light this time of the year, and Sherrilyn drove well, not fast but with confidence.

She pulled up to the stop sign in a town consisting of a railroad crossing, a gas station, and a general store with bearded old men rocking in chairs out front. Neither of them had spoken for several miles, David feeling relaxed in the sunshine and the company. Sherrilyn looked both ways and said, "Your people . . ."

"Beg pardon?" David said, coming out of a daydream.

The old men watched the pickup move through the intersection. "Your folks, I mean," Sherrilyn said carefully.

She'd taken him back to her place, where he'd slept most of the day, awakening to join her for a supper of ham and mashed potatoes and three glasses of milk, and gone back to bed a few hours later. When he awoke on Saturday, he found a note explaining she was working the day shift. He did some reading, and in the evening they watched her videotape of *E.T.* It was Carrie's favorite, she told him. They sat curled at opposite ends of her sofa, growing comfortable with each other.

In the truck Sherrilyn said in response to his silence, "I don't mean to stick my nose in."

"No, it's okay," David said quickly. "My parents died when I was very young—in a car accident."

"I'm sorry."

"It was a long time ago," David said. "Now I live with Uncle Harry and Aunt Cecilia in Vermont half the year, and Grandpa and Grandma in New Orleans the other half. I'm on my way down there."

"Won't they be worried about you?"

"See, that's where the poker comes in," David said brightly. "Uncle Harry taught me how to play, and I got real good, so now, each year, he gives me some money, and then he doesn't tell Grandpa I've left until a week after I really do. Meanwhile I play cards, and if I win, I split with Uncle Harry." David shook his head in a show of regret. "I guess he'll be disappointed this time."

Sherrilyn looked at him. "Really?"

"Sure," David said confidently.

When he'd first made up the story, adjusting the geography and the timing as necessary, he'd been just out of the Facility and thought it was pretty clever. Now, with some months and a lot of miles and experience behind him, he could see that it was, on its face, a fairly unbelievable tale that owed more to all the TV sitcoms he'd watched than to the experience of real life he'd been denied. But that didn't matter now, not since he could make people believe anyway.

"Aren't you missing school?" Sherrilyn asked.

"A little," David admitted. He had not been in a classroom since the first week of second grade. "But I read a lot, and I'm pretty smart." He felt himself redden. "I don't mean to be bragging."

Sherrilyn tapped her fingernails on the steering wheel. After a while she smiled at him. "Carrie's smart too. She'll be like you." She pursed her lips and stared straight ahead through the windshield. "I miss her when she's with her father."

When they'd finished their sandwiches, on a blanket spread beneath a sprawling live oak in a little natural park a half mile up a winding trail that skirted the bank of a spring-fed creek, Sherrilyn lay back for a while with her eyes closed. Without opening them she said, "I like you, David."

"I like you too, Sherrilyn," David said, for all the world meaning it.

He was always heartened by reminders that good people were not that rare after all. He wished she could sense and he could tell her more, but all that brought him was another pang of recollection of Linda Gaylen. He lay on the blanket crosswise to Sherrilyn and worked hard to put Linda from his mind.

She came back into it that night.

They were walking on a beach near the water's edge where the sand was wet and packed and each step left a clean, molded relief of their bare feet, two sets of tracks, her imprints larger than his but the length of their strides about equal. They were close but not touching, and she was wearing a lineny dress that the high sun illuminated, so when she stopped and turned, he could see the silhouette of her figure through the material.

The image dissolved and drew into itself and became a tiny darting point of light that danced for a moment before growing once more, the sand and the water and the woman. . . .

But now she was Sherrilyn, and her dress was shorter and finer, and the wind wrapped it tight against her thighs. She opened her arms, and he moved within them. Now he was wearing bathing trunks, and her hands were moving on his back, spreading to cup his shoulders and then coming together between the blades, tracing down the ridge of his spine.

He felt the pressure of her, and her hands went on stroking, and her warmth oozed into him and grew. It made him press closer and hold her and went on growing like something straining within his belly to burst free, and nothing could make him stop holding her like that, not until the warmth was un-dammed—

David opened his eyes and stared up into dimness. He knew he had awakened from a dream, and yet he felt a very real warmth being released, and his hips as he lay on his back were thrusting up against the weight of the blanket. After a few moments he lay still, the urgency melting into a sense of lazy well-being.

His vision adjusted to the darkness, and he saw the light fixture in the middle of the ceiling of Carrie's bedroom, and when he turned his head, her stuffed toys and dolls on her pink dresser. He knew what had happened and felt kind of excited.

He'd read about it in library books, and anyway there were plenty enough references to how boys changed in all the movies that were about guys only a little older than he desperately chasing after girls. Besides, he'd noticed the transformations in himself, especially down there. He reached into his jockey shorts and touched at the wetness on his thigh. Turning into a man was nothing to be ashamed about. He wished he had some buddies his own age to talk about it with and was thinking that maybe he could discuss it with Sherrilyn—she'd know about that stuff and understand—when he heard her sharp cry through the half-opened bedroom door.

As David threw off the cover, Sherrilyn cried out again, a low, shuddering moan. He pulled on his pants.

Her door was adjacent to Carrie's bedroom, and

open far enough for him to see the foot of her bed. He hesitated, but when she made the sound a third time, he pushed the door and stepped through, said her name.

Sherrilyn was lying on her back, the bedclothes half off her so David could see her down to the waist. Her eyes were closed, but she was twitching spasmodically. David stared at her breasts for a moment, flattened and quivering. Moonlight streamed through the window to illuminate the twisted expression on her face.

"Sherrilyn?" David said more loudly. He was worried about her and felt embarrassed.

Sherrilyn arched her back, and the blankets fell down around the bottom of her stomach. She shuddered massively and threw out her arms, then lay still, her eyes remaining closed. David moved into the room, took the hem of the blanket, and started to pull it up.

Sherrilyn opened her eyes and looked at him, a foot away, her face blank for a moment before turning angry. She snatched the blanket from his hand and jerked it up to her chin. "What are you doing?" she said sharply.

"Nothing . . ." David felt uncomfortable. "You were making noises. . . . I was afraid you were hurt."

Sherrilyn's expression softened. She tucked the blanket around her, drew out a hand, and patted the bedside. "Sit with me a minute, David."

David sat. "Did you have a nightmare?"

She shook her head. "A good dream, but it seemed so real. . . ." She gave him a long look. "Were you asleep?"

"Of course." David hesitated. "I had a dream too." He knew from the books that what happened was normal and okay, but he still blushed a little when he told her.

She didn't say it was okay. She didn't say anything for a long time, just stared at him in an odd, discomforting way.

"Who was in your dream with you, David?" she said finally.

"First it was this woman I knew once." David paused again. "Then it was you."

Sherrilyn pulled the covers up tighter and moved a little away from him. He sensed confusion and something else, something out of place that he couldn't isolate for a moment. He concentrated and got it.

It was fear, but of what? There was no one here but him. . . .

He saw the way she had been in the moments before she'd awakened, the writhing and then the shuddering end to it, remembered movies he had seen. . . . "What did you dream about?" he asked.

She shook her head.

"Did you dream about me?"

"No," she said quickly.

If this were a poker game and she was betting a full house against his three of a kind, he would have gone all in to raise her. He was that certain she was lying.

"I . . . I'm tired now," Sherrilyn said. "We'll talk in the morning."

David started to speak, but her look stopped him. He rose reluctantly and went out, closing the door behind him.

A moment later he heard the snick of her lock. He could still sense fear, only slightly diminished.

In the morning she made him blueberry pancakes and tried to act as if everything was the same and fine, but David didn't need to sense to know it wasn't true: It was in her tone, her nervous gestures, the way she avoided his gaze. He told her that he'd better be moving along before Grandpa started worrying about him. She didn't protest. At the bus station she waited with him, and before he boarded, she kissed him on the forehead and said she was sorry. He thanked her for the hospitality and told her there was nothing to be sorry about.

She had done nothing wrong, but he was not so sure about himself.

His powers had become stronger, strong enough to take off on their own. He didn't blame Sherrilyn for being scared. He was scared himself.

The point in his mind: This time it had appeared by itself, and how could he be sure it wouldn't happen again, and if it did, that it wouldn't be something more destructive than a sex dream? What if he could not control it even when he was conscious? What if he got angry at someone and went right over the edge?

David stared out the bus window at the hills and hollows whizzing by. He could control it; he had to. Otherwise he would have to give up his freedom voluntarily, to turn himself over to the Facility and let Dr. Breunner cut him so he would not be a public menace. He couldn't run around like some time bomb that could be triggered by a bad word, or his own dreams. . . .

The idea was so bleak that he drifted into sleep to evade it, and when he awoke, it was late afternoon, and the bus was crossing the Louisiana state line. He remembered something his mother had told him when he was very small: Life always looked better in the morning. Well, it wasn't morning, but he did feel better. He wasn't like the others, Mr. Simic and Dr. Breunner and the cold-faced Frieda Kohl. He had morals; and he would not hurt those weaker than he, could not.

He slept again while the bus rumbled south through the lush flatness of Louisiana, was occasionally roused to semiconsciousness by the frequent stops, but did not come fully awake until the bus pulled into the New Orleans terminal at dawn. A ticket agent gave him directions, and out in front of the terminal, he caught a bus to Bourbon Street, because on television when New Orleans came up, that's where they always mentioned. It turned out to be a noisy, busy, and kind of run-down area, though the hotel he found was decent. After breakfast he returned to the room and tried to read a book of mathematics puzzles he'd been carrying around for a week, but the solutions came too easily, and anyway he was having trouble concentrating.

He turned on the TV, but all he got were game shows and soap operas and a monster truck rally on ESPN, so he clicked it back off and lay on the bed. He had to do something; he couldn't just move around from place to place and wait for them to make their new jammer and track him down.

He thought about going to Linda Gaylen again, but that was a dead-end street. For starters he didn't know where she was. Three weeks earlier, after he was certain he was not being followed anymore, he'd phoned information in a moment of weakness and asked for her number in Washington. It wasn't listed. When he called *American Weekly* magazine, he was told she was no longer an employee. He asked where she could be reached, but the woman wouldn't tell him. If he wished to leave a number where he could be contacted, the woman would try . . . David hung up, guiltily accepting the folly of his hopes.

He couldn't put her in that spot. If she was there when the new Voss found him, the guy would sense her too, and then she'd really be in hot water. "The lousy creeps," he said aloud, lying on the double bed. He would not mourn if they were all dead. Simic was a killer, and Breunner and Frieda were mad doctors who experimented on people. They deserved to die—

The thought bubbled and burst in his mind: He could kill them. He could wait until they found him, and probably he would be stronger than their new

Voss, he was growing stronger every day, so he'd let them take him back to the Facility and then kill them all—

David rolled off the bed to his feet and stood shaking. The sudden rush of awful thought had left him weak and damp with sweat. Two wrongs never made a right, and the fantasy of murder only reminded him of his fears of losing control, of doing something bad that he had no right to do, in God's eyes or his own.

He went into the bathroom and washed his face. He had to think of another way, one he could live with. Maybe he could hide out where there weren't any people, or only a few, a place so remote the Facility's APB would not reach it. But that would be worse than running, as bad as being locked up. He was lonely enough already; in cities he had contact with people, and some of them, like Sherrilyn, weren't strangers, at least for a little while.

David stared at himself in the mirror and watched his face brighten with a new thought, the first one that truly had possibilities. He left the bathroom, fetched his jacket from where he had neatly hung it in the closet, and went down to the street.

He had to go way north, near the University of New Orleans, before he found what he was looking for, near the end of Elysian Fields Avenue. It was still only ten in the morning. The store was a combination copy service and computer-rental place, and as he entered, he saw booths in the back. The guy behind the counter looked like a college student.

"Do you have Macs that people can use?" David asked. He'd learned Macs in first grade.

The guy nodded toward the booths. "Five dollars an hour," he said.

"Great." David gave him two twenties. "Probably I'll need it for the rest of the day," he said.

CHAPTER NINE

Stephen A. Shaner wore a Pittsburgh Pirates baseball cap, no shirt, and cutoff jean shorts. He sat slumped in a modernistic hardwood-and-canvas lawn chair, his sockless, penny-loafered feet propped on a low marble table. His hair had been expertly bleached to surfer blond and moussed into a casual shag that accented his open, boyish, clean-shaven features. Every few minutes he touched at his hairline in an affected gesture that Linda had noted soon after the interview began. It was contrived to show off the ring on his left pinkie, a gold setting with a diamond not quite as big as a Ping-Pong ball.

"Would you like a refill?" Shaner offered.

Linda was drinking mineral water. She said, "Thank you," and Shaner snapped his fingers and said, "Nick."

Nick was a hard-bodied man in his early forties. He had salt-and-pepper hair and was dressed more neatly than his boss, in khaki slacks and a short-sleeved Oxford shirt. He slid off the rattan stool in front of the outdoor service bar, went around to the refrigerator, and fetched a Perrier and another Dos Equis for Shaner. Shaner didn't look at him, and when Linda said, "Thank you," Nick gave her a quick grin from behind Shaner that was conspiratorial and self-deprecating at the same time. His features were high-cheeked and handsome.

"Your press bio says you started out in the NBC

mail room," Linda said to Shaner. "Isn't that sort of a cliché?"

"Sure, but in my case it's true." Shaner gave her a brilliant smile, revealing toothpaste-ad-perfect teeth.

Shaner had plenty to smile about. At the age of twenty-eight he owned and ran Essayess Productions, a company with five series running on the networks, including *Rattigan's Rangers*, the top-rated one-hour action-adventure show for the second year in a row, and *Ham on Wry*, a new sitcom that had put a hammerlock on the number-four spot by the end of its third month on the air.

"Essayess is privately held," Linda said, "but your per-episode production costs are available in *Variety*, along with the licensing fees the networks pay you, the foreign-rights income, and the projected syndication value of your shows." Linda took a sip of her drink. "Would it be reasonable to estimate your income at a million a month?"

"That's in the ballpark," Shaner said complacently.

Linda glanced across the sweeping backyard. Beyond a tennis court was a free-form swimming pool that had to be twenty-five yards long, and near it a guest cottage as big as the average suburban home. Paved paths cut among luxuriant gardens occupying what must have been two acres of prime Bel Air real estate. A high brick wall topped with cast-iron spikes enclosed it, the effect softened by cascades of bougainvillea.

Linda smiled prettily at Shaner. "I wonder how I can get my readers to conceptualize a number like that."

"Write that Steve Shaner makes more in a week than the average Joe makes in a lifetime," Nick said from the bar.

Shaner gave Nick an elaborate look. "I beg your

pardon," he drawled, "but I don't recall anyone requesting your input."

"I could go upstairs and polish my gun," Nick said, "although, in my professional opinion, Ms. Gaylen doesn't look like she's planning to take a crack at you."

Shaner gave Linda a put-upon frown, and she shook her head in feigned sympathy. She caught Nick looking at her, as if he knew she was softening up Shaner for the kill.

"I don't relish my necessity for a bodyguard," Shaner said primly. "But in this day and age . . ."

"Do you think you're particularly lucky?" Linda said.

Shaner shook his head no. "Not particularly smart, either. I seem to be good at one thing: coming up with ideas for shows that people will watch. If the networks are stupid enough to pay me ridiculous amounts of money to do it, I'm sure as hell not stupid enough to turn it down."

"You think there's ever such thing as having enough money?" Linda asked. "Or even too much?"

"What do you mean by too much?" Shaner said.

"More than you need. More than you could ever spend. Money you obtained just to show you could."

Shaner looked puzzled. Nick was watching her with shrewd amusement.

"I've got an idea for an episode of *Addison and Steele*," Linda said. *Addison and Steele*, about the adventures of two L.A.-based reporters named Jill Addison and Mike Steele who worked for a tabloid called *The Tatler*, had been Shaner's first green-lighted show and was still drawing a respectable audience share after four seasons.

Shaner gave her an indulgent nod. Linda knew what he was thinking: In L.A., the gag went, every cabbie, car-hop, and bartender was prepared to pitch a script at any opportunity.

"There's this actor," Linda said. "He's in his sixties, very famous—long, distinguished movie career. He's rich, and though he doesn't have to work, he's a professional who wants to continue to practice his craft."

"A Burt Lancaster or Robert Mitchum type," Nick said, enjoying this.

"Since there aren't many film roles for his persona and age," Linda went on, "he does TV now and then. One day his agent hears that some producer is doing a four-hour, two-part remake of *Huckleberry Finn*, and he figures his guy, the actor, would be perfect for the part of the Duke. The agent requests a copy of the script, it turns out it's terrific, his client the actor agrees, and he puts in for the part."

"You know," Shaner said thoughtfully, "it's not a bad idea. Doing *Huck Finn*, I mean, with Lancaster. It's by Charles Dickens, right?"

Nick snickered and Linda pressed on. "The producer is pleased to have the distinguished actor, so the producer asks the agent to bring his client down to the office so they can touch base, meet each other, and so on. The actor shows up, along with his agent, which is fine with the producer because he has business on his mind."

Linda glanced over at Nick, who continued to watch the exchange with a carnivorous smile. "The producer and agent have already agreed on an even three hundred thousand for the actor. Now, in his office, the producer asks the actor to kick back twenty-five—under-the-table cash—in exchange for the part. The actor, who happens to have principles, flatly refuses and stalks out."

"Where do Addison and Steele come in?" Shaner said.

"The actor is steamed over the producer's greed, so he goes to Jill Addison with the story, hoping she'll expose the guy."

Shaner furrowed his brows. "This guy—the producer—is hot, right?"

Linda nodded.

"If he's so hot," Shaner said, "what does he care about a lousy twenty-five grand?"

Linda shifted in her chair. "It's not just twenty-five. The producer has several shows on the air, and he's working the same grift on virtually every actor he hires. And it works, because most of them, unlike the older actor, need the work too badly to refuse, and besides, they know the producer is powerful enough to blackball them if they don't cooperate and keep their mouths shut."

"But Jill has no proof." Shaner lowered his legs and straightened in his chair, gave Linda a long, hard look. "She's looking at a libel suit, isn't she?"

Linda shrugged disarmingly.

"Isn't she?" Shaner repeated, more insistently.

"If I remember what I learned in Reporting one-oh-one," Linda said smoothly, "truth is an absolute defense against libel."

Shaner stared at her for a long moment. "I'm not so sure I like what I'm hearing," he said finally.

"Well, you're the producer."

"What's that mean?" Shaner snapped.

"Would you like to hear how Jill Addison gets her proof?"

Shaner took a deep swig of his beer.

"She makes up a list of recent guest stars on the producer's shows," Linda said, "and goes around to each of them with what she suspects. Some deny it. Some have Jill thrown out. But she and Mike Steele convince enough of them that there's power in numbers, and in the end they nail the guy."

"It works for me," Nick said from over at the bar.

"Shut up!" Shaner stabbed a finger in Nick's direction, then slowly lowered it, drew a steadying breath. "So your producer guy is pulling in maybe an extra hundred grand a week," he said to Linda. "He's still risking his career and his reputation for pocket change. Why?"

Nick had risen again, and now he stood facing Shaner. "It's like the old joke," Nick said in a hard tone. "Why does a dog lick his balls?" Nick smiled. "Because he can."

"I think you're on a power trip, Mr. Shaner," Linda said.

Shaner came to his feet. "Think what you want," he snapped. "But print it, and I'll sue your ass."

Linda gazed up at him. "Do you want to tell me your side of the story?"

Shaner turned to Nick and said, "Throw her out."

Linda stood and turned toward Nick. He smiled at her and said to Shaner, "No." Nick spun on his heel and went toward the sliding glass doors that opened on the mansion's sunken living room.

"Where do you think you're going?" Shaner said to Nick's back.

"To pack," Nick said. "I quit." He looked back at Linda. "You mind giving me a lift? I won't be long."

"I'll wait in my car," Linda said.

Steve Shaner did not bother to escort her out.

"What comes after Nick?" Linda said ten minutes later when he climbed into the Porsche. In D.C. it was probably gray and drizzly, but here in Los Angeles the day was summery and blue-skied, and she'd put the top down.

"Delvecchio." Nick tapped a forefinger on his cheekbone. "You probably noticed the Italianate good looks."

Linda went down the long curve of Shaner's driveway, turned left to Bellagio. "Where to?" she said.

"I owe you."

"How do you figure?"

"I've been thinking about walking out on the jerk for weeks," Nick said. "You got me off my butt. How about lunch?"

Linda turned right toward Sunset. "Lunch would be good." Maybe there was more he could tell her about Shaner. "How long did you work for him?"

"Two months last Tuesday. I don't think I'll miss it much. It wasn't like he was the brother I never had, if you know what I mean."

At the corner of Bel Air Road, a young woman in very dark glasses and a silk scarf over blond hair had stopped to let a Pomeranian on a leash piddle against someone's wrought-iron gate. "What did you do before that?"

"This and that." Nick shrugged, as if the subject bored him. "I technical-advised on one of those buddy-cop movies that they're turning out by the six-pack lately. That's how I met Shaner—he was doing an MOW on the same lot. For a while before that, I did legwork for a detective agency in Century City. Once upon a time I repoed cars for a finance company in El Monte, but I got tired of running into doped-out losers with guns."

The light changed, and Linda pulled into the streaming traffic on Sunset. "Cop?"

"Long ago, in another life," Nick said, in a tone that put the lid on that topic. He changed the subject. "Maybe you've got something for me. I could help you nail Shaner," Nick said.

"Let's start with lunch," Linda suggested.

At two in the afternoon, Nate 'n' Al's was mostly empty. So was the rest of downtown Beverly Hills at that hour on a Wednesday; everyone was in air-conditioned offices making deals, except for the odd bored-and-rich housewife in the tony shops along Rodeo Drive, spending her deal-maker husband's deal money. In one of the deli's corner banquettes, a reedy man in an expensive but nonetheless evident wig raised his voice to say, "Four points of the gross is as low as he'll go." He was addressing a guy in a loud jacket.

Nick Delvecchio waved one-half of an overstuffed corned-beef sandwich. "Keith Framingham, right?"

Keith Framingham was indeed the established actor who'd first approached Linda with the revelation of Shaner's kickback scheme. She hesitated a moment, then decided to trust him. "You knew what Shaner was doing?"

Nick bit a large half-moon out of the center of his sandwich. "Shaner considered me part of the furniture. He didn't worry about what he said in front of me. He doesn't really need a bodyguard, but it's the latest status symbol. I was on a par with his pinkie ring. You noticed it, right?"

Linda nodded.

"Who do you write for?" Nick asked.

"I'm free-lancing. I think the *Times* will take this one. I was with them once, and I've still got some ins there."

Nick thought for a moment. "Okay, so Framingham came to you, and you believed him. Then what?"

Linda scooped up a forkful of scrambled eggs and lox. "I talked to a half-dozen other actors and actresses who'd worked for Shaner," Linda said.

"Who?"

Linda named them.

"And?" Nick asked.

"I got a half-dozen denials."

"They were lying," Nick said.

"Five of them were, anyway."

Nick looked at her curiously. "How did you know?"

Linda shrugged. "I've been a reporter long enough so I can sense a lie."

"Just like that?" Nick said skeptically.

"Uh-huh."

"Okay," Nick said. "Which one was telling the truth?"

"Philip Campion," she said. Nick's look told her she was still on the right track.

Philip Campion was a leading-man type with twenty-five years of solid television work, mostly in made-for-TV movies and miniseries. He had a reputation for being untemperamental, hardworking, and eminently honest. "Campion told me off the record that he'd heard rumors about Shaner, but that wasn't any reason not to work for him. Campion has been with the same agent for most of his career, trusts her completely, and is sure she wouldn't agree to a kickback. Apparently Shaner decided Campion was too risky and never asked for one."

"But the other five Shaner could push."

"Uh-huh. The second male lead in the same MOW that Campion was in. Two actresses with small regular roles in his sitcoms, the next-door neighbor, whatever. The Bolivian bad guy in a six-episode arc of *O'Flaherty, DEA,* and the mother-in-law on *Welcome to Wonderland.*"

"You couldn't get confirmation from any of them?"

"I didn't say that," Linda pointed out. "I told each that I knew they were holding back on me, and I understood why. Hollywood is a small, gossipy town on a perpetual power trip. They're afraid Shaner could get them blackballed, and they're right. I promised to protect their identities, but I said that if someone else got hold of the story—and sooner or later someone will—they might not be so lucky." Linda smiled. "After that they talked."

"What now?"

"Give Shaner a chance to deny, and then ask him to promise to cut it out."

"If he does . . ."

"I'll kill the story."

Nick looked surprised. "Why would you do that?"

"Because it's the only leverage I have and the only bargain I can make."

"Why do you want to make a bargain? I thought your job was to report, period."

"I did too. Lately . . ." She hesitated. "A couple months ago something happened that made me change my mind. That's one of the reasons I'm free-lancing. I want the autonomy to decide where I'm going to stick my nose, and what I'm going to do about whatever I sniff out."

"Scumbags like Shaner deserve to be exposed."

"No argument," Linda said, "but what good will it do? If I write the story, it won't change a damned thing. The fact is that no matter how creepy he is, Shaner is very good at making a lot of money for a lot of people. Outside of buggering six-year-old boys at the corner of Hollywood and Highland in broad daylight, there's little he can do to make those people kill the goose that lays the golden eggs. But if I can get him to stop ripping off people powerless to object, I've accomplished something, and these days that means a lot to me."

Nick stared at her for a long moment, then tried to snap his fingers, which turned out to be impossible since they were slick with corned beef. "Wait a minute, I know where I've seen your name. You used to write for *American Weekly*."

"I took a leave of absence."

She'd been in L.A. since before Christmas, long enough to feel comfortable with the move. She'd liked the city when she'd reported for the *Times*, and now, on returning, she found she liked it still. If she decided to go back to staff work, *American Weekly* had a large bureau here, and Brian Dancer had promised her a spot whenever she said the word.

After a while she thought she might take him up

on the offer, but for now she was keeping her options open. That was one of the reasons she was still living "temporarily" in an apartment hotel on Wilshire and clinging to the freedom of working piece rate for the *Times* and other local publications. "I needed to turn my back on some bad luck I'd had," Linda said. "When people want to escape, it seems like L.A. is the place they think of."

Nick put down his sandwich.

"I meant me," Linda said.

"Sorry." Nick gave her a long, frank look. Finally he said, "You hit the nail on the head. I'm a runaway myself."

"I've been doing most of the talking." Linda pushed her plate aside. "I'm not bad at listening, though."

The waitress came up, and they asked for coffee. "Detroit," Nick said. "Uniform, then detective division. Fifteen years, all told. I was a good cop." It came out more self-effacing than a brag.

Nick looked away, as if his past were being projected onto the restaurant's wall. "But then one day I got shot."

Linda watched him stir sugar into his cup.

"I'm on this bad-check case, about as routine as they come," Nick said. "I'm supposed to talk to a woman who was one of the check-kiter's victims. I get the wrong house. Officer in charge transposed two numbers when he typed the address on the prelim report. Something as dumb as that."

"Those things happen," Linda said.

Nick smiled wryly. "Things happened, all right. I go up to the place, I hear familiar sounds: shouting, swearing, things being smashed. Domestic altercation. Okay, I'm a detective, this isn't my business, but I'm still a cop. I ring the bell, guy opens the door, he smells like he's been swimming in an ocean of gin. I identify myself, and he says . . ." Nick fiddled with his spoon. "You can guess the sort of thing he says."

"And then?"

"Then he pulls out a Smith and Wesson thirty-eight, and it goes off." Nick winced at the memory. "But I'm moving, instinct I suppose, and he only gets me in the side. Nothing vital is drilled, but I want to tell you that at the time it hurt like nothing I've ever felt before."

Nick tasted the coffee. "There's not much more," he said. "I got out my own gun out and shot him three times in the chest, nice, tight grouping. Any one of the slugs would have been enough, the coroner said. There wasn't any trouble with the department, either, no question about whether I used justifiable force. As for the guy, he was nobody, some mope with a long record, a history of drinking and spouse abuse, and an unregistered revolver." Nick gazed across the table at her. "Does this strike you as stupid?"

"Of course not."

"The point is," Nick said, almost angrily, "I didn't like killing someone, and I didn't want to do it again, so I quit. I think that about covers it."

"Were you married?"

Nick nodded. "Some cops make lousy husbands. I was one of them, even before this happened." He looked up quickly. "I don't mean I was cheating on her."

"I understand," Linda said. "Long, odd work hours, a lot of stress that you couldn't help taking with you. I've known a lot of cops."

"You've about covered it," Nick said. "Then, when I kind of went into a funk, the relationship went right to the bottom of the well."

"You blame yourself," Linda said gently.

"Who else?" Nick shook himself, as if trying to shed the recollection. "Thanks for listening," he said.

"Anyway, that was three years ago, and like you said, L.A.'s not a bad place to find at the end of the trail."

Linda drank the last of her coffee, cleared her throat awkwardly. "I'd better get back to work."

Nick pushed back his chair. "That business about you dropping the story if it'll bring about some changes?"

"Yes?"

"I like that."

"Thanks."

"Listen," Nick said, and stopped abruptly. Linda waited. Nick went on with schoolboylike awkwardness. "You want to have dinner sometime?"

Linda hesitated. She'd been asked out by several men since she'd come to L.A. and had turned them all down. It was not from some sense of respect for Richard's memory. She was sure that he would wish her to go on with her life.

But the idea of becoming involved remained threatening. The psychologist that she'd seen after Richard's death had predicted the reaction and suggested its root was an ultimately neurotic fear that to care was to risk another loss.

"You're seeing someone," Nick said.

"No. It's just that I'm pretty busy these days," she said lamely.

"Can I call you?"

Linda managed to grin. "Or I'll call you. They let girls do that nowadays."

She dropped him at his place, a rented bungalow in Venice. As she drove back up Wilshire, she found Nick Delvecchio replacing Steve Shaner in her preoccupations. She liked him, she decided. She liked him quite a bit. She smiled to herself. Something was telling her it was time to take a chance.

CHAPTER TEN

It took David a lot longer than he'd expected before he was satisfied he'd left out nothing important, but he enjoyed the chore and looked forward to returning to the computer place each morning. It was true what people said about getting something off your chest.

He finished toward the end of his third day hunched in front of the Mac in the work booth. Printed out, it came to sixteen pages. He scanned each to make sure there was no computer glitch and that it was all down on the paper, then fetched a pair of long scissors from the supplies table, pried the plastic disk case open, and cut the thin oxide-coated wafer inside into four pieces before discarding them. When he paid the rest of the bill for the computer time, he also bought a large manila envelope.

On the way back to the hotel off Bourbon Street he picked up a cheeseburger, fries, and large milk to go. Up in the room he set the printout on the desk, then sat Indian-fashion on the bed and went to work on his supper. He was hungry; writing was hard work.

It was funny, he thought as he dipped a fry in catsup, how up to now he'd done a pretty good job of keeping the past at arm's length. Most of the time it was the healthy way to go, because you couldn't change things that were done and over with.

David touched at the scar on his forehead as he remembered where he'd first learned that lesson.

• • •

The summer before they took him away, he joined a Cub Scout pack and made the minors in Little League. He was pretty good at learning knots and memorizing the Scout oath and all, though he found the rituals a little bogus, but he was only decent on the baseball diamond and didn't make the starting team until a week before the end of the season, when he was put in right after the regular fielder fell out of a dead apple tree and broke his wrist.

In his first game as a starter, in the top of the third with the score tied at two runs each, the lead-off batter on the other team—the Eagles, they were called—hit a lazy pop fly. David only had to move two steps to get under it. He saw himself standing with his feet set, his glove up, and his right hand ready to cup the ball within it, remembered it growing bigger as it plunged down toward him. It hit the glove's pad, bouncing to the side. David grabbed and missed. An angry shout rose from the dugout as he chased the errant ball down, pegged it toward the cutoff man, and missed by five feet, and he heard cheers from Eagle fans as runners crossed home plate.

His error was the beginning of a five-run Eagles' rally. The coach lit into him good when he and his teammates finally managed to retire the side, and some of the other kids took it up. They had a right, he supposed. Through the mesh fence around the dugout, he could see his mother and father in the bleachers, watching the scene. His mother caught his eye, gave him a wink to tell him it was okay.

David already knew that; everyone made an error now and then. The thing was to try to do better.

He had his chance in the top of the last inning. By then the game was pretty much lost; the Eagles had scored five more, while David's team hadn't advanced a man past second base. In his at-bat David had gotten to first, but only because the shortstop made a throwing error on his weak grounder.

With none out the Eagles had men on second and third, and if those runners scored, the Eagles won because they'd be twelve runs ahead, and when that happened, the game was called. The batter was the Eagles' clean-up man, a big eight-year-old lefty. He stepped into the first pitch, and the ball came soaring in David's direction.

It was going over his head, David could tell that right away, maybe even over the fence, but that didn't mean he couldn't try for it. Backpedaling wouldn't get him there in time, so he turned and ran, looking over his shoulder as the ball arced high above the field and began its descent. His cap blew off and cartwheeled across the grass. David ran harder, keeping his eye on the ball, and then he launched himself into the air, dived with his glove extended. The ball plopped into the pocket, and he folded the leather around it, and a split instant later his head plowed into the fence.

David scrambled to his feet, saw the cutoff man isolated a third of the way into the outfield, flung the ball. It hopped in front of the baseman and into his glove, and the other kid whirled and rifled it toward third. As David caught his breath, he saw that both base runners had neglected to tag up, certain he'd never catch the deep fly. The lead runner was heading back from home, but he was miles away when the baseman tagged the sack, turned, and chucked the ball to second to beat the other returning runner. David heard a loud cheer, but now it was hard to see, because there was blood in his eyes. He wiped it away impatiently. The second-base umpire was crouched in the classic pose, his thumb in the air indicating "Out" for the triple play.

The game stopped while a couple of the other kids walked David off the field. His mother, who was

an R.N., wiped away the blood with professional gen-
tleness and said, "Looks like you'll need a couple of
stitches."

"Can we stay until the game is over?" David
asked.

It didn't take long; after David's team went hit-
less, the Eagles won when their second batter drove a
towering hit over the head of David's replacement,
and it rolled all the way to the fence, but after they'd
lined up and shook hands, David was surrounded by
his teammates, everyone hollering, "Great catch,
Dave," and that sort of thing. When they were done,
the coach took him aside and said, "I wouldn't have
yelled at you if I'd known it would make you ram
your head into the fence."

"I was watching the ball like you always tell me,
Coach," David said. The coach rumpled his hair, and
David grimaced because it made his head hurt, and
the coach apologized again.

In the car on the way to the emergency room,
David said, "Do you think I'll have a scar?"

"Why, do you want one?" his mother said, teasing him. But actually he didn't mind when, after the
stitches came out and the wound finished healing, he
was left with that little ridge of raised puckered skin
just above his hairline, where it couldn't be seen but
where he could feel it and remind himself that there
wasn't any use moping when things went bad, only
in working to make them better.

In the hotel room David finished his dinner,
balled up the dirty wrappings, and dumped them into
the wastebasket. He sat down at the desk, opened the
drawer, found a ballpoint pen with the hotel's name
etched into the plastic, and drew the printout in front
of him. With the pen poised over it, he began to go
over what he'd written.

> My name is David McKay. I was born in Iowa
> City, Iowa. My parents' names were Philip McKay and
> Jennifer Perkins.
> They met while they were going to school at the
> University of Iowa. When I was three, we moved to
> Hanover, New Hampshire, so my father could study
> at Dartmouth for a doctor's degree in English. My
> mother was a nurse and got a job at the Mary Hitch-
> cock Hospital.

His father was tall and broad-shouldered, with
sandy hair like David's and a face that laughed easily,
and his mother was only a few inches shorter and
handsome, with long blond hair that she banded up
in a ponytail when they went on hikes. His earliest
memories of being with them, when he was three and
a half or four, centered on those trips in the White
Mountains, a couple of miles at first and then longer
as he grew bigger and stronger. He'd always carried
at least some of his own gear, a daypack when he was
real little and later a full one, twenty-five pounds with
his sleeping bag, and on the last trip, two weeks before the end, they'd camped out for three nights.

It always seemed to David that their relationship
was different from most of the kids in his school; his
mother and father made rules like all parents, and on
the infrequent occasions when he broke them, they
punished him fairly and without anger. They got
along; David loved them but more than anything
thought of them as his friends.

Life was comfortably ordinary. He had plenty of
pals in school, girls as well as boys; he'd never shared
some of the other guys' dislike of or discomfort with
girls. He happened to be the brain in the class, the
one who always knew the answer and got the best
grades, but that was because schoolwork came easily
to him. He didn't think it made him special or better,
and even as a little kid, he understood that the few of

his classmates who held it against him were just insecure.

I met Dr. August Breunner during my first week of second grade. On the night I told my parents about him, we were having meatloaf. One of my mother's patients had died during the day. The man was only thirty-five years old, but very overweight, my mother said, and he'd had a heart attack.

I remember the meatloaf and the fat man because my mother was feeling bad about him and needed to talk even though it wasn't her fault. After she finished her story, she told me she was sorry that she had forgotten to ask me how school had been that day. So I told her and my father about Dr. Breunner, except that when he'd come to my class that day, he called himself Dr. Rossbach.

Our teacher told us that Dr. Rossbach was a scientist who had permission to test us for an important project. She explained that the results would be given to the school so the school could use them to help us, but as far as Dr. Rossbach's project went, he wouldn't even have our names, just numbers so he could match up the tests. Our teacher said if our parents asked, we could tell them that everything would be kept private.

First he gave us IQ tests. I knew that's what they were because they'd given them the year before. My mother told me that time I scored one hundred and fifty-something. I know now that's very good, but I'm not writing it down here to brag, only because it might have something to do with the way I am.

Next the doctor showed some pictures on a screen with an overhead projector and asked us to write little stories about them.

The third test was with Zener cards.

I figured out later that the whole business of testing everyone in school, and the IQ tests and the business with the pictures, was baloney. All that Dr. Breunner really cared about was to test me on the cards, and later at the Facility when I asked him, he said I was right.

At the Facility I also asked Dr. Breunner to give me books and articles I could understand explaining the cards and some other things, and he did. Zener cards were invented in the early 1930s by Dr. J. B. Rhine and a scientist named Carl Zener who specialized in how people perceive things. The cards are used to test people for what they call "psi" powers, which aren't much different from what the science-fiction books call mental telepathy, except that psi really exists. I guess if anyone knows that, it's me.

Anyway, there are twenty-five cards in a Zener deck, five each with the same symbol—a star or circle or rectangle or cross or wavy lines. The experiment is pretty simple, or as Dr. Breunner called it, elegant, because it doesn't depend on language or intelligence. It can be used on anyone who can tell one shape from another, even a kid.

The way it works is, a person turns the cards one at a time so the other person can't see the symbol. At each turn the first person concentrates on the symbol, and the second person tries to guess what it is.

Odds are another thing I learned about, especially later in my stay at the Facility, when I got the idea about playing poker. The odds of calling the Zener cards, if you're just guessing at them and have no psi, are what you'd expect, which is one chance out of five. That means that if you go through a full deck, plain guessing will turn out to be right five times in twenty-five cards, over the long run.

In school that first time, Dr. Breunner ran me through six decks. My scores were nine, eight, eight, ten, seven, and eight again.

When I told my parents all of this, right away they were upset. My father got up without finishing his meatloaf and went into the guest bedroom he used for a study, and when he came back, he had a set of Zener cards of his own. I wasn't surprised, even though I'd never seen Zener cards before that day. I was seven years old, I didn't know that they had to do with psi experiments, and I supposed Zener cards were some game that adults did all the time.

My father had me turn my back to the table, and then he did the cards with me. I scored ten, twelve, and nine, and then on the fourth deck, fourteen. My mother said Oh shit, so I knew she was plenty upset, though I couldn't figure why.

They asked me about the man who called himself Dr. Rossbach. I described him and said he talked with a German accent. Actually, I didn't know the accent was German; I said it was like the enemy soldiers talked in old war movies.

David looked up from the page and rubbed his eye with a knuckle. Dr. Breunner was indeed his enemy, and yet there were times he almost felt sorry for the old man. Still, he wasn't about to let sympathy get in the way of clear thinking. If it came down to a choice between his own freedom and Dr. Breunner's safety, well . . . Dr. Breunner would have to look out for himself.

Their relationship hadn't started off on the right foot, that's for sure. For openers Dr. Breunner had lied to him. When his parents found out about that part, they got really bothered.

After they finished asking me questions about the doctor, my parents went back in the study and left me to watch TV. I could hear them in there talking. Arguing was more like it, and it made me feel bad, because I didn't know what I'd done to start the argument. I wanted to stop them, and also I'd remembered something else, so I went and knocked on the door. My father was at his desk, figuring on his calculator, and my mother was sitting on the bed. As I went in, my father was telling my mother that the probability of me doing so well if I was just guessing was some high number.

They'd taught me it was okay to have secrets, but I told them that I knew this secret was about me, and it was scaring me. My mother said she was sorry and gave me a hug. I asked them if they'd noticed that I'd done better on the cards just then than I had in school.

They had. My mother said maybe it was because I was reading someone I was close to, and my father said that also I was reading someone else who had psi. I shook my head and said that I thought it was because the doctor cheated me.

Dr. Breunner wanted me to concentrate on doing as best I could, and I know now he is a good-enough psychologist to have figured out I liked to compete and win. So he'd turned the guessing into a game. With each kid he tested, he said whether the kid was right or wrong after each card, and someone at the chalkboard would mark it up, like a score. Well, I told my parents that sometimes he'd called me wrong when I'd guessed right.

Later Dr. Breunner admitted to me that he'd been afraid the teacher might be smart enough to figure out that what I was doing was extraordinary, so he'd kept my score down.

My parents were shook up and sort of jumped on me, wanting to know how I knew Dr. Breunner lied. I thought they were calling me a liar, and I got a little angry. I said I didn't know, at least I couldn't prove it. I said that for cripe's sakes, you could tell when someone was lying to you.

What I'd really done, though, was sense, which I'll explain in a while. I'd been able to do it for a couple of years, though I didn't know it was sensing. I'd ask another kid to borrow a toy or something, and he'd say he didn't remember where he'd put it, and I'd know that was bull. I didn't mind. If the kid didn't want to lend it to me, that was his right, and besides, I really did think that anyone could tell when someone was lying to him.

David reread the line and laughed. His sensing was an accident of fate and genetics, and all it had gotten him was in trouble. He never much liked using it, especially in poker—he felt vaguely guilty that it was sort of cheating—but he had to eat.

The thought made him realize he was hungry again; at least he could stand dessert. He locked the door carefully behind him and went down to the street. At the end of the block, there was one of those ice-cream places where you could pick whatever toppings you wanted. David got a scoop each of jamocha fudge and chocolate-chocolate chip, with Reese's Bits and Red-Hots, to go. On the way back to the hotel, he passed the café where he'd gotten his dinner and almost went in for another bag of fries to go with the ice cream but decided there was no point in overdoing it.

French fries played a pivotal role in an old piece of McKay family folklore: the story of how his mother and father had met. His father had been reading a textbook in the college snack bar, and his mother sat down with her tray across from him. His father was so into his book that he didn't even glance at her, and after a minute he reached out absentmindedly and snagged one of her fries, thinking he was taking it from his own plate. He finished them all before he finally looked up and saw her for the first time, studying him and trying not to laugh out loud.

David unlocked the hotel room, set the ice-cream container on the desk, and pulled over the printout.

He went on reading as he attacked the sundae with a plastic spoon, careful not to dribble on the pages.

It was only fair that my parents explained to me what was bothering them, and they did, but at first I couldn't see what their story had to do with anything.

Since they were students when they got married, they were pretty broke most of the time, they told me that night. A way they made extra money was to volunteer as subjects for research experiments, mostly in the psychology department, and one of them used Zener cards.

Both of them did well, but nothing like me, maybe two or three cards better than average. Still, it was statistically significant, I found out from Dr. Breunner, and he knew, because the researcher my parents worked for was getting money from the Facility. What caught the researcher's attention was that at the time, my mother was six months pregnant with me.

Dr. Breunner, who was calling himself Dr. Morgenstern then, had this theory that psi was hereditary, and this was the first time he'd ever run into two psis who were having a baby together. A week after my parents thought they were finished with the experiment, Dr. Breunner showed up in Iowa City and asked to meet with them.

He offered my parents a lot more than they'd ever been paid before if they'd do the cards for him. After they did, with about the same results, Dr. Breunner started asking questions about the baby my mother was going to have. He wanted to know if the pregnancy had been normal, and if my mother had taken tests to find out if I was going to be a boy or a girl.

There was something about Dr. Breunner that bothered my parents. First, they checked and found out he wasn't with the college. Second, they didn't like the way he seemed so interested in me. But I think now that the most important thing was that they could sense some in those days, and they sensed Dr. Breunner was not someone to trust. By the time I'm writing about when I was seven, my parents weren't nearly as good as they'd once been at the Zener cards, and maybe their sensing power had begun to fade. According to what I've read, this happens with some psis.

Anyway, Dr. Breunner told my parents that he might like to do follow-up tests over the years and offered more money if they'd stay in touch with him. My parents said no. Now, when they found out what had happened at school, they were wondering if Dr. Breunner had managed to keep track of them anyway, so he could test me once I was old enough and see if his heredity hunch was right.

It was. He told me so himself.

That same night my father called my school principal at home and found out that the man who called himself Dr. Rossbach was still in Hanover, so he went to see him. Sure enough, it was Dr. Breunner. Dr. Breunner pretended to be surprised, then told my father he was glad to see him. When my father told Dr. Breunner what he was thinking, Dr. Breunner laughed and said my father was being paranoid.

Dr. Breunner did admit that he was still working on experiments having to do with psi. He said he was traveling around the country giving the cards to a lot of schoolkids, and it was just coincidence that I turned out to be one of them. But when my father asked why he had been Dr. Morgenstern in Iowa and he was Dr. Rossbach now, Dr. Breunner wouldn't answer.

The next day, during afternoon recess, the principal came out and got me and took me to his office. I could tell something bad had happened, but the principal wouldn't tell me what.

A man in a state policeman's uniform was waiting in the office. He said my parents had been hurt bad in a car crash and that he was going to take me to them. I was really worried and too confused to sense that the man was lying, so naturally I went out with him to his police car.

Another man, dressed in white, was in the backseat. I thought we'd be going to the Mary Hitchcock Hospital, but instead we went south out of town along the Connecticut River. After about five miles we turned into a plowed-over cornfield, and in the middle of it was a helicopter with the blades turning. The man in white grabbed my arm and jabbed me with a needle that made me unconscious.

A couple months ago I went to the Boston Public Library and looked up the Manchester Union Leader for the day that happened. It covers the whole state of New Hampshire, and I found the story on page two. It said that at about the same time I was being loaded onto the helicopter, my parents' car had a head-on collision with a cattle truck. My parents died right away, and so did five of the cows, and according to the article another seven had to be destroyed.

David found himself staring at the painting hanging above the desk and realized that he had stopped reading several minutes earlier. In the painting people in all sorts of gaudy harlequin costumes were capering around in the street during a Mardi Gras parade. David had to blink to keep it in focus; his eyes were moist.

It was past ten at night. He set the printout aside and went into the bathroom. As he washed his face and brushed his teeth and undressed, he felt hollow weariness, but after he turned off the light and settled into the pillows, sleep was perversely long in coming.

Once again his mother's old advice proved correct; life did look a little better the next morning, if only because the day was bright and warm and pretty, and David had things to do, a purpose aside from drifting to a new city and keeping his sense on full alert. He set an Egg McMuffin, an order of potato cakes, and a large milk on the desk, and went back to work on his printout as he ate, a napkin in his lap and another near to hand.

One thing I do know is that the Facility is able to pull off some pretty neat tricks, and one of the neatest was when they "killed" me. It sure was the easiest way to not have to answer questions from the school and relatives and other people who knew me. All Dr. Breunner would tell me—it was the truth—was that the boy the two fishermen found in the Connecticut River near Northampton, Massachusetts, ten days after I was kidnapped, had died in a legitimate accident.

I can guess the rest. The boy's body would have been pretty mangled, and Mr. Simic got the local police to identify it as me. Maybe he made out I had fallen in the river, or maybe that I was glum about my parents' death and had killed myself. That doesn't matter. But I know I was the only person in my parents' will, because they told me so, which means whatever they left, the Facility stole from me, and there is another thing I have against them.

Speaking of relatives, I did try to get in touch with my grandfather once I escaped, but while I was at the Facility, he'd died. Mr. Simic never told me that. The Facility was pretty lucky there, because besides my granddad there was no one else. He was my mom's father, he'd gotten divorced before I was born, and neither he nor my mother got along with my grandmother, so I never knew her. My father was brought up in foster homes and had no family except for one sister. But I don't think my aunt is even capable of knowing I ever existed, because she has a mental illness, schizophrenia, and is in the hospital and on medication.

> So all in all I've had some tough breaks, but like I said, I always try to remember there's no point in worrying about what you can't change. It isn't always easy.

The four years he spent at the Facility was time stolen from him; it was as good as if they had thrown him into prison for a crime of which they knew he was innocent, and for that he held Simic responsible. On the other hand, though everything they did to him and demanded of him was motivated by their own ambitions, they paid attention to his needs. For four hours each weekday, Dr. Breunner or Dr. Kohl tutored him in the basic subjects: math, reading, history, and so on. Also, on Dr. Breunner's insistence, he was given sports equipment—a baseball glove, a basketball, a mountain bike on his ninth birthday, and a skateboard on his tenth. Dr. Breunner encouraged him to spend some of his time in play, with one of the guards, or sometimes with Voss when the ex-convict— he had told David about his crimes, to get a rise out of him—felt like it. When he wasn't playing or studying, he read books on his own, and he watched a lot of television. Dr. Breunner knew the combination of study, recreation, and free time was important to the preservation of his physical and emotional health.

Dr. Breunner believed that as David matured, his powers would increase. Periodically he ran David through the Zener cards, and the results confirmed his theory. By the time he turned eleven, he was averaging seventeen out of twenty-five over any number of decks, a score that was unheard of in all the years since Dr. Rhine invented the experiment.

At the desk in the New Orleans hotel room, David remembered something he'd forgotten to put in his story. That was okay; it wasn't necessary, though it struck him as interesting now: It was about the same time as his eleventh birthday, a little more than a year ago, that he'd first thought about escape.

Had he somehow sensed that Simic would soon push Breunner to invent ways to speed up David's development? He knew he hadn't; though clairvoyance was a kind of psi that many researchers thought was real, David had never shown any signs it was among his powers. He hadn't seen the future; he'd just gotten tired of being the Facility's prisoner, and he was ready to think about getting away.

David made his first move the next time Dr. Breunner ran him through the cards. Dr. Kohl was in the isolation booth, and David sat at a table with his back to her and facing Dr. Breunner. Breunner could see Frieda's head but not the cards; each time she turned, she nodded, and Breunner said to David, "Card," and David gave his call.

They took a break after ten decks, and David went out into the cinder-block-walled hall to stretch his legs. When Breunner called him back into the lab, the doctor seemed upset, as if David had betrayed him—which he had. David was pleased it hadn't taken Dr. Breunner long to figure it out.

"Something is wrong, David," the doctor said, his accent a little thicker than usual. "Let us try the cards again, if you please."

They took their places at the table, and Dr. Breunner began to say, "Card," and David to make his calls. He identified nine of the first twelve correctly, to show he still could. For the thirteenth time Dr. Breunner said, "Card."

David said, "Star."

"Card."

David read a rectangle and said, "Circle."

"Card."

"Rectangle."

Dr. Breunner stared hard at him, said, "Card."

"Star."

The doctor sighed heavily, looked past David at Frieda Kohl. "I think that will be enough for today." He waited until Frieda Kohl had left the room, then said, "I am very disappointed in you, David. You are deliberately calling cards incorrectly."

David nodded calmly.

"Why?"

"I want to be rewarded for what I'm doing," David said.

"Rewarded how?"

"I want to be paid a dollar for every correct card over ten," David said evenly.

Dr. Breunner stared at him for a long while. Finally he said, "I'll have to ask Mr. Simic."

"Tell him if he doesn't agree, I won't call the cards at all."

"He will be angry."

"I guess he will," David said.

In fact, when Simic confronted him, his first words were, "You little bandit."

David almost told him it takes one to know one. Instead he said politely, "I bet I'm worth a lot more to you than a dollar a card, Mr. Simic. I think it's a pretty fair bargain."

Simic studied him. "Fifty cents."

David wanted to laugh but only shook his head no. "You can afford it, Mr. Simic. I'd like you to pay me in cash, each time I call the cards."

David didn't have to sense to know what Simic was thinking: David would never have the chance to take the money away from there anyway. "Deal?" David said.

After a moment Simic grudgingly said, "Deal," and then he stalked off, looking sulky.

David was pleased at how it had gone. It proved his powers were valuable enough to give him some leverage. The money itself was important as well; if he did get free, he'd be on his own and have to pay for food and a place to stay. The problem was, what happened when the money ran out?

In the room David laughed. You read a lot about how TV warps kids' brains, but in this case TV had provided him with his solution.

The Facility is run by a man named Simic, though most of the time he is not there, and I think he has another job. I never heard anyone say his first name. Dr. Breunner and another doctor named Frieda Kohl do the Facility's research. Both of them are medical doctors, but Dr. Breunner is in charge of doing the operations. Dr. Kohl does more of the work of coming up with theories, which they test on computers. Both have German accents, and Dr. Breunner's gets thicker when he's excited. Mr. Simic has an accent too, more faint and harder to figure out. One night I was fooling around with the TV satellite dish they have at the Facility and started watching a rerun of a show called *Mission: Impossible*. Mr. Simic's accent is like the ones the good guys used when they were undercover in some country in Europe and trying to talk like communists.

The building where the Facility is located is one story, made of concrete blocks, and is about the size of a warehouse. Nearby is a smaller building where the guards live. The two buildings are surrounded by an electrified fence with rolls of barbed wire along the top. There's one gate, with a guardhouse. The fence is pretty far out from the buildings, and the space inside it is about as big as five-by-five city blocks.

Like I said, when I was kidnapped, they drugged me, and when I came to in the helicopter, I was blindfolded. All I knew then was that the Facility was somewhere in a desert, and about a two-hour helicopter ride from Denver.

I know that because three times they took me places, or four times if you count when I got away.

Anyway, on each trip we flew in a helicopter and then took a plane from Lowery Air Force Base in Denver. The first trip was to San Francisco, the second to Atlanta, and the third to Washington, D.C. I figured out the cities from the billboards we passed on the way from where we landed to where we were going.

Mr. Simic wanted to inject me with drugs again for the trips, which scared me. I didn't know what was in the needle, or what it would do to me, and I told Dr. Breunner that if they shot me up, I wouldn't do what they wanted when we got where we were going. Dr. Breunner told me that he convinced Mr. Simic that there was no harm in my knowing, because I'd never be able to use the information, so Mr. Simic gave in.

The purpose of the trips was to have me read the Zener cards in front of a person, like a demonstration. I don't know who the first was, the one I did the cards for in San Francisco. He was a Japanese man who talked English well. Later I found out who the other two were because I saw them on TV. The woman in Atlanta was Sister Sarah Stilwell, who has a show on the religious channel where she asks people to send her money. The man in Washington was Jason Carver, who is a Republican senator from Utah. All of them were plenty interested in my powers, but why is something I still don't know.

This is as good a time as any to say what my powers are. I understand that this is going to be hard to believe—like maybe a lot of what I've said already—but I can prove it's all true, or at least I could prove it if it wouldn't get me into even worse trouble, like I found out. But that part comes later in the story.

First off, I can't read minds. I mean, I can't go into someone's head and tell what they are thinking. That's not what the Zener cards are about. What I can do, what's called telepathy, is get someone's thought if they are concentrating on some object.

But second, and this is called empathy, I can

also read if someone has a strong feeling or emotion, like lying, or anger, or if they want to grab me, as right now they do.

Dr. Breunner and the Facility knew about my telepathy and empathy, of course, and like I said, they had a theory it would get stronger. What they didn't know was that I would get whole new powers as I grew older. I had to get away before they found out, or they would perform their zombie operation on me, like they operated on Mr. Voss.

One of the new powers was actually something I had been able to do for several years. I discovered it on the trip to Washington when I did the cards for the senator, though I didn't think much of it then. I call it cosensing; that means I can recognize another person with psi. The Facility doesn't know about this.

In Washington I sensed a woman whose name I found out later was Linda Gaylen.

David stared at the name on the paper before him, raised the pen, and started to black it out. Even though he was writing this story for her, he'd omitted that fact up to now. He didn't want to put her on the spot; he'd already done so once, and look where it had gotten him.

On the other hand, he had to trust her to decide what to do once she understood why she could be in danger from the Facility, just as he was. David put the pen down and went on reading.

The way I could make money once I escaped came to me one night about six months ago, while I was watching a black-and-white show on the satellite. It was called *Maverick,* and it was about two brothers who traveled around the old West, living by their wits and gambling at poker. The next day I asked Mr. Voss to teach me how to play.

I'd thought that maybe my idea was dumb, figuring a way to live from a TV show, but what Mr. Voss said made me think that it wasn't so dumb after all. He told me he'd teach me the game, but he sure as heck (actually, he didn't say heck) wasn't going to play with me for money, not when I could read whatever cards he had. But he did show me how it worked, and after a while I even got him to bet for nickels and dimes, even though I had to let him win most of the time.

The fourth power I have, the one that forced me to, like they say in the movies, make my move, is what I call transmission. I learned about it by accident, but the problem was that Mr. Simic found out about it at the same time.

One day when I was outside playing one-on-one hoops with a guard, Mr. Simic came and ordered the guard to get lost. When he did, Mr. Simic told me that he was getting impatient. He said he knew I could do better, that ever since I had talked him into giving me money for the cards, I'd been getting too big for my britches, and that he wanted to see some results, like Dr. Breunner predicted, or else.

Which made me mad, so mad that I thought that I would like to hurt him. All of a sudden Mr. Simic looked pale and sick. He went away, and I shot some buckets, though I was worried about what had happened and didn't hit too many of them. After a while Dr. Breunner came and took me inside. When we got to the laboratory, Dr. Breunner asked me what I'd done to Mr. Simic. I said I hadn't done anything.

It turned out that I had, though. Mr. Simic had a terrible headache, though otherwise there wasn't anything wrong with him. Dr. Breunner thought I had given him that headache.

I said I hadn't. I admit I wanted to hide the truth from him, but also that's what I wanted to believe. I was as scared as I'd been since they'd taken me there. I didn't want the power to hurt people. I don't want it now.

But I do have it, and the other day I figured out why it has gotten so much stronger all of a sudden. I'm changing, and not just my head. What I mean is, and this is embarrassing to write, but I've got to because I want this to be clear, I'm becoming a man. Puberty. That was where the new transmission powers came from, and once he got over his headache, Mr. Simic knew what he had to do.

He told Dr. Kohl to figure out some operation to make my transmission stronger, and at the same time work it so that they could be sure I wouldn't use it on them. I think Mr. Simic was a little afraid too. That headache must have been pretty bad.

He never knew for certain that they meant to cut his brain, but he suspected they were planning something, and now, from what Mr. Voss had said before he died, it was a fair guess that was it.

What he did know was that a few days after the headache incident, Dr. Breunner started acting jumpy. Something was bothering him, and David's sense of Dr. Breunner's guilt was so strong that it was like having a live wire in his head.

Finally he'd asked Dr. Breunner flat out if he was going to hurt him. Dr. Breunner said no, and then he'd done something that had surprised and revulsed David at the same time.

Dr. Breunner hugged him. His cheek was stubbly against David's, his breath sour. Still, the gesture would have been meaningful, David thought, if he didn't sense beyond doubt that Dr. Breunner was lying.

A few days later the helicopter came again, and this time they did inject me. I guess they could have the other times too, because it was as easy as Mr.

Simic holding me down and telling Dr. Breunner that if he didn't give me the shot, Mr. Simic would see that Dr. Breunner spent the rest of his days in a jail cell, if they didn't just execute him. Dr. Breunner made a sad noise, and I felt the needle in my arm.

The injection didn't knock me out all the way. Instead it was like I was in some kind of outer limits like on the TV show. I couldn't move, but while they were loading me into the helicopter and it took off, I could make out some of what they were saying. I don't know if that was because Dr. Breunner didn't give me enough drugs, or because my powers were stronger and it took more to knock me out.

They were arguing again. Mr. Simic wanted to know why Dr. Breunner couldn't do the operation at the Facility, and Dr. Breunner said that he was the surgeon and he would decide. Dr. Kohl said that Dr. Breunner was wrong, but I got woozy, and I don't know how Dr. Breunner answered her.

When I woke up, I was lying on a cart in a hospital kind of room. Both doctors were wearing green gowns, and Dr. Kohl was preparing another needle, pushing it through the stopper in a bottle and drawing a clear liquid into it. Mr. Simic was there too. None of them knew that I wasn't unconscious, and when Dr. Kohl pointed the needle at my arm, I made her drop it. I heard it break on the floor.

Mr. Simic swore, and I gave him another headache. He fell down. I didn't care. I didn't have the money I'd earned reading cards, because when they stuck the first needle in me, I didn't have a chance. I sat up on the cart and told the doctors I'd hurt them worse than I hurt Mr. Simic.

I told Dr. Breunner to give me my clothes and all the money he had. I was really angry because they had robbed me again, and they could tell. After Dr. Breunner did what I said, I told him to give me Mr. Simic's money too, and also Dr. Kohl's. When I counted it later, I had two hundred and seventy-seven dollars, lots less than what I'd left behind.

While I got dressed, Dr. Breunner tried to talk me into not running away. I called him a name.

On the way out a guard tried to stop me, but I wouldn't let him. It was about sunset when I got outside, and I was surprised that the building was not some big hospital, but a house out in the country. I think now it was what they call in the movies a safe house. There was a fence around it and more guards. I didn't hurt any of them, but I kept them away, and then I ran.

Wherever I was, the houses were far apart, and they were all surrounded by fields of cattle grazing behind barbed wire. It was getting dark quickly now, and with the drugs they had given me and all, I was awfully tired. But before I found a place to sleep, I learned two new things. One was that ranches had ranch dogs, and the other was that I couldn't transmit to them.

The first three places I tried, the dogs chased me away. At the second place, before that happened, a woman came out and stood under the porch light, wiping her hands on her apron. She looked nice, and I considered going up and asking her to help me, but then I thought that maybe by now the Facility had put out word on me, that my picture had been on the television and there was a reward. Even if not, the woman might think I was a runaway and turn me in to the police.

The dog at the fourth place was a golden retriever, who just came up and licked my hand. The dog followed me when I snuck in the back of the barn, and when I lay down on some straw, he curled up next to me, and we went to sleep together. That dog was the best friend I'd had in a long time.

David checked his watch—it was nearly noon—and then shuffled the rest of the pages: There were three sheets left. He got up from the desk and began to pack his few articles of clothing into his gym bag.

When he awoke in the barn at dawn, he'd petted the dog one last time and headed down the ranch's drive. A guy who must have been the rancher was working a hay baler and called out to him. David ignored him and ran on down to the main road. Off in the distance he could see tall buildings. He crossed the road and stuck out his thumb. The first vehicle that came along was a stock truck. He told the guy driving it that he'd gotten lost and simply refused to answer any other questions. The man dropped him near the center of the city, which turned out to be Houston.

In the nearest café David ordered hot chocolate and bacon and eggs. While he was waiting, he went over to the pay phone. The book was missing, but the waitress had one behind the counter. He found the address he was looking for in the blue pages, under "U.S. Government."

Even though I'd figured that if I was able to get away, I'd be on my own, once I did it, I decided that I was wrong. This was America, and we had laws that stopped things like the Facility, and those laws would help me. So the first place I went was to the FBI.

Here was one of those times that there's something to what they say about not believing TV. Before that first day was over, I learned that some FBI agents aren't like Efrem Zimbalist, Jr., on the show.

I went to where the phone book said the FBI had its office in Houston, in the Federal Building on Rusk Street. I knew the woman at the desk wouldn't believe the real story, so I told her I had been kidnapped. Pretty soon after that a man named Tom Parkhurst took me into his office. He was a special agent, but I knew from the show that all FBI men were called special agents.

I told Mr. Parkhurst my story, but when I finished, I could tell he didn't believe me either. So I asked him if the FBI office had a psychologist that they used when they were dealing with criminals.

The psychologist was named Humbolt, and he had never heard of Zener cards, but he did find a deck of regular cards, so I called suits for him, spades and hearts and so on. I got forty-one out of fifty-two. Dr. Humbolt was smart enough to understand that this was strange, so he called some other psychologist who did know about Zener cards. I did ten decks for him. Afterward the FBI put me in a hotel downtown, with Special Agent Parkhurst to watch over me.

I was tired from sleeping in a barn, but not so tired that the next morning, when another special agent came to the room and said he was from Washington and he was going to take me there, I didn't sense that he meant to do about the same thing with me as the Facility had.

Since then I've read in books that the FBI, and the CIA too, know all about psi. They've been doing experiments for as long as the Facility, trying to find someone who has it that they can use.

I didn't stay around long enough in the hotel room to find out how they meant to use me, but I didn't hurt any of them, not badly at least, when I got away.

The point is, I realized that I could never depend on them. I could never depend on anyone. For better or worse, and maybe for the rest of my life, I was on my own.

David turned the last page facedown atop the rest, reasonably satisfied with his work. He took a sheet of stationery from the drawer, dated it, and wrote "Dear Ms. Gaylen," then paused, sucking thoughtfully on the end of the pen.

This letter is going to sound a little crazy, but I hope you'll believe me and understand after you read the story that is enclosed with it. I am the one who was with you in Arizona the night that man fell off the butte and died.

The reason I have arranged to have this sent to you is I trust you to do the right thing. If you have gotten this, it means either that the Facility has found a way to get me back, or I am dead. Either way, I hope you will figure how to stop them.

I know that even if you believe what I've written, and I think you will or I wouldn't be sending it to you, you will still have trouble getting anyone else to believe it. But you can prove it because you also have psi. Both Mr. Voss and I sensed it, and I believe your powers are pretty strong. You may not know about them, because maybe you've never had any chance or reason to use them, but I am positive that if you try, you can discover them.

But you must be very careful who you reveal your powers to, because if they are as strong as I think, you could put yourself in a lot of danger from the Facility. You may decide that it is too risky to reveal your abilities to anyone, and maybe it is, because the Facility is awfully powerful. If you feel you can't help, I will understand.

David reread the letter, then signed it, "Thank you, your friend, David McKay." He squared it atop the other pages, slipped them into the manila envelope, and sealed it carefully. When that was done, he looked one last time around the room to make sure he had forgotten nothing, then took his gym bag and went down to check out.

The first lawyer was irritated to learn that the "Mr. McKay" with whom he had an appointment was twelve years old. He was officious, impatient, and not at all interested in whatever David had to say. David thanked him and excused himself within a minute of entering the office.

The second lawyer was smooth, pleasant, and dishonest. "I'd be happy to accommodate you, young man," he said, smiling. "My fee would be fifty dollars a month for as long as you wish to continue the arrangement." This one had a cubbyhole office on the edge of Algiers and looked as if he could use an extra fifty dollars a month, though David sensed that once he had the money, he would have no qualms about ignoring David's instructions.

David went back to the phone book and chose a third name as he had the first two, at random. Gavin Reed's office was downtown on the seventh floor of a building on Decatur Street. The stencil on the door said there were two other lawyers in the firm; behind it a nice-looking middle-aged woman presided over a reception room. She was surprised to see that David was a boy but too polite to make an issue of it. Instead she offered him a soft drink, which he declined with thanks. The woman said Mr. Reed would be with him in a moment.

On the waiting-room table were copies of several magazines, including *American Weekly*. David chose *Time* instead. He was reading a review of the new Bruce Willis movie when Gavin Reed came out. The lawyer was about fifty, balding and portly, with a smooth, almost babylike face that smiled cordially when he shook David's hand. David sensed that he was less startled than the receptionist and supposed that lawyers saw a lot of strange things in their work. The good ones probably learned not to pass judgments until they had information on which to base them. Gavin Reed apologized for keeping David waiting and escorted him into a modern-looking office with a window overlooking the barge-clogged Mississippi.

Gavin Reed molded his form to the chair behind his desk, clasped his hands on his stomach, and said, "How can I help you, Mr. McKay?"

David grinned. "You can call me David."

"Well then, you must call me Gavin." The lawyer glanced at the manila envelope David placed in front of him.

On it he had written Linda Gaylen's name and the address and phone number of the Washington office of *American Weekly.* "I'd like to give you this to keep somewhere safe," David said. "Once a week I'll call you up." David turned the envelope so Gavin Reed could read what was written on it. "She doesn't work there anymore, but because you're a lawyer and all, would you be able to talk to someone at this magazine and find out if they know where she is and can get this to her?"

"I think I could."

"If they don't know, could you hire a detective or someone to find her?"

"Most likely."

David frowned thoughtfully. "That would cost money, though. I've got some. . . ."

"We'll talk about money after you've told me the rest of what you wish me to do," Gavin Reed said solemnly.

"Okay," David agreed. "If I don't call you some week, you get this to her. All right?"

Gavin Reed studied him with kindly eyes. "Are you in trouble?"

"Yes."

"Can you tell me about it?"

David shook his head. "I'd prefer if you didn't read what's in here."

"Then I won't."

David sensed that the promise was good as gold.

"A lawyer's business is secrets, David," Gavin Reed said. "Secrets people tell me, and secrets that they keep from me. I tell you that I'll help you however I can; you tell me as much or as little as you're able."

"It's not that I don't trust you," David said. "There are things I know that if other people knew, it might hurt them. I don't want you hurt."

"As you wish," Gavin Reed said gravely.

"I think there better be a code," David said.

"I beg your pardon?"

"When I call. So you know it's me." David grinned sheepishly. "I know that sounds like something from a dumb movie, but I guess it's better to be dumb than careless."

"If much time passed in which I failed to be dumb," Gavin Reed said, "I would begin to doubt that I was paying proper attention to myself. What shall we call you?"

David touched at the scar on his forehead. "The right-fielder," he said. "When I call, I'll say I'm the right-fielder."

Gavin Reed nodded. "I believe I can remember that. Now, as to my professional fee, taking into consideration my costs in executing this trust, along with my time, I would suggest twenty dollars per annum."

"That's too little, Mr. R—Gavin," David protested.

"I'm sorry," Gavin Reed said. "That is my offer, and you must take it or leave it."

"All right," David said. "But isn't there something like, you know, on TV, they talk about a retainer?"

"That slipped my mind," Gavin Reed said. "All right, the retainer shall be an additional ten dollars."

When David took out his money clip, Gavin Reed was surprised for the first time. David removed a twenty and a ten, laid them on the desk. Gavin Reed picked up the money, regarded it thoughtfully. "I'll say only this, David," he murmured. "I believe everything you have chosen to tell me. I will follow your instructions, and when you call each week, I hope you will be able to assure me that you remain all right, because that will be a concern of mine. I will also endeavor to help you as best I can, if you ever decide to solicit that help."

"Thanks," David said. "There is one other thing."

"Yes?"

David remembered the names on the door of the office. "One of your partners is a woman, right?"

"Yes."

"Does she travel much?"

"She does. I believe that next week she will be in Chicago for two days to take depositions."

"Chicago should be far enough away," David said, thinking aloud. "Okay, just before she leaves to come home—at the airport would be best—I'd like you to ask her to make a phone call."

Gavin Reed offered a pen and legal pad. On it David wrote the number he'd been trained to memorize, and was quizzed on weekly, since he arrived at the Facility. If by any circumstance he was ever separated from the Facility, he was to dial the number and they would come to him. Just what he wanted, David thought bitterly.

He passed the pad back to Gavin Reed. "Have her tell them she's the person David said would call. She should ask for Mr. Simic, and when she gets him, say that what I told him is true, and that she promised to do what I asked. After that tell her to hang up and get on the plane. She shouldn't say anything else, and not answer any questions—*any* questions, even 'How are you?' " David chuckled. "Although I doubt they'll ask that."

Gavin Reed stared at the number. After a moment he nodded.

"I guess that's it." David stood, and Gavin Reed came around the desk and walked him back to the reception room. When they shook hands again, Gavin Reed gave David his business card and said, "I'll look forward to your calls. Good luck."

"Thanks," David said. "And don't worry too much. So far my luck has been okay."

David dialed the same number himself the next morning, from a pay phone encased in a plastic bubble in a waiting lounge in the New Orleans International Airport west of the city. After he identified himself, he heard a series of electronic clicks and beeps. "Don't bother to trace this," he said to the woman who answered. "I'm at the airport in New Orleans." He was scared, and because of that he mouthed off. "I'll give you the number I'm calling from." He read it off the label plate on the phone. "Please put Mr. Simic on," he said.

"He's not available," the woman said.

"I won't talk to anyone else." David checked his watch. "If he really isn't there, and you can't contact him and patch him onto this line in the next five minutes, I'll have to hang up."

"Don't!" the woman said sharply.

David knew she might be stalling, but he wasn't too worried. Unless they had their new Voss ready to roll—along with the ability to teleport him to David's location, something he doubted even the Facility was capable of—he was safe for the moment. He could see the departures monitor from the phone; his flight would begin boarding in seven minutes.

Three of them passed before Simic came on the line. In the interim the woman asked him questions, to which he responded with silence, even when she said, with evident concern, "Are you still there?" Noises crackled in the background again, and then Simic said, "I'm displeased with you, David."

"That's not what I want to talk about, Mr. Simic," David said firmly.

Five minutes later he was in the plane, strapping on his seat belt. When the cabin attendant came on the intercom to remind the passengers that this was the flight to Salt Lake City, David was mildly startled. Reviewing the conversation in his mind, he had forgotten for the moment where he was going. He'd done well enough, he decided, but it had reminded him that it was never a smart idea to underestimate Mr. Simic, who was as tricky as a snake.

Salt Lake City, David thought. For now it was as good as anywhere.

CHAPTER ELEVEN

The only personal item in the office Simic used when at the Facility was a two-by-three-foot photographic blowup, mounted on the opposite wall so it faced him when he sat behind his desk. In the picture he stood smiling at the camera, dressed in a white down parka, insulated pants, and wool hat, holding a Harrington and Richardson M-317 Ultra Wildcat bolt-action rifle cradled in his arms. The H and R, with its seventeen-caliber cartridge, was nominally a varmint gun, but the animal that lay in the snow at Simic's feet in the picture, a thin ooze of blood depending from the little hole in the side of its majestic head, was no varmint. The snow leopard that Simic had shot three years earlier on Rongbuk Glacier in Tibet, nine miles inside the Chinese frontier, measured over two meters, including its luxuriant three-foot tail, and weighed forty point seven-two kilograms, which was very close to a record, though it would never be recorded. That did not trouble Simic; he enjoyed hunting endangered species for the sport of it.

He had been in his regular office at the Agency when the boy called, a lucky break. Comm-Sys did not know the boy's significance but was under standing orders that should he phone, he was to be given directly to Simic, priority Triple-A Three. The call was traced and recorded automatically; immediately on its conclusion Simic had personally hand carried the tape to the Facility.

Before him on the desk was the transcript that Frieda Kohl had made, reluctantly and with much whining complaint. Under the best of circumstances, she was, in Simic's frank opinion, a brass-plated bitch, and she particularly abhorred secretarial duties as beneath her, an objection she emphasized by riddling the transcript with typos and strikeovers. She must have gone to some trouble to do so, considering that she had done the work on a word processor.

Simic squared the sheets and started through them for the third time, searching for nuance behind the boy's words, as well as reviewing his own performance. When a threatening pose failed to shake the boy, Simic had quickly adopted neutrality. He began to read at the top of the second sheet.

McKay: You understand what this means, Mr. Simic?

Simic: You tell me, David.

McKay: If you catch me and take me back to the Facility, and a week goes by and I don't call this lawyer, she'll send what I've written to this person. You can't make me call her, and I don't think even the Facility can question every lawyer in the country to find out which one has my story.

Simic frowned thoughtfully. If Kohl was correct about the surgery she posited, they could indeed get the boy to make his weekly calls. They could get the little bastard to do any damned thing they wished.

McKay: This person, the one that will get what I've written . . . [Pause] He'll tell about the Facility, about what you've done to me.

Simic: Whom will he tell?
McKay: Everyone.
Simic: But will they believe him?
McKay: You can count on it.
Simic: Why?
McKay: Because . . .
Simic: Because what?
McKay: Because he can prove it's true.
Simic: How can he prove it?
McKay: He can. Take my word for it.
Simic: All right, I will. You've never lied to me before.
McKay: [Laughter]
Simic: Why do you need this other person? Why don't you tell your story yourself, if you think it will save you and destroy the Facility?
McKay: You're a smart man, Mr. Simic. You know why. If I went to the authorities, how do I know you don't have some way to get them to give me back to you? Or maybe they'll try to use me the same as you.

The transcript indicated another pause here. Simic had given several moments of careful thought to his next comment before deciding it would gain him more than he would be giving away.

Simic: You mean like what happened when you went to the FBI?
McKay: [Audible breath] How do you know about that?
Simic: As you said, David, I'm a smart man. I know a lot of things. I know where you are.
McKay: I told you that. I also told you I won't be here five minutes from now.

Simic: Wherever you go, I'll know, just as I knew about the FBI. And incidentally, you were right. No one, the FBI or anyone else, is going to let someone with your unique skills go free.

McKay: That's not what I want to talk about.

Simic: David, do you know what a Mexican standoff is?

McKay: I guess.

Simic: It's when antagonists each have some weapon powerful enough to keep the other from attacking. For example, at the moment I can't harm you, and you can't harm me.

McKay: I can harm you, Mr. Simic.

Simic: You'll go down with me, son. Your mysterious friend and your document revealing all are basically worthless. You can't prove a damned thing without putting your own ass on the line. You won't be doing your friend any favors either.

McKay: [Pause] Whatever you say.

Simic: For the moment I'm stymied too. If my people try to take you, you'll zap them, as Voss used to say.

McKay: I can zap you too, Mr. Simic.

Simic: That could change.

McKay: I did it already. Remember?

Simic: I'm still around to tell about it, am I not?

McKay: I've got to go now.

Simic: All right. Nice talking with you.

McKay: [Pause] Do you have someone to take Mr. Voss's place?

Simic: Can you sense over the phone, David?

McKay: [No answer]

Simic: In case you can't, assume for your own sake that I'm telling the truth: The answer is yes. Does that scare you, David?

McKay: [Pause] Good-bye, Mr. Simic.
Simic: See you soon, David.

Simic set the transcript aside and sat motionless,
looking unfocusedly at nothing at all. Ten minutes
passed before he roused himself. He unlocked a drawer
in the desk and removed the secured phone, then made
four calls that had nothing to do with the boy. There
was other business to take care of—there always was—
and it helped clear his mind. He terminated the last
call by saying, "Do it!" and slamming down the receiver.

For a time after that, he sat motionless and gazing at the photograph of himself and the dead snow
leopard, remembered saying the same two words—
"Do it!"—to the helicopter pilot when the man objected to the incursion into Chinese territory. Over the
years those two words had been damn useful in end-
ing discussions, and by now he had learned to speak
them in a way that never left room for argument.

Breunner's knock on the office door brought a
sharp, "Wait!" from Simic. Breunner did as he was
told; either Simic was busy with some secret of per-
ceivedly grave importance or was making Breunner
languish merely to remind him who gave the orders.
A minute passed before the door's electronic lock
clicked and Simic called, "Come." Breunner turned
the knob and entered.

Simic said, "Well?"

Breunner was carrying the original tape of the
phone conversation and a stack of fanfold paper on
which a stylus line traced sharp spikes of varying am-
plitude. Simic let him stand there for a few moments
before waving him into the visitor's chair facing the
desk. Its seat was three inches lower than Simic's.

"He lied twice," Breunner said, "about the

lawyer and the person to whom he addressed this document of his."

Simic was surprised. "You mean he didn't actually set up a fallback?"

"Oh, indeed he did," Breunner said. "Everything he told you was patently true, except he reversed their genders. The lawyer he referred to as 'she' is actually male; the other person is a woman."

Simic had to smile. "Where's the kid get these ideas anyway?" Both of them knew that the boy had an excellent imagination. Breunner suspected it was a factor in his psi abilities, particularly transmission.

"Is he scared?" Simic asked.

"Of course. He has reason to be." Breunner consulted the fanfold results of the stress analysis. "His degree of fright was appropriate to the situation, except at two points."

"Which were?"

"When you made what was essentially a cruel joke, and he laughed. That had nothing to do with mirth. It was a defense mechanism directed at regaining composure he had momentarily lost."

"What I figured."

Breunner gestured with the sheaf of paper. "Perhaps you don't need me at all."

Simic looked amused. "Something eating you, Doctor?"

"Nothing extraordinary," Breunner said, keeping his tone even.

"Then go on."

"He was decidedly nonplussed when you revealed your knowledge of his approach to the FBI."

"That was the idea."

Breunner refolded the papers and set them on the desk, tapped a forefinger on them. "Otherwise, he is self-confident without having an unrealistic sense of ego or power. He shows no indication of physical or mental illness. He feels a bit prideful at his success in eluding you. Oh, yes," Breunner added, "he dislikes you rather strongly."

"No shit," Simic said. "All right, aside from what the machine tells you, what do you think? You knew the kid best. Is he going to fly off the handle? Will he attempt to expose the operation?"

"I think it highly unlikely. He acknowledges the accuracy of your analysis of the risk he'd be running."

"So for the moment we're okay." Simic leafed through his copy of the transcript from back to front, checking the notes he'd scribbled in the margins. "He believe me about Rogan?"

"Probably. He knows from Voss that we have the wherewithal to develop another person with the power to interfere with his transmission ability. No doubt he assumes we would do so."

"That's fine." Simic went on paging through the transcript. "What about the woman who's supposed to get his story?"

"What about her?"

Simic gave Breunner a sharp look. "What has she to do with him?"

"I have no idea," Breunner said blandly. In fact he had a hunch but saw no reason to share it. "A family friend," he suggested. "A former teacher he trusts, a member of the clergy, a relative we overlooked. It doesn't matter. As you said to David, she can prove nothing."

"The kid said she could."

"No doubt he was lying."

"Then why didn't the lie show up on the stress analysis?" Simic asked shrewdly.

"I . . ." Breunner licked his lips. "Perhaps it did. I will recheck."

"Are you holding something back from me, Doctor?" Simic demanded.

"Certainly not," Breunner said firmly. "Are you

ready to brief Rogan?" he went on, to change the subject.

Simic rubbed his palms together slowly; they made a dry scraping sound. "The question is," Simic said, "is Rogan ready to jam the boy?"

Breunner pursed his lips. Six days earlier he'd declared Rogan recovered from the surgery, and motivated at least for the moment to follow orders. More important, to Breunner's relief, Rogan showed no transmission ability. From the Facility he and Frieda had taken Rogan to two universities and a private nonprofit medical-research institute, each of which, working under grants covertly funded by the Facility, had uncovered subjects showing positive if nonsignificant psi results. At each Rogan was placed in an observation room behind one-way glass through which he could watch the subject do a Zener reading.

The first subject was unable, deck after deck, to do as well as the expected five of twenty-five. For the second subject Breunner had Rogan carefully intensify the jamming. That subject averaged less than two of twenty-five. Again with the third Rogan slowly intensified. After a deck in which every call was incorrect, this subject complained of inability to concentrate, then inability even to remember the five symbols, and finally a blinding headache.

"He can jam," Breunner told Simic in the office, "and he is much more powerful than Voss." Breunner leaned forward in his chair. "Perhaps we can further enhance Rogan," he said earnestly. "Why not use him and leave the boy be?"

"Because the boy isn't crazy." Simic stood. "I'm not a scientist, but I'm not a dimwit either. Kohl's projection of a correlation between preexisting mania, particularly sociopathy, and the successful surgical enhancement of psi has proved correct, two out of two."

Simic leaned forward, steepled his fingers. "Kohl

also projected other abilities in Rogan. Was she correct?"

Breunner wondered how much Simic already knew, and how much of this questioning was a loyalty test. He'd already been informed that the surgery was successful in regard to jamming, Breunner was pretty certain. He'd walked into Frieda's office unannounced three days earlier and found her in a phone conversation, which she abruptly terminated. He was certain she was reporting to Simic; she had done so behind Breunner's back on other occasions. She was a suspicious, cynical woman who believed the show of lapdog loyalty would win Simic's favor.

She was wrong. The day she became unnecessary to Simic would be her last on earth, and the same was true for Breunner—and Rogan, for that matter. Ironically the boy was keeping all three of them alive.

"Like Voss, Rogan can sense other psis," Breunner said.

Simic smiled, sat down again. "So can the boy," he said.

Breunner stared at him, startled. He had never told Simic that David had found them on the butte in Arizona by sensing. "I don't know."

Given that Voss had developed cosensing ability, Frieda correctly hypothesized that Rogan might have it as well. To test the theory, at one of the colleges they had arranged to have students known to possess psi placed in a large group of people. At a time when the subject was attending a lecture, in a location known to Breunner and Kohl but not to Rogan, the two physicians had walked Rogan around the campus, beginning at its periphery.

Although neither subject had more than a minimal gift, Rogan sensed the first at five hundred meters. The next day, with a similarly endowed subject, he was able to sense at nearly one and a half times the distance, suggesting his cosensing power continued to grow. In both cases Rogan led the doctors to the correct lecture hall and identified the subject from among several hundred students.

"But Rogan is damned strong," Simic said, again revealing Frieda's informative hand.

"I said he was."

"And as to the question of who is stronger, he or the boy," Simic said, "we'll find out soon enough."

The idea of loosing Rogan on the boy appalled Breunner almost as much as the idea that Rogan might fail. Simic seemed to have dropped the question of side effects for the moment—so he did not know everything after all—and Breunner debated whether to bring them up himself. Would it change his plan? Breunner had to have time to think.

To terminate the interview, Breunner resorted to sarcasm. "You are correct, of course," he said. "You are always correct."

"Don't you forget it."

Breunner stood. "Will you see him now?"

Simic jerked a thumb in the direction of the door. "Lead the way, Doctor," he said.

In his own office August Breunner slumped into his chair and wiped thought from his mind for the moment. On his desk was the latest 486-series computer, with thousands of times more power, speed, and memory in a few cubic feet of case than in the room-sized computer that had been the Facility's first machine. Bookcases lined two of the office's walls from floor to ceiling, their shelves a jumble of texts, technical journals, and precarious stacks of research papers. But while Simic at least had his disgusting photograph, nothing in Breunner's office betrayed the personality of the occupant. That was deliberate, because Breunner saw himself as a man whose personality had long ago been stolen by others.

A few minutes earlier he had escorted Simic to

the lab where Rogan awaited. Breunner was dismissed as soon as Simic was satisfied that he was safe with Rogan—and the machine-gun-carrying sentinel who was one of a team that kept twenty-four-hour guard over the man. Simic wished Breunner to know no more than was necessary, and that was fine with Breunner. He knew enough already.

Breunner roused himself from his slouch to slide open the lower drawer of his desk and remove a bottle of schnapps and a thick-bottomed shot glass. He was not much of a drinking man—that at least was a vice he had managed to avoid—but he found that a thimbleful of the thick liquor helped to free his mind to new approaches to vexing problems. This time the libation evoked no insights into his present difficulties nor future solutions but only opened gaping windows on the past.

In the late summer of 1945, two days after his interview with the man who offered salvation in exchange for his soul, Breunner found himself in a prison cell once more. There he remained for the better part of six months.

He was not mistreated, beyond endless interrogation. He answered their questions freely and honestly, because he had no loyalty to the Nazi masters who had forced him to prostitute his Hippocratic oath, and because cooperation meant survival. When the inquiry was complete and their proposition offered, he accepted immediately. He was removed from his cell, taken on a long flight by cargo plane, and installed in what appeared to be a farmhouse. In time he learned it was in the Virginia countryside about twenty-five miles southwest of Washington, D.C.

His mandate, along with that of the half-dozen or so other researchers of various nationalities resident in the well-equipped building, was to devise and improve methods of mind control. He was never told anything about his subjects except that they were expendable, and that results would be expected without regard to effete sensibilities about human life. He was encouraged to explore all avenues of method, which came to include brainwashing, drug therapy, patterning and depatterning, and on occasion torture. When in 1959 a book called *The Manchurian Candidate* by the writer Richard Condon became a best-seller, it spurred demands for greater excesses in quest of more profound results, as if it were true fact rather than a skilled and imaginative fiction.

That whimsy as much as anything led to the exposure and downfall of the project to which, by then, Breunner had been attached for nearly twenty-five years. All of it came out: the withholding of treatment from mental patients, the excessive administrations of medications and electroshock, the emotional tormenting of legitimate defectors through sensory deprivation, and finally, the death of a biochemist who, convinced he had gone mad while under the influence of a surreptitiously administered dose of LSD, had defenestrated himself from a room on the tenth floor of the Statler Hotel in New York City.

The congressional investigations that shut down the mind-control experiments in the midsixties confirmed what Breunner had long suspected: His masters were associated with a legitimate American intelligence agency that could only be the CIA. How else to explain their power, sufficient to keep his own name from the public eye? Sufficient, Breunner thought bitterly in his office, to retain his services for the far more covert project that became known, to those few who knew of it at all, as the Facility.

The interview with Simic, on the first occasion Breunner met the man two decades earlier, recalled the postwar interview with Simic's predecessor. On the one hand, Simic told him, Breunner was a potential embarrassment: No one relished the revelation that a government agency was employing an ex-Nazi torturer masquerading as a physician. Of course there were many ways to insure Breunner's silence, Simic noted. He could be killed or perhaps turned over to the Russians or the Israelis. Simic suggested that death might be preferable to either of the latter alternatives.

After successfully frightening him, Simic had flattered him. Of those researchers who had left the project through death or been purged for refusal to cooperate, Breunner was by far the most brilliant. Therefore, Simic offered an alternative: Breunner could accept Simic's protection and do as he was told.

With sharp-focused clarity Breunner saw himself back then, a still relatively young man sitting in a nondescript room somewhere near Washington, levelly meeting Simic's gaze. "I see no difficulty," Breunner heard himself say, over the distance of decades. "I have made a distinguished professional career of doing as I am told."

If Simic heard the sarcasm, he gave no sign.

In his office Breunner turned to the computer and entered an apparently random command sequence, then stared at his watch. After exactly fifteen seconds he entered a second sequence, and only then did the screen prompt for password. Breunner typed the German word *Diener,* chosen as a self-deprecating injoke. At the next prompt he entered the subdirectory of files that contained the few secrets that had never been coerced from him.

The file he opened comprised a single screenful of data, boiled down from days of postoperative psychological and physical tests on the man Rogan. Here were the answers to the questions Simic had failed to ask, the proof that once again Breunner had given Simic all that he had requested.

And more.

●   ●   ●

"What you call your disinterested observer," Rogan said conversationally, "might conclude I got a few reasons to hold a grudge."

The Simic guy was leaning against the isolation booth, his ankles crossed. He watched Rogan blankly, letting him have his say.

"For starters you've got me locked up." Rogan sat in a folding chair at the unadorned deal table where they put him when they made him guess the cards.

"You already were locked up," Simic pointed out. "We could take you back, if you preferred it there."

"I didn't, but I was working on it," Rogan said. "But then you came along and sliced my brain open." Rogan fingered the scar, about an inch and a half long and a half inch above his forehead. His hair had mostly grown back. "That's the other reason I might be a little steamed: You kind of forgot to ask me to sign a consent form before you had the kraut scramble my frontal lobes."

"Dr. Breunner did you no damage." Simic straightened, came around, and sat in the chair opposite Rogan. The guy in the corner with the M-16 kept an alert eye on Rogan, who'd noticed the gun was off safety. "Besides, you'll be out of here quite soon—perhaps within the week."

"There's the third thing I'm not so sure I like." Rogan turned over in his mind what Simic had outlined to him during the last ten minutes. "Lemme see do I have this straight. This kid you want me to fetch: He can do with his mind what the kraut can do with a scalpel."

"But you can stop him."

"Maybe." Rogan had always prided himself on his ability to distinguish bullshit from buttermilk, and now he stared hard at Simic.

Simic did not look away. "Drs. Breunner and Kohl are eighty percent sure you can control him completely. They are ninety-eight percent sure you can jam him sufficiently to keep him from doing you any significant harm."

It was the truth. "Okeydokey," Rogan said. "Next thing is, why am I going to do this?"

"For money."

Rogan smiled. "Now we're cooking with butane."

"One hundred thousand dollars."

It was too much for a snatch job, even a specialized one like this, and Simic knew it. Rogan went on smiling. "A quarter million."

"You're in no position to bargain."

Rogan had been around the block often enough to recognize that Simic was not a person with whom to fuck. Rogan smelled government on him, but he smelled something else as well. "Let's try a hundred and fifty," Rogan said. "In cash, seventy-five up front."

"Expenses up front," Simic said. "A hundred fifty when you deliver the boy."

It was the answer Rogan expected; they weren't about to set him loose with money in his britches, but there were ways cash could be raised once he was out on the town. "Done," he said. "You think we ought to shake on it?"

Simic ignored the wisecrack. "Be ready to move at short notice. You'll go out as soon as we locate the boy."

"I can't hardly wait," Rogan said.

The guy with the M-16 followed three steps back when he walked Rogan down the hall, just far enough so Rogan couldn't make a grab for the chattergun. Not that he meant to; there'd be time enough for that kind of play later. When Rogan was back in his quarters, the guy shut the door and locked it from the outside.

The room wasn't bad, compared to other places in which he'd been confined. They'd provided him with new clothes, a bunch of Louis L'Amour novels he'd requested, and a TV, VCR, and some tapes. He turned the set on, picked out a cassette, and slid it into the machine. The move was *True Grit;* he'd been in the middle of it when they'd taken him to see Simic. On the screen John Wayne was horseback and facing Lucky Ned Pepper and his band of desperadoes across a grassy plain. John Wayne put his reins between his teeth, drew his six-guns, and hollered, "Fill yer hands, you sons of bitches."

Rogan lay back and let the movie play out. The part he liked best was when Glenn Campbell got snakebit, the candyass. When the last of the credits faded from the screen, Rogan went on staring at the white noise crackling across it.

As near as he could tell, the kraut hadn't screwed him up in any serious ways. In fact, since coming out of the operation, he felt occasionally insightful flashes of unusual clearheadedness. His instincts told him they were right: This mind-reading kid they wanted him to take care of presented no real danger.

It was Simic he had to worry about.

The reason the guy had started the bidding so high, and then had given in too easily, was he had no intention of paying a penny, let alone a hundred and fifty thousand smackers. Once Rogan did the job, Simic meant to bump him off. Rogan grinned; hell, that's how he'd handle it, if he were in Simic's shoes.

Rogan didn't plan to let him. The first order of business was to get out of here, and that would happen soon enough. After that, get the kid.

Because once he had him, all sorts of new deals could be cut.

CHAPTER TWELVE

The woman was so archetypal that Linda Gaylen wondered if the restaurant had called central casting and asked them to send over an Italian waitress. She was in her fifties, with the girth of a beer barrel and huge heaving breasts to match; her jet black hair was tied back severely, and her plump olive-skinned face was handsome despite the pronounced mustache. She wore a white half apron over a voluminous dark dress, a crucifix joggling on the swell of her bosom. She said nothing while she dealt out plates of salad, veal, shrimp, pasta, an overflowing bread basket; to talk, she needed her hands free.

When she was done, Nick Delvecchio spoke in Italian, and the woman laughed gaily and responded in the same language, accompanied by extravagant gestures that required no translation: Nick was a rascal of the first order. When she left them to their meal, Linda said, "What did you tell her?"

Nick twirled linguine on his fork. "That you were my cousin from the black-sheep side of the family," he said, "and that I was only with you because I owe your father money. I said that once I managed to ditch you, I'd come back and make mad, passionate love to her."

Linda nodded judiciously. "Sounds reasonable. Did she go for it?"

"She said she was too much of a woman and was

afraid that I'd never survive the experience." Nick tasted the pasta. "Guess I'm stuck with you."

Linda laughed, and Nick said, "Dig in." The restaurant was on the Pacific Coast Highway a few miles north of Newport. Inside it was warm, full of delicious smells, and decorated with checked tablecloths, dripping candles in old wine bottles, and Cinzano ashtrays, all as clichéd as the waitress. Over the door a discreet sign identified it as Mario's, but unless you were looking, you'd easily pass it by. Yet now, on a Saturday night, it was full of people who all seemed to know each other, a place for regulars and friends, among whom Nick was clearly numbered. Linda followed his example and found the food wonderful.

"Glad you came?" Nick said, his mouth full.

"Yeah," Linda said. "I think I am."

"That's a start."

A week had passed since she'd met him at Steve Shaner's house. When he didn't call, Linda found she was disappointed. Maybe he had sensed she needed to work through her fear of involvement; if so, it worked. When one night she returned to her apartment hotel and found the desk was holding a dozen white roses for her, it worked. The card, unsigned, informed her that her name had been specially selected to receive the flowers and a delicious meal. She'd put down the card, condemned herself for being chicken, and dialed his number.

In the restaurant she lay down her fork. "There's something I want to share with you," she said.

Nick looked up from mopping marinara sauce with a hunk of crusty bread. Linda took a deep breath and plunged into the story of the accident, and Richard. . . .

"I'm sorry," he said when she was finished. "I really am."

"I know, and I appreciate it. I was sure you'd understand."

"We've both got to work through some things."

She was touched at his kindness. Nick saved the awkward moment by clearing his throat and asking, "Did you talk to Shaner?"

Linda nodded. "He said he'd cut it out."

"Did you believe him?"

"No."

Nick raised his eyebrows. "So?"

"So I told him that if he didn't, I had ten people willing to go public—and that I had their sworn depositions in a safe place."

"Did he believe you?"

"I think so."

"You told me none of those actors wanted to risk it."

"Shaner doesn't know that," Linda said.

Nick looked at her with frank admiration. "Every Thursday night I get together with some guys to play poker. If there's ever an empty seat, remind me not to invite you to fill it."

"By the way," Linda said lightly. "I forgot to tell you Shaner's got a new bodyguard. He's lots prettier than you."

"Thanks," Nick said. "I needed that."

The rest of the dinner passed in easy banter, and a full moon illuminated the ocean to their left as they drove back toward the city. As they pulled up in front of her building, Nick said, "Can I come up for a nightcap?"

Linda hesitated. "Next time, okay?" Afraid she might change her mind, she opened the car door, so Nick had to get out quickly to walk her into the vestibule of her building.

"There will be a next time," he said, touching her arm. "That's good enough."

Linda smiled wanly. "I feel like I'm confirming every cliché about women and indecision. They're going to make me turn in my NOW membership card."

Nick shook his head and kissed her lightly, then waited politely until she got the building's door unlocked and was safely on the elevator.

Upstairs, as she undressed, she felt the oddest flash of guilt. It came not from what she had made of her life, and especially not from some neurotic shame at living while Richard and their child had died, but she could not put her finger on it until she was in bed and flicking off the nightstand light.

From her subconscious emerged the gnawing memory of that consummately bizarre night two months earlier in Arizona, and the boy she had met. He had seemed frightfully needy, and in some irrational yet undeniable way, she was certain that she had failed him.

Toward four in the afternoon the traffic through the border crossing at San Ysidro, fifteen miles south of downtown San Diego, began to pick up, and over the next hour it continued to thicken. By the time the bottom edge of the sun touched at the Pacific, cars were backed up three or four deep at each of the tollboothlike passages under the sprawling length of canopy, even though most of the vehicles were waved through after a brief consultation between the driver and the border-patrol guy. The pedestrian traffic increased as well, especially between five and six. The majority of the people crossing on foot looked Mexican to David, from his vantage point at the rail of the walkway a hundred yards or so from the gate through which they passed. Some were asked to show documents, though after a cursory glance at the papers, all were quickly admitted through.

This was a Friday, and David assumed the traffic would be at least as heavy the next evening, clogged by Mexicans returning from shopping in the U.S. and Americans bound for Tijuana for the wild nightlife for which the border city was notorious. He'd make his move then, he decided.

David crossed the highway to the bus stand. He let the first one, marked City Center, go by and took the next, whose destination was North Island Naval Air Station. Most of the other passengers were young men in blue uniforms; a lot of them were hung over and a few were still drunk. The one David sat beside showed him a crooked grin and said, "When are you sailing, shipmate?"

David smiled and gave him a salute. The sailor made a funny, solemn face and said, "Sorry, Admiral, didn't recognize you without your stripes." For the rest of the ten-minute trip, the sailor told him a raunchy story about a girlie show he'd seen the night before.

David got off a half mile before the air base and went across Silver Strand Boulevard toward the entrance drive of the Hotel Del Coronado. The previous evening, in a poker game in which David had won six hundred, a couple of the guys had been talking about the place. It was nearly a hundred years old, they said, and truly fine and different. He'd probably recognize it, the guys said, because it had been in a movie. It did look familiar as David walked up the drive, an elegant, sweeping fairy castle of turrets and lacy-railed balconies facing out on the Pacific.

When he checked in, the desk clerk didn't make remarks or ask intrusive questions about him being a kid or paying cash. They never did anymore, not after he gave them a little shot of friendliness and reassurance. In the elevator David snapped his fingers and said to the bellman, "I know, the one where at the beginning there are all these chopped-up bodies on the beach, but then you find out they're just actors in a picture."

The bellman smiled. "You want me to tell you, or you want to guess?"

David thought a moment. *"The Stuntman."*

"With Steve Railsback and Peter O'Toole." The bellman nodded with approval. "A lot of people remember, but I bet nineteen out of twenty can't name it."

"I watch a lot of them," David said.

"I was in it," the bellman said. "I even had a line."

"No kidding?"

"I'll do it for you." The bellman struck a pose. " 'Right away, sir.' "

In a spacious room overlooking the ocean, David waited while the bellman turned on the air-conditioning and so on. David tipped him three dollars, even though all the luggage he had was, as usual, his gym bag. The tip was an extravagance, and so was the room, which had cost him one hundred and sixty-five dollars, at least twice what he'd ever paid before. But what the hell, David thought. He deserved to pamper himself just this once, considering it would be his last night in the United States.

Instead of going to the coffee shop according to habit, David made an eight o'clock reservation for the main dining room. It was ornate and high-ceilinged, with potted palms, dark wood tables, snowy linen, and china plates with curlicue patterns around the hotel's monogram. David had a small filet mignon, baked potato with sour cream, salad, a large glass of milk, and for dessert a scoop of vanilla ice cream in a puff pastry, with a lot of fudge sauce poured over it. It was more than he usually stowed away, and at a later hour, but he wanted to be stuffed and dopey with caloric overload by bedtime. The next day might be tiring and would surely be disorienting, and he needed to preface it with a solid night's rest.

But back in the room, when he was washed and undressed and between crisp, immaculate sheets, sleep refused to come. After a time he got out of bed and turned on the television, trying channels until he found Arsenio Hall. Arsenio was interviewing a white movie actor whose career hadn't been going so hot lately, and Arsenio was being his usual combination of sweet and provocative. Before the commercial Arsenio said that when they came back, the movie actor would demonstrate some martial-arts moves.

David turned the set off and got a book from his bag, a collection of Ray Bradbury stories that he'd been working through on and off since buying it in the airport at Salt Lake, but after a few minutes he set it aside on the night table. His mind was too full of other thoughts, and questions to which he was still unable to match completely satisfactory answers.

Still, he was learning some things, such as there were all sorts of edges one guy could have over another. That's why he had decided, even if he couldn't sense over the phone, that Mr. Simic was telling the truth: They did have another jammer to replace Mr. Voss or at least would have one soon enough. Which meant he was down to two choices: go on the offensive, or run.

Poker had taught him something about risk versus reward, and the risk in the first alternative was simply unacceptable. If he faced Simic's new jammer, he might have to kill the man to stop him. He was as unwilling to do that as he was to yield to him—and besides, he'd be betting his life that he was more powerful than the jammer.

That left running, which presented its own set of problems.

If he continued to frequent places where there were plenty of people, he'd be spotted. They'd found him in New York and a half-dozen other places, and they'd find him again. But in a small town he'd stand out and be forced to make up a lot of stories that would eventually be revealed as lies, and besides, how would he find a poker game?

But he could leave the country altogether. There was no way the Facility could be so powerful that its reach stretched around the world. Still, he'd need a passport, meaning he'd have to apply and then wait for it to be issued. The idea of wondering in the meantime if the passport people were busy alerting the Facility was one that David did not much like.

There were two places you could go, though, where all you needed was a birth certificate: Canada and Mexico. David didn't have a birth certificate either, but he knew it was lots easier to obtain than a passport. He'd learned that from a movie.

Everyone in Salt Lake City had been kind as could be. The librarian dug out microfilm reels of the *Deseret News* from around David's own birth date and showed him how to use the projector. He scrolled through the obituaries until he came across a boy named William Oswald, born three days after David, who had passed away at the age of six weeks from sudden infant death syndrome. The woman at the Salt Lake County Courthouse had been equally helpful in providing him with an official notarized copy of William Oswald's birth certificate, which cost David seven dollars and fifty cents. Like the movie had said, there were still very few places where birth and death records were coordinated.

David turned off the light in the room in the Del Coronado, lay in darkness with his hands folded behind his neck. It could work, he thought; it had to. He fell asleep against inchoate thoughts of bad things that might happen to a boy alone in Mexico but, to his relief, did not dream.

Although David had counted on a lot of traffic in which to get lost, the line at the pedestrian crossing was longer than he'd anticipated. There were maybe a hundred people ahead of him, and either the border-patrol guy was paying extra attention to each, or David was being paranoid. Whatever, the line sure seemed to move slowly; nearly a half hour passed before he found himself near its head, behind a guy whom the guard questioned quickly in Spanish and then passed through. David stepped forward, the birth certificate in his hand.

"Nationality?" the guy said.

"American. United States." David smiled. "I guess Mexicans are American too, is what I meant."

"Purpose of visit?"

"Just to see things. Tourist."

The guy looked at him longer than David liked. "You by yourself, son?"

"Uh-huh."

"Hold on a second, would you?" The guy ducked back into his kiosk. Behind David people murmured impatiently. Inside the booth the guy was flipping sheets on a clipboard. He found the one he wanted, stared at it, and picked up a phone.

David slipped out of the line, forced himself to walk deliberately but quickly, in the direction he'd come. Behind him the man said, "Hold on there!"

Now David did break into a run. He made a half-dozen steps before he saw other men in the border-patrol uniform closing on him from either side.

His first impulse wasn't so much fear as outrage. He couldn't stand the idea that the Facility's intrusive arm reached even to these people, who probably didn't even know who he was, or who the Facility was, or why anyone wanted him, only that if they saw this kid who wasn't doing any damned thing wrong but fit some description they'd been given, they were supposed to arrest him and hold him until someone from the Facility could take him away and mess up his brain—

David touched at his temples and transmitted.

Someone cried out. He didn't care; they couldn't do this to him—

He saw one of the uniformed men on the black asphalt, his face white, his breath forced. David bolted for the break in the circle, his running feet passing within a yard of the man's head. The man did not grab for him. Others hollered.

David ran.

Ahead of him, at the bus stand, he heard the wheezy sound of a door closing. At the same instant someone behind him said, "What'd he do to Murphy?" Someone else said, "Get the little bastard," and a third voice moaned, "Oh Jesus!"

David pounded at the side of the bus below the driver's window. The driver scowled down at him. David concentrated and projected indecision. The driver hesitated, then gestured David around the front of the bus. David raced in that direction, the door sighing open as he got to it. He pulled himself on board, dropped coins into the box.

The driver put the bus in gear, said without looking at him, "What's your story, kid?"

"Late," David got out, breathing hard. "My mom is gonna kill me."

The driver pulled out, a puzzled look on his face as he gazed in the rearview mirror. David sensed him wondering why he had stopped to help someone obviously a fugitive from authority. "My father too," David said to distract him, scanning the bus for an empty seat.

The driver jerked a thumb over his shoulder. "Them guys don't seem so fond of you either," he said.

It was ten at night when the Greyhound pulled into the terminal, and David was thoroughly tired and more than a little disgusted with himself. For the moment he was at least safe; beyond that he could think of little in the way of cheering thoughts. "Stupid idea," he said aloud. "Gol-damned stupid."

"Wha's that?" The woman in the seat next to him roused from bleary sleep and grabbed at the shopping bag between her feet. "Wha'd you say?" She looked around groggily. "We there?"

David shook his head, and the woman seemed to take that as a negative answer to her question. She looked out the window, said, "Yeah we are." She stood and pushed past David's knees.

At least he'd gotten away. No one tried to stop the bus and board it on the way into San Diego, no one had bothered him as he went into the terminal and bought a ticket for the first intercity bus out, which was going to L.A. Now he roused himself, got his bag from the overhead rack, and went down the aisle after the last of the passengers, climbed out into neon glare, the routine as familiar and depressing as always, except—

Someone was focusing on him; the sense hit him strong and clear as a dousing of ice water.

David stopped short on the walkway in the bright light at the head of the bus. People streamed past, boarding or debarking. He looked around, homing in on the sense. . . .

A dark unmarked Ford was parked across Sixth Street. There were two of them, which explained the strength of the sensing.

The anger that had been simmering in him since those stupid border-patrol guys had tried to arrest him now flashed to a boil. David touched at his temples and started toward the car. He could handle these guys too. He'd put the fear of God into them—or the fear of David McKay.

The car pulled quickly from the curb—they knew, they'd been told, not like the border guys—and David broke into a trot, touching at his temples to summon the point in his brain, turning his anger into transmission. He saw the car slow at a light, veer, and almost sideswipe the vehicle beside it, stall, and then jerk forward through a red signal. Horns blew. The car went on, its taillights disappearing around a corner, and the connection broke as they escaped beyond his range.

David turned, trudged up Sixth toward downtown. He hated what had just happened, losing control like that, hated and feared it. Judging from what had happened at San Ysidro, he could broadcast now, transmit to a bunch of people at once. Maybe he'd just get stronger and stronger until his brain blew up, but before then he would take a few people with him. There was a happy damned thought.

He went into a café at the corner of Broadway, moved through the buzz of chattergun conversation in Spanish, punctuated by quick laughter, and took a seat at the counter. The waitress came down and said, "Isn't it past your bedtime, *niño*?"

"I guess I wouldn't be here if it was," David said meanly.

"Such a mouth." The waitress looked hurt.

David forced himself to smile. "Sorry," he said, and gave her pleasant thoughts. "Hot chocolate, please."

The waitress smiled back. "That's better," she said, not angry anymore. She went away to get his drink.

Easy, David said to himself. Flying off the handle wasn't going to get him anywhere except wearier and more muddleheaded, and this was a time for clear thinking if there ever was one. He was in a pickle, no two ways about it.

The waitress returned with his hot chocolate, and David said, "*Gracias.*" The Spanish brought him a smile. He took a sip and nodded. "How do you say 'good'?"

"*Bueno,*" the waitress supplied.

"*Bueno*," David repeated.

The drink perked him up a bit, and he began to work things through in earnest. The significance of the business at the border, confirmed by the two men waiting when he got off the bus, was that after a month of leaving him alone, Mr. Simic had put his network back on alert—and that meant Simic had his replacement jammer.

"Why so sad, *muchacho*?" the waitress said from where she stood a little ways down near the coffee maker. When David looked at her quizzically, she did an exaggerated imitative sigh. David hadn't realized he'd sighed himself, but he sure enough had reason.

Leaving the country had been a stupid idea. He didn't speak any languages, which meant he'd have a heck of a lot of trouble getting into any games, and anyway an American boy on his own was bound to raise curiosity. What if he was detained, on suspicion or for some made-up crime? He'd probably end up in the custody of the U.S. embassy, and it was a fair bet that people there were part of Simic's network too.

When he left the café, in the process learning "*Buenas noches*" from the waitress, he went past a couple of crummy-looking rooming houses and then found himself in the heart of downtown Los Angeles amid more modern buildings, some of them hotels. But they'd be too expensive, and besides, staying in one would break a rule that he had already broken the night before, that a kid alone was more likely to attract attention in either a flophouse or a deluxe place. In the former some do-gooder might get curious; in the latter the service was too good, with too many employees learning too much.

He got into the first cab at the taxi stand in front of the Bonaventure, asked the driver to take him to a moderately priced hotel within a mile or so, and immediately sensed greed and notions of rides via roundabout routes. David said, "Forget it," ignored the guy's protests as he climbed out again, tried the second cab in the line. Its driver took him west on Wilshire Boulevard about twenty-five blocks to a place called the Hotel Chancellor that looked about right. David gave the driver five dollars for the three-fifty fare. Inside, the hotel had a good feel to it. David paid cash for one night.

The room was neat and clean, except that the maid had forgotten to empty the wastebasket, and in it was a newspaper. After flicking on the television, David dug it out, unfolded it atop the desk.

It was the *L.A. Times.* The headline on the front said there was strife in Central America, but David decided he'd had all the strife he could handle for one night, and so he put the top section aside.

Beneath it was the section called "Style." The lead story was headlined, "Steve Shaner Hosts Beverly Hills Benefit for Homeless." David recognized the name; Shaner was like the Spielberg of TV. He had one show on that David halfway liked, about this actor and his son Kenny. The actor was supposed to be so bad he was almost good; anyway he was always getting these parts and nearly screwing them up until Kenny helped him out. The show was called *Ham on Wry.*

The article was about some charity thing and didn't look too interesting, but one of the boxes over the masthead said there was a review of the new *Star Trek* movie on page D-6. David started to turn to it when the headline about Shaner caught his eye again, the headline and what was beneath it.

He sat down heavily in the chair and muttered, "Oh shit." He ran his forefinger over the page, as if to confirm by touch what he was seeing.

At the top of the column of type, a line of italics said, "By Linda Gaylen."

CHAPTER THIRTEEN

The twitchy punk leaning against the front window of the bar on Eastern unfolded his arms and scratched his crotch. He wore black jeans, engineer boots, a cutoff jean jacket over bare chest, one gold earring, and a tight net holding greased dark hair. A leather satchel hung from a strap over his shoulder.

A dinged-up low-rider Chevy pulled to the curb. The driver, a black man, left the motor running and approached the guy with quick, mincing steps, stood before him swaying a little. The two of them went around the corner into the dimness of an alleyway. A block north traffic rushed past on the Santa Ana Freeway. After a half minute the two men reappeared, the black continuing to the car and easing away, the punk taking up his post beneath the neon Coors sign in the bar's window.

In the shadow of the recessed doorway of a closed bodega across the street, Rogan grimaced and ran his tongue over his front teeth. It was the sixth transaction he'd observed in the twenty minutes he'd staked out the scene. He worked a finger inside the collar of his white shirt, loosed the damp cloth from his thick neck. Although it was supposed to be winter, L.A. was having a heat wave; at two in the morning, the night remained warm and stank of smog, and the oppressiveness of the unfamiliar suit coat and tie didn't improve Rogan's already piss-poor mood.

Across the street the punk fished out a cigarette

and patted at his pockets. Rogan came out of the
doorway and crossed the street, saw as he drew closer
that the punk was a mongrel, spig with a healthy
touch of the tar brush. Rogan brought up a Bic lighter,
flicked flame.

The punk hesitated, then coolly mouthed the cigarette and stuck its end in the fire, watching Rogan's
eyes. Rogan pocketed the lighter and brought out a
pair of handcuffs, grabbed the punk's left hand and
twisted it up, clapped one cuff around his wrist. The
punk's eyes went wide with pain and panic stoked by
a noseful of dope, and he tried to pull away. Rogan
went with the motion, wrenched the uncuffed arm up
behind the punk's back, and frog-marched him around
the corner.

"Listen, man . . ." the punk said.

Rogan pushed the punk front first against the
bar's brick sidewall. "Police officer," Rogan said.
"Don't say another fucking word."

"I wanna see a eye-dee," the punk said.

The little shit was asking for it, and Rogan was
getting steamed enough to give it to him. He drew a
steadying breath, got the wallet from the inside pocket
of his suit coat, flipped it open, and put the badge a
few inches from the punk's nose.

"You got to read me my rights," the punk said.

That just about did it; for a long moment Rogan
hung suspended above the notion of how nice it would
be to mash the bastard's face into the bricks. The image was nearly hallucinatory; Rogan could see the act
played out, the scene veiled with a misty red film, like
atomized blood.

Rogan heard a snap, and the punk moaned, "Oh
Jesus, man. Jesus God," and Rogan came around and
realized he'd broken the punk's arm.

"You should've shut up when you had the
chance," Rogan said, not exactly certain what had
happened. It didn't matter; it was time to move things

along. A length of electrical conduit ran down the side of the building a couple feet to the left. The punk whimpered pathetically when Rogan turned him around. Rogan slipped the loose cuff behind the pipe, snapped it on so the punk was propped up and facing him.

Rogan produced a knife, held it where the punk could see it when he pressed the release to expose six inches of stiletto blade. Rogan slid the steel under the strap of the satchel and cut it free.

The satchel had two compartments. Inside one Rogan found a jumble of vials. He drew out a handful: Each was glass with a black plastic top, enclosing a tiny white rock. Rogan flung the vials away and heard them bounce and shatter on the alley's buckled pavement. In the other compartment was a trash pile of crumpled currency.

A white man and a black woman turned the corner and took a few steps toward Rogan. The man stopped, held the woman's arm. Rogan said, "Piss off." The man steered the woman back toward Eastern.

Sweat glazed the punk's face, which had turned pale beneath its darkness. "Here's what's gonna happen," Rogan said as he pulled the money from the satchel. "I ask you one question, you answer the truth, I'm out of your life." Rogan straightened the bills into a lumpy stack. "You lie . . ." Rogan finished the sentence by waggling the knife under the punk's nose.

"You ain't no cop," the punk said sickly.

Rogan folded the money in half and put it in his coat pocket. "I got the badge," he said to the punk. "I got this knife, and right here"—Rogan patted at the left lapel of his jacket—"I got a big gun. What do you got?"

The punk blinked at him.

"I tell you what you got," Rogan said. "You got three seconds to tell me where to find the guy you're working for."

• • •

Earlier that evening over his restaurant dinner, Rogan had read a column in the *Los Angeles Times* about how social problems turned people into dopers. The college guy who wrote it said that people living in poverty and unemployment were forced to turn to the drug trade to stay alive. Rogan figured that if the egghead came down from his ivory tower and took a look around, he'd see what a load of crap he was spouting. People lived like pigs because they *were* pigs.

After he got his answer from the punk, Rogan pulled his gun and laid the barrel against his temple, hard enough to knock him cold for a good long time. A few minutes later Rogan steered his rental Olds into what had once been a gas station. Frayed ends of wire and pipe sprouted from pump islands, and weeds grew in the cracks of the concrete. The windows of the garage were boarded with plywood covered with a mosaic of spray-painted graffiti.

From there Rogan could see the house the guy had told him about. It was halfway down the block, a one-story bungalow behind a fence that had once been white but was now a string of peeling, weather-warped, mostly broken pickets framing a gate hanging drunkenly from one hinge. It fit into the neighborhood like a lame dog in a pound: All of the houses on the street were of similar architecture, with patchy browning lawns, sway-bottomed porches, and miscellaneous trash scattered everywhere. Lights glowed dimly in a few of them, but most were dark.

As Rogan watched, a woman hurried up on the house's porch. She crouched by the door until metal creaked, grabbed something, and went back through the broken gate, disappeared down the street. Rogan pulled out, drove past the house, U-turned at the end of the block, came back, and parked across from it, facing toward the freeway. He dug out the pile of money he'd taken from the satchel, rough-counted it in the yellow light of a street lamp. The bills were mostly tens, with a few twenties and one fifty, maybe four hundred all told. Rogan replaced it in his pocket, got out, locked the car door. A skinny guy darted up to the house, bent, came back to the sidewalk, and moved on, not looking at Rogan. When he was out of sight, Rogan crossed the street and went through the gate.

The door didn't match the rest of the house: It was sheathed in steel, with a lensed spy hole at eye level and beneath it a metal door a foot square. Rogan pulled on the handle. Inside was a V-shaped drawer, like the night drop at a bank. Rogan released the handle, and the drawer made a sharp clang as a spring mechanism drew it closed. Rogan stepped to one side. After a while something behind the spy hole clicked. Rogan waited until it clicked a second time, then went down the walkway and through the gate.

At the end of the block, he turned and went to the head of the alley that ran behind the houses. A guy materialized from behind a cluster of trash cans, flashed a knife, and said, *"Tienes dinero, pendejo?"*

Rogan reached under his left arm, and the guy lunged at him. Rogan showed him the .357 Magnum and said, "I got this, asshole." The guy stopped, poised on the balls of his feet, then spun and raced down the alley past the back of the house. The gun felt light in Rogan's grip, and he thought it might be nice to use it. . . .

In his head he saw Simic, curtained behind misty red, and he felt a lightning-bolt flash of anger. Hell with him—he'd been doing for the bastard since dinner, and now it was time to do for himself.

He was in the shadow of a dilapidated garage, frozen in position except that he was trembling some. He muttered, "Fuck it," put the gun back under his arm, and pulled the knife instead, bared the blade.

The gate in the fence behind the house was rickety but whole. Rogan pushed through, and the back door opened, splashing light across the jumble of auto parts and dented beer cans littering the yard. Rogan saw the silhouette of a man and something smaller and animate at his feet. He heard the snarl, and then the dog was racing toward him, leaping for this throat.

Rogan caught the dog's neck and squeezed hard as he drove the knife into its gut. He ripped up, and the dog mewled into his face. He tossed it aside. The house's back door slammed shut. The dog was a pit bull; Rogan watched it twitch and whine at his feet. He bent, grabbed it by a hind leg, dragged it up to the door. He kicked the dog in its bleeding belly, and the dog howled. Rogan stepped to the side of the door. While he was waiting, the dog died.

The guy who'd sicced the dog was behind the door, scared and angry and for a few moments full of indecision. Rogan sensed the guy's anger rise—he'd probably sniffed some dope—and all of a sudden the guy was pure fuck-all kick-ass crazy mad. Rogan set himself, and the door opened.

A spig voice said, "You want to play, mother-fucker?" and a hand holding a machine pistol shot out next to Rogan.

Rogan slashed down, and a gash opened in the guy's forearm. As the guy screamed, Rogan clamped his free hand over the machine pistol's receiver, jerked it away. It was an Ingram MAC-10, an oversized magazine jutting out of the grip. Rogan stepped around and smashed the gun into the face confronting him. The guy fell away. Rogan pulled out the magazine and ejected the cartridge in the chamber, then flung the whole works out into the darkness. The hell with chatterguns; the Magnum would do for this little wingding. Rogan took it out, stepped over the guy into the house, and said, "Anyone home?"

He was in a short hallway beside a door opening

on a kitchen. A half minute passed, and then a shoe scraped on floorboards, and another guy appeared at the hallway's far end, a gun up. Rogan laughed and shot the guy in the middle of the chest, the Magnum's report caroming off the walls. A hand clamped weakly around Rogan's ankle. Rogan jerked loose, bent, and put a bullet in the other guy's temple. "Shoulda played possum, pal," Rogan muttered.

Two minutes, he decided; around these parts he figured he had at least that much time before someone got worried enough about gunfire to call the cops. A glance at the kitchen table told him that he'd struck pay dirt, but he passed it by to check the bedroom. A naked woman lay on a bare mattress, her eyes glazed. She might have been dead; in any case she wasn't going to bother or remember him. Rogan considered doing her, quick and hard and brutally, so when she came back from whatever planet she was on, she'd know she'd been done good. But he didn't really feel like it; you had to be worked up and pissed off for that kind of fun. But his anger had passed, and all he was interested in now was seeing to business.

He slammed the door on her and went back to the kitchen, where a case of empty vials sat on the table beside a mirror on which rested a razor blade and a baseball-sized rock of crack. Beside the mirror was a balance scale and a Kleenex box. Rogan knocked the cocaine to the floor and ground it to dust under his heel, then pried his fingers into the dispensing slit in the Kleenex box and ripped it open. This time most of the bills were fifties and hundreds. He balled them into his coat pockets and went to the front door, undid a safety chain and threw two dead bolts, and got the hell out of there.

A kid was huddled over the door of the rental car while his lookout lounged against the front fender. Rogan emerged from the shadow of the crackhouse's porch, and the lookout straightened, hitched at his pants, and took out an ice pick, made a come-on gesture with his other hand. Rogan pulled the Magnum, and the lookout said, "Aw shit." His buddy glanced back, saw the gun. The Slim Jim he'd been using on the car window clattered to the pavement, and the two of them took off like comic darkies in some old ghost movie.

Rogan unlocked the car, fired it up. As he pulled away, the street in the rearview mirror looked still and desolate as a fresh-dug grave.

Rogan drove up Eastern to Brooklyn, turned left toward town, went three blocks. He parked the car in front of a discount record store and left it unlocked with the keys in the ignition. He doubted if anyone would have taken down the license even if they heard the shots, but it was always possible that a cop had cruised by and been curious enough about a rental Olds in that neighborhood to note the tag number. He went into an after-hours joint two doors down, used the pay phone to call Hertz, and reported the car stolen. When he went back out, it had been.

He had to walk a dozen blocks before a cab would stop. Five others cruised right on by, and Rogan didn't entirely blame them, though of the few people he passed on foot, none were stupid enough to mess with him. He gave the cabbie the name of the hotel in Westwood, which he had chosen because it was about halfway between the city center and the airport. He might have to move fast, either way.

He was a little pissed at himself about the rental car, even if there was no real harm done; the Hertz woman had seemed mostly bored with the idea of one of their vehicles stolen and promised to have a replacement delivered to the hotel within the hour. Still, he couldn't pull that trick again; next time he needed transportation while promoting pocket money, he'd hot-wire some junker.

"Live and learn," Rogan said aloud.

"How's that?" the cabbie said. He was a hippie, with long hair and tinted glasses, even though it was the middle of the night, for chrissakes.

"I been cooped up lately," Rogan said laconically.

The hippie gave him a wise grin in the rearview mirror. "You interested in a woman?"

Rogan figured any women the hippie knew came with a free dose thrown into the bargain. "I'm queer," Rogan said.

"Me too." The cab went through MacArthur Park on Wilshire. "What were you in for?"

Rogan positioned himself so the cabbie would see his mean grin in the mirror. "Boosting cabbies," he said.

The hippie laughed nervously and shut up. When they got to the hotel, Rogan stiffed him, and the hippie didn't say a word. Rogan knew he wouldn't. He couldn't stand hippies.

On the TV David Letterman was interviewing Arnold Schwarzenegger, Letterman asking his smirky questions, and Schwarzenegger answering as nice and pleasant as you please, knowing he was bigger than the asshole behind the desk and always would be. With muscles like that you could see he was full of himself, but you had to give it to the big lug for making it. Letterman said, "You just came back from a location shoot in Thailand, Arnie."

Arnie? Rogan thought. What a dickhead.

"What was your most profound impression?" Letterman went on, smiling his stupid smile like if Schwarzenegger didn't quite understand, Letterman would be pleased to use smaller words.

"David, if I learned one thing," Schwarzenegger said on the tube, "it's that America is the greatest country in the world."

Letterman laughed, and the band played a few jazzed-up bars of "The Star-Spangled Banner." The camera cut to Paul Shaffer so he could shoot a knowing wiseass look to Letterman.

Rogan clicked the channels until he found some black-and-white movie, turned down the sound, and went back to the bed where the money lay scattered. He uncreased the bills and sorted them into piles, adding the cash he'd taken from the street dealer's satchel. It came to one thousand nine hundred and seventy-three dollars. Old Arnold had said a mouthful; America *was* the greatest country in the world. If there was another place with more thieves per square mile, Rogan was ready to book a ticket.

When they held a contest for crooks, Rogan guessed Simic would at least make the final cut. Barely ten hours had passed since the man had come into Rogan's room at the Facility to tell him he was leaving in fifteen minutes. They blindfolded him for most of the chopper ride, but they couldn't dope him because they needed him awake and kicking. A few minutes before they landed, the blindfold came off, and Rogan saw they were flying over desert. Near the horizon line toward the setting sun, Rogan saw a lot of neon. "Vegas?" Rogan guessed.

Simic nodded curtly. "We'll land at McCarren. You're booked on a commercial flight to L.A. leaving in forty-five minutes." Simic passed him the credit card and the cop ID, which said he was an officer with the Federal Defense Investigation Agency. If anyone called the phone number on it, Simic said, Rogan's identity would be confirmed. Simic also gave him a small leather case, which was now locked in Rogan's suitcase. Within was a syringe of something that would knock the kid out for plenty enough time for Rogan to call in Simic. "When you get to LAX," Simic said as the chopper landed, "rent a car, get a room, and contact me. I expect to hear from you by eight o'clock."

It was nearly nine before Rogan made the call, so of course Simic was pissed. Rogan let him rant on until he got to the point, which was that since the two chickenshits had lost the kid at the bus station the night before, he had not been spotted. "Too bad," he cut in. "If they find him again, let me know. Meanwhile I'll be getting some shut-eye."

"Don't be an idiot," Simic said. "You can sense him."

"If I'm close enough," Rogan said, not sure what Simic was getting at.

"We know he hasn't left L.A. by bus, train, or plane."

"He could have hitchhiked," Rogan pointed out.

"Figure he didn't," Simic said, striving to sound persuasively reasonable. "Move around. Start at the bus station and circle out from there. It worked once before."

Rogan told Simic that he'd get right on it, then hung up and turned his thoughts to more pressing matters, like building a bankroll that would allow him to show the asshole who was running this circus.

But once he'd decided that East L.A. was the best place to raise ready cash with no kickback, he decided that maybe Simic had the right idea. No harm in trying, and there was a lot to be said for finding the kid before Simic's people. Anyway, it would make it easier to rig a way to get his money and haul ass before Simic could hit him. So he'd cruised for three hours before the crackhouse job, though he'd not caught a whiff of the kid.

On the box in the hotel room, the movie was interrupted by a commercial: The Doublemint twins were on some beach, making cow eyes at a pair of lifeguards who were also twins. They wiggled their asses—the lifeguards, not the Doublemint twins—and all four of them Barbie-dolled off toward the rolling surf. Rogan rose and stashed the money in his coat in the closet, then got a water glass from the bathroom and splashed in two inches of bourbon from a pint bottle on the desk. He took the drink and an ashtray over to the night table, flopped back on the bed, and fired up a smoke.

The money gave him room to operate. Better yet, there was more for the taking, plenty of other crooks a guy could rip off without worrying about a squawk. Rogan gurgled down bourbon, drew deep on the cigarette, let out a thick cloud of smoke that was bluish in the TV's light. No, money was no problem, but that was not to say he did not have problems.

The kraut had cut into his head to make him different, and it had worked in more ways than one. Rogan thought back to when he was standing at the back door of the crackhouse, how he'd felt the guy on the other side go from fear to crazed, dope-fed determination. He'd sensed the exact moment the guy would give in to it and throw open the door, and then the fear returning when he stepped out of the shadow and cut him good. That ability was going to make Rogan tops in his trade, as soon as he got unhooked from Simic and back into business.

After they'd operated and he began to flex his muscles, so to speak, the sensing had surprised him and, though he'd never admit it to Simic or the doctors, scared him a little as well. He realized that his lifelong ability to tell when people were lying to him was more than instinct. He had been different then, and he was a hell of a lot different now. At the crackhouse something clicked in the part of his brain they'd messed with, and for a flashing moment the dishonesty, the fright, the uncertainty of the other person was part of him as well.

But with the click came the other change, the one that scared him: the red-misty anger that ate at him in the alley when he'd cuffed the pusher, again behind the house when he'd thought of Simic. Hell, there'd been no reason to break the guy's arm; if he'd lied, Rogan would have known it.

He wondered if the kraut and Simic had meant to give him the anger along with the sensing, but that didn't figure. They wanted to control him, not drive him over the deep end.

But he wasn't going crazy, because he refused to let it happen. Still, he hated being scared, and as he thought of the kid, anger began to take over, the room taking on an odd redness, the bloody mist. . . .

Rogan closed his eyes. The redness remained, as if it were being projected on the backs of his eyelids, and mad fury rose in his mind—at Simic, the kid, the kraut, and his scalpel.

Rogan gasped and concentrated and pushed at it, and it began to yield, slowly at first and then more rapidly as if fleeing from a stronger power, and after that it was gone. Rogan opened his eyes. He was trembling a bit, his skin was clammy with sweat, and then he felt a sharp pain—but a physical pain, from the fore- and middle fingers of his right hand, where the cigarette had burned down to sear his skin.

He dropped the butt in the ashtray and rubbed at the burn blister. He got up, treated himself to another shot of bourbon. He could beat it, goddammit, and for sure he could beat some snot-ass mind-reading kid.

The phone rang. He snatched it up and said, "Yeah?" A woman said she was reception, and his replacement rental car was out front. Rogan said, "Thanks, babe," and put down the phone.

He was clearheaded and strong, and not at all tired. If the kid *was* still in L.A., he had to be in the sack, and dawn was four hours away. Rogan unlocked his suitcase, took the syringe and replaced it with the money from his coat, relocked the case, and stowed it back in the closet.

At the desk in the lobby, the clerk was sleeping standing up, bent over with his head cradled in folded arms. Rogan slapped his hand on the desk a few inches from the guy's ear, and the clerk jerked upright, gave Rogan a stupid, sheepish smile.

"Just checking, see if you're still breathing," Rogan said.

The clerk blinked at him. Rogan laughed and hit the road.

CHAPTER FOURTEEN

"**M**s. Gaylen isn't on staff," the woman on the phone explained.

"She does articles for you sometimes, right?" David asked.

"Yes, but I'm afraid she doesn't spend much time in the office."

"Thanks anyway." He sighed; he should have known it was a dumb idea.

"I'd be happy to give her—" The woman interrupted herself. "I'm sorry, she *has* signed in. I didn't see her name."

"May I speak with her?"

"One moment."

Drippy music came on the line. David gazed absently at the television in the hotel room. On the *Today* show a guy was telling Bryant Gumbel that the president would have a comment on that issue some time in the near future. David felt a flash of anticipation as the music cut off, but it was the newspaper's operator again. "She's on another line," the woman said. "Could I have her call back?"

David hesitated, then gave the woman the number of the hotel and his room. The woman said, "Your name?"

"I'm the boy who was in Arizona," David said. "Could you just tell her that, please?"

"Certainly."

David heard the click of a keyboard. "Will you

ask her to call right away?" he said. "I won't be at this number long."

"I'll give her the message," the woman said cheerily.

David thanked her, hung up, and looked vacantly around the room. He had to get out of town—he'd put it off too long already—but to where, and more important, how? If Mr. Simic were able to get the border patrol to watch out for him, it was a sure thing that he'd have people staked out everywhere there was public transportation. He could hire a cab to take him out of the L.A. area, but what if the cabbies all had his picture too?

The whole business was just too depressing, and more than anyone ought to have to handle alone. That was the real reason he had called Linda Gaylen. Sure, he'd pretended to himself it was because he was afraid that if he got caught by the Facility again and Gavin Reed sent her his long letter, she might not believe it, but the truth was he had an overwhelming need to hear a sympathetic human voice. There wasn't anything wrong with that, was there?

"Yeah, there is," David said aloud. When she called back—if she called back—the switchboard operator would answer with the hotel's name. She'd know where he was and, if David judged her correctly, would come running. Forget the whole thing, he told himself, and get the hell out—

The phone rang.

David reached for it, hesitated. It buzzed again, a third time. *Let it go,* David thought desperately. *You've got no right—*

He snatched up the receiver, held it poised over the cradle, then raised it to his ear and said, "Hello."

David heard a brief hiss of line noise, and then her voice saying, "Who is this?"

"Miss Gaylen—"

"Who are you?" She sounded angry.

David sat on the edge of the bed. "My name is David McKay," he said. "I've written you a letter—"

"You've put me through some changes, David McKay," she broke in. "I want to talk to you—in person."

He needed so much to see her, to confide in her, yet—

"You're at the Chancellor, on Wilshire," she said. "Give me ten minutes."

"No!" David said sharply. He made himself calm. "I shouldn't have called you."

"I want to help."

"Please," David said—

—and was rocked by a mental invasion so jarring he could not go on.

It was as physical as the point he felt when he transmitted, but vastly more profound, as if his brain itself were straining against the bonds of his skull. Yet there was no pain, only a scramble of confusion from which he could barely draw thought.

This was nothing like sensing; whoever was in his head wasn't one of Simic's regular people picking up his track. This was someone far stronger, maybe even stronger than—

David dropped the phone and touched his fingers to his temples and—*pushed*. After a few moments he heard the tinny sound of Linda's concerned voice coming from the headset lying on the carpet, and with it his mind cleared.

He catapulted off the bed, grabbed up his gym bag, and began stuffing his things into it. Damn if he hadn't been stupid, and now he was going to pay.

But not her, not if he could help it. He was on his own, always had been and always would be; there was a fact it was past time to face.

"What's wrong?" Linda said into the phone, loud enough so that several reporters in the *Times*'s editorial bullpen turned her way. "Goddammit, what the hell is going on?"

The line clicked, and the dial tone buzzed. Linda slammed down the receiver, pulled over the telephone book, and shuffled pages until she found the address of the Chancellor. She bolted from her chair and almost ran head-on into Nick Delvecchio.

"I was in the neighborhood, so I thought I'd stop by and see if you were interested in an early lunch." Nick gave her a narrow look. "Trouble?"

"Nick, I've got to go."

"You're on a hot story."

"Yes." Linda forced a smile. That evening they were to have dinner at a place near the Santa Monica pier that was the new hip spot, and after that, maybe . . .

"Pick me up at seven?" she said.

"Sure. I'm looking forward to it." ·

"I really have to run. I'll fill you in tonight."

She squeezed his hand and then pushed past him, went out into the hall, glanced at the indicators above the elevator bank, and passed them up for the stairs, taking them two at a time. She was sorry she'd been so short with Nick, but at the moment she was more interested in answers.

Rogan felt the sense fade as he drove slowly past the hotel, a Spanish-style place with one drooping palm in the island formed by the drive curving under the canopy fronting the office. He turned right at the next corner, drove up a steep hill, turned right again, and circled back. The sense waxed. He pulled into the near end of a bus stop and levered the shifter into park, turned off the ignition, put his hand on the door handle, and let it rest there.

He'd found the little bastard. The question was, could he take him?

The kid was moving toward him. Rogan jerked open the door and got out. He had to steady himself,

and when he stared across the street at the hotel's fa-
cade, it was draped in red.

The sense abated slightly. Rogan, preoccupied
with shuttling the mist aside, didn't get it right away,
but then he understood. The kid had sensed him too
and was taking it on the lam.

As Rogan started across the street, horns blatted
at a sports car pulling precariously across traffic and
into the hotel's drive. A good-looking babe was behind the wheel.

Rogan froze. Another horn sounded, this one right
on top of him. Rogan turned, saw the front of a bus
a few feet to his left. The bus driver was gesturing
angrily at the rental car parked in his spot.

Rogan flipped him the bird. The son of a bitch
jerked on the emergency brake, levered open the bus
door, started to rise from his seat.

Rogan reached up and slammed his fist against
the windshield, shot a forefinger at the driver. The
guy stared and sat down. Rogan stepped back, and
the bus pulled past. As the big vehicle cleared his line
of vision, Rogan saw the woman get out of the car.

It was like you were listening to the car radio,
and all of a sudden you came into range of another
station, and it blocked out the first one, crackling and
staticky and overpowering. The woman was doing
that to him, coming between him and the kid, broad-
casting like a clear channel—

She was one too. She was like the kid, except for
one thing.

She could not hurt him.

The woman went into the hotel, and Rogan
crossed the street after her.

David ran down the alley, fleeing the sense of
Simic's jammer as if it were a bad smell. The gym bag
in his right hand unbalanced him, and he stumbled
against the side of a Dumpster, righted himself, half

trotted toward the flow of traffic at the alley's end. As he exited onto the sidewalk, a taxi cruised toward him, and he waved it down. He could no longer afford the paranoiac luxury of worrying that his picture was clipped to every cabbie's visor.

The taxi drifted to the curb, and David jerked open the back door. The driver leaned over the seat and peered at him, said, "You look like you just saw your great-grandmother's aunt's ghost, son."

David gasped for breath.

"Where to?" the driver asked.

He tried to reply, but his head felt like a hive full of bees, and he couldn't have formulated the words even if he had known the answer to the cabbie's reasonable question. He sensed Simic's jammer but felt someone else as well, a multitude of sensing filling his brain and defying understanding or segregation.

"Oh Lordy," he heard himself say.

"Got to shut that door if we're going anywhere." The driver laughed hollowly. "Them's the rules."

"She's here," David said, "and he's sensed her."

"Say what?"

David demanded control and forced his demand to be answered. "The Chancellor," he said.

"I heard of it. Around the corner is all you want to go?"

"No," David got out. "Just drive to the front." He managed to dig out his money clip, work free a twenty-dollar bill. He shoved it over the top of the front seat, and it disappeared into the driver's mitt. "Please," David said.

The driver shrugged, said, "It's your money." He U-turned, went left at the corner.

"Pull over," David said, as the cab neared the hotel's drive. Ahead he saw her get into a late-model Porsche convertible. The engine started, and the car pulled to the exit, hesitated, entered the stream of traffic. As it did, David caught a glimpse of her face, confused and scared.

"She after you, kid?" the cabbie said. David studied him for the first time. He was ruddy-faced, with red hair and an oversized nose. "You do her dirt?" the cabbie kidded.

Her sense receded, but another sense—Simic's jammer, but where was he, dammit?—remained strong and steady. David dropped his concentration long enough to give the cabbie good feelings and fellowship. "You know how it is," David said.

"Sure," the cabbie said, as if he understood what was going on.

A big man came out of the hotel and ran across the street to where a Buick was parked in the bus stop. He was limping a little. He jumped into the car, pulled across the six lanes of traffic as if they did not exist. Another car careened away to avoid him, climbed the curb, and knocked over a newspaper box. A cacophony of horns filled the air as the man's car straightened, went off in the direction she had taken.

"Your dad, right?" the driver said. "He been beating on her?"

"That's right," David said quickly.

"I don't cotton to that," the driver said. He pulled the cab into drive, hit the accelerator, gave David a reassuring look in the rearview mirror. "Like they say in the pictures, follow that car."

A horn blared on her left, and a Mercedes flashed by with no more than a foot of clearance. Linda veered back into her own lane. She was shaking and short of breath, and the steering wheel, which she held with both hands, felt slick to her touch. She looked for a place to pull over, saw the Los Angeles Country Club's drive curving uphill to the right. The wide lane was bordered by high hedges, and she went far enough up so she was out of sight of the traffic passing on Wilshire below. She jerked the hand brake up violently, then hit the switch to raise the convertible top, because she felt exposed.

The events of five minutes earlier were indistinct in her mind, like dreams at breakfast: the desk clerk telling her the boy had checked out moments before, and no, he left no forwarding address nor said where he was going. Hesitating, wondering how to go about looking for him, knowing it was vital she talk to him, frustrated at missing him. Turning, seeing the man standing just inside the lobby door, looking at her . . .

He was frowning, as if perhaps he thought he knew her but couldn't place her face. From habit Linda took a mental snapshot: six five or six six, big-bodied, with hard, wide shoulders, large, thick-fingered hands, a barrel chest, at least two hundred and fifty pounds. His black hair was bristly, his face hard, his frown wreathed in leathery creases. He wore a lightweight sport coat over a white shirt and black-and-red rep tie, khaki slacks, dark brown brogans. The coat was cut full though not particularly well. It draped loosely in a style that Linda recognized; she'd seen it on police detectives and federal agents who carried a gun in a shoulder holster, though this man did not look like a cop or a fed.

Remarking him occupied her only for a moment, and then she was thinking about the boy, knowing she wasn't going to find him by standing still, and even if it was a long shot, it was the only shot she had, at least get in the car and cruise and hope that he'd left on foot. She crossed the lobby and reached out for the revolving door, and the man grabbed her wrist.

He shoved some kind of badge under her nose and took it away before she could examine it. Linda said, "You're hurting me," but he did not loosen his grip. His face was too close to hers, and he was peering at her through darkly angry eyes. "You mind if I ask some questions?" he said, his voice tight.

"Yes. Let go of me."

The man's frown twisted savagely. "I don't think so," he said.

She did not frighten easily, not in a hotel lobby on Wilshire in broad daylight with the clerk ten yards away, and yet, as she met the man's gaze, she was for a moment panicked beyond rationality, and she screamed.

The clerk looked up in alarm and said, "Sir!" and the man twisted her wrist and barked, "Shut up!" and tried to get his other hand over her mouth. Linda kicked him as hard as she could, driving the point of her shoe into his shin. The man grunted but held on, so she kicked him again, clawed at his face with crabbed fingers, fear fueling her strength. The clerk picked up the phone, punched buttons, and said, "Get me the police. Emergency." The man turned his dark look in the clerk's direction, and Linda kicked him a third time, raked at his eyes, missed, and scraped down his greasy cheek. The man let her go and fell to one knee. Linda pushed frantically through the revolving door.

As she worked to calm herself in the country-club driveway, a Rolls with tinted windows drove past and paused at the guard booth. Linda took a deep breath. She understood about the man now. He was like the one in Arizona who had died. . . .

He was after the boy, and he wanted her as well.

But why? Why the boy, and especially why her? She had to find the boy now, had to make him tell her why she was in this peril. She knew his name; there must be some way—

Linda heard another engine, jerked her head up.

A Buick pulled into the frame of her rearview mirror. Linda said, "No," hit the central door-lock button, thought: It was impossible, he hadn't been following her, she was sure, so how could he have—

The Buick stopped bumper-to-bumper behind

her, the face of the man behind the wheel twisted into
something brutal and ugly.

Linda jammed the Porsche into gear. Rubber
squealed on pavement as she shot up the hill. The
guard stuck his head out of his booth, and Linda considered stopping and telling him to call the police, but
what if there was no phone in the kiosk—or if the
man behind her—he *was* behind her, accelerating up
her tail—if he pulled his gun and shot the guard dead?
She did not want that on her conscience, and besides,
she would be okay if she could get to the clubhouse
and the press of people inside, so she went through
the entryway at speed. The guard shouted angrily,
then jerked his head back as the Buick barreled past.

She slowed, looking for an empty slot among the
cars angle-parked in front of the sprawling rococo
two-story building. As she was realizing the inanity of
the thought—*just leave the car and get inside, dammit,*—the Buick pulled around and screeched to a
stop, wedging her against the tail ends of a Saab and
a Corvette. The big man leapt from the car, came in
her direction. Linda shifted into reverse, started to
tromp on the accelerator, and checked the mirror at
the last moment. A cab, empty except for the driver,
was blocking her to the rear.

The big man tapped on the window glass with
the point of a nasty-looking knife. His muffled voice
said, "Open up, babe, or I'll slice my way in like I
was gutting a trout." The knife disappeared from her
sight above the window, and Linda froze, expecting
at any moment to see the blade slashing through the
fabric over her head.

Instead the man spun suddenly on his heel, took
a step away from the car. Linda looked past him, but
from her low angle she couldn't see over the cars to
whatever had diverted his attention. Linda glanced in
the rearview mirror again: The cab was backing
away.

She unlocked the door and carefully opened it, poised to slam it the moment the man turned on her. But instead he bolted for his own car, cranked open the back door and ducked the upper half of his body inside, reappeared a moment later with a small leather case.

Linda climbed warily from the car, but he paid her no attention. He tossed the case into his vehicle, and now Linda saw a hypodermic syringe in his hand, a rubber sleeve over its needle. He hesitated, looked around as if he'd lost something.

A voice called out, "Over here," tremulous, cracking in the middle of the second word. Linda looked in its direction.

The boy was in the middle of the first fairway, perhaps fifty yards from the foursome at the tee, two men and two women who looked irritated.

The boy caught her gaze and met it, and even at the distance Linda saw his distress and fear. He shook his head, and she stayed where she was.

The big man started after him. The boy turned and ran, out into the lush green vastness of the golf course.

David cupped his hands around his mouth and hollered, "Come and get me!"

The second fairway sloped down from the tee. David stood on the edge of the brushy rough into which he'd ducked for a moment to catch his breath. A hundred yards up the hill, the man had just pushed through another foursome. As David called out, the man turned from the golfers. They had outraged expressions on their faces, as if he'd just said something bad to them.

David trotted on toward the hole. The important thing now was to lead him away from Linda Gaylen. He slowed and glanced back to make sure the man was following. He was.

David felt frightened but calm, nothing like panic, plenty clearheaded enough to know what he had to do. First off, give Linda plenty of time to escape. Of course she'd run; he could sense her pulsing fear clear as the warm breeze.

Second, face the man and hope to God he was the stronger.

David crossed the second green, went down another slope of fairway, glancing at his watch. Five minutes had passed since he'd attracted the man's attention. He'd give her three more, to be sure she was out of the man's range.

Behind him the man shouted, "Give it up, kid." He had a mean, tough voice.

David ran on, past the flag in the second hole and up the next fairway. Someone called out, "Fore!" and the man said, "Fore, my ass." David turned to see him jerk the club from a golfer's hand and fling it away.

David went over a little hill and down another fifty paces to the perfectly round green. He slowed to a walk, the grass beneath his feet regular as carpet. This should do, he thought calmly. He stopped beside the pole, glanced up at the pennant printed with the number 3 in a circle, watched the man continue toward him.

Now he could see the man was carrying a syringe. He didn't much like that, but Simic would never take a chance on seriously hurting him. Being doped was better than being knocked unconscious with a blackjack or something.

David shook his head and swore to himself. Neither was going to happen.

He backed away slowly, no longer retreating, just making space. When he reached the edge of the green, he stood with his hands on his hips, his feet a little apart. The man was breathing hard, swinging his arms as he trotted, the needle in his right hand.

The man looked up and stopped, surprised to see

David waiting. He took the last few steps that brought him onto the green, on the point of its circumference opposite David. He glowered and drew breath so he could speak, but David beat him to it, said, "What's your name?"

The man looked at him narrowly, and David returned a slight, humorless smile. He'd learned a few things about bluffing, especially in the situation when you had pretty good cards but weren't certain you were holding a winner.

"Rogan," the man said. "The name is Rogan." He matched David's smile. "And your name, kid, is mud."

The breeze gusted, and David felt its warmth tousle his hair. "You know who I am, Mr. Rogan," he said. "And I know who you are, and who sent you. But there's something they maybe didn't tell you."

"There's plenty they didn't tell me," Rogan growled. "But that's my beeswax."

"Did they tell you I can kill with my mind?" David said levelly. That part *was* bluff. In the cab David had come to a decision: He would not kill unless a life—his, or Linda's—was directly threatened. It might not have to come to that, at least not yet. . . .

"Everyone else," Rogan said. "Me you can't touch."

"I think I can," David said, and threw fear.

He'd been using his powers a lot lately, mostly to give kindness or confidence or acceptance when necessary to get into a game or deflect questions, and now, as he saw Rogan take an involuntary step back, he knew he could do it on the fly, dammit he could, and he felt a rush of elation—

Rogan stood steady, closed his eyes, and David felt the first tickling sensation of reinvasion, the jamming, as Voss had called it. David touched at his temples, and when the point appeared, he drew from it an image he'd seen in a movie and committed to memory like a photo in a family album, a man on fire, the flame feeding on his greasy skin and biting down into his flesh—

Rogan grunted, his eyes still closed. He loosened his collar, and within David's mind the fiery man distorted, began to break apart like a TV picture from a distant channel. David bore down and revealed the man's face, blackened and shriveled and skeletal, his eyes bubbling and sputtering in their sockets like eggs frying in hot fat.

Rogan said, "No," and jerked off his jacket. Beneath it he was wearing a gun, but he did not reach for it. His face was dripping with sweat, and the jacket fell from his fingers. He started forward, and now his eyes opened a bit, red slits searing toward David, and on his gaze drifted the distortion, the blocking—the jam—

David wiped at his own forehead, called up every ounce of concentration he could muster.

Rogan stopped, slapped a hand to his cheek as if real fire had bloomed there. David swayed, woozy under the strain, and Rogan came on.

Behind Rogan an automobile horn blared. Rogan whirled around, and David felt the jam lift.

The Porsche came over the rise of the fairway, all four wheels lifting from the grass before the car came crunching down again, slewed a little, straightened, and raced toward Rogan.

Rogan flung himself to one side, and the car missed him by inches. David saw Linda behind the wheel. The car braked hard and slid sideways, tearing great earthen ruts in the green's perfection. The passenger door popped open, and she cried, "Get in."

David hesitated. On the other side of the car, Rogan was on hands and knees, looking groggy. David threw quick makeshift fear at him, and Rogan slumped to the ground.

"Get *in*," the woman said.

"No . . ." David said.

Linda ducked toward him so he could see her face. "Get in the goddamned car," she said.

David barked out a brief, hysterical laugh. He couldn't help it; she sounded like a mother giving an order to a bad kid.

Rogan rolled over on the now-muddy grass and pulled his gun from its holster.

David dived into the car. Linda reached across him, jerked the door shut. The car skewed around, and David heard clots of dirt bounce off the undercarriage. He sat up in time to see Rogan off to the side, the gun held in both hands.

"Look out!" David cried, but she was already turning in Rogan's direction. Rogan hesitated a split second too long, tried to dodge the car again. David heard the thump as it struck him. When he turned, Rogan was on the ground again, rolling into a sitting position, bringing up the gun.

It went off, but there was no corresponding sound of impact, and then the car was over the fairway hill, and Rogan disappeared from David's sight. Linda cranked the wheel, and the car swerved around an astonished golfer, shredded grass rooster-tailing into the air. The car barreled across the first tee, and golfers scattered. Sirens sounded. As Linda accelerated past the kiosk, where ten minutes earlier the cabbie had stopped to occupy the guard while David slipped out, two police cars came up the drive. Linda went past them, slowed at the foot of the hill, laid more rubber as she peeled into the traffic on Wilshire.

The light at Beverly Glen flashed red, and Linda pulled to a ragged stop. She turned in her seat, looked at him fully for the first time. She was as pretty as he'd remembered.

"All right," she said. "Let's have it."

"What?"

"Your story," she said, "and it better be good."

CHAPTER FIFTEEN

"This is insane," Linda Gaylen said.

David watched her pull a pile of underwear from a dresser drawer, toss it into the yawning suitcase on the bed. "You've got a right to be angry," he said.

"Thank you," she said sarcastically. She hesitated, hands on hips, glared at him. "Are you making me do this?"

"No."

"You did once," Linda said. "Made me do something, I mean."

"That night on the butte." David nodded. "I had no choice." He felt weary and nervous; the confrontation with Rogan had drained him more than he liked, and if he was to find them now, David wasn't sure he could stop the man. "I can do a lot of things," he said. "Not that I'm proud of it."

"You're scaring me," Linda said. "I want to know what the hell is going on."

David looked at his watch. Twelve minutes had passed since she'd rescued him. "Do you trust me?" he asked.

David felt her sensing him, though he doubted she realized what she was doing. "Yes," she said.

"Then believe me when I tell you we have to get out of L.A. as quickly as we can."

"Where?" Linda demanded.

"North, to start with." When he saw her curious look, he added, "I've got a plan."

Linda looked around her hotel apartment, its closet now empty, the drawers of the bureau gaping. She shut the suitcase, did up the clasps. "A plan," she repeated.

David picked up the suitcase. "I know what I'm doing," he said earnestly.

"Great," Linda said. "I'm glad one of us does."

He startled her when he awoke as she pulled into the gas station, stirring and shifting sleepily in the bucket seat one moment, sitting bolt upright and straining against the shoulder belt the next. "Where are we?" He jerked up his arm, looked at his watch.

"Are you all right?" Linda said. "You look pale."

"I'm fine. Where are we?"

Linda regarded him. "You always this snappish after a nap?"

He looked sheepish. "I'm sorry. I was sort of beat, after . . . what happened."

Linda nodded. She had plenty of questions, but a lifetime of reporting had taught her that often the best way to find out what you wanted to know was to give the other person time to tell it. "We're in Mojave. L.A.'s a hundred miles back, and you've been asleep two hours. You look like you're getting your color back. The tank is almost empty. This is why we have stopped at"—Linda ducked her head to look up at the sign over the station—"Goofy Gary's Gasatorium. Any other questions?"

David smiled. "Sorry," he said. "I didn't mean to come on so strong."

"You want to pump the gas?"

"I don't know how."

Linda gave him an odd look and felt a little bad when he turned away, embarrassed. She opened her door. "Come on," she said. "I'll teach you."

• • •

North of Mojave the road was two-lane blacktop, desert stretching off to the right and sere rolling hills to the left, over which ran the immense black pipeline of the Los Angeles Aqueduct. The sky was cloudless, and heat waves that never grew nearer shimmered on the highway before them. Traffic was sparse. As Linda got the Porsche up to speed, David said, "The best thing for the moment, I think, is someplace with a lot of people. Do you have a map?"

"Under your seat," Linda said. "Isn't it about time you offered some explanations?"

David dug out her Thomas Brothers California Road Atlas, let it rest unopened on his lap. "I shouldn't have called you. I'm sorry."

"Would you stop saying that?"

The boy looked puzzled. "Saying what?"

"That you're sorry."

"Sor—" He caught himself. "All I mean is I messed up your life good and proper. I guess that's worth an apology, at least."

The road was straight as a city street. Linda checked for oncoming vehicles, downshifted, and passed a Winnebago.

David waited until they were back in lane. "Why did you come after me at the country club? You were pretty scared."

"So were you."

He looked at her. "You maybe saved my life."

"I owed you," Linda said. "You saved mine in Arizona." When he didn't answer, she said, "Didn't you?"

"I guess. But it was my fault in the first place, and now you're stuck with me, at least for a while."

"I can stand it. Why am I stuck with you?"

"Because your life is in danger again," David said evenly, "and I'm the only one with a chance to protect you."

"How good a chance?" It was supposed to come out flip, but she was rattled.

"I don't know. He's lots stronger than Mr. Voss was."

Linda drummed her fingers on the steering wheel. "Why is it the more you say, the less I understand?"

"Miss Gaylen—"

"That's *Ms.* Gaylen. 'Linda' would probably be okay."

He gave her a weak smile.

"Look," Linda said, "I *am* scared. I've had a rough day, and it hasn't nearly started. First, a strange kid—and you are strange, David, if you don't mind my saying so—a kid who tailed me around D.C. three months ago and then to Phoenix and refused to tell me why, this kid calls me up and *still* won't tell me why. Then some thug—"

"His name is Rogan," David interrupted.

"This Rogan strong-arms me and obviously means to do me extreme dirt," Linda pressed on, "so I end up trashing a good part of the country club's first three holes saving your ass, you'll excuse the expression, and now I'm driving who knows where."

Linda went on before he could interrupt. "So the reason I came for you, aside from my generous nature and an understandable reluctance to see the thug eat you for lunch, is that I want to know what the hell is going on and how I'm involved. You're going to tell me, before I really get irritable."

David turned, cocked a leg up on the seat. "Did you ever feel like someone was looking at you? You're in a restaurant or some other crowded place, you think someone is staring in your direction, and you turn around and they are?"

"Sure. That happens to everyone."

"Were you ever with a person you were close to, a lover or a relative, and you were thinking about something, and all of a sudden they speak up about the same thing?"

"Yes," Linda said slowly.

"Okay," David said, warming to the subject. "You're a reporter."

"I was, until you sort of came between me and my career."

He didn't rise to the crack. "And you're good at it, right? Why? What can you do that other people can't?"

The question was rhetorical. "I'm going to take a guess," he went on. "When you ask them things, you know if they're telling the truth."

"I've got good instincts," Linda said.

"You *know*," David insisted. "When you sense they're lying, are you ever wrong?"

"No," Linda said slowly.

"Concentrate on a number from one to ten."

"Huh?"

"Come on. Think of it as a game."

Linda glanced at the speedometer. David said, "Six."

"Cute," Linda said skeptically. "We're going sixty, and you saw where I looked."

"Try it again."

"Okay."

"Two," David said. "Again."

"Go."

David laughed. "You cheated. Fourteen."

Linda gave him a sharp look. "How'd you know?"

"I'm different, Linda. So are you."

"Now wait a damned minute," Linda said. "I can tell when someone lies to me. You, on the other hand, are able to give me hypnotic suggestions, like on that butte when you made me stay while you lammed out. Now I find out you can also read minds."

David shook his head. "If you're concentrating on something specific, like a number, I can sense it. I can also sense strong emotion, but I can't read minds."

"The point is," Linda said impatiently, "we're hardly in the same league."

"I think we are," David said. "Sometimes psi—
that's the term for what we're talking about—sometimes
it's latent, even if it's very strong. I know it's strong
in you; it would have to be for me to sense you, like
I did the first time in Washington. Rogan sensed you
too, remember. When he tells the Facility, they'll be
after you as well as me. But if you can't transmit, and
probably you can't—"

Linda cranked the wheel and hit the brakes, skid-
ding to a stop in the loose gravel. She put the car in
neutral, jerked up the parking brake, turned, and shot
a finger at him.

"Facility," Linda echoed. "Sensing. Transmitting. What the hell are you talking about?"

David frowned. "You like me, don't you?"

"Yes, I like you," Linda snapped. But it was true.
There was something about him that Linda liked a
lot, something vital and vulnerable.

"I like you too." He pointed through the windshield. "Let's get going."

Linda sighed heavily, levered the Porsche into
gear, and pulled back onto the road. "I wrote you a
letter," David said.

Linda felt unmoored. "Why?"

"It's a long story," David said.

The café in Bridgeport was on Main Street near
the traffic light that marked the center of town. David
knew its sort, a place where older men and a few
women hung out during daylight hours, nursing coffee and talking in low voices, and too reserved to ask
intrusive questions to a boy traveling on his own. Now
that he was with Linda, they hardly looked at him.
They figured he was her son, he supposed. Something
about that deception made him feel good.

The waitress brought water in thick plastic
glasses, poised her pen over her pad. David ordered a
cheeseburger and milk. Linda asked if there was a

dinner salad, and the waitress said, "Sure. It's like the lunch salad, only bigger. Italian, Roquefort, or Thousand Island?" When she went away, Linda folded her arms on the table and said, "I don't think I could digest anything too rich. I'm having enough trouble digesting what you've told me."

It was five hours since they'd left Mojave, cruising through the featureless desert until they hit U.S. 395 and then following it down into Owens Valley. David did most of the talking, Linda occasionally looking skeptical but not interrupting except to interject a perceptive question now and then. She believed him; reluctantly, a little resistantly, but she accepted, and that was a relief. There had been times since he'd escaped when David feared that no one would, ever.

The smell of his burger frying rekindled David's appetite. He fished a packet of Saltines from a bowl, stripped off the cellophane, and popped a cracker into his mouth. "Want one?" he offered.

"I think I can wait," Linda said dryly. "There's a couple things I don't quite get."

"Shoot," David said through a mouthful of crumbs.

The waitress returned with David's burger and Linda's salad. "You two on vacation?" she asked.

"Yup," David said brightly. "We're going to Lake Tahoe."

"We are?" Linda said.

"It's only another fifty miles or so," David said. "Are you tired?"

Linda rolled her eyes. "I think I can hold out."

"I been to Tahoe," the waitress said abstractedly. "We saw Rodney Dangerfield. You want catsup?"

"Please," David said.

The waitress snagged a red plastic squeeze bottle from the next table, placed it in front of David. "There's a man with an attitude," the waitress said. Linda didn't get it, but David ran a finger around the collar of his T-shirt, lowered his voice, and said, "I don't get no respect." The waitress laughed and left them alone. David gave his attention to spiraling catsup over the top half of his hamburger bun.

Linda waited until he looked up. "Why are we running?"

"The Facility knows who you are."

"How?"

David took a bite of burger, mopped a puddle of juice from his plate. "Unless Rogan is real stupid— and I didn't get the sense he is—he memorized your license number." David chewed thoughtfully. "Incidentally, we'll have to get rid of the car."

"The hell we will!"

"We'll talk about that. How's your salad?"

Linda gingerly prodded a lettuce leaf with her fork. "Wilted."

"Some people like it that way."

Linda snorted and began to eat. "Why don't we go to the police?" she asked.

"Too risky. Like I told you, the Facility has all sorts of connections. Chances are they've already got the word out."

"What word?"

David shrugged. "If I was Mr. Simic, I'd make out that you had kidnapped me."

"That's grand," Linda said. "That is just grand."

"Sorry," David muttered. "Whoops, I forgot I'm not supposed to say that. Sorry."

Linda gave him an exasperated look. "Are you working at driving me crazy, or does it come naturally?" She stabbed at her salad. "All right, so what *do* we do?"

"I'm working on that."

"I've got a life," Linda insisted. "I can't just disappear. For starters I've got to make a call."

"To who?"

"None of your business."

"I just meant . . . it wouldn't be such a hot idea for someone to find out what really happened to you. Probably they wouldn't believe it anyway."

Linda sighed. David said, "You've got a guy."

"You're doing it again."

David did not rise to her irritation. "Someone you care about."

"His name is Nick, I *do* care about him, and we were supposed to have dinner tonight. He and other people are going to wonder where I am."

"How about if you wait until we get where we're going?"

"Where's that?"

"I'm not sure. It's another thing I'm working on."

Linda set down her fork, leaned forward. "David," she said in a low voice, "I've trusted you, and considering what I've had to accept so far, that's saying a lot. You've got to trust me too. As you said, we're stuck with each other. I'm not entirely unhappy with that. I do like you. But if we're going to be partners—if we're ever going to get out of this pickle—we have to work together."

"I know that."

Linda breathed a deep sigh. "All right," she said. "Let's take it a step at a time. First off, we're going to need money. I've got about twenty thousand in the bank in L.A., along with some stocks—"

He was shaking his head no. "They'd have to send it to you, and we can be pretty sure the Facility will be keeping an eye on your accounts. Anyway, money is no problem."

"That's a load off my mind," Linda said ironically.

"It's why we're going to Tahoe."

"*What's* why we're going to Tahoe?"

David popped the last of the burger into his mouth, pushed his plate aside, showed her his smile. "Have you ever played blackjack?" he asked.

∙ ∙ ∙

It was winter for true in the mountains. Snow frosted their tree-covered flanks, ice rimmed the shallow edges of the lake, and David could see his breath in the crisp twilight air. They'd bought down parkas in Bridgeport after dinner; his was bright blue with a hood. Linda was going to use her American Express, and the saleswoman had given David a funny look when he'd stopped her and produced his money clip to pay cash. In the car afterward he tried to explain to her again how easily the Facility could find out things, and though she believed him, he could see she still had trouble accepting the situation. Not that he blamed her . . .

The used-car place was called Jumpin' Jack Sampson's South Tahoe Import/Export. The lot was surrounded by poles supporting strings of colored lights and triangular plastic flags that made a wet sound as they flapped in the stiff breeze. David was checking out a Mustang convertible when he heard Linda say, "I could get twenty thousand in L.A."

David went over to where she was facing a guy in a checked flannel jacket and porkpie hat. The guy took a cigar out of his mouth and said, "So sell it in L.A."

"I'll go seventeen five," Linda said.

They were standing outside the little wooden hut that served as the dealership's office. "Fifteen," the guy said.

"Fifteen is fair," David said as he came up.

"Wait a minute here," Linda said to him. "Whose car are we selling anyway?"

David smiled politely at the bemused used-car guy. "Could you excuse us for a moment?" David took Linda by the arm, drew her over under the string of lights. "I know you're attached to the car."

"He's trying to rip me off," Linda said hotly.

"We've got to get rid of it."

"We?"

"Just pretend I know what I'm talking about. Okay?"

Linda looked down at him. "I'm reminded of something they say a lot in Hollywood: 'What he really wants to do is direct.' "

David smiled. "Okay?" he repeated.

Linda gave an exaggerated sigh. "Why is it I keep going along with you?"

David remembered the article she'd written about Steve Shaner, the guy who produced *Ham on Wry*. On the show the kid had a line he always said when he talked his father out of some stupid scheme, and the father asked the same question. David turned up the smile and said, "Boyish charm?"

It was almost seven o'clock, and the used-car guy couldn't get the money in cash until the banks opened in the morning, so they drove on up Lake Tahoe Boulevard to where it curved along the beach, then through town and past the five casinos bunched up only a couple yards over the Nevada state line. David picked out a small motel called the Lakeside another half mile on.

"Would you rather get separate rooms?" he asked.

Linda was a little surprised. It was a sensitive and mature gesture.

"I mean if you want privacy," he said, mistaking her silence for discomfort. "I'll be all right."

She did not want to be separated from him, and not only from fear someone was after them. "I can stand being roommates," she said.

"Good," David said. "It'll look more normal."

He seemed preoccupied after she registered. In the room he watched her unpack her toilet kit, take it into the bathroom. When she came out, he said, "Did you ever want to have a kid of your own?"

Linda stopped in the doorway, stared hard at

him. David went pale, stumbled back, and sat down hard on the bed. "Oh geez," he said. "I didn't mean to . . . Sometimes I can't help it."

"What are you talking about?"

"When I asked you about having a kid," David said. "You were so sad all of a sudden. I wasn't trying to sense you, but . . ."

Linda colored. "I have a right to my own thoughts. I don't like this one bit."

"I know, I know," David said miserably.

"Can you control it or not? Let's get that on the table right now."

"Most of the time . . ." David shook his head blankly. "I don't want to make you angry."

Linda came over and sat on the bed beside him. "Easy does it," she said gently. "When you asked me that . . ."

Partway through the story of Richard and the child they had been expecting, Linda reached out to him, and when she was finished, David looked down at his hand in hers. "Is it okay if I say I'm sorry?" he asked after a moment. "Just this once?"

Linda nodded. "I'm sorry too." She put her arm around his shoulders. "I don't mean to put my problems on you. You've got enough of your own."

David felt awkward. He slipped out of her embrace, stood. "Are you very tired?"

"I'm kind of jacked up," Linda said. "Why?"

"Since we're here," David said, grinning again, "let's go work on our bankroll."

David squeezed Linda's shoulder, and Linda tapped a finger on the faceup cards in front of her, a jack and a six. The dealer slid a hit card from the plastic shoe, flipped it atop the other two: a seven, for a bust. The dealer's hand passed over the felt layout, and Linda's twenty-five-dollar green chip disappeared. David squeezed again, not in signal but as reassurance.

He was having a good time. He'd wanted to play blackjack for a long time, but no casino would let a kid gamble, and the one private game he'd run into, in a hotel in Austin, was honest but a sucker proposition, with the house winning tie hands and only paying even money on blackjack. It frustrated him, because he knew he could win at the casino version—it suited his talents even more than poker, with its fast action and rigid rules—and this evening had proved him correct. Playing twenty-five dollars a hand, they had doubled a thousand-dollar stake in two hours.

Linda drew a jack-ten, and David kept his hand relaxed, though by now she had learned enough about the game to know she had a probable winner. The dealer drew a king to bust a fourteen and paid her off.

It was eleven at night, and Harrah's Casino was fairly crowded. David liked the bustle, the waitresses in their short-skirted costumes, the clang of the slot machines occasionally punctuated by the whoop of a big winner, the smoke whirring up toward a ceiling that was set with irregular panels. Some of them were one-way windows, through which bosses watched the action; a guy David had met in a poker game in Chicago told him about the men upstairs, and how winners in particular attracted their interest. So they kept moving, changing tables and then casinos as their stack grew.

Linda drew a natural blackjack. As she collected her winnings, David said, "Let's take a break."

"Not while I'm finally starting to get ahead," Linda said, as he had prompted her when he'd gone over the plan in the motel room, demonstrating the game with the pack of cards he always carried in his bag. Over the course of playing, she had continually drawn chips from the table and stashed them in her purse or took out more chips and scattered them carelessly on the felt. David wasn't sure how effective that strategy was, but at least it didn't leave large, neat piles so it was obvious she was ahead.

"Come on," David whined. "I'm tired."

Linda sighed dramatically, gathered up her chips, and slid off the stool. When they were in the coffee shop, she gave him a wide smile. "What are you, a method actor?"

"I'm not really tired."

"What you are," she said, "is pretty amazing."

"I'm getting better," David said. "I'm almost never wrong now."

David ordered hot chocolate, and Linda asked for herb tea. "Are we going to play some more?" Linda said.

"We might as well, if you feel okay."

"The tea will help." Linda leaned across the table. "How are we doing this?"

"Blackjack has the best odds of all the casino games," David explained. "There's a basic strategy—what to do with any two cards, depending on what the dealer's up-card is. That might sound hard to learn, but it's not; there aren't that many combinations."

"How do you know all this?"

"From a book." David was showing off a little, but what the heck. "If you play the basic strategy and don't make mistakes—and I haven't been—"

"You ought to get a load of yourself, chum," Linda said. But she was smiling.

"If you do," David went on patiently, "the house has only about a two percent advantage. That means out of a hundred hands, you'll win forty-nine and lose fifty-one."

"Is that what it means?" Linda said, needling.

"I'll bet you didn't know that," David said. "Most people don't."

The waitress returned with their drinks. David scooped up some whipped cream from his hot chocolate, licked at his spoon. "But if you know what the dealer's hole-card is," he went on, "the game is way in your favor. You've got an edge of almost ten percent, even if you never double down or split pairs."

"Say what?"

"Those are other plays you can make. I'll teach them to you later."

"Why thank you, Professor," Linda said. "I can hardly wait."

David sighed. "If the dealer doesn't look at his hole-card, I can't sense what it is. But he has to look if the up-card is a ten or a face-card or an ace, to see if he has blackjack, because if he does, the game is over, and all the players lose except anyone who ties him with another blackjack. Are you following this?"

Linda gave him a look that made him laugh. For a day that had started out so lousy, he was feeling pretty darned good right now.

"Five out of every thirteen cards is a ten or ace or face-card," he went on, "so the dealer looks—and I know. Now you've been playing long enough to see the patterns. Say you're dealt fifteen, and the dealer shows a ten, but when he looks, he doesn't have blackjack. If you didn't know what he had under, you'd take another card, because probably he's already got you beat. But if you know he has a six and will have to take a hit himself, you'd stay, because chances are he will bust."

"Look," Linda said, "let's just leave it at this: You squeeze, I take a card. You don't, I don't."

David smiled over the rim of his mug. "It's worked so far," he said.

•   •   •

Linda opened the bathroom door, and in the moment before she flicked off the light, David caught a glimpse of her in panties and bra. The room went dark. "You awake?" she said.

David felt embarrassed and almost feigned a snore. "Yes," he said instead.

He heard the sheets rustling as she got into bed. "You know, before we went out, when I sort of sensed you by accident?" His eyes dilated, and he could see her form a few feet away.

"I'm not mad about that anymore. I don't hold grudges."

"I know. It's not that exactly."

Somehow the darkness made it easier to tell her the story of the erotic dream he had involuntarily transmitted to Sherrilyn Casey, and more briefly how he had felt a loss of control when he lashed out at the two agents who were waiting at the bus station in Los Angeles. When he was done, Linda said, "They wanted to abduct you. She sounds like a nice lady."

"That's the point," David said, relieved she understood. "You don't have to be afraid."

"I don't quite follow."

"I thought maybe I couldn't control it, but I figured out I mostly can. My control is getting stronger just like the rest of what I can do. Even if I did slip, maybe transmit to you by accident, I can't hurt you. I'm not sure how I can be positive about that, but I am."

"Like hypnotism maybe," Linda said from her bed. "You can't get a subject to do something he wouldn't normally."

"Exactly," David said happily. "You're safe with me. . . . Well, maybe not *safe* exactly, but . . ."

"Don't start again," she said, but lightly.

David lay still for a few moments. "You want to hear something funny?"

"What?"

"I'm no good at lying. Maybe because I know if other people are."

"Me too, remember?" Linda said.

"I guess that means we can't lie to each other," David said.

"Why would we ever want to?"

David felt better than he had in a very long time. It was awfully hard to be with Linda and not believe that with her help he couldn't somehow get the Facility off his back for good; already life seemed more full of possibility than it had in a mighty long time.

David smiled and after a time drifted down into untroubled sleep.

CHAPTER SIXTEEN

A voice tickled at Rogan's mind and drew him driftily up toward consciousness. Phrases: ". . . as if his current were turned off . . . voluntary physiological functions . . . CNS remains unimpaired . . ."

Rogan's eyes were open.

". . . allow us to perform the necessary brain scans without impediment." Kohl's voice.

"Can he hear us?" This was Simic, a little farther away.

"Probably. Even so, he will not remember."

I'll remember, Rogan thought. *Count on that.*

"What did you use?" Simic asked.

"An ichthyotoxin derived from *Sphoeroides testudineus.*"

Rogan saw uniform soft-focused off-whiteness. He tried to blink it away.

His eyelids would not move.

"The crapaud de mer, or sea toad." Breunner's voice was to Rogan's other side and close by. "Also known as the puffer fish."

A liquid splashed the lens of Rogan's eyes, one then the other. He could not feel its wetness, but its runny film curtained his sight. "His lacrimal glands are shut down, so the cornea must be artificially irrigated." Breunner's voice moved away.

Rogan's vision cleared, and the off-whiteness resolved into stippled ceiling tile. Simic said, "Did we develop it?"

"*I* developed it, under Agency sponsorship," Kohl said. "At the Pennwood lab, in 1961. Unfortunately it is useful only in rare situations."

Rogan tried to turn his head in her direction, and then just his eyeballs.

He could move neither.

"Paralytic at the indicated dosage," Breunner said. "Its administration to enemies as part of Haitian religious culture is the basis of the zombie myth."

Rogan screamed. The cry reverberated against the walls of his skull, and when it stopped, he realized he had made no sound.

". . . assume time is of the essence," Kohl was saying.

"Obviously," Simic said.

"Then we will operate this afternoon, if the scan results are as expected."

Jesus God, Rogan thought, *they'd made him into the living dead, and now they were going to cut him again, and he could not stop them, could not move the tiniest muscle, could not even talk, to tell them about—*

"The woman," Kohl said, as if he had spoken. "Has the trace on her provided any information that will help us find them?"

"Are you familiar with the proverb regarding the result of curiosity on the cat?" Simic said.

Kohl muttered something. Rogan felt the red mist coming up to blot out the ceiling, the anger overpowering the sound of their voices. He forced it aside, commanded it to leave and take the panic with it. The tiles told him he was at the Facility; it was morning, probably the day after the business with the kid. The goddamned kid . . .

Let it go, Rogan insisted. *Pay attention, and put the energy into finding some way out of this, like you always do. . . .*

Breunner asked something about the time frame.

"We'll find them soon enough," Simic said.

"But must we do this immediately?" Breunner asked.

"Yeah, you must," Simic said in his wiseass voice.
"We've identified the woman as a reporter named
Linda Gaylen."

So they knew about her, Rogan thought. But he
bet they didn't know the part that counted. . . .

"Can she expose us?" Kohl asked.

"Not without exposing the boy," Simic said.

"Let us hope."

"Do your job, Frieda, and fast."

Breunner hovered into view, and more droplets
splashed into Rogan's eyes. Simic said, "I'll leave you
to your tests. Let me know if there are any glitches."
A door opened and closed.

Breunner said, "You are certain about your model?"

"You went over it," Kohl said.

"I had less time than I wished."

"It will enable him to absolutely control the boy."

"What else?"

Silence passed. Rogan tried to move again, could
not. They wouldn't hurt him; they needed him, and
how bad could the operation be? The kraut bitch said,
"What are you insinuating, August?"

"I am not insinuating. I am asking if the procedure is fail-safed against . . . unwanted effects."

"Yes," Kohl said firmly. "As long as you do your
part." Her voice turned sickly sweet. "And you will,
August. You are very good, you know."

It was almost as if she were flirting with him.
Rogan found himself wondering if the two of them
got it on—Christ, there was a sickening thought. *Concentrate, goddammit. They're talking about you.*

Breunner said, "It is gracious of you to say so,
Frieda," sarcastic. "Still, without prejudice to your
own finely honed skills, I would treasure the opportunity to make a thorough analysis of the model. It
would take no more than twenty-four hours."

"Would you like to tell Simic that? We proceed

today. Don't we?" More silence, and then she repeated, harder toned: "Don't we?"

When Breunner didn't answer, she said, "Go analyze the scan results, August—and please, do not attempt to contrive some objection. If you do, I will learn of it."

"And tell Simic."

"With whom do you think my loyalties lie?"

The door opened. "With yourself, Frieda, and no one else." The door closed.

Rogan forced possibilities to present themselves. He'd always had a high tolerance for dope; could be he'd come out of it before they started to cut.

If so, it would be time for some smart moves—smarter anyway than his moves twenty-four hours earlier.

When the babe had clipped him with her sports car and snatched the kid right out of his goddamned hands, Rogan was knocked goofy but not out. He came around within a half minute, in time to see the car disappearing over the hump of the fairway, back toward the clubhouse.

The second thing he saw, as he dragged himself to his feet, was a faggy-looking guy in white pants and polo shirt, facing him with a golf club cocked over his shoulder. Rogan squared himself and waited for the guy to come on, and for a moment thought he would. Instead the guy turned away, gestured with his free hand at the deep twin ruts the babe's car had cut in the grass, and said, "My God, look what you've done."

That should have been funny, except the red mist was tickling at the edge of Rogan's vision. He knew from the night before, the business at the crackhouse, that even though he could maybe control it, there was a quicker way, and that was to give in to the mist, feed it. It was like they'd installed a pressure valve in his brain, and every once in a while, he had to let off steam—like right now, when he needed to be clear-minded as fast as possible.

A woman cried out, "Edmund!" She was back by the edge of the green, a blond in a short skirt. The guy half turned toward her, and Rogan took the golf club away from him, double-handed it like a baseball bat, and slammed its head into the guy's stomach. The guy gasped and bent, so Rogan chopped him across the back of the neck, and the guy went down face first into one of the muddy ruts.

The woman screamed, and behind her sirens sounded. Rogan went in the other direction through a brushy rough until he came to an adobe wall. He leapt and got a grip, drew himself over. There was more brush on the other side, and beyond it the curb-side along Wilshire.

By then Rogan felt normal once more. The kid had scared him, sure, but he hadn't done any real harm. The jamming had worked that well, at least. He could deal with the kid some other day, if it came to that. Right now it was time to regroup.

First thing was to hit the road. The get-out-of-jail-free card that Simic had provided might not be enough to chill the rap on the beating he'd just given the golf guy. The babe would give the cops a description, and besides, they'd pull prints from the rental car, which would give them a name; his prints were on plenty-enough cop computers. Odds were that Simic would find out as well, and he wasn't apt to be too pleased that the kid had given him the slip. No doubt he'd soon have guys bird-dogging him. So: boost a car, point it away from here, and haul ass.

Traveling money would help, and the Magnum might come in handy too. Rogan checked his watch; less than ten minutes had passed, and the hotel was only another five away. Rogan crossed Wilshire to the Holiday Inn, jerked open the door of the first taxi in line. He gave the cabbie his hotel's name and added, "Twenty bucks if we're there inside of five minutes." They made it in three, with the meter showing four-eighty. Rogan gave the cabbie a five-spot and told him to keep the change.

The clerk who had been dozing at the desk ten hours earlier was still there; he must have owned the fleabag. "Call for you," he said as Rogan crossed the lobby. "A guy named Jackson. You want the number?"

"I got it." "Jackson" was Simic's nom de spook. Rogan heard the phone ringing while he unlocked the room door, and it went on ringing as he checked the money in the suitcase, added to it a few changes of underwear and a couple of shirts. The ringing stopped while he took a piss, then started up again as he came out of the bathroom. Rogan sneered at it, threw the room key on the bed, and hoisted the suitcase.

The phone started up again as he went out. Before he could press the button, the elevator doors parted to reveal the desk clerk. He looked at Rogan's suitcase and said, "You weren't thinking of jumping your bill, were you?"

Rogan gave him a look, got in, and punched the "G" button. The clerk cleared his throat. "That guy called again." He waved a piece of note paper. "Said he heard about your round of golf, wants to congratulate you in person."

The elevator shushed to a stop, and the doors parted. Across the lobby two men came through the revolving doors. They wore vested suits, brogans, short haircuts, hard looks on chiseled faces.

"When'd he call?" Rogan said.

"Just now." The clerk pushed wire-rim glasses higher on his nose.

"You tell him I was here?"

"Why not?"

The mist teased at the corner of Rogan's vision. He

stepped out of the elevator. The two men were in front of him, standing a little apart. One said, "Mr. Rogan?"

Rogan did not try to push the mist away. "Maybe," he said. "And then what?"

"Would you come with us, please?"

Rogan stared through the redness that outlined the man like an aura. "Sure," he said. He extended his arms. "You wanna cuff me?"

"If you don't mind."

One came around his flanks. Rogan said, "I don't mind," stepped forward, and drove his foot into the other guy's balls.

The guy doubled up, and Rogan threw him aside, half turned. The other guy had his hands full with the cuffs. Rogan put a fist into his face. Nose bone splintered.

"Back way," Rogan grunted.

The clerk was cowering in the elevator. He pointed. Rogan went past the desk, down a corridor, pushed open a fire door.

Cookie-cutter replicas of the first two guys were waiting in the alleys with guns drawn. Rogan slapped at the nearest weapon, saw it skitter along the buckled pavement. Someone jumped on his back, and another gun jabbed at his ribs.

Rogan said, "You gonna shoot me?" and slammed his forearm across a windpipe. The guy grunted, "They fucking didn't tell us—" Rogan kicked back at his shin and missed. Others were running down the alley. Rogan spun around, unloosed the guy on his back, flung him toward them. One went down, but the other leapt clear.

Rogan squared and drew his Magnum. Behind him someone said, "Son of a bitch," and a blackjack cratered into the base of Rogan's skull. He staggered, clawed for the face before his. The blackjack bored in with a second blow, and an explosion of pain blew the red mist into a cloud of ruby shards.

•   •   •

Frieda Kohl's pinched face swam into Rogan's field of vision. Somewhere behind her Breunner said, "His fingertips. Motor reflex?"

Rogan realized he'd attempted to clench his fist.

"He's regained rudimentary neurological control," Kohl said. "He can do nothing to harm us."

I can tear your fucking arms off and make you eat them for dinner. Rogan tensed himself, tried desperately to work sensation back into his muscles.

"Isn't that right, Mr. Rogan?" She smiled awfully.

Rogan squeezed together all of his strength, lunged at her, his fingers grappling for her eyes through the consuming red mist. He missed but caught her flesh under his fingernails, raked down, felt it part, and tried again, straining upward at her sunken sockets and finding them, the pulpy grapelike balls within—

"You see, August?" Her voice was soft and cold at the same time, insinuating. "Our poor little man."

He had managed to barely raise his head, and though the strain made his neck muscles spasm, he held the position. He could see his fingers at the end of arms lying woodenly at his sides, their tips twitching spasmodically as if attached to a puppeteer's strings. More than anything he had ever desired, he wanted to grab her throat and crush the life from her.

Use it, his mind screamed. *Use it to fight whatever they give you. Stay strong.* He let his head fall back.

Kohl's taunting expression hovered before him. "Go away, little man." He felt the pressure of a needle in his arm, but not the prick. The drug flooded into him, and he fought it, tried to ignore the rise and fall of her maddening voice singsonging, "Little man, our little man."

BOOK
THREE

CHAPTER SEVENTEEN

L/inda missed a gear, swore, and wrenched at the stick shift. This time it slid into place, but not without a grinding protest from the transmission.

"You've got to press the clutch all the way to the floor," David offered.

"Is that right?"

"That's what I hear," David said, unperturbed.

The two-lane blacktop curved along a bench above the Kootenai, the river's surface ice glazed except for a narrow channel where the deep water flowed. Mountains rose steeply on either side of the valley, their skirts forested with Douglas fir and ponderosa pine except where clear-cut logging operations had left snow-covered bald spots.

"The clutch on this thing is stiff as a rusty door," Linda said.

"Maybe you should use both feet," David said, giving her an exceedingly solemn look. He liked the truck, a six-year-old Chevy Silverado half-ton pickup for which they'd paid sixty-five hundred in Tahoe the morning after they'd sold the Porsche. It had almost new steel-belted radials, a canopy topper, a big V-8 engine, and four-wheel drive that allowed it to climb anything short of a sheer cliff.

"I figure you've noticed, since you're trained to be observant and all, around here there's more trucks than cars," David went on. "It's a western sort of rig. Fits in with the scenery."

He remembered that he had almost messed up on that account; in Tahoe he'd forgotten until the last minute that the title to the truck would go into some computer under Linda's name, just the kind of thing Simic would be keeping tabs on.

So David had slipped the used-car guy two hundred dollars extra and a shot of goodwill, in exchange for putting a different name on the truck's title than the one on the Porsche's. At the Ravalli County Courthouse in Hamilton, Montana, they'd used the title to exchange the temporary plates for regular ones. Now the truck was duly owned and registered to someone named Lilly Magee.

A sign pointing to a dirt road on the left said, "Sugar Mountain Cross-Country Ski Area, 4 Mi." Linda jounced onto it. "We've fit in too," she said.

David peered through the snow lashing at the windshield. "So far," he agreed.

With nearly a week between them and the trouble in L.A., Linda was beginning to relax. As hideouts went, this remote northwestern corner of Montana had a lot to offer. From her days in journalism school down in Missoula, Linda knew the country, and more important, the ways of the people. David's primary reason for steering them in this direction was more pragmatic: Poker was legal in bars. Kids couldn't play, of course, but they were permitted inside if with an adult—there remained that laissez-faire, do-what-you-want-as-long-as-you-don't-bother-others frontier ethic to the state, something else that worked to their advantage.

"I told you it would probably happen," David said.

"It still scared the hell out of me." Linda gave him a sharp look. "Hey, cut it out."

"I can't always help it, you know," David said, a little hurt. "It's like you accidentally overhear a private conversation so you move away, but you still catch some of it."

She had been thinking of an evening three days earlier in Kalispell, when the most vivid awakening of her own psi powers had occurred. David had talked her into trying some poker, even though they didn't need the money yet; their bankroll was up to nearly twenty grand, what she'd gotten for the Porsche plus more than ten thousand they'd won in various casinos as they made their way across northern Nevada.

The game, in a saloon called Mike McGurk's, was seven-card hold-'em, three cards down to each player and four common cards that were part of everyone's hand.

Their system was simple: David, at the rail enclosing the tables, placed his right hand on it to signal her to fold, his left to call, and both hands to raise. Once he was sure she understood the rhythm of the betting and the ranks of the hands—it didn't take long—he'd leave the rail every half hour or so and let her play a couple of rounds by herself, so no one got suspicious he was helping. He didn't need to sense to know these country folk were savvy poker players; fifteen minutes of watching the game showed him that.

It was after eleven when David returned from one of his breaks, toting a Coke in a paper go-cup. As the last cards were dealt, an older guy in coveralls, a well-chewed pipe stuck in the corner of his mouth, opened thirty dollars, the pot limit. Except for Linda he was the only player who'd been steadily winning. While the two between him and Linda dropped out, David scanned the common cards in the middle of the green felt: a three, five, nine, and jack, all hearts. One of them had to have the flush; judging from the old guy's big bet, David guessed he held the heart ace or king.

When David focused in, he sensed confidence. He set his right hand on the rail. Linda looked up at him, frowned, and raised thirty bucks back. David shrugged. Maybe she was the one with the ace of hearts—except the older guy's confidence remained rock steady.

He fingered his stack of chips, showed Linda a gap-toothed smile, and said, "Three jacks, little lady?"

Linda smiled back. "Nines."

They sat like that for another minute, and at its end, as David sensed the confidence washing away like water down a drain, the guy picked up his hole-cards, hesitated another moment, and said, "Nines win." He flipped two aces and a deuce, none of them hearts.

"I was lying a smidgen." Linda showed her hand. "Three of a kind, but they're fives."

"That's good enough, little lady," the guy said, with no trace of rancor. "Always a pleasure to see a fine card player in action."

"Popular win," another player agreed, as the dealer gathered in the discards and squared them in preparation for the next round.

Now, as Linda piloted the truck up a long switch-back of logging road, David said, "Tell me what you felt."

Linda pursed her lips. "As long as they looked at their cards, you were able to sense them, and then remember for the rest of the hand, right?"

David nodded. "The sensing part is like with the Zener deck. When the players are concentrating, I can read them. As far as memorizing, I've had a lot of practice the last couple months. It's not that hard if you put your mind to it."

Another pickup passed them on the straightaway of the switchback, two sets of skinny skis protruding above the truck's rear gate. "You could read them too, couldn't you?" David said.

"A little," Linda said. "I found out I couldn't

handle everyone at once, so I paid attention to the older guy, because he was the big winner."

"Besides you."

"That time I thought he had black cards down. Of course he still might have beat me if he had a better three of a kind, or a straight, even a full house."

David grinned. "For just having learned it, you've got a pretty good handle on poker, Linda."

"What I always wanted to be," Linda said. "A card shark." She downshifted to take the elbow at the switchback's end, hitting the gear smoothly this time. "Anyway, since I sensed he didn't have the flush, I decided to take a flyer."

"You knew."

"I wasn't certain. . . ."

"Yes you were."

The road widened, and up ahead the pickup that had passed them was parked with a couple other vehicles by the roadside snowbank. "I remember staring at him when he looked at his cards. I didn't close my eyes, but all of a sudden there was a point in my head, and out of it this image came, black pips, spades or clubs." Linda pulled over, shut off the motor. "I wasn't kidding that it shook me."

"I know." David undid his seat belt and faced her across the bench seat. "Linda, sometimes when I'm feeling down, the psi seems like a curse. But there's nothing you or I can do about it."

Linda pulled the key from the ignition. "I don't have to like it."

"*I* don't like it," David said. "There's not a damned thing I like about it."

"Sorry," Linda mumbled. "I guess it's worse for you."

David levered open the door. "I thought of one good thing about psi."

"Which is?"

"It got me together with you."

When Linda didn't reply immediately, David looked uncomfortable. "Of course," he went on, "the other side of the coin is you got stuck with me."

"Hey," Linda said sharply.

David started. "What?"

He thought he owed her, but to Linda's mind she had received as much as she'd given. Despite the danger—and the conviction that sooner or later they would have to face up to it—she felt more alive and complete than she had in many months. In a revivifying way the child she lost had been replaced—by a child she had come to cherish deeply.

David's specialness for her rested not in his psychic powers, but in his warmth, his kindness, his perceptive sensitivity to her own feelings; he had gentled her into a new and hopeful outlook on her own future as a woman and a human being. One *could* take control of one's life; David was living proof and constant reminder. However this all turned out, she did not want to let him go.

Linda cleared her throat. "You mean a lot to me."

"I was pretty lonely," David said. "I've been thinking about that a lot, wondering if it's why I need you so badly. I don't guess it is. I hate to get mushy, but . . ." He shook his head almost angrily. "Oh hell."

"What?"

"Sorry."

"*What?*"

"I love you," David barked. He stomped out into the snow, peered into the truck's cab, only his head visible above the high seat. "I love you, okay?" He disappeared toward the back.

Linda got out quickly, slammed the door, went around to find David jerking out the skis. David looked at her; his cheeks were red, and not from the cold.

"Could I get a hug?" Linda asked.

David came into her arms. She rested her chin on

the top of his head, after a while murmured, "All right, skiing it is," but she did not release him, not right away.

The depth of her grateful acceptance of the trick of fate that brought them together had come to Linda three mornings earlier in an unlikely pose: She was on her knees, a brush in one hand and a container of Sani-Flush in the other, staring into the rust-stained bowl of a wooden-seated American Standard toilet. They'd found a house, and at that moment she saw an outside chance of making it into a home.

When David had spotted the for-rent sign, they were northwest of Kalispell heading toward the Canadian border, tired and running out of country. A snow-covered pasture separated the one-story frame house from the road, a mile outside a place with the evocative name of Brave Horse; the sign directed prospective tenants to Penelope at the Lumberjack Bar and Grill, which turned out to be one-quarter of a downtown otherwise comprising a MiniMart with gas pumps, a True Value hardware, and a tiny white-washed church.

Penelope was a large middle-aged woman with bluish hair. She told them the house rented for two-twenty-five a month, but then she looked from Linda to David and back to Linda and said, "I don't know. . . ."

Before Linda could figure a plausible reassurance, David climbed onto a stool and folded his arms on the bar, looked around confidentially as if to confirm the three of them were alone in the dimly daylit saloon, and said, "Ma'am, can we trust you to keep a secret?"

His solemn tone amused her. "Call me Penelope," she said. "Everyone does."

"The thing is, Penelope," David went on, "we're in some trouble."

"Law trouble?"

Linda put a cautionary hand on David's shoulder, which he ignored. Penelope didn't seem to notice, and Linda realized that David was gently transmitting to her.

"Sort of," David said. "I don't mean we did anything wrong," he added stoutly. "We didn't."

"That's a relief." Penelope brushed back a strand of hair with a dishwater-reddened hand. "I was afraid you were the reincarnation of Bonnie and Clyde."

"It's my dad," David said earnestly. "He's the one who did the wrong thing." David hesitated.

"There's not much I haven't heard, son."

"He's a doctor," David went on. "Like . . . you know, a pillar of the community. So nobody would believe me if I told what . . . what he does to me."

"I get the idea," Penelope said. "You don't need to go into chapter and verse."

"And see, Mom here"—David flashed Linda a loving smile—"Mom had this problem with drinking."

Penelope gave Linda a penetrating look.

"She's okay now," David said quickly. "She got dried out in the hospital. But while she was being cured, my dad got a judge to say he could have me. I was really scared of being with him, and Mom was afraid too, so as soon as she got out, we ran."

Penelope went on studying Linda. Finally she said, "Good for you. You done the right thing, and I'll stand by you."

"Thanks, Penelope." David looked at Linda again. "See? I told you she'd understand."

A half hour later Linda was flinging open windows, exchanging chill but fresh air for the musty odor that permeated the old house. David came in the back door with an armful of split cordwood, dumped it in front of the fireplace. "Where do you get this stuff?" Linda asked.

"There's a pile out near the shed."

"You know what I mean," Linda said.

David looked sheepish and instead of answering went out for more wood. Linda was in the bathroom working over the toilet when he returned. He must have found some old newspapers; she heard them crinkle as he put together a fire. By the time she was done cleaning the stained bowl, the fire was crackling, and she was warm enough to doff her parka. She put the brush aside and stood. David was in the bathroom doorway.

"The part about me being an alky was a little much," Linda said, still in a snit.

"Come on," David protested. "It was a good story. She believed it, anyway."

"Where *did* you get it?"

David shrugged. "Some TV show."

Linda laughed explosively. "You are really something."

"Thanks," David said modestly.

The morning after they moved into the house, David said carefully, "You've had psi for a long time. You just didn't know what it was."

Linda was at the elderly gas range, scrambling eggs and onions. "You want to get out the milk?"

David took the carton from the refrigerator and brought it to the table, poured himself a glass. "There's two things I better explain. One is, it usually gets stronger with use."

"Makes sense—as much as any of this makes sense."

"The second thing," David said, and paused. "One way they do the experiment with the Zener cards is to test a group of people all at once. One person turns the cards, and the others write down their guesses. A bunch of times when they've done this, the group does way better than average, but the individual subjects on their own don't show much psi at all."

"How about popping in some toast." She watched him work rye bread from the packet. "You get all this from your reading, Professor?"

"Uh-huh. What they think it means is, when two psis are together, their psi adds up."

Linda refilled her coffee cup. "May I assume that pretty soon you're going to tell me what this is about?"

"It's about Rogan."

Linda said nothing while she served the eggs, caught the toast as it popped up, arranged a slice on each plate. She slid one in front of David, sat down. "Eat before it gets cold," she said.

David buttered his toast. "Your psi is potentially very strong, which is why I sensed it."

"Strong enough that I know you're hungry. Eat."

"If we worked on it," David said doggedly, "I bet that we could communicate through psi, like say we got in trouble or separated or something. What I mean is we ought to practice."

Linda looked at him for a long moment. "With the cards, you mean."

"You could also practice sensing." David piled eggs on his toast, took a healthy bite. "Then there's transmitting. I've got a hunch that if you're teamed up with me, you can—what's the word, you know, make my powers stronger?"

"Augment?"

"That's it."

Linda frowned. "How do we test this theory?"

"We can't, unless we try it with strangers, which probably isn't that great an idea. But I can practice my transmissions."

"On me?"

"There isn't anyone else. If we're going to stop Rogan—"

"Are we?"

David knew what she meant. "This isn't over. Sooner or later—well, anyway, we've got to be ready."

Linda ate in silence for a while. "I'll try it," she said finally.

"I won't hurt you."

"That's a comfort," Linda said skeptically.

When the dishes had been cleared and cleaned, David washing and Linda drying, they sat opposite each other at the table, a third cup of coffee at Linda's elbow. "Try to resist, okay?" David said.

"Why?"

"It might make it harder. Also, it'll exercise your psi. You ready?"

Linda nodded tentatively.

David touched at his temples and gave her love.

It wasn't sexual love; he remembered how invasive he'd felt with Sherrilyn Casey. From the point in his mind came the vision of his own mother, the way she had been and made him feel, how he missed her—no, he pushed that projection away, replaced it with a time in school when he'd gotten mad and been mean to another kid who didn't deserve it, then talking about it with his mom, and her reassurance. . . .

Linda gasped. David ignored the distraction, maintained the warm image.

Linda began to cry.

Her eyes were closed, tears oozing from the corners and lining down her high, smooth cheeks, and David was about to break it off, but her mouth was curved in a slight sad smile but a smile all the same. He held the image a while longer, then slowly eased it away from her.

Linda took a tissue from the box on the table, wiped at her face. Her smiled grew radiant.

"Oh, David," she said.

"Are you okay?"

She reached across the table and took his hand. "Better than okay. I saw Richard."

"I didn't try to give you grief or sadness."

"You didn't," Linda said, her voice rich with emotion. "What were you seeing?"

David told her.

"And you were remembering that it was good, right?"

"Yes," David said.

"So was I. I saw that no matter what had happened—even if he has been taken from me and nothing can change that—I still have the memories." She squeezed his hand. "You didn't give me grief, David. You took it from me."

"I . . . I feel a little embarrassed."

Linda wiped the last of her tears away. "Me too," she admitted. "Maybe we ought to work on this in the privacy of separate rooms from now on."

"I think I can do that," David said solemnly.

Linda laughed. "I think you can do a lot of wonderful things."

After that they spent time on it each day. David, to his profound relief, learned that his control was near total now. Linda got stronger as well, and as the days passed, their closeness grew.

When Linda had balked at spending two hundred dollars on a couple of ski packages, complete with boots and poles, David said, "Come on, Linda, would you like it better if I wanted a Nintendo and a Super Mario Brothers? This is good for me. It's exercise." Then, when she replied, "Yeah, but I'm the sedentary type," he needled, "Afraid you're going to fall on your butt and look dumb?"

"Wrong," Linda insisted.

"Then it's settled," David said. "I've been wanting to try this for a long time."

"Ever since you saw it on TV?"

David gave her a guileless look. "How'd you know?"

A squall of snow flurries came up while they figured out how to get their boots into the three-pin bindings and stopped as quickly when they pushed off, awkward at first but soon picking up the technique. Within a quarter mile David had gotten into the rhythm of putting his weight on one ski while sliding the other forward, swinging one pole before the other and chivvying himself along, and pretty soon Linda was able to match his pace. By then the sky had confirmed Montana's reputation for changeable weather by clearing to reveal a sun that glared with painful intensity off the smooth stretch of snow-packed track. When it straightened, David took off like a sprinter, poling and gliding with such effortlessness that Linda called out, "Hey, wait up."

David snowplowed to a stop where the track turned off down a grade, propped his arms on his planted poles. Linda skied up beside him. "You're quite the hot dog, aren't you?" she gasped.

"I guess. Fun, huh?"

"Like having your lungs crushed under a cement roller," Linda agreed.

David gestured down the slope. "Race you to the bottom."

"Are you kidding?" Linda said. "If you think I'm going to risk my ass—"

She pushed off down the hill, hollered "Go!" She had a ten-yard head start by the time David got going. Linda set her skis parallel, poled hard. As the grade leveled off, her tips spread. She tried to bring them together, overcorrected, and went down in a snow-spraying, head-over-heels fall. When David caught up, she was trying to get upright and brush snow from her hair at the same time. He glided to a stop and said, "Cheater."

Linda planted her poles and levered herself erect. "It's a cruel world, chum," she said.

"Race you back up," David challenged. "Double or nothing."

"Did we have a bet on this?"

"Sure," David said. "Five hundred."

Linda ran her mitten over her mouth, left a smear of snow that immediately began melting against the warmth of her overheated skin. "I've been thinking."

David's smile went away. "What's wrong?"

"Would you cool it?" Linda said. "Nothing's wrong. That's what I've been thinking about."

David unstrapped his daypack, dug out his water bottle. He shook it to loosen a skim of ice, offered it to Linda. She took a long drink. "How do we know this Facility of yours is still after us?"

"They are."

"What if they can't find us?"

"They can."

Linda drank again, passed the bottle back. "That's what I thought. I wanted to be sure my sense of security was definitely false. What do they want with you?"

"Nothing good." David cocked his poles. "Come on. I'm getting cold standing around."

Linda matched his pace as they short-stepped back up the hill. David's face was grim, and not from the exertion. At the top he stopped again. "They've got to be connected to the government," he said, as if she had contradicted him. "How else could Mr. Simic get all those people on my trail, find me so easily?"

"They have pull with the regular authorities," Linda agreed, "and obviously they're covert. I mean, if what they're doing is mind-control experiments—"

"And killing people," David pointed out. "Always remember they're killers. They killed my parents."

Linda brushed snow from her cheek with the back of her glove. "I know how you feel."

"You lost two people you loved too," David said. "Life can be pretty unfair, can't it?" He shook away the thought. "I'll give you one last chance and race you to the truck."

Linda made a big deal of sighing. "All right," she conceded. "On your mark—"

"Go!" David hollered, and pushed off.

But she was ready for that and on his tail immediately, poling as hard as she could, the cold air stinging at her cheeks, her breathing regular and deep. As they hit the last straightaway and the pickup appeared ahead, she came abreast of him. David looked over, grinned with determination, and stepped up the pace, but she matched it.

David swung out his pole and caught its basket around hers, jerked up. Linda teetered, flailed with her other pole to steady herself. Its point glanced off to the side, and she went down in a cloud of snow.

David was laughing so uproariously that he lost his own balance, toppled over a few yards ahead. He went on guffawing to beat the band.

"You little shit," Linda said. She tried to form a snowball, but the dry powder crumbled in her hands.

David could hardly speak. "Geez," he gasped. "You should see yourself."

David set the brown paper sack on the kitchen counter and removed a six-pack of Coke and two of Miller High Life, a packet of Doritos and another of Ruffles, a can of bean dip, and a couple of deli bags, one of sliced Swiss and the other of pastrami. "You're some shopper," he said. "I should have kept an eye on you." When they'd stopped at the Safeway in Eureka, a few miles up from the ski area turnoff, he'd gone to browse the magazine rack while she picked out the groceries.

Linda shrugged out of her damp parka, hung it on the rack by the door. "I had a junk-food attack," Linda explained. "They come over me sometimes, just like that. I don't know why—must be my time of the month."

David remembered a crack Jo-Jo had made in the poker game in New York. It seemed a lot longer than four months ago. "My body is my temple," David told Linda.

"Sure it is," Linda snorted. "You could write a book: *The David McKay Cheeseburger Diet: Thirty Days to Better Health on the Run.*"

David worked one of the beers out of its plastic sleeve. "Can I have this?"

"May I have this, please," Linda corrected maternally.

David sighed. "May I have this, please?" he echoed.

Linda took the beer from him, popped its top, and took a long swig. "Absolutely not," she said.

"That's funny," David said darkly. "That's really rich." He hung up his own coat, then opened a Coke and tore off the top of the Doritos, dug out a handful.

"Come on into the living room," Linda said. "Bring the refritos, would you?"

"Yes master," David said. He gathered up the Doritos and the dip.

When he got into the living room, she was pulling off her boots. She wore jeans and a sweater, and the tips of her hair were frizzy damp with melted snow. She sprawled back on the couch. "You mind opening that?"

"Certainly not, master." David worked the seal off the can, set it and the chips on the coffee table where Linda could reach them. "Will there be anything else, master?" he asked.

"Not for now, thank you," Linda said properly. The living room of the farmhouse was furnished with

aging but comfortably upholstered chairs and a fairly
new television, and cheaply framed Charlie Russell
prints hung on the walls. Snow had drifted into the
corners of the window's mullions, and outside the day
was descending swiftly into dusk. Linda drained the
can and crushed it in her fist, sat straighter, and lined
on the wastebasket beside the fireplace. The can
bounced off the rim onto the striped carpet. David
picked it up, fake-dribbled to the center of the room,
spun around, and launched a jump shot, hitting his
target with a satisfying rattle of metal on metal. David forked fingers toward the floor and said, "Two!"

"Hey, Doctor J," Linda said, "you wanna fetch
me another?"

David gave her a superior smirk. "Don't you
mean, 'May I have another beer please?' "

"Right."

"Say it."

Linda sighed. "May I have another beer please?"

"Nope," David said with immense satisfaction.
"You've had enough."

"I've only had one," Linda protested.

"Just say no."

"Look, if I have to get off this damned sofa just
because you—"

"Take it easy," David said. "I was kidding."

"Nothing funny about coming between a lady and
her beer," Linda pouted.

David laughed, went into the kitchen, and came
back with a second can. He took a handful of chips
over to the easy chair and plopped into it.

Linda opened the beer. "What we were talking
about," she said carefully. "The Facility, the bad
things they've done to you . . . your parents."

David gave her a curious look. "Yeah?"

"Wouldn't you like to do something so they don't
hurt other people?"

"What?"

"Stop them."

"Oh sure," David said. "Maybe we can hire Rambo to go in and gun them all down."

Linda belched. "You're the one who's so sure they're going to find us. You want to sit around waiting for it to happen?"

"You got a better idea?"

Linda nodded. "Expose them. Look, David," she went on quickly, "if they *are* plugged into the government, if they are covert, all we've got to do is shine the light of day on them."

"We've gone over this," David said. "Try to think back through the alcoholic haze."

"Nice talk." Linda drank.

"You go to the cops or write a story, what happens?" David went on doggedly. "How are you going to reveal them without revealing me?"

"I'll figure that out," Linda insisted. "I'm a reporter; I know how to protect sources. Part of the story could be enough. If I convince them to perform an autopsy on the brain of that guy Voss, or if we get Rogan to tell his side of the story—"

"Get real," David said skeptically. "I bet he's been itching to do us a favor, ever since you ran him over on the golf course."

"Pardon the cliché, but knowledge is power. If we find out who's behind this, then just maybe we can figure how to stop them and cover our own asses at the same time."

David frowned pensively. "I don't know. . . ." He rose, came over to the sofa. "Let me just have a sip of that. Please," he added quickly, before Linda could get on his case.

"One sip." Linda handed him the beer can.

David hefted it. "Hey, there's only one sip left."

"Then it works out perfectly, doesn't it?" Linda waited while David chugged it down. Outside the window full darkness had settled. "How about another for me, while you're up," Linda said. "Please."

"I guess you're not going to be doing any driving tonight," David said judiciously.

"What are you, my father?" Linda said.

"No, your bartender."

"Any chips left?"

David retrieved the bag. "Uh-uh. You want a sandwich?"

"You making?"

"Sure."

"Then I'm eating."

She sipped the fresh beer while she listened to him in the kitchen, the refrigerator opening and closing, the rattle of cutlery. She hated the chance that what she had in mind could get them into trouble, but dammit, they were already in hot water, and she was not used to doing nothing.

"Mustard or mayo?" David called, and she asked for both. He returned with two plates and a couple of paper napkins. He'd piled pastrami and cheese on split Kaiser rolls, slathered on the condiments, and added sliced tomato. "I put it in the toaster oven for a few seconds," he said. He was waiting expectantly, so she took a bite.

"Good," Linda said, meaning it. "I take it all back what I said about your culinary habits."

David brought his plate and a fresh Coke over to the chair. "Who do you want to tell about me?"

"How many people know about you now?" Linda gestured with her sandwich, answered her own question. "There's this Simic, plus the doctors. All of them have a good reason not to say anything, especially if they're caught: They'd be admitting to complicity in kidnapping and murder."

"That leaves Rogan," David said. "Even if we put the Facility out of business, he probably has someone else he could sell me to. Or if he's caught, he might turn me in as part of a deal." David's expression suddenly turned grave.

"What is it?" Linda said.

"There's only one way to stop a killer." He stared at her. "I don't know if I can do it. I don't think I want to know."

Linda paused in midswig.

"That's what this is really about. You tell me this, Linda: If the only way is for me to kill with my mind, am I supposed to do it?"

"David . . ."

"That's what I've got to decide. Me."

She set down her beer can. "You think I like it any more than you?"

David looked away. "Tell me your idea."

"There's someone who maybe can dig up info that—"

"This boyfriend you told me about?" David interrupted.

"Are you jealous?" She was irritated by his mean tone and did not bother to hide it.

David, to his credit, looked embarrassed.

"It's been rough, not being able to call him," Linda said. "I'd hate it if I never saw him again. Nick is one of the two best people I've run into in some time." Linda smiled at him. "You're the other."

David wanly returned the smile. "I got testy."

"Yeah, and for nothing," Linda said lightly. "I wasn't thinking of Nick in the first place. There's someone else I know and trust—you can too. I'd like to ask him for help, but I won't unless you agree. I'll never do anything behind your back."

David nibbled thoughtfully at his sandwich. After a time he nodded, as if concluding an argument with himself. "What the heck," he said finally. "I don't see how it could hurt us any worse than we already are."

CHAPTER EIGHTEEN

Binary Bob Berkowich keyed up a printout, then leaned back wearily in his swivel chair. As the H-P LaserJet began ejecting pages, he rolled his head on his shoulders in a vain attempt to get the stiffness out of his neck.

What he needed, he decided, was food. He unfolded his skinny frame from the chair as the printer chuffed on, went through the thick steel door that protected his basement enclave. Daylight ambushed him when he emerged at the top of the stairs; he glanced at his watch and saw he'd been at it nearly ten hours.

He'd found out what Linda wanted, though he wasn't especially elated at his success. In fact, he was more than a little nervous. He made sure the front and back doors were locked, then went into the kitchen and stood before the open refrigerator. He settled on a half quart of orange juice and a Ball Park Frank, took them downstairs. As he finished the cold wiener, washing it down with juice swigged from the carton, the printer went silent.

He wiped his slippery fingers on his sweatshirt and was reaching for the printout when a new idea tickled at him. Instead he sat down at the keyboard again, began to input. Password prompts and then text appeared. He scrolled through several screens, his dread mounting with each. Three minutes later he was in his VW van, trying to get the key in the ignition and doing a bad job of it. His fingers were slippery again, and not from hot-dog grease.

Binary Bob misdialed, swore, and punched at the telephone buttons a second time. As the long-distance line hissed and clicked through the cordless phone's earpiece, he stared at the wall, covered with photos and descriptions of gracious Virginia countryside homes. The office belonged to a real estate guy named Ralph McCaffey who let him use it outside of business hours. It cost Binary Bob two hundred a month, but it was money well spent; now was damned sure a time when he needed more privacy than a phone booth. The first ring sounded, and he muttered, "Answer, goddammit."

Linda's voice interrupted the seventh ring. "We were outside shoveling the driveway," she explained after Binary Bob identified himself. "It's snowing like hell." Linda paused. "Is everything okay? You don't sound so good."

"I was up all night. I got it."

"Great," Linda said. "You want to go punch some dogies?"

The reference was to the Cattlemen's in Elizabeth, a town ten miles up the highway from Brave Horse. She'd given him the number of the café the night before when she'd called from there.

"I better lay it on you now." Binary Bob set the printout on McCaffey's Leatherette-bordered desk blotter, heard someone else in the background—the boy, he figured.

"This Breunner," he began. "When you gave him to me a couple months back, you didn't have a first name, remember? Also, I made the mistake of assuming he was alive."

"He isn't?" Linda said, surprised.

"Not according to the Pentagon. The August Breunner they've got was convicted of war crimes by an Allied military tribunal and executed in March of 1946."

Linda made a vague sound. "Frieda Kohl?" she asked.

"Like Breunner a physician, research neurologist. University of Vienna, 1952. In 1956 she did a post-doctoral residency at a private psychiatric hospital in Saint Paul. She got nailed for unauthorized and arguably unethical drug-therapy experiments on patients incompetent to give informed consent. Wait a minute," Binary Bob said abruptly.

"What is it?"

He turned to the second page of the printout, found the hospital's name. "I've run into this place before, on another job. There was an allegation—never proved, except I happen to know it's true—that several doctors were accused of the same kind of monkeyshines."

"Involving what?"

"Mind control," Binary Bob explained. "Behavioral conditioning, doping, hypnotism, whatever—methods for getting people to behave in programmed ways."

"Why?"

"For money. The Agency was funding them."

"The CIA?"

"Where your pal Simic works."

Binary Bob heard Linda speaking to the boy. When she came back on, he said, "I'll get to Simic in a minute. The bottom line on the Kohl woman is that some patient's husband got wind of what was happening and took exception. When they tried to shut him up, he brought a lawsuit. Before it could get very far, Kohl was deported, and after that she disappears from the record."

"Is it possible she returned to this country?"

"She was never issued a visa, for what that's worth."

"All right," Linda said. "What about Simic?"

"Simic was easy—he's virtually public record. His official title is Assistant Deputy Director, Directorate of Operations."

"The euphemism for covert skulduggery."

"Yeah. He also liaises for the Agency with domestic law enforcement on all levels—federal, state, and local. Does that fit?"

"It . . . it explains some things."

Binary Bob shuffled through the printout. "I found two Rogans matching the description you gave me. One's an aide to the governor of Oklahoma. The other is basically an international hired gun. He crops up maybe six dozen times in Interpol's bad-guy list, but they don't have any present whereabouts on him."

Binary Bob turned another page. "As to you and your young friend, you seem to be in a fair deal of trouble. Do you want to tell me about it?"

"I can't, Bob."

"Okay. I'm not sure I want to know. You're on the feds' teletype for abducting your child, to whom you lost custody. Local law-enforcement agencies are asked to be on the lookout, et cetera. I assume this is bullshit, unless you had a kid while I wasn't looking. I wish you luck, for what that's worth."

"I appreciate that, and I appreciate what you've done. I owe you one."

"There's more. That Facility you mentioned."

"I thought you'd draw a blank on that one."

"I've got bits and pieces, but they don't seem to total any coherent whole."

"Run them down, and we'll put our heads together."

Beyond the window of Ralph McCaffey's office, the morning sky was slate gray. Binary Bob felt depression, tried to credit it to weariness. "First, Breunner and Kohl were both involved in experiments that were a long way from kosher," he said. "Second, back in the sixties Simic was in the pipeline to those experiments."

"How did he avoid getting taken down?"

"There wasn't anything to avoid. The little people took the fall, and not many of them. Even when the Agency gets caught in dirty tricks, life goes on. You know that, Linda."

"Let's have it, Bob. Don't hold back on me."

He cleared his throat. "I got into Simic's own computer."

"You can do that?"

"Not usually."

"I'm impressed. Find anything interesting?"

"Simic has a file of entries that go back to about the time the mind-control experiments were supposedly shut down—but the file indicates they never were. They went underground—very deep underground, is my guess."

"He's still running it?"

"I think so." He licked at his lips. "I'm going to give you some people, then I'm going to get the hell off the line. This conversation has already gone on too long for either of our good. You got a pen?"

"Of course."

He dictated four names and scraps of background on each. "I don't know how they're connected," he finished, "but they're all listed in the same file."

Linda was silent for a moment, then said, "Something's wrong, Bob. I can hear it in your voice."

As if a tap had been opened, the fear that he had been fighting gushed forth. His mouth felt chalky dry. "I may have fumbled the ball."

"What do you mean?"

"I left fingerprints." He took the phone to the window. A cold snap had set in overnight, and passersby on the sidewalk were unusually bundled up for the D.C. area. "There's no one hundred percent bombproof way you can lock out hackers. Not if they're good—and I am."

"I know."

"But you program so that if there is a break-in, you can trace to its source. I got a hunch that had happened, so I went back to check. Simic's software was rigged to make the trace."

A thin drizzle began to fall. Through its veil Binary Bob could see his VW van parked at the curb across the street. Behind its tail end a man in a topcoat had taken shelter under the awning of a florist's shop. On the phone Linda said, "Is there someplace you can go?"

"Sure," he said distractedly. The man across the street seemed to be looking right at him, but it had to be a trick of the flat daylight. "The hell with it," he muttered.

"What's going on, Bob?"

The man *was* staring at him, and he felt his stomach spasm with fear. "Too late," he got out. "They're on me."

"Bob . . ." Now the fear had infected her voice as well.

"Linda, I promise, I won't tell them a damned thing, even if . . ."

"Get out of there, Bob."

"I didn't mean to screw you up."

"You did me a big favor—someday I'll be able to tell you how big. Now take care."

"Sure."

He was staring at the cradled phone when Ralph McCaffey let himself into the office a minute later, said, "Hey kid, how they hanging?" Ralph McCaffey was a florid-faced middle-aged man who favored loud ties and vile-smelling breath mints. Binary Bob roused himself, said good morning. A whiff of breakfast bourbon cut through McCaffey's minty stink as Binary Bob went out past him.

He had to go back. If they had tracked him that quickly and knew his van, they'd have his address soon enough. Before that happened, he had to do some housekeeping; once they got into his computer—and they would—they'd find a wealth of data, encoded but breakable over time, that could screw up a lot of people who had trusted him.

He left the van where it was and flagged a cab. Seven minutes after he'd slipped out the back door of McCaffey's office, the taxi turned onto his street. His neighbor across the way was taking off in his station wagon to whatever it was he did. A dog relieved himself at the curb, and two joggers trotted past. The neighborhood looked as banally ordinary as only an American suburb could. Binary Bob drew a deep breath: Quarter of an hour to copy onto floppy disk the stuff he had to keep, erase the rest, and grab his credit cards and a change of clothing. He speared a twenty at the cabbie and said, "Wait for me, would you? I'll be going to Dulles."

"Sure," the driver said cheerfully. "Dulles is a thirty-dollar fare."

As Binary Bob got the key into his front door, he heard the cab's engine rev up. He turned to see a man step back from the driver's side as the cab pulled away. The man wore a topcoat.

Binary Bob pushed open the door, and the man came up and said, "Mr. Berkowich?" pleasantly, as if he were offering something for sale.

Binary Bob licked at dry lips.

"Could we speak inside?" the man said.

He was somewhere between forty and sixty and spoke with the slightest of accents. Beneath the topcoat he wore an expensive-looking business suit. Binary Bob said, "I don't think—" and the coat parted to reveal a gun.

The man wrapped his hand around the gun's grips. "Thinking will not be necessary," he said.

Binary Bob sat in the Barcalounger in his living room. The gun in the man's hand was an automatic, and a silencer was screwed onto its muzzle. "Are you Simic?" Binary Bob said.

"Yes I am," the man said pleasantly. "And you are quite the computer whiz, are you not?"

"Why the trapping program?"

Simic's gun was pointed at the carpet between them. "From here on," Simic said, "I will ask the questions, and you will answer them. Understood?"

"Yes."

"Now then," Simic said, "as a person familiar with computers, you understand the concept of an if-then statement. Am I correct?"

"Yes." Binary Bob sat up straighter in the chair. He felt the need to urinate.

"All right," Simic said, his voice still pleasant. "*If* you tell me immediately where the woman Linda Gaylen is, *then* I will not harm you. If you do not, I will hurt you badly, and you will tell me anyway, and then you will die."

It was a lie. At the end of twenty minutes, Simic had hurt him very badly indeed, with his fists and a blackjack and a long thin-bladed knife, though Binary Bob had talked until he could talk no more. In the end he found himself staring through the blood pooled within his eye sockets into the round dark hole at the end of the silencer, and then the world exploded into ether, and drew him down into its inescapable thickness.

CHAPTER NINETEEN

David spun on his heel, flung his gym bag against the bedroom wall. It flipped over, spilling socks and underwear. "Jesus Christ," he said.

From the doorway Linda said, "How do you think I feel?"

David slumped onto the edge of the bed. "You screwed up, Linda."

"That's not fair."

David looked up at her, his face a mask of fear and frustration. "You're right," he said. "It wasn't your fault."

"Or yours," Linda said firmly.

David stared at her for a long time. "You really believe that?" he said finally.

Linda leaned against the doorjamb, rubbed hard at her forehead in a futile attempt to push back the guilt that had been gnawing at her.

She'd known she could not hide her apprehension from David, and when she told him about the tail Binary Bob thought he'd spotted, David became frightened as she. When she said, "Simic wouldn't . . ." David had turned away without answering. Linda stared at the phone a long moment, then called Brian Dancer. Since he of course knew she was a supposed fugitive, Dancer was more than a little interested in knowing what the hell was going on, but she managed to put him off with the assurance she was all right, and a promise to tell all when she was able.

Linda watched David get up from the bed, retrieve the gym bag. Dancer had gotten back to her five minutes earlier. Acting on his tip, Falls Church police found Binary Bob in his basement computer room, shot once in the face. On the floor beside him was a half kilo of uncut cocaine. The authorities surmised that in the course of using his hacking skills in furtherance of some drug scheme, Binary Bob became either the victim or failed perpetrator of a double cross. Dancer told Linda that the police didn't seem much interested in what they saw as scum bumping off scum and would probably close the case as soon as possible.

"The Facility killed him, not us," Linda said in the bedroom.

David finished repacking the gym bag. "I still feel crummy about it," he said. "That's why I barked at you."

"I know." Linda watched him jerk the zipper closed. "What are you up to?"

"What do you think? We're getting out of here."

"Not right now. Probably not today."

David's eyes flashed angrily.

Linda crossed the room, pushed back the drapes. The bottom half of the window was glazed with ice, and outside, wind-lashed snow streamed down so thickly the pickup truck was barely visible a dozen yards away. "Radio says Morton's Pass got three feet overnight," she said. "The highway is closed until at least this afternoon."

"We'll go back through Kalispell."

Linda shook her head. "There's a seven-car pileup northwest of town, and they're not having much luck finding wrecker drivers crazy enough to go out in this mess."

"So we're sitting ducks," David said bitterly.

Linda turned from the window. "Maybe Bob didn't talk."

"They killed him because they got what they wanted," David insisted. "Face facts, Linda: Simic knows where we are."

A chill draft seeped around the edges of the window. "And you want to run."

"I'm getting real good at it."

Linda sat down on the bed. "Now might be the time to stop."

"Give up?"

Linda shook her head. "Take a stand. You can stop them."

Across the room David glared at her. "Let's say it out loud. We are talking about me killing them." When she didn't answer, he advanced, stood over her. "All right, thanks for the permission."

Linda's stomach felt hollow and sickly. "I won't ask you to do that."

"All the same," David said, "that's what it could come to."

Linda patted the bed. "Sit down."

He hesitated, then came over and dropped woodenly to the bed beside her. She put her arm around him. His shoulders were hunched and stiff.

"We've got some leverage," Linda said. "We know that Simic is running a highly nonsanctioned operation. The authorities will have to shut him down if we blow his cover—and we can do it through Breunner, probably Kohl, maybe Rogan—definitely without involving you."

"If they don't kill us first."

"I want the truth to get out." She hesitated. "No matter what happens to us."

David frowned at her. "You're thinking about this Nick."

"He's a good man, David. If it comes down to it, he'll pick up where we left off."

"You just want to hear your sweetie's voice," David said.

"What if I do?" Linda said, genuinely irritated. "I've already told you I miss him, and right now I don't much care if you like that or not." Linda drew a calming breath. "But if you think I'd deliberately endanger him or us . . ."

"I don't." David rubbed at his forehead. "I'm being a jerk."

Outside the wind howled, and snow tattooed against the house's walls. "We owe it to Bob, if for no other reason," Linda said.

"You'll be putting Nick in the same kind of hot water."

"I'm not going to drag him into this," Linda said patiently. "I only want to arrange a fallback like you did, to make sure the story gets out if . . . if something happens. Will you call your lawyer and arrange for what you wrote to go to Nick?"

"I suppose." David's shoulders slumped, as if he had lost interest in the whole topic.

"Hey." Linda pulled him closer. "Whatever happens, we're going to make damned sure it isn't in vain."

David sighed. "That's something, I guess."

Linda rumpled his hair. "That and each other are going to have to be enough."

By nine the February day was blossoming into cloudless, sun-drenched warmth more typical of June. Nick Delvecchio wiped sweat from his forehead as he jogged up the curving asphalt walkway through Venice Beach, past street musicians and barrel-jumping roller skaters, the caged paddle-tennis courts and the weight-lifting area, the guy who juggled bowling balls and chain saws. Nick turned inland past a vegetarian restaurant, running loose and easy. Since moving to L.A. he'd lost ten pounds, quit smoking, cut the booze down to a beer with dinner, and gotten into a routine of four miles a day. *Mens sana in corpore sano*, he thought; life goes on.

He slowed to a walk a half block from his bungalow on Twenty-seventh backing on the canal, and by the time he reached the door, his pulse rate was down to normal. He clicked on the answering machine while he went into the kitchen and got the pitcher of iced tea from the refrigerator.

The machine beeped, and some guy said that Nick had won two nights and three days at the Big Bear Time-Share Condos, gave the phone number of his L.A. office, and urged Nick to arrange an appointment for his personal sales presentation. Nick filled a glass while the machine beeped a second time and a tape of a chirpy woman asked him how he was today and offered him a free lifetime supply of thirty-five-millimeter color film, then paused for him to give his name. What a wonderful country, Nick thought. He was willing to bet that in Russia they didn't have phone machines that talked to other phone machines. Nick was on his way to turn it off when it beeped a third time, and Linda Gaylen's voice said, "Nick, are you there? Pick up if you are, please."

A stretch of static played back, and Linda's voice said, "It's . . . it's almost nine, your time. I'm at area code four-oh-six, five-five-five, seven-three-two—"

The machine made a coughing sound, then hissed like a cat. Nick punched the stop button twice, and the tape lid rose ponderously. He snatched at the cassette, but it wouldn't come out cleanly. Nick peered into the workings, saw loops of tape wrapped around the heads. He jerked it loose, and the tape parted.

He threw it across the room, snatched up a pen and a used envelope from the telephone table, swore, and wrote down as much of the number as she'd given, hoping to hell he'd remembered it right. He was still cursing when the telephone rang. He snatched up the receiver, thinking that if this was someone trying to sell him a table at the fireman's ball, he was going to jump down the line and rip the sucker's eyes out.

To his relief Linda said, "Nick?"

He took a deep breath. "It's good to hear your voice."

"I wish I could have called earlier." Her tone was cool, flat, as if a lot were on her mind.

"You're in trouble."

"No . . ."

"That wasn't a question, Linda." On his coffee table was a copy of the "Metro" section of a week-old *Times,* folded to the fifth page. Nick dragged it over, stared at the headline that said, "Woman Makes Thousand-Yard Drive from First Tee, Leaves Large Divot."

"Nick?"

"I'm here. Listen for a second." He read her the headline and the five paragraphs beneath it. "I know a lot of this is bull," he went on when he'd finished the article. "Who's really after you?"

There was a pause, and then she said, "No one."

Nick carried the phone over to the sofa, sank into the cushions. "I'm not mad at you, Linda. I want to help. Let's get that straight right off, okay?"

"I know that," Linda said. "Now please, if I don't phone tomorrow by this time—"

"Where are you?"

"I can't—"

"Where are you, goddammit?"

He heard another voice, and then Linda said, "I . . . It's dangerous."

"For whom?"

"For us."

"And me?"

Linda said something sharply off phone. "I don't want you involved. Probably I shouldn't have called in the first place. Please, just listen to the rest of it."

He sighed, said, "Shoot."

The ice cubes were melting in his glass when she finished, apologetically yet abruptly, refusing again to answer any questions. She had not been able to maintain the cool tone, though; by the end Nick heard fear creep in.

The phone buzzed impotently in his hand. He stabbed the cutoff button, dialed the number of the Century City detective agency where he'd briefly worked. A voice answered, "Carmody."

Nick identified himself and said, "Jimmy, you remember Munoz? Little guy with a big knife and an idea about sticking you with it?"

Carmody sighed. "I owe you, is what you're about to say, right?"

Nick picked up the envelope, stared at the six digits he'd written. "That's right," he said.

Simic cradled the cordless headset between his shoulder and cheek while Comm-Sys patched the radio link through. When the operator picked up at Malmstrom Air Force Base in Great Falls, Montana, Simic gave his name as Charles Jackson and asked for the intelligence liaison officer. A few moments later a Captain Isaac Fairbairn identified himself.

"Captain, could you access the clearance subdirectory on the DOD mainframe and punch up seven-alpha-two-three-romeo?" Simic said.

"Yes sir," Fairbairn said. Simic heard the click of computer keys. The code would bring to Fairbairn's screen a verification ID for "Jackson" and the instructions that he was to be given full cooperation. Fairbairn said, "How can I help, sir?"

"I need a chopper and pilot at the Kalispell airport, fifteen hundred hours." Simic glanced around the passenger compartment of the Learjet Longhorn. "Four passengers, including myself."

"Uh, sir . . ." Fairbairn said.

"A couple of other things, Captain," Simic interrupted.

When Simic had finished running them down, Fairbairn said, "The weather's a little dicey, sir. We've got heavy snow, and visibility is a hundred meters. You might want—"

"I told you what I want, Captain."

Fairbairn cleared his throat. "It'll be ready when you land, sir," he said stiffly.

"Thank you, Captain," Simic said, and cut the connection.

Simic frowned at his watch. According to the phone company's computer, the call between Berkowich and the woman had ended almost exactly three hours earlier. Berkowich had spilled his guts a half hour after that, and ten minutes later Simic was in the air. By now the Janitors had dressed the scene for the local cops, and the Computer Dweebs would be down in the asshole's basement, picking his electronic brains like ripe cranberries.

Simic unfolded a topo map of Montana, turned his attention to its northwest corner. The black dot representing the town of Brave Horse was about midway along a thirty-mile valley with only two ways out, and at the moment, he had learned in a previous call, roadblocks had the valley bottled. State police were stationed at the foot of the snow-clogged pass to the north to keep anyone from trying to get over it, and to the south where a bunch of idiots had done Simic the favor of piling up. He'd merely had to pass the word through channels that the cops were to watch for the woman and the boy. Even if the kid got them through, Simic would have a plate number and the direction in which they were fleeing—and Rogan to track them down.

Simic pronged the handset on the receptacle attached to the plane's concave wall. Frieda Kohl was in the front right passenger seat, a Toshiba laptop on the fold-down table in front of her. She wore a severe, high-necked black dress, and her gray hair was done up in a bun contained within a snood. Behind her Rogan's comatose bulk was stretched across two seats; Breunner stood over him. The detour to the Facility to fetch the three of them had cost an extra hour, but with any luck they'd still have the boy before dark. Simic stood, said, "Want anything to drink?"

Breunner said, "No, thank you," but Frieda gave Simic an angry look, as if he had just insulted her mother. A cigarette was smoldering in her armrest ashtray. She turned back to the computer, her fingers pecking arrhythmically, her scowl fixed in place. Hell with her, Simic thought. He went back to the drinks cabinet at the passenger compartment's rear and found a pint carton of orange juice. He sipped at it, said, "Dr. Kohl."

She turned her head and furiously blew smoke into the aisle. "I am trying to work, Mr. Simic," she announced, as if it were news.

Rogan was breathing shallowly but regularly. Simic studied him a moment, said, "The drug for the boy—"

"Will render him unconscious and incapable of transmitting within moments after Rogan administers it." Breunner sounded weary. "Its effects will last for approximately four hours."

Simic turned to Kohl. "You're certain the operation succeeded?"

Her head snapped up. "Why do you keep asking me that?"

Simic kept his temper. "And the operation you're preparing for the boy?"

She shrugged elaborately, trying to needle him. "He will lose none of his abilities. He will merely become tractable."

"He'll do what we tell him?" Simic pressed. "He'll no longer have the free will to harm us?"

Breunner took his seat and stared at Kohl. "He will be all that you wish," he said, "and more."

Simic glared at him, and Breunner gazed back through hooded eyes. When Simic turned to Kohl, he saw she was staring at Breunner as well, almost warily. Simic gestured at Kohl's computer. "You making sure you dotted the i's and crossed the t's?"

Kohl kept her gaze on Breunner. "I am doing research. I am a research scientist."

"Is that what you are, Frieda?" Breunner said.

"What's with you two?" Simic said, genuinely perplexed. Neither answered. Simic had had enough of the both of them for the moment. "Try to keep from tearing each other's eyes out," he said stiffly, and went back to the toilet.

They had almost lost Rogan, not on the operating table but to a guard's gun. Once the ichthyotoxin had worn off, the general anesthetic should have maintained his comatose state, but as Frieda bent over his skull with the razor, Rogan twitched massively and bolted to a sitting position.

He clawed for Frieda, managed to catch her wrist. The electric razor clattered to the floor, and its plastic case shattered. Rogan jerked, and Frieda tumbled atop and then over him, her weight dragging Rogan from the gurney. His sheet fell away, and his naked body went down on her, pinning her in an obscene embrace.

"Bitch," Rogan grunted, his voice tight and twisted and to Breunner's ears utterly insane. One of Rogan's hands closed around Frieda's throat and cut off her scream.

The guard stepped from the corner of the operating room, bringing up his automatic weapon. Breunner shouted, "No!" The guard hesitated and Rogan reached out, grabbed the guard's ankle and yanked. The guard sat down on the floor but kept the gun pointed at Rogan. Breunner saw his finger tighten on the trigger.

Breunner kicked out clumsily at the guard, who swatted his foot aside. Breunner heard cloth rip, and this time Frieda got her scream out. A burst of rifle fire exploded deafeningly within the room's confines, and holes stitched into the concrete wall, but Rogan's hand was gripping the barrel now, pushing it up.

The door swiveled back on its hinges, and Simic came in, his own gun out. Rogan saw him, got to his knees, pulled the rifle from the guard's hands. He nearly got it turned around, his finger groping for the trigger, when Simic slammed the frame of his own weapon into the side of Rogan's head. Rogan swayed, and Simic hit him again, harder. Rogan's hairy torso flopped face forward back onto Frieda.

For a moment no one moved, and then Frieda began to sob. The guard retrieved his weapon, stepped back to hold it on Rogan.

Breunner blinked at Simic. "If you've concussed him . . ."

"Help her, you idiot," Simic barked.

Breunner bent, wrestled Rogan to one side. Frieda got to her feet. Her blouse was torn open to the waist. She looked down at Rogan for a long beat, choked back one last sob, then swung back her leg and kicked him in the ribs.

"Oh for chrissake," Simic said. He holstered his handgun, pulled Frieda roughly away by the forearm. "Give her a sedative," he ordered Breunner.

"I am all right," Frieda's voice was thick.

"Well then, give him one," Simic said, gesturing at Rogan. Simic was as angry as Breunner had ever seen. Breunner kept his eyes averted as he went about filling a syringe and injecting Rogan. Other guards appeared and struggled to worry Rogan's mass back onto the gurney.

When Breunner had disposed of the needle, he

saw that Frieda was paying no attention to Simic either. Her eyes were on Rogan, and in them was something deadly.

Now, in the Learjet, Breunner waited until he heard the lock on the bathroom door snick shut, then took the seat across the narrow aisle from Frieda. *"Erfolg,"* he said. " 'Success.' Your ego is showing, Frieda."

Her eyes widened. *Erfolg* was the password to her computer; Breunner had uncovered it by running a permutations program he'd written himself. "I've been spying on your work for years, Frieda, as you have been spying on mine," he said. "But I did not break the encodement of your latest file on Rogan until last night."

"Shut up, August."

"Oh, I have shut up, Frieda. I haven't told Simic, have I?" Breunner shrugged. "But if he *were* to learn how you lied to him—"

"I'll say it was your idea." Her voice was hard as glare ice. "The operation will increase Rogan's jamming ability, as Simic requested. He will be able to subdue the boy."

"But the model predicts side effects," Breunner said. "You mean to make him subject to your command."

Frieda carefully lit a cigarette, her eyes never leaving his.

"First, you will use him against Simic," Breunner said. "After that, I assume you plan to employ him to your own ends."

"And we will be free, and so will the boy," Frieda said. "Isn't that what you want?"

"If you miscalculated, Frieda? If your model is flawed and there are other effects?"

The bathroom door clicked. Frieda leaned toward Breunner and repeated in a fierce whisper, "Is not that what you want?"

Simic came out, started down the aisle, drew up short as he saw them, their conversation frozen. He frowned suspiciously. Breunner looked up at him, looked back to Frieda, said nothing.

Frieda smiled, answered her own question. "Apparently it is," she said, her tone perfectly normal.

Rogan thought: *Okay, pal, you screwed up twice, but third chance is the charm.* It had better be, another part of his mind cautioned; at this moment Simic had his nuts in the wringer, and it didn't look like there would be a fourth chance.

He'd been conscious for maybe an hour now, and near as he could tell in his right mind. Whatever they'd done to him—the side effects he'd heard Breunner talking about as he came around—they couldn't have fucked him up too bad.

In one way it looked like he was lots better. When she went on talking about him like he was a piece of meat, he'd been damned pissed off, mad enough to take another shot at her if he hadn't realized that was not the move of the moment—but he *had* realized it, and though the anger was genuine and heavy-duty, the red mist was nowhere to be seen.

He lay still, trying to assemble the framework of a plan. Simic made a call to check on a chopper that was supposed to meet them, then another to arrange for an ambulance. Rogan felt strength returning to his limbs and body. The only discomfort was in the pit of his stomach; he was hungry as hell.

The plane began to nose down, and Rogan heard the pilot rogering control-tower instructions. All right, he thought, pretty soon now you're going to be outside of this tin can. That might be the last chance for a break, before they get you loaded on the next pony. Figure Simic to be the dude with a heater, and if it was a public airport he might not be so quick to use it. Once they were out of the plane and on the ground—

Something fuzzed into his mind and pushed the planning aside. It felt vaguely familiar, but for a moment he could not put a mental finger on it, strained—

And sensed so clearly he almost cried out.

The woman and the boy, but they were not near, not by a long shot. This wasn't the mind-filling sense he'd gotten from them in Los Angeles, but more like they were beaming to him on a high-power narrow-band channel.

The plane jolted down on tarmac, and Simic's voice said, "Get ready to move out. You stay with him until I return with the ambulance crew."

Kohl said, "If they ask—"

"They won't," Simic said. "They'll strap him into a gurney, and we will wheel over to the chopper." A button clicked, and Simic said, "Pilot, pull in close to the military craft."

"Do we revive him first?" Kohl asked.

"I don't advise that," Breunner said.

"No need," Simic said. "The chopper will have a stretcher basket on the skids."

The plane eased to a stop, and the door sighed open. Simic's voice came from that direction. "Is he ready to be moved?"

Through slitted eyes Rogan saw Breunner standing above him. "He's fine."

Careful not to smile, Rogan thought, *Bet your ass, on that, bub.*

Swirling snow blew down his neck, and Simic turned up the collar of his topcoat. Although it was only a few minutes past three in the afternoon, the day was dim as dusk; the Kalispell airport was on a flat south of town, with few trees to hamper the searing wind that drove billowing flakes across the apron and blotted out sight of anything beyond the termi-

nal, fifty yards distant. The chopper was parked near
the runway's end, out of sight of prying eyes. Its pilot,
a youngish-looking air-force captain in a fleece-
collared leather jacket, had said nothing beyond his
name and "Yes, sir," twice to Simic's orders.

The ambulance was between the chopper and the
Lear, its red lights rotating dimly in the storm. As
Simic watched, the two medical technicians worried
the stretcher out of the Lear's hatch. Breunner and
Kohl exited behind it. Breunner carried his medical
bag. The EMTs popped the wheels on the gurney and
pushed it toward Simic.

"On the basket," Simic said as they came up.

"In this weather?" one of them asked.

"Follow orders," Kohl said behind him.

Simic stepped around the stretcher. "Good advice."
He pinned her with his gaze. "Is there something you
haven't shared with me, Dr. Kohl?"

Frieda squared her shoulders. "I beg your pardon?"

"On the plane, when I came out of the head,"
Simic said. "What were you two talking about?"

Her eyes went wide with fear and surprise. Simic
said, "If you think—" and Breunner said, "My God!"

Simic realized Kohl was looking past him, and he
spun on his heel in time to see Rogan rip the chest
strap from the stretcher and come off it as if he were
on springs. Simic reached under his arm, but Rogan
was coming at him, and as the hammer of the revolver caught on the cloth of Simic's lapel, Rogan's
arm went around his throat.

Simic was jerked back, and the cold metal of the
barrel of his own gun pressed against his temple. Rogan manhandled him so they were facing the pilot,
who was half-turned in the seat reaching for something. Rogan said, "Ease off, fly-boy." The pilot put
both hands at shoulder level.

The gun's hammer clicked back. "Don't," Simic said. His voice was reedy.

"Why not?" Rogan breathed in his ear.

Off to their right from the direction of the terminal, a voice said, "Police officer. Freeze!" A woman in brown slacks and a leather jacket with a badge held her own weapon on them in firing-range stance. "Airport security," Simic said. "She saw the lights and got curious."

"So?" Rogan said.

"Listen to me," Simic said in a low voice. "You'll have to kill us all, including a cop."

"Give me a better idea," Rogan said. "And remember if I don't like it, you're the first one dead."

"Drop it!" the deputy called.

"Officer!" Simic shouted. "I'm a federal agent. Please do not interfere." Simic lowered his voice again. "Let me get out my ID."

Rogan hesitated. "You're wasting time."

The gun muzzle brushed Simic's short-cut hair. "Use me as a hostage to get out of here," he said.

"Where am I going?"

"To get the boy."

Rogan laughed.

Through the lashing snow Simic saw Frieda take a step forward. "*Gehorche,*" she said in a firm, toneless voice.

Rogan stiffened, heard her mumble, "You see, August." She raised her voice. "Emile, give me the weapon."

From the periphery of his vision, Simic saw the gun move toward the ground—and then up toward Frieda. She repeated the word, and Rogan snapped, "Shitcan the pig Latin."

"Get back, Frieda," Simic ordered. To Rogan he said, "Our deal still stands. You turn him over to me, and I'll pay off. I'll tell you where to find him."

"I know where—" Rogan said, and shut up. The deputy shouted, "This has gone far enough."

"She's right," Simic said quietly.

"You got the babe's phone number?" Rogan said. "Yes."

"Call it. Hour from now, every ten minutes after that. Anyone but me answers, hang up." Rogan shifted his weight. "Tell the kraut to hand over that needle."

Simic relayed the order.

Breunner opened his bag, dug out the syringe case. Frieda said to Rogan, "You don't need that."

"Shut up, Frieda," Simic barked.

"Why don't I?" Rogan said curiously.

"I have fixed you so you do not."

Rogan's finger stabbed out in her direction. "I'm gonna fix you, bitch."

Frieda took an involuntary step back.

"You better have the money," Rogan said in Simic's ear.

"I can get it. There must be a local bank that—"

"I don't care how. Just do it."

"All right," Simic said. "Now use me for cover, and we'll move out toward the parking lot." Simic nodded toward the terminal. "You can hold me until you find a car to steal, and then—"

Rogan laughed again, and his grip around Simic's neck tightened. "Fuck that noise," Rogan said. Simic was dragged back toward the chopper. "I'm riding in style," Rogan said.

On the television Alex Trebek welcomed everyone to *Jeopardy*. There was no cable, and the single station that came in was as snowy as the air outside the house. David fiddled with the tuner, but it only got worse.

Behind him Linda said, "I can't stand you acting like this."

"How am I acting?" David did not look at her.
"Like an asshole."

On the TV a player chose "Movie Classics" for
one hundred. The answer in the box was "He had
a one-night happening with Claudette Colbert." "Who
is Clark Gable?" David said. The contestant guessed
Cary Grant, and Alex Trebek said he was sorry.

"I just don't want to talk about this anymore,
okay?" David said.

Linda came over to his chair. "I'm going out for
some wood. You want to help?"

David shrugged without looking at her.

"Jesus," Linda said disgustedly.

She was right. He felt treed and helpless, but that
wasn't any reason to act out. Cold drifted in from the
kitchen, and he heard the door slam shut. A contestant said, "Literature for two hundred, Alex," and got
the clue: "He whitewashed a fence without getting his
hands dirty." In unison the contestant and David said,
"Who is Tom Sawyer?"

David got up and went to the window. No matter
how pissy he felt, he should have gone with her. He
peered through the snow in rising alarm, then made
her out near the shed, piling wood in the cradle of her
arm.

He turned back to the television, froze suddenly,
and said, "Oh God."

He rubbed frantically at the frost on the window-
pane, but it didn't help. Linda was no longer at the
woodpile. David listened hard, heard nothing—didn't
have to—the sense grew, tried to overwhelm his
mind—

He raced through the kitchen, flung open the
door, stepped out into the whirling storm. Snow stung
at his eyelashes, and he blinked it away. "Where are
you?" he screamed into the wind.

The wind screamed back.

The sense throbbed, and he was frightened. He

wasn't ready for this after all, wanted to go back into the house and lock the door and hide but could not, because Rogan was out there, and—

He had Linda.

David stepped forward. A knee-high drift clutched at his blue-jeaned legs, and the wet chill chapped his face. He hollered again, "Where are you?"

Through the blizzard's near whiteout he saw them, Rogan with his arm around Linda's neck and a gun in his other hand. David pushed aside the fear and touched at his temples, and image exploded in his mind: a human brain, warty and wrinkled and pustulated with a tumor as he'd seen it in a copy of *Gray's Anatomy* that he'd found in the rented house and pored over until it disgusted him, because—God help him—he'd thought he might need that image, might have to put it into Rogan's brain and make it rot and—

"Shut it off, kid."

Across the snow-swept yard David saw Rogan put the gun to Linda's head.

"It ain't doing any good anyway."

But it was, or he wouldn't say that. David called, "Shut what off, Mr. Rogan?"

David felt the jamming, but it wasn't nearly strong enough, he knew he could beat him. He sensed the rising panic as Rogan felt the pain of the transmitted tumor. David pushed it toward him through the veil of crazed snow.

Linda shouted and kicked out, caught Rogan in the shin. Rogan half let go of her, and David felt the jam slip. Rogan lashed out with the gun, caught Linda a glancing blow on the temple. David was jolted with fear for her, and with it he lost concentration, and the picture in his mind blurred. Rogan barked, "Ha," straddled Linda, and pressed the muzzle of his gun against her forehead. "Count of one and I kill her," Rogan said. "One."

David blanked his mind. Linda rubbed at her head, and David felt a terrible pang of guilt and impotence. He'd let her down—he'd let them both down. "David," she said levelly.

"Can it!" Rogan raised the gun again.

Linda ignored him. "Do what you have to, David. For me."

Rogan whipped the gun in David's direction, said, "I'll kill you first, and then the babe. Give me one little reason."

She was right, David thought, eerily calm. *Do what you have to.* "Mr. Rogan," he said.

Rogan's face was wrinkled with anger and fear and madness, and that scared David more than the gun. David said, "Do you have your needle, Mr. Rogan?"

"David, no," Linda said. She crabbed away, leaving a track in the deepening snow.

Rogan jerked her back, said, "Yeah," almost to himself. He produced the hypodermic from the pocket of his jacket.

David knew Rogan could kill her while he was unconscious, but he was going to kill her right now if he did not cooperate. When the drug wore off, David thought grimly, he would be back at the Facility, and this time there would be no escape, Mr. Simic would see to that by making Dr. Breunner operate. But that was later. At this moment Rogan was at the brink of madness, ready to shoot them both. David could buy time and hope that Rogan was at least sane enough to understand they were more valuable to him alive. . . .

David rolled up the sleeve of his flannel shirt, showed the puckered skin of his arm. "Hurry up, please," he said politely. "I'm getting cold."

CHAPTER TWENTY

On the phone Rogan said, "You're asking *me* why you'd want her? Geez, Simic, haven't you figured it out yet? She's one too."

Linda sat in a straight-backed wooden chair in the house's kitchen, her wrists bound with cord Rogan had cut from the venetian blinds. She was glad for her bulky sweater; Rogan had turned down the heat in the house on entering. Outside full dark had fallen; the old-fashioned wind-up clock over the stove said it was a few minutes past six.

"You park where I told you," Rogan said on the phone. "You blink your lights three times, and the play goes down. Incidentally, you get hold of another gun?"

Rogan fished a cigarette from the pack in his shirt pocket. "Never mind," he said. "Just bear in mind that I'll kill both of them if you try anything funny."

He listened a moment. "You gonna nail me for destroying government property, Simic?" His grin turned to a frown. "That so? Guess I did hit him a little hard. I was hungry and pissed. You can write him off on Kohl's account."

Rogan lit the cigarette, blew out smoke. "Enough palaver," he said. "Be there." He pronged the phone.

He stood staring absently at Linda as if surprised to find her present, then opened the refrigerator and took out a beer. Linda said, "Did you leave the heat on in the bedroom? There's a thermostat by the door."

"Good idea." Rogan went into the hall.

Linda blanked her mind and into it came the point and from it an image—of a man clutching at his chest, his eyes wide and his face crimson—

Rogan reentered the kitchen and said matter-of-factly, "You can't do it, babe."

She had not expected it to be strong enough, but David *had* been drilling her. Rogan wasn't angry. "Whatever it is you got," he said, "this psi like they call it, I can sense if you try to turn up the juice. But you ain't anywhere as good as him."

"Neither are you," Linda said.

He sat across from her. "He's sleeping like a baby, by the way."

"If you can stop him with your mind, why did you have to drug him?"

Rogan shrugged. "This jamming shit is hard work. I let down my guard, he scrambles my brains good and proper. Course, truth to tell, I'm already a little scrambled."

Food was scattered on the table between them, plastic envelopes of cold cuts, blister packs of barbecued chicken and pork chops, smoked sausage, a stick of salami and a large jar of dried beef, dozens of candy bars. Rogan tore open a package of pepperoni, began to pop slices into his mouth.

"They must have cleared that wreck blocking the road," Rogan said conversationally. "Some cop got through, anyway. Simic says he found the chopper a mile south of here, where I left it. I shot up the control panel, and then it looks like I kind of fractured the pilot's skull."

She wasn't sure what he was talking about, but his tone arrested her. At the moment, despite the topic, it was purely rational, though at times since he'd shown up, it had veered toward madness.

"What did they do to you at the Facility?" Linda said quietly.

Rogan force-fed himself more of the meat. "They cut me. The kraut dame figured it'd make me so I could beat the kid. I'm not sure I want to find out if she was right."

The honesty surprised her.

"Her I am gonna kill. You wouldn't blame me, you'd been through what I have." He tore open a package of turkey ham. "At least I brought my own chow. You can't say I ain't a polite guest."

After he had deposited David in the bedroom and tied her to the chair, Rogan went back outside. To her astonishment he returned a few moments later with two snow-frosted sacks filled with the groceries now strewn between them. "I got hungry," he said to her now, "so I made a pit stop." He chewed. "I don't eat, I lose it. That's another thing she did to me."

Rogan threw the empty packet on the floor. "We're in the air, I got the gun, and I'm giving the orders. Get out of the country is my first thought, except thoughts are not coming so clearly anymore. I'm so starving, my gut is starting to chew on itself."

He took a deep swig of beer. "I spot one of them gas-and-food places, tell the pilot to land. He thinks I'm nuts. The guy behind the counter thinks I'm nuts. What do you think?"

"Go on," Linda said neutrally.

"The guy is so scared, he doesn't make any noise about me rifling his refrigerator case. He's telling me how he just reopened, the road got clear, and he figured what the hell someone might need gas, he's still chattering when I leave."

Rogan crumpled the beer can, got up for another. It was his fourth by Linda's count, though the alcohol seemed to affect him no more than the cold. "The food clears my head," he said, "and I decide Simic is not a man with whom to fuck. Maybe even outside the country he's got contacts, I'm looking over my shoulder the rest of my life. Maybe the deal really does go down, I get my money, and I'm out of here. Maybe I have to kill him after all. Too many maybes. So I decide, bottom line, I got to have you and the kid in hand. There's my main leverage."

"And Simic knew where we were."

"Yeah, but I didn't need him," Rogan said. "This sensing business?"

"Yes?"

"Mine got a lot stronger. I could read you nine by nine all the way from Kalispell."

"That's twenty-five miles away." Linda considered. "But if that *is* in range, why didn't David sense you?"

"*My* range, not his," Rogan said. "I told you I could beat him."

"I don't believe you."

"Sure you do. You just don't understand it. Neither did I, at first." He belched. "You give up? On how I could sense you two without the kid knowing?"

"Tell me."

"I read a book or two, once upon a time. Hardly even moved my lips. It's like with magnets."

Linda got it then. "The inverse-square law," she said.

"Say what?"

"Something I remember from high-school physics. With two magnets the attraction is proportional to their mass, divided by . . . I don't exactly remember, except the larger they are, the more they attract, and over greater distance."

Rogan looked pleased. "What I said: You and the kid together—your power added to his—it was like a bigger magnet, plenty bigger than me." Rogan drank, wiped his mouth with the back of his hand. "Snatching folks sure works up the old thirst."

"Once you've got your money from Simic," Linda said.

Rogan regarded her over the top of the beer can. "Yeah?"

"You'll kill us."

Rogan shook his head doggedly. "I got nothing against the kid." His eyes were half-closed. "You're thinking about what he did at the golf course, but that don't count. I meant to wax his ass, so he had the right."

"I *was* thinking about the golf course," Linda admitted. "I also sense you're lying."

Rogan broke into genuine laughter. "Goddamn, this mind-reading crap is a laugh a minute, ain't it? We ought to just talk with our brains, like aliens from the planet Zircon."

"You know I can't do that."

"I'm not sure what you can do, babe." Rogan stared at her. "Killing you both does have its appealing aspects."

Rogan stripped the wrapper from an Almond Joy. "You think you got me figured, babe. Here's a few things you don't know."

He stuffed half the candy in his mouth. "First, I don't like the idea of greasing a kid. I will if I have to, but I hope I don't. You tell me if I'm lying this time."

He wasn't.

"I'm not even sure I like the idea of giving him to Simic," Rogan said, "but I'm gonna if it works out that way. There's the second reason: If I don't turn him over alive, Simic'll kill me. That's an idea I know I hate."

Rogan drank and grinned again. "Hell, me and the kid could make a damned good team, you ever think about that? With his brains and my, how you say, loose moral code, we could cut some folks a new asshole."

"There's a third reason," Linda said quietly. "You want to get him off your hands, because he scares you."

"Hell yes he scares me. He's a scary kid."

"And you see a way to use him—as bait."

"Bait?" Rogan echoed throatily.

"Whether you give David to Simic or not, Simic intends to kill you," Linda said. "Unless you kill him first."

Rogan looked almost impressed.

"You'll have to kill Breunner as well, and Frieda Kohl."

Rogan nodded. "They're witnesses. You got any objections?"

"We're witnesses too."

His hard look made Linda wonder if she had taken this one step too far, but she was telling him nothing he did not already know.

"You two go your way, I'll go mine," Rogan said after a moment. "You promise not to put my name in the paper, get my ass in a sling, far as I am concerned, we're quits."

"You'll take my word on that?"

"You giving it?"

Linda nodded, and Rogan said, "Deal."

Their gazes locked, and it was almost funny, because he knew she could tell if he was lying—

And yet the sense she got was mixed. She realized he wasn't sure himself what he would do with them if he came out of this the winner.

She was betting her life on Rogan defeating Simic—and then deciding to let them live. It was a slim chance, but she could see no better one looming on the horizon.

The clock over the stove chimed once to mark six-thirty. Rogan stared at it. "All right," he said. "Now that we're talking each other's language, let's go over your part in this swell plan of mine."

CHAPTER TWENTY-ONE

"**H**e intends to kill all three of us, of course," Simic said.

Frieda Kohl gave him a sharp look.

"Don't worry, Doctor," Simic said. "I won't let him."

Breunner leaned forward in the backseat of the Ford Bronco four-by-four they'd rented at the airport in Kalispell. "There is one factor we must consider. The boy could regain consciousness prematurely."

"I thought you said four hours."

"I could not chance harming him," Breunner said, "so I based the dosage on his size four months ago. If he has gained weight or otherwise grown . . . in any case, it would be best to get this finished."

"My sentiments exactly." Simic worked the charger on the weapon in his hands, an AR-15, Colt's semiautomatic civilian version of the M-16 full-auto combat rifle. It belonged to the Kalispell police chief, as did the attaché case lying on the front seat of the rig between Simic and Frieda; the chief had fallen into line right smartly once Simic had given him a number to call and then explained to him the deleterious consequences noncooperation would have on his career. Simic would have preferred a fully automatic weapon, but it would serve.

"Everyone know their lines?" Simic asked. He wore black pants, a black parka over black sweater, and a black wool hat; dark cosmetic goop was smeared on his face.

"I'm cold," Frieda said.

Simic whirled on her. "You could get a lot colder. Right now I do not want to hear your whining, Doctor. I've got a lot of reasons to be displeased with you—don't give me another."

Simic waited long enough to give her a chance to go on, but she was smart enough to shut up. He levered open the door. "Three minutes," he said. "Then hit the lights."

Simic stepped out into the blowing snow, crouched low behind the cover of the rig. He drew three deep breaths, then moved out.

Linda was almost out of the bedroom when she spun on her heel, peered through the dimness at David's form. His position was unchanged, yet she was certain she had sensed him. He was coming around—

And if he was, Rogan would know.

She closed her eyes, projected with all her strength: *David, not yet . . .*

The sense dissolved so suddenly, she was not sure she hadn't misperceived. On the bed he lay still, his breathing regular.

When she returned to the kitchen, she found Rogan gnawing on a salami stick and staring intently out the window. He glanced back at her and said, "Time to roll."

She peered past him and saw the headlights flash from the road across the pasture. She took her parka from the peg near the door, shrugged into it. "What if . . ."

"If Simic's got the same idea as me?" Rogan grinned. "He does. He's out there already."

"You can sense him?"

"Sure."

Linda felt relief. Concentrating on Simic, Rogan

had failed to sense David. As long as David kept still, his mind blank . . .

"Don't matter anyway," Rogan said. "This jungle fighting is my meat and potatoes."

"You're going to leave David alone?"

"No, I'm going to drag him along." Rogan showed her a sarcastic smirk, then flicked off the interior lights before jerking open the door. "Go."

But as Linda started into the snow-clotted darkness, Rogan grabbed her by the forearm. "You rooting for me, babe?" His stubbly face was close to hers, and she could smell the spicy salami on his breath. "Funny, ain't it," Rogan said, and pushed her out.

Wind bit at her face and blinded her until she could blink the flakes away. She refocused on the headlights, started toward them. She almost walked into the barbed wire surrounding the pasture before she saw it, pried the strands apart, and ducked between them. Drifts clutched at her legs as she crossed the field. When she tried to move out of the headlights' direct glare, she heard the vehicle's engine rev, and the lights pivoted to keep her in their spot. Impacted snow had nearly buried the fence at the roadside so she was able to step over it, but the other side of the bank was steep and slick, and she went down on her bottom, sliding into the barrow pit.

As she picked herself up, a woman's voice said, "Stop there."

Linda said, "Where's Simic?"

A compact form was silhouetted in the headlights' glare. "You're supposed to give me the money," Linda said evenly. "Once I turn it over to Rogan, he'll leave in our truck. David is with him. If you don't do as I say, Rogan will—"

"Shut up." The woman spoke with a Germanic accent.

A door opened and slammed. "What do you think

you are doing, Frieda?" The man's voice was similarly toned: Breunner.

"Here is your money," Frieda Kohl said.

Her arm blocked more of the light, and at its end a briefcase flopped open. Sheets of newspaper blew out into the wind.

"Frieda, have you gone mad?" Breunner's form appeared beside her.

"Listen, August." A gun was pointed at Linda now. "Listen and do exactly as I say, or I will shoot you as well."

Rogan watched the dark form move to the edge of the field, where the slope of foothills rose. He lined on it, but the range was too long. He wished he'd brought some of the food; once this was done, he'd need a good feed. "Simic!" he hollered.

Three shots pinged into the snow a dozen paces to Rogan's left, where he'd been a moment earlier. "Play it your own way," Rogan hollered, and moved again. "Just remember you called the game, you lying sack of shit."

"What do you want?" Simic didn't sound too scared—yet.

"Your pecker on a plate." Rogan crab-walked across the face of the slope where it rose above the pasture behind the house. Simic was somewhere off to the right, within fifty yards, Rogan judged. More shots drilled into the snow, closer this time.

"You pulled your last double cross." Rogan crouched and ran a couple of yards, stopped, listened. The Gaylen babe and the kid were okay, that much he could sense, but he'd seen some kind of shit going down in the rig's headlights by the road. It was time to wrap this show. "Simic," he called again.

He could no longer hear the soft tread of the man's footsteps, but he could sense him coming. Rogan scrambled back up the slope, stumbled into brush.

Something made a pocking noise to his back, and he spun in that direction, fired. The shot echoed, and the pocking noise sounded again, in front of him this time: rock hitting a tree, oldest trick in the book.

He came out of the brush, turned upslope. A third pock struck behind him, but he ignored it. His gut growled insistently, and with the hunger came the anger. He tried to blink it away and peer through the white-walled dimness to movement, but he saw nothing. The anger spoke and told him that this was going to be good. Put a slug into something nonvital, the bastard's knee or shoulder, then finish him off with his bare hands, feel his flesh under his fingers and watch his face while the life was squeezed from it—

A gun barrel jabbed into the small of his back.

Instinct pushed aside the anger for the crucial moment he needed, and Rogan rolled away without hesitating, tumbled to his knees, and started to bring his gun up.

Simic had expected the move and was awaiting it, stood six feet back with his weapon trained on Rogan's chest. "Drop it."

Rogan held his pose.

Simic cradled the gun against his shoulder, sighted down the barrel. "It's over."

If he didn't move, he was dead, so Rogan tensed to spring and could not understand why he did not, knew only that the anger seemed suddenly paralytic— he could not move, but he could—

—*transmit*—

He had killed before, but never had he so much wanted another man dead, and from the white heat of that craving, the means seethed into being. A point in Rogan's mind winked and then exploded, into an image of his hands clawing at Simic's throat and then into it, his fingers wrapping around sinew and blood vessel, ripping them free like rotten wiring—

Simic screamed.

Rogan focused in on the photo-vivid image, felt his fingernails cutting through warm, wet meat and the tissue flapping loose—

The sound of Simic's scream was like nothing he'd ever heard before.

Rogan got to his feet in time to see Simic's weapon arc into darkness and the man fall backward, both arms flung outward, his body spasming.

Rogan no longer needed the image and made it collapse upon itself, the point in his mind was sucking it up, and then he extinguished the point. It was easy as making a fist, like he'd been doing it for years.

He straddled Simic, bent, placed his hands where they had been in his mind picture. Simic stared at him through fish eyes, and Rogan squeezed, dug his fingers into the flesh and felt the beat of pulse beneath. It was weak and stuttery, and then after a few seconds was gone.

Rogan picked up Simic by the throat and tossed him aside. He landed facedown. Rogan stared at the corpse, while unassuaged anger seeped up from the emptiness in his gut.

From below came a car engine, and lights moved slowly along the road. Through the trees Rogan could make out the dark form of the house; as the vehicle reached it, the kitchen lights came on. He could sense the Gaylen babe inside, her fear; the krauts had the drop on her.

For a moment he studied Simic's broken-necked form, snow collecting in his hair and eyelashes. He and the world were well rid of the son of a bitch, Rogan thought. Probably crossed him on the money too. . . .

A sense of the boy brought him around; the kid was groggy, but he was coming out of it—and that meant it was time to shit or get off the pot. Rogan's stomach rumbled.

Only one sure, once-and-for-all way out of this

mess: Kill them all. It couldn't be helped. Always have to worry they might talk, or even turn on him.

Yet he still didn't like the idea, and through his crazing hunger, rationality struggled: He didn't deserve this crap, and they knew it because they were like him, might even help him. . . .

Anger sent the thought packing.

Linda heard the vehicle pull to the end of the drive, and a moment later Breunner came into the kitchen carrying a medical bag. Frieda Kohl said, "You heard the shots?"

Breunner nodded. "Pray God Rogan is dead."

Kohl stood by the counter, the handgun aimed at Linda. Linda sensed out toward David, felt nothing for a few moments and then the faintest of responses. He continued to fight the drug, but too slowly, too late. . . .

"Prepare a sedative for the boy," Kohl said. "We must move quickly."

Linda shifted her weight, got her legs under her. Breunner's participation in this was reluctant, she sensed. If she could disarm Kohl . . .

Linda came halfway out of the chair. Kohl stepped back, leveled the gun on her midsection. "We have the boy," she said. "We can do without you."

For a giddy moment Linda thought she would shoot. Kohl gestured with the weapon and said, "Get him."

Linda let out a breath, moved carefully through the door and down the hall, Kohl at her back. Linda leaned over the bed, got her arms under David, lifted him with difficulty.

As his cheek fell against hers, she sensed him growing stronger. She got the image of a man . . . not Rogan, but someone else. The sense lapsed, though she felt David stir in her arms.

She carried him back to the kitchen and knew

immediately something was wrong. Breunner stood across the room by the door, a hypodermic in his hand and alarm in his expression. Linda lay David on the table, and behind her Kohl grunted angrily in German.

Linda came farther into the room and saw Nick Delvecchio put a hammerlock on Kohl and jerk her gun away. Nick pushed Kohl into a chair, and she stumbled and went down on one knee as Nick stepped back into the hall doorway from where he could cover the room. "Drop the needle." Breunner blinked, did as he was told. The hypodermic broke, and thin liquid drizzled across the linoleum. Nick said, "You all right?"

Linda gaped at him. "What are you doing here?"

"Arriving in the nick of time, is what it looks like."

"How did you find us?"

"You left most of your number on my machine, remember? It was enough."

Kohl dragged herself to her feet, looked murderously at Nick as she sidled over to Breunner. Nick said, "Is the boy okay?" As if trying to answer, David muttered something.

"Come on, Linda," Nick said roughly, "fill me in."

"Sorry." Linda drew a deep breath, let it out. "Jesus, Nick, is it good to see you."

Nick allowed her a smile. "Are there others out there?"

"A man named Simic."

David wriggled in her arms. "I'm okay. Put me down." But he was unsteady on his feet, and Linda helped him ease into the chair. "Not Simic," he said thickly.

Frieda Kohl whirled, stared at the door as if beyond it there were monsters, swore fearfully in German.

David rubbed his eye sockets with his knuckles. "He's crazy mad," he said to Linda, "and my head is all fogged up. I'll do my best, but your friend . . ."

"What are we talking about?" Nick said.

Before Linda could answer, the kitchen window exploded.

Rogan ducked back behind the shed. Hunch told him he could not transmit to all of them at once; he needed to experiment with the new power, like a kid learning to walk. But he could still take them the old-fashioned way. He dropped the clip out of Simic's AR-15: About a dozen rounds remained. He reseated it.

On the tail-end echo of the shots and the shattering glass, he heard the house door slam open.

Rogan darted three steps and dropped behind the woodpile, saw Frieda Kohl dive through the driver's-side door of the idling Bronco. Rogan laughed into the wind. She'd thought the operation would make him her slave, but she was wrong. She'd changed him, though, and she was going to regret it.

Rogan brought the point of light into his mind, massaged it, and turned it toward Kohl, began to draw forth an image—

The picture shattered. The kid was transmitting too, strong enough that Rogan needed all his concentration to jam.

Snow rooster-tailed from the Bronco's rear wheels, and it slewed down the driveway. Rogan fired four times, heard the ping of the slugs drilling metal and glass breaking. The Bronco skidded wildly, bucked off the drive, and tore through the barbed wire like he'd gotten her, but then it came careening out of the barrow pit, and the taillights receded down the main road.

Rogan turned to the house, put two shots into the door. The kid transmitted again, and this time it rocked him, foggy, dull pain creeping into his head. Rogan moved out across the snow-packed yard, and the pain waxed. Rogan jammed, fought the kid's pain and the anger in his brain and the vacuum in his belly. The door loomed in front of him, and he fired. Yellow light seeped from splintered holes.

Rogan threw his weight, and it gave like cardboard. The broad screamed, and the boy sent out a bolt of hurt and—

Rogan fell away from the doorway light into shadow but too late, heard the shot and felt the slug creasing into his gut, saw the new guy with the gun. Rogan darted back out the door, ran for the shed. The guy fired again, and Rogan twisted out of the way, went down on his knees, let go of the rifle as he pulled himself behind the woodpile. He clamped his hands over his stomach, felt the warm ooze of blood between his fingers.

He sat like that for a minute, staring at the rifle between him and the house. He could do without it, he decided, and with the thought strength returned, enough so he could make it to his feet. He circled around the house toward the highway. Seconds earlier he had been able to think only of rest, but now he saw that could wait. There'd be plenty of time for rest once he took care of business.

"Until we know the score, I think we'd best move out," Nick said in the kitchen. His voice was a little shaky, his face only a bit less pallid than when he had returned he had come to them after the shooting. "Can you walk?"

David stood. "I'm okay." He offered his hand. "David McKay. And you're Nick."

Nick gave him a funny look, shook hands. "Thanks for what you did," David said.

"Sure," Nick said. "What did you mean about doing your best?"

Impatiently Linda said, "Is Rogan dead?"

"I can't sense him," David said. "Can you?"

"No."

"I got him point-blank," Nick said. "If he's not dead, he will be soon."

"Maybe he's just out of range," David said to Linda.

"Hey," Nick said. They looked at him. "Would somebody mind telling me what we're talking about?"

"Later," David said briskly. "You're right about leaving. Do you have a car?"

Nick hesitated and then gave it up. "I'm parked down the road." Nick's arm was around Linda, her head resting on his shoulder. Even in his weariness David sensed how pleased she was to see him.

Breunner slouched in one of the kitchen chairs, his face in his hands. "Come on, Dr. Breunner," David said. Breunner stood painfully, his eyes down.

Linda held Nick closer, murmured, "I missed you a lot." David cleared his throat and said, "Hey."

They both looked at him.

David sighed wearily. "I thought we were getting out of here," he said.

Stiff wind sluiced snow through the shot-out rear window of the Bronco, and its pressure made the beastly vehicle even more difficult to control. Frieda Kohl gripped the wheel with two frigid hands, wrestled to keep the truck on the road and pointed straight through the blowing whiteness.

The high headlights of a semitrailer truck flooded the Bronco's interior. It swerved out and its huge bulk barreled past, buffeting her in its slipstream and stirring up a great white cloud that enveloped her for a few seconds, cutting off visibility entirely. Frieda clutched at the wheel and eased down on the brake until the whiteout cleared. A reflective sign on the edge of the two-lane highway said she was three miles from Flathead Lake and ninety-seven miles from Missoula.

Her fear was irrational, and she had tried to reject it as paranoia. She could not; somehow she knew with moral certainty that Rogan was after her.

She had been fine once away from the house; well before she reached Kalispell, she was realistically assessing the future. She rated the threat represented by the boy or the Gaylen woman as minimal; even if she was wrong, there were others who like Simic could use her skills and offer protection in exchange. She could go directly to one of the board members; Eshkol the Israeli mercenary, for example, might find her surgical abilities a valuable aid.

At the Kalispell airport she found she'd missed the last flight by twenty minutes, and the only charter pilot available declined to fly in the storm. By then she was calmed enough to take the time for a meal in the terminal restaurant. When it was finished, she made further inquiries. In Missoula to the south, the weather was predicted to clear soon. Confidence welled as she retrieved the Bronco, turned south onto the highway, accelerated—

And knew.

Rogan was coming, radiating hate for her benefit alone. She had made him so much more powerful than she'd imagined, strong enough to touch her as if she had the sense as well.

The road reached the lake and turned to the right, and its course became a nightmarish snaking of endless curves. The lake was huge, its inky surface stretching south to the horizon, broken here and there with the wooded mound of an island. There was no beach, only a skirt of cliff with the highway atop. The snow was falling hard and steadily, and wind gusted up off the water every minute or so to jostle the vehicle. She glanced tremulously at the abyss of black water below the road. Fewer cars passed. She pressed

down on the accelerator and bent over the wheel,
peered frantically into the onrushing rays of snow.

She remembered her terror when he had come
conscious in the operating room, his naked form
pressed atop her. The recollection brightened and co-
alesced, and his image rearranged itself into a new
whole and would not leave her. His body thickened,
nostrils flared above gap-toothed mouth, arms and legs
bulged and turned shaggy, and he became a beast
with penis rampant.

The beast struck her across the face hard enough
to bring piercing pain yet leave her conscious. She
heard the rending as the fabric of her clothing parted,
saw the redness of the eyes of the beast and the gleam-
ing white sharpness of its teeth, smelled its rank sexual
breath, felt the hardness between her bare thighs.

A moment of clarity: The road unreeled before
her, her course unerring. She steered; her hands on
the wheel moved and her foot pressed the gas pedal
to the floorboards, the car shooting faster and faster
down through the tunnel of encasing snow.

The moment passed, and the beast was back and
ripping into her. The pain was terrible, and she felt
as if she were being torn in two, blood gushing from
between her legs and from her throat as the beast's
jaws closed on her. Then she was floating, but it was
not release because with the sensation came the beast's
final thrust, and her body ruptured as the organ came
through and out of her, and even death would not
end the fiery pain.

CHAPTER TWENTY-TWO

Linda pushed open the sliding glass door and said, "I don't believe this."

Nick gave her a sheepish look. "I didn't hear you come up."

"Nick's teaching me to spit," David said proudly.

"I can see that."

"A guy has got to know how to spit," Nick said

"Don't girls spit?" David asked.

"Certainly not," Linda said. "We expectorate, and only in the privacy of the powder room."

From the deck at the rear of the motel, they could see across the Clarkfork River to the University of Montana campus. They'd reached Missoula thirty-six hours earlier, drained from the violent events at the Brave Horse house and the hundred-and-fifty-mile drive south on U.S. 93 through the enshrouding snowstorm.

But the next morning the clouds lightened, and by the time they got to the airport, sun began to creep through. It turned out the storm had canceled a half-dozen flights and backed up reservations, and it would be two days before they could get a plane connecting with a Los Angeles flight. They considered driving, but they were still tired. Besides, Linda recalled from her college days that the U had a pretty fair library, and after some rest she had retired there to begin the work that had to be done.

This second day had begun blue and cloudless,

and now, as it neared noon, the temperature was rising past forty and felt warmer. Joggers in sweat suits were trotting across the footbridge upstream from the motel, and below the deck a man in hip waders was fly-fishing from the rock beach.

Linda waved the notebook she was carrying. "Would you prefer to continue this exploration of the hawking of goobers, or do you want to hear what I've ferreted out?"

Nick made a sweeping gesture and accompanied it with a bow. "Lead on, oh mighty news-hen," he said.

David shut the door behind them as they followed her into the single room. The men were sharing a kitchenette next door. Nick had suggested the roommate assignments, though Linda thought he'd prefer a more intimate arrangement. In the brief time since they'd come together, she was growing closer to the same idea. It was fine to have him with them; it made their party complete.

"Where's Breunner?" Linda asked.

"Taking a nap."

"He's been awfully sad," David said.

"He'll be all right," Nick said.

He was fully part of the team now; no discussion had taken place, but it was tacitly understood. Still, the previous morning, as David had fleshed out the brief story Linda had told Nick on the phone, Nick's skepticism was obvious. Finally Linda said in exasperation, "Give him something."

David shook his head. "Not to Nick."

The two of them had hit it off immediately. Beneath Nick's hard-boiled exterior lay the instincts of a born father. Already she had caught him and David tête-à-tête—talking, no doubt, about her. She didn't mind.

Finally David got up and dug a sealed deck of cards from his gym bag. He stripped off the cellophane, removed the jokers, and executed several expert riffle shuffles. "You play poker, Nick?" he asked guilelessly.

"Sure."

David sat across from him on the bed. "Dealer antes five, ten-dollar limit, twenty on the last bet, three raises." David glanced at Linda. "You want in?"

Linda rolled her eyes. "Spare me."

An hour later David was up four hundred and twenty-three dollars, and Nick looked like a kid who had just learned that Santa Claus was a parental fiction. But Linda still sensed resistance, and apparently David did too; he squared the deck, put it aside, and said to Linda, "All right, all right." To Nick he said, "Think of something."

"Like what?" Nick asked.

"Something important to you."

Nick closed his eyes. David hesitated a moment, then laughed. "Should I tell her?" David said.

Nick's eyes flew open. "Hey," he said. "I was thinking—"

David was grinning at Linda. She said, "I know what you were thinking. You've got a lot of nerve, Nick Delvecchio."

"It wasn't that bad," David said, getting a kick out of this.

Nick was blushing beet red. "Okay, I'm a believer."

David squared the currency on the bed, gave Nick back his losings. "I don't play for money with friends."

"I can see why," Nick had said.

Their bonding was a good omen. Nick had not only delivered them from Simic but had brought them the luck and hope that they most sorely needed. They had a chance now. In the motel room Linda opened her notebook and said, "You ready for me to run it down?"

"Not yet." David gave Nick a broad conspiratorial grin. To Linda he said, "Do you know what today is?"

"The swallows are returning to Capistrano?" Linda guessed.

"Tell her," David said. Nick looked sheepish.

"Heck, I'll tell her," David said. "It's Valentine's Day." He got down on hands and knees, slid a shopping bag from under the bed, and from it produced a huge heart-shaped box of candy. "It's from Nick," David said, presenting it to Linda.

"It was your idea," Nick protested.

Linda set the box on her lap, looked from one to the other. "Lordy me," she said, "you two are a pair to draw to." She worked the lid off, selected a piece, and passed the box to David. "No fair biting into one and then putting the other half back," she cautioned. David laughed and judiciously selected two of the candies. "Hey," Linda said. "This is really sweet of you both."

"We're sweet guys," David said, his mouth full of chocolate. "Now that we've had dessert, anyone want lunch?"

David dialed room service, relayed their orders. When he hung up, he turned abruptly to Linda, seated at the desk, said, "What's wrong?"

"Would you cut it out?" Linda said, too sharply.

"Couldn't help it," David mumbled, abashed.

Linda shook her head resignedly, tapping a forefinger on the notebook lying before her. "I just . . . well, something about this gives me an extra case of the willies."

David came around behind her, studied the page. "You can read that?"

Linda looked up from her squiggles. "Yeah, me and no one else," she said. "That's the beauty of it."

She flipped pages. "Binary Bob gave me some names, before . . ." She squared her shoulders. "Anyway, he gave me some names. His idea was that they have to do with the Facility, though the connection is less than obvious."

She ran her finger down the page. "Sister Sarah Stilwell, Jason Carver, Randy Tukai, Morris Eshkol."

"Sister Sarah is the TV Jesus-beater with the seventy-five-million annual take, and Carver is the war-hawk senator," Nick said.

Nick frowned thoughtfully while David told him how the Facility had trucked him around for demonstrations. "What I figure now," David concluded, "was they were trying to persuade these people that someday my abilities would get stronger and pay off."

Neither of them moved when a knock on the door sounded, so David got up to admit a white-jacketed waiter pushing a cart loaded with a cheeseburger and fries, steak and baked potato, a big salad with strips of ham and cheese, two mineral waters, and a pint carton of milk. When the food was dealt around and the waiter had departed, Nick asked, "Who're the other two?"

Linda dressed her salad. "Tukai is the CEO of Nippon-Transatlantic Technologies Limited," she said. "If you've ever used a computer, odds are it contained chips his company manufactured. Clean as a whistle, which is more than you can say for Eshkol."

"I remember now," Nick said. "Some spy scandal."

Linda nodded. "Morris Eshkol was a colonel in the Mossad, the Israeli intelligence agency. About ten years ago, when he was on liaison assignment to the CIA, it came out that his real mission was to spy for his own people."

"I thought the Israelis were our pals," David said. Linda and Nick both looked at him. "Well, I can read, for crying out loud," David said.

"We're allied, but that doesn't mean we don't spy on each other," Linda said. "Eshkol was paying off State Department and Agency employees to supply him with information to which he wasn't supposed to be privy."

"You mean he wasn't entirely kosher?"

"That's a good one, Nick," Linda said dryly. "Let me make a note of it." She turned another page. "Eshkol dropped out of sight for a couple of years, then resurfaced as an international arms dealer. As such he made a bushel basket of money. That's one of the two common threads."

Nick sawed into his steak. "First, all four are rich," he said, puzzling it out. "Second, each is rabidly prodemocracy, in the way that always gives me the hives."

"Nuke a commie for Christ," Linda agreed.

David cleared his throat. "What do they want with me?"

"Your powers."

Nick stood abruptly, put his hand on David's shoulder. "We know that this Facility of yours is some kind of clandestine continuation of a sanctioned experiment into mind control, right?"

"Yes."

"We also know that if it is a deep layer in the spookdom setup, it isn't funded through normal channels. So who is funding it?" Nick pointed at Linda's notebook. "I'll give you four guesses."

"You're scaring David," Linda said.

"I'm okay," David said.

"All right then, you're scaring me," Linda snapped.

"You should be scared," Nick said. "Take Eshkol. A guy in his business makes enemies, and David could sniff them out."

"Shit," David said. Neither of them responded to the swearword.

"Tukai wants to take out a competitor," Nick went on, "or maybe win out in a business negotiation. David confuses his opposition. Sister Sarah needs a miracle or two to keep the faithful panting at the bit— write your own scenario."

"Last presidential election Carver made noises about running," Linda said. "I covered the story. The GOP powers that be got him to back down—he was too far off the right end of the spectrum to do anything except split the party. But there are other ways to become president."

"Such as?"

"Next time around he throws his support to the mainstream candidate in exchange for the promise of a cabinet position. He's powerful enough to cut a deal like that. That puts him in the line of succession. If he's named secretary of state, for instance, there are only four warm bodies between him and the Oval Office."

"And with David it's a cinch," Nick picked up. "No evidence, no motive, and no M.O. He gets David within range at a public appearance of his victim, David gives a suicidal impulse, and the goose is cooked."

"He was crazy," David said. "I can sense that too."

The door opened, and Breunner came into the room. His eyes were red-rimmed with recent sleep. "They are all crazy," he said.

"You mean literally?" Linda asked.

"It does not matter." Breunner slumped into an armchair. "Suffice to say that they all remain amenable to Simic's vision."

"Which was?"

Breunner sighed. "Simic was and always had been of the species known as superpatriot. That is, he wished only the best for his nation—and trusted no one but himself to decide what that was. In the mind-control project he saw the instrument of his vision, and so, when it was supposed to be disbanded, he instead turned it into a nonsanctioned covert enterprise."

"I get it," David said slowly, working it out. "It would cost plenty of money, and if the government wouldn't give it to him anymore . . ."

"Exactly," Breunner said. "Simic brought together

what he called a board of directors, people who financed the Facility in furtherance of their common dream."

"And furtherance of their bank balances, I'll bet," Nick said.

"Of course," Breunner said, "but a bit of pious rhetoric has propaganda value in an undertaking of this sort. You see, they are prepared to claim that the situation has become critical. Supposedly our cities are choking with drugs, the media are saturated with obscenity, crime has turned the streets into combat zones. They insist democracy is impotent against such threats."

"What do they plan to do about that?" Nick asked.

Breunner peered at him. "What do you know about coups d'état?"

"That they're impossible in a large industrialized country," Linda said tartly. "You have to cut off the means of supply, isolate the prevailing government and its officials, take over the communications media. How the hell—"

Linda stopped abruptly. Breunner and Nick were gazing at David.

"Simic and his supporters intended to suspend the Constitution and civil liberties, seize manufactories and industries, and enforce a military dictatorship." Breunner rubbed at his eyes wearily.

"Let me get this straight," Nick said. "Simic told these people that if they funded the Facility, he'd pay them back by giving them the country?"

"Yes," Breunner said. "And if they have David, they remain well able to win their goal, even in Simic's absence."

"Not if I can help it." Linda pushed back her chair, took off her reading glasses. "I say we use our knowledge to make them cut it out. It worked with Shaner."

"These guys make Shaner look like a Benedictine

monk under a vow of poverty." Nick pushed his plate aside. "Still, it might fly, if—"

Nick turned, stared hard at Breunner. Breunner paled. "Can you get David back into the Facility?" Nick asked.

Breunner straightened his bent frame. "If we move quickly, while the helm is rudderless."

"I go in behind them," Nick said, "we wipe out its records, then we tell Carver and the rest to drop the project. They try to cheat, David will sense it— and if he does, he'll throw a little something their way, nasty enough to make them toe the line."

Linda's gaze sharpened. "I thought we agreed not to use David that way."

"Have you been talking behind my back?" David said, annoyed.

Neither of them paid attention. "We'd better re-open negotiations on that point," Nick said to Linda. "We can't do it without David's powers, and if we don't shut them down for good, sooner or later we're all three of us dead ducks."

Linda looked helplessly at David. A faint milk mustache clung to the fuzz above his upper lip, and Linda felt the maternal urge to grab a tissue and wipe it away. "I don't much like this, Nick," she said.

"Neither do I," Nick said evenly.

Linda stared up at him for a long moment. She pushed her salad aside, picked up her satchel. "I've got more work," she said unhappily. "I'd better get to it."

Four hours later when Linda returned from her second research foray, she didn't need her sense to perceive the pervasive glumness. David lay on the bed half reading *Treasure Island* and half watching Oprah, the sound turned low. Nick was drinking a beer and paging through that day's *Missoulian*. Breunner sat slumped in a chair, his eyes half-closed.

Linda tossed her satchel on the desk, stood with hands on hips. "What happened to the Valentine's Day cheer?"

"Frieda Kohl is dead." Nick folded the newspaper, passed it to her, indicated an item in the "Montana Briefs" column headlined "Single Vehicle Accident Claims Unknown Woman." Linda scanned it: The victim had been found the previous day in a Ford Bronco that Lake County Search and Rescue personnel had winched out of Flathead Lake after a vehicle-sized hole in the ice had been spotted by a trucker. The condition of the body indicated it had been submerged since approximately ten o'clock the night before. Identification was being withheld pending notification of relatives, which, Linda knew, was police-ese covering a variety of circumstances.

"How do you know it's her?" Linda asked.

"I had a pretty good hunch—the timing, vehicle, and gender all fit. I played cop and called the Lake County Sheriff's Department, got a description."

"It was indeed Frieda," Breunner confirmed. "You understand what that means."

"We never talked about it, but I guess we all knew it was possible," Nick said.

"Talked about what?" Linda said.

"Rogan is alive."

"Wait a minute," Linda said. "What was the official cause of Frieda's death?"

"Drowning," Nick said. "Her lungs were filled with a couple gallons of solid ice."

"No traumatic injuries?"

"Cranial contusion, consistent with banging her noggin on the steering wheel."

"So?" Linda demanded. "She was driving a heavy rig with which she was unfamiliar, on a curvy two-lane blacktop in a near blizzard. She lost control and went into the drink. Where's Rogan come into the picture?"

"For one thing," Nick said, "they didn't find his

body at the Brave Horse house. Or Simic's, for that matter."

"They had to suspect foul play," Linda objected. "The shot-out window in the kitchen, the glass in the driveway, our sudden disappearance—they must have learned Penelope owned the place and asked her if it was tenanted—why didn't they follow up on that?"

On their way to Missoula, they had stopped in Kalispell long enough to call the police. They assumed Rogan had killed Simic before Nick had taken out Rogan, and it might help confirm their story later if both were found and identified.

"The Janitors." Breunner roused himself. "In my association with Simic, I have witnessed occasions when events have . . . not worked out. Simic summoned these people to clean up the mess and quiet any local authorities who might have stumbled upon it."

"Who called this time?"

"The cops who found Simic," Nick said, piecing it out. "When I asked what they found at the house, they got real circumspect."

"Makes sense," Linda nodded. "As Agency, Simic was probably carrying some kind of specialized ID, 'if this man is detained, injured, or killed,' and then a number to call, highest national-security priority, and so on."

"That still leaves Rogan," Nick said.

"Maybe these Janitors handled him as well," Linda said.

"He's alive," Breunner said.

"I shot him in the gut," Nick said.

"I have been reviewing in my mind what I know of Frieda's operative model," Breunner said. "The operation may have affected his recuperative powers—" He cut off, stared at the television.

David was already off the bed and turning up the sound.

On the screen a superimposition reading "Special

Bulletin" was stitched across an anchorwoman's chest. Over her shoulder was a grainy black-and-white insert. The anchorwoman was saying, ". . . security camera at First Federal Security Savings and Loan in Butte. Authorities are at a loss to explain why patrons and tellers suddenly began fighting among themselves during the course of the robbery. Police report three injuries, including one teller whose back was broken when she was struck by a chair wielded not by the robber but by a colleague. Another teller suffered a skull fracture when he inexplicably ran into a wall. Police ask anyone who can identify this man . . ."

David turned off the set.

"Why hasn't he run?" Linda said.

"Maybe he's decided to clean up the loose ends," Nick said woodenly.

"That doesn't figure," Linda said. "He can sense David and me together from lots farther than David can sense him. He's had plenty of time to get us if he meant to."

Breunner sat straighter in his chair. "Maybe he himself does not know what he wants. His mind . . . we have done so much to it."

Linda remembered him in the kitchen of the house, the simmering mad anger that only food could keep tenuously at bay. "We'll have to go to the authorities with what we know," she said.

"We can't," David said.

"I promise we'll find some way to keep you out of it."

"That is not what the boy means," Breunner said. "The model predicted that Rogan would develop the ability to transmit. The deaths of Simic and Kohl suggested the model was correct. This melee at the bank proves it."

"Meaning," Nick said, "that if we cause some cop to confront him, we condemn the guy to death."

"Anyway, I don't want to go through life wondering when he'll pop up," David said.

"You mean to go after him?" Linda glared incredulously at Nick. "You've asked David to kill?"

Nick shook his head. "I'll do the killing."

Linda gestured angrily. "How can you talk about it so casually?"

"I sure as hell don't feel casual." Nick took a long drink of beer. "I killed men in Vietnam, and I hated it then and every day since. But they were trying to kill me, and I didn't have a choice. We don't have a choice now."

Nick dropped his beer can in the wastebasket, stood with his back to them. "All David has to do is what he did back at Brave Horse, distract Rogan long enough for me to take him out."

Linda looked bleakly at David. "Do you want this?"

"No," David said without hesitation. He came over to where Linda sat, faced her. "But Nick's right. It's Rogan or us—us and everyone else he'll hurt—and that's not bull from a movie."

Linda got up and went unsteadily toward the bathroom. She started to close the door, hesitated, came out and faced them, her arms crossed. "Now that I think about it," she said, "I don't see how locking myself in and crying is going to help that much."

Nick went to her, and she let him hold her. After a while she put her arms around him and rested her head on his shoulder. "It's two hours to Butte," she said finally. "We can beat dark if we get started now."

CHAPTER TWENTY-THREE

The clerk squatted on his haunches, his forehead propped on a low shelf beneath the cash register. His arms hung limp with his knuckles brushing the floor, and in one of his palms lay a little twenty-five-caliber five-shooter. Above him on the counter, in the open space between the register on one side and a postcard rack and a jar of beef jerky on the other, a magazine lay open to pictures of a naked woman with her legs spread.

Rogan pawed the page and felt himself thicken. He swept the magazine away, and it fluttered to the floor. He stared down at it absently for a moment, then dug a piece of jerky from the jar, gnawed on the rich salty meat. Coolers lined the convenience store's walls, and racks of shelves ran between, everything too brightly lit by garish neon ceiling fixtures. When he'd finished the jerky, Rogan went around the counter, took the squatting clerk by the shoulder, and flopped him onto his back. The gun fell out of his hand. Rogan left it where it lay. Blood stained the low shelf and the clerk's forehead.

The clerk had said, "Don't do anything stupid," obediently opened the register with a key, and then ignored his own advice, bending to the shelf and taking up the gun. Rogan could sense his aggression as if the counter were transparent, so he leaned over it and hit the clerk on the back of the head with both of his cupped fists. The clerk was dead before his brow struck the shelf; Rogan had felt skull bone crunch under the power of his blow.

On the rear shelf hot dogs rotated on spits in a glass warmer. Rogan couldn't see where it opened, so he punched out the front pane. He plucked two of the franks from the prongs, ate them in four quick bites.

The money from the cash drawer went into the pocket of his nylon windbreaker, all the coat he needed to keep warm despite the winter night's subfreezing temperatures. Beneath the counter he found a brown paper sack. He whipped it open and dumped in the remainder of the jerky, topped it off with lunch meat from the coolers. A woman came in the store's door. Rogan said, "Get the fuck out of here," and she rushed back into the night. He stacked a bunch of six-packs of randomly selected beer in a second sack.

No other business in this place came to mind, so he kicked the door open and took the sacks out to the Land Rover parked by the pumps, where he'd gassed up before entering the store. When he tossed the bags into the rear compartment, one split and spilled a jumble of plastic-collared beer cans across the uncarpeted metal floor. Rogan took two of them and a handful of lunch-meat packets, slammed the rear gate.

He let the rig idle while he popped a can of beer and tore open an envelope of corned beef with his teeth, folded two slices of meat and shoved them in his mouth. He shifted into gear, went past a sign that said, "Leaving Ennis, Fly-Fishing Capital of Montana."

Rogan glanced at the backpack lying in the passenger seat. He'd taken it from a store in Bozeman some hours back, as afternoon turned to twilight. He'd found the Rover in Bozeman too, parked in front of the store. Three days had come and turned to night since the kraut bitch had died, and in that time he'd had plenty of different rigs. People in these parts left keys in ignitions.

Another sign said that West Yellowstone was seventy-one miles down the pike, and Yellowstone National Park West Entrance was seventy-three. This was open country, and few other vehicles passed as he drove on, drinking beer and stuffing down meat. A couple of times he touched at his stomach a few inches above his belly button. The wound there and the exit hole in the small of his back had scabbed up cleanly. It had hurt like hell when the broad's sweetie pie had put the slug in him—gut shots were always a bitch, Rogan knew from experience—but not for long; within five minutes Rogan had made the pain go away.

Five minutes after that he was in the middle of the highway. When the first car appeared, he didn't bother to raise his arms to flag it down. He just made it stop. The driver got out and ran the wrong way in his panic and the darkness and tumbled into the barrow pit. He'd either come around or he'd die from the cold; Rogan left that up to him.

His wound was no longer bleeding when he drove off, and by the time he caught up to Kohl and transmitted her into the lake, he could feel his tissue rebinding and healing. He didn't know if it had to do with his powers, or if he was just a healthy, lucky son of a bitch, and he didn't much care.

The town called West Yellowstone was a little bigger than Ennis, six-by-six blocks, with plenty of motels and places advertising snowmobiles for rent. The buildings on the street at its south edge were fronted by canopied raised boardwalk, like in a Western movie. Rogan parked the rig, pulled on a wool hat to cover his stubbly scalp, and went into a saloon called Greg's Geyser. It was like in a Western too, with the long hardwood bar and worn unpadded stools, round cigarette-burn-scarred tables, a poker game, and a back bar with mirrors and curlicue trim around the booze bottles.

Rogan took a stool next to a guy and a good-looking babe. He gave her the eye for a time, and the guy started to say something and instead lowered his head and spoke softly, then took the babe's arm and drew her away. He left half a mug of beer, so Rogan finished it. The bartender came over, a big guy in biker colors, with long hair and an earring. He pointed at the mug in Rogan's hand and said, "You just grazing, or you want to buy something?"

Rogan ordered a beer and a shot and didn't get mad. The bartender brought his drinks and picked up the fiver Rogan placed on the bar. When he returned with Rogan's change, he said, "No offense meant." Rogan lit a cigarette and pointed to a two-gallon jar on the back bar that was filled with lumps floating in a milky liquid. "What're them?"

"Pickled turkey gizzards."

"Gimme a half dozen," Rogan said. " 'Nother shot." He stayed in the saloon until it closed, drinking steadily and eating half the jar of gizzards.

The motel clerk was a good-looking blond in a bulky sweater and stretch ski pants. "You work all night?" Rogan said as he put some name on the registration card.

"Until eight in the morning." She smiled, but she was scared.

He took the meat and a couple of the six-packs up to the room, turned on the television. He wasn't drunk, and not particularly tired; he didn't need much sleep as long as he kept himself fed. A few stations were still on the cable, so he cranked the dial until he got some old movie, turned down the sound, lay back on the bed, and put his boots up on the spread.

Time passed. He skinned off the wool hat and touched at his head, the two spots that gave spongily where the skin was stretched over the holes they had drilled in his skull. He reached for more food, and its weight in his stomach tamped the anger down.

With his head clear he wondered as he had each time he'd managed to feed himself into clarity why he had not put more distance between him and Montana. Simic was dead, and he had his revenge on the Kohl bitch. Without them Breunner was a dickless old fart. He didn't much have to worry about the kid or his sidekicks, either. Even if they talked, anytime he wanted to, he could return to his old foreign stomping grounds and take up where he'd left off. Besides, here or anywhere else no one could touch him.

With the discovery that he could transmit, born of his survival instinct and his hatred of Simic, had come the recognition of his other powers. Nobody could sneak up on him; he'd sense 'em and zap 'em before they got close.

But even though rationality told him he was safe to do what he goddamned wanted, instinct nagged that first he should tie off the loose ends. He'd needed food and money, sure, but that wasn't the main reason he'd been ripping off places and greasing assholes.

They knew he was alive and were following. Meanwhile he was sending what shrinks called mixed messages. He moved on, running when his stomach was full but not going anywhere, yet stopping to draw them on when the hunger possessed him. . . .

"Jesus Christ," Rogan said aloud. He stared at the television and went on eating and drinking, the meat and beer mixing and cooking in his belly and the warmth illuminating his brain. He didn't really want to kill the kid, and if he did, he'd have to do the others as well. There was still time to change his mind and get out. He remembered a beach on the Thailand panhandle near where it bordered on Malaysia, with babes, brown chicks and white. Maybe there he could make himself get better.

He slept lightly and dreamed continually, and all

the while his sense was as alert as animal instinct; it was like his brain was sleeping with one eye open. As dream dissolved into dream, he saw the boy and the woman with him, in snow and dark and not near, but not far away either.

Rogan awoke with a hard-on and full sensing. They *were* somewhere within range. His gut rumbled.

He could beat the kid now; he could give pain and fright and death. Pick a spot, he thought. Pick a spot and get it done.

He ate what was left of the lunch meat and finished the beer, but it was not enough. Dawn was two hours away, and they had settled in. He smoked a cigarette, and after a while the issue resolved.

He'd make the boy come and in the morning lead him to where cold and weariness and most of all his strength would finish the kid once and for all. He dozed back into sleep, and this time his dream took him to the motel's lobby, the money in the cash register, the good-looking woman and her fear. . . .

David sat up in the folding cot and said, "Nick, what's wrong?"

Nick paused in the act of pulling on his pants, tried to hop on one leg to regain his balance, failed, and sat down hard on the bed. "I need some fresh air."

David frowned into the darkness at the lie.

"Go back to sleep," Nick said. He got into his pants, stood, and put his parka on over his bare chest. In the folding cot Dr. Breunner rolled over and snuffled out a sinusy snore.

The motel-room door opened to admit cold air and indirect street light that was eclipsed by Nick's bulk before the door shut again. David stayed still for a few moments, then crawled from the cot and went to the window. He crouched beneath it, shivering in his underwear, and pushed the curtain aside a crack. After peering out for a few moments he sighed and let the curtain drop back into place. The cold got to him then, so he returned to the bed and snuggled under its covers.

"I'm scared," Linda said. "I'm scared for me and you, and most of all I'm scared for David. I'm scared sick for David."

Nick stared up through the falling snow at the motel's sign: The place was called the Rainbow, and the logo was a neon arc-backed trout, the lighting animated so its tail waggled up and down. "Yesterday was a long day," Nick said. They had driven nearly three hundred miles and hadn't gotten to bed until after midnight. "You should be tired."

"I couldn't sleep," Linda snapped. "Can you?"

"No," Nick said gently, "as you may have noticed."

She wore her parka over a nightdress whose hems brushed the snow that once more had begun to flurry down. "I don't care anymore who got whom into what," she said softly. "None of this is David's fault, including my involvement—or yours."

"I never thought it was." Nick cleared his throat, said lightly, "If you want out, freezing to death would be one way."

"Come on." Linda took his hand.

Nick unzipped his coat and sat on her rumpled bed while she put coffee on the minipercolator. Rogan had killed three more people, in Whitehall and Three Forks and the previous evening here in Ennis. Each killing was associated with a robbery, and to the first two there were witnesses. The one in Whitehall ID'ed Rogan from the police book as a convicted rapist who had escaped from the state prison in Deer Lodge a week before. In Three Forks a customer present in the bar Rogan had ransacked was certain he was a short fat man. The very fact of the confused descriptions confirmed they were on his tail.

Linda filled two Styrofoam cups and brought one over to Nick. "It's de-caf," she said.

"De-caf is fine." Nick watched her return to the desk and rummage in her suitcase, come up with a pint bottle of Jim Beam. "You want a little jolt in that?" she offered.

"Sure." Nick smiled as she poured. "You haven't started hitting the bottle on the sly, have you?"

Linda splashed some bourbon in his cup. "You think anyone would blame me?"

Nick sipped at the hot, slightly sweet drink. "We'll get him. Rogan isn't bullet proof."

She sat down at the head of the bed, drew her legs up under the nightgown. "You make it sound simple."

"Maybe it will be."

"God I hope so. I'd feel so guilty if—" She cut herself off, buried her nose in her drink again.

"I'll be with him."

"I've lost enough people I love."

"So have I," Nick said carefully.

Linda peered at him over the rim of her cup, set it aside on the night table. "I'm warm again," she said. She unzipped the parka.

"Linda?"

"What?"

"I think I'm going to kiss you." Nick moved up on the bed beside her.

Linda shrugged out of the parka, put a hand against his bare chest. "I think I'm going to let you," she murmured.

Nick tumbled from the bed, fell automatically to a one-knee crouch, grappled at the night table, and swore. The gun was on the night table all right—in the room next door. The door rattled again with the pounding of a fist. Linda sat upright in the bed, clutched the sheet to her breasts. Faint daylight leaked around the edges of the window curtains as sleep cleared from Nick's mind.

"Mr. Delvecchio, Miss Gaylen, please." It was Breunner.

"Shit," Nick said.

Linda got up, went to the chair where her robe was draped. "You look good," she said languidly.

Nick retrieved his pants, pulled them on. "You don't look so bad yourself." As Linda fastened the robe, Breunner banged on the door once more. Linda came over and kissed Nick on the lips. "Better let him in," she said.

Nick unlocked the door, and Breunner pushed through. He wore trousers and a sleeveless undershirt, and his wispy gray hair was whorled and peaked like meringue. "He's gone," he said.

"Jesus," Nick said. "When?"

Breunner looked at his watch. "An hour ago." His accent had thickened.

"Why didn't you stop him?"

"I tried. He put me back to sleep."

Linda took Nick's arm. "What's he doing?"

"Trying to save our asses," Nick said. "Come on."

CHAPTER TWENTY-FOUR

For a dozen mostly straight miles, U.S. 287 cut through flatland range, and then mountains rose and opened, and the road plunged within a deep river-cut canyon. "See that, son?" Elmer Frain said.

From the backseat of the club-cab pickup, David peered obediently out the side window at the massive fall of scree on the slope to the right.

"The seventeenth of August, 1959," Elmer Frain said. "Few minutes before midnight. Gol-damnedest earthquake Montana has ever seen."

"Language, Elmer," the missus said. She was a sweet-faced grandmotherly type in an orange hunting parka, her gray hair done up in braids. Their truck was the first vehicle to emerge from the bleary dawn, a minute or so after David took his place across from the motel in Ennis. He climbed in and thanked them, as if they'd stopped of their own free will. "Name's Elmer Frain," the large-boned cheerful man had said, "and this here's the missus."

Now, as they passed the landslide in the canyon, Elmer Frain winked at David in the rearview mirror. "Whole danged mountain came undone and stopped up the canyon like a cork in a bottle. Plugged the Madison River so solid it made a whole new lake—Earthquake Lake, they call it now. Washed away a bunch of houses and most of the road. You'll see, up ahead, there's drowned trees sticking up out of it."

"Boy," David said, politely impressed.

"So," the missus said carefully, "you heading down to West Yellowstone, are you?"

"Is that where this road goes?" David asked.

"About the only place it does go," Elmer Frain said. "Oh, I suppose you could continue on, but Targhee Pass is a nightmare this time of year, and there's lots easier ways to get to Idaho Falls. I'd wager most folks on this route are bound for the park to do some beeling."

"Beeling?"

Elmer Frain jerked a thumb over his shoulder to indicate the two snowmobiles riding on the flatbed trailer hitched to the truck. "You never been beeling, son?"

David was silent for a moment. The flash of sense he'd gotten from Rogan had not reoccurred, not since that moment after Nick had left the room and Rogan had bored into his mind, brief but unmistakable. "Can kids do beeling?" he asked Elmer Frain.

"Sure enough. Why hell—" Elmer Frain glanced at the missus, corrected himself. "Heck, I had Elmer, Jr., on a machine soon as he was big enough to reach the handlebars."

"He's a heart doctor now," the missus said. "In Seattle."

"Now don't be bragging," Elmer Frain reproached.

"What are you going to be when you grow up, son?" the missus asked, to change the subject.

"I'm not sure, ma'am," David said. "Something to do with people, I guess. I'm pretty good with people."

It was colder in the mountains, fifteen degrees above zero according to the time-and-temperature sign outside the bank in West Yellowstone, and the sky was a smeary slate promise of storms brewing. The first flurries began to drift down as David reached the Yellowstone Park gate, where the ranger gave him a map and told him to have fun and be careful, then waved him on without paying him much attention. The light snowfall wasn't any bother, and the wind had not come up, but David had spent enough time in Montana by now to know that if it began to storm for real—and it felt like it would—it would blow as well. He was glad for the polypropylene jersey and long johns he'd bought in town, and especially for the wool headmask that, with its eye- and mouth-holes, made him look like a bank robber.

The rented snowmobile wasn't hard to handle once he got the hang of it, and it could hit forty when he opened up the hand throttle on the straightaways. It would have been fun if he hadn't been preoccupied with sobering thoughts.

That Rogan had become so much more powerful—that he seemingly could reach out to him at will—scared the hell out of him, no two ways about it; still, he had to believe he could beat the man. But in the end it was a showdown like in some Western movie, and whoever was quicker and stood his ground would walk away.

The other would die.

Rogan deserved death; he had killed Dr. Kohl and Mr. Simic and all those strangers and meant to do the same to David, Nick, Linda, and who knew how many others. Nor could anyone get close enough to stop him, especially Nick—and David cared for the guy too much to let him try.

But David could, because Rogan was letting him. David had been sensing him for the past three hours, ever since he'd arrived in West Yellowstone.

The sense was faint though unmistakable; Rogan was dangling it like a lure in front of a trout.

The bulk of a snow coach appeared up ahead, and David slowed. The road straightened past a curve, and the driver's arm appeared out the window and waved him on. As David went past the blocky vehicle—it was like a bus with treads instead of wheels—he saw people through the foggy windows. One of them waved, a boy about David's age, looking envious of David's more rakish mode of transport. David waved back. Cross-country skis were racked on the roof, and the sign above the windshield said it was going to Old Faithful Lodge.

David accelerated along the snow-packed road. One possible edge was that the madness driving Rogan was tainted by his nature; even sane, he was a man of violence and evil. David on the other hand felt no emotion beyond the fear he was managing to keep in check, along with a vague sadness at being forced to do this. Even if in an odd, sick way he and Rogan were brothers, the fact that he was on the side of good might be the winning factor; it worked that way in the movies, anyway.

It was near noon when he reached the fork at what a sign called Madison Junction. David pulled over, worked off his gloves and the ski mask, and got the map from the pocket of his parka. The right-hand turn, which from the trampled condition of the snow saw most of the traffic, went to Old Faithful. Fourteen miles up to the left was another junction called Norris.

A green two-person treaded vehicle with the Park Service symbol on the door lumbered to a stop. A ranger slid down the window, stuck his head out, and said, "Need any help, son?" Before David could answer, the ranger pointed and whispered urgently, "Look there!"

In a meadow above the riverbank were a huge bull moose with a great spread of flat antler blade, a cow only slightly smaller, and a juvenile. They were tearing boughs off a cottonwood and chewing contentedly.

"Mom and Dad and Junior," the ranger said.

"They're something," David acknowledged. The moose ambled off, the bull in the lead.

The ranger studied David. "You're not out here alone, are you, son?"

"My folks are back there somewhere." He put on a sheepish kid's grin. "I like to go faster than them."

"Don't get too far ahead," the ranger said. "Looks like it's fixing to storm."

"No, sir," David said. "I'll be real careful."

The ranger tipped two fingers to his brow and drove off, working the steering levers. David watched until he was out of sight, then sat waiting, his mind open. Behind him branches crackled as the moose plunged into the brush.

The sense of Rogan simmered and bloomed.

David tensed, stared up the road toward Norris. Rogan was beckoning: *Here I am, kid, come and get me if you can.* David could almost hear the words.

The time had come. David gunned the snowmobile and turned left, feeling more than anything an anticipatory excitement. As he advanced, the strength of the sense remained the same, as if Rogan were modulating it, teasing at him in case he got cold feet.

David worked the throttle, shot down the snow-paved road.

There was no time to be subtle or polite, so when the clerk at the Rent-All smiled and said, " 'Fraid not, friend," Linda snapped, "He's lying."

Nick took a fifty-dollar bill from his wallet, smiled. "Maybe you forgot."

The clerk was a prematurely balding kid in a bulky turtleneck. "I'm not supposed to rent to anyone under eighteen. Insurance regulation."

"You don't have to worry about us."

The clerk looked at the money and licked his lips. "Okay, I guess he was in here. I rented him an Arctic

Cat." The money disappeared into the pocket of his wool pants.

"He slipped you a little extra?" Nick asked.

"Uh-uh." The clerk shook his head, puzzled. "Now that I think about it, it was the damnedest thing. He said it'd be all right, and I just had the feeling it would. I never broke the rules before—I got a five-year-old boy and a wife that ran off with an Amway salesman from Glendive. I need this job." The clerk shook his head. "Still, it sure does beat all, don't it?"

"Did you rent to anyone else this morning?" Linda asked. They'd already tried three other places. Linda described Rogan.

"About an hour before your boy," the clerk confirmed.

"Were both of them going into the park?"

"About the only place you can go from here."

"I suppose there are a lot of different trails."

The clerk shook his head. "Off road is out of bounds, so the wildlife don't get hassled; they're real fragile in the winter."

The clerk indicated a spot on the map of the park taped to the underside of the counter's glass. "From here to Madison Junction and then on to Old Faithful is always open because the snow coaches keep it tromped down. If he went that way, he might be able to get a few miles past the geyser, but once the road starts to climb toward Craig Pass, it closes out. The machines bog down in deep snow, and on the Divide we're talking twenty, thirty feet."

The clerk traced his finger in the other direction from Madison. "Most beelers kind of look down on the ski folk and shy away from Old Faithful, enough of 'em so the Norris road is passable. Beyond Norris depends on the snowfall, and this year there's been plenty. So there ain't too many places he could have gotten to, and only one way out."

"I want to rent a machine," Nick said.

The clerk glanced at Linda. "Just the one?"

"That's right."

Linda took Nick's arm, not gently. "Dear," she said, with forced sweetness, "may I have a word with you?"

Linda steered Nick past air compressors, power tools, shop vacs, and Roto Tillers to the front window. The car was parked at the curb, Breunner slumped in the backseat staring at nothing. "This time I'm going with you," Linda said in a low, hard voice.

"There's nothing you can do."

"I love you, and I love David, and I'm going."

The clerk cleared his throat. "You can ride double on one of them machines, if driving her own is what's troubling the lady."

Neither of them looked in his direction. "You like to get your way," Nick said lightly. "That's something to know."

"Oh Jesus, Nick," Linda sighed.

Nick allowed himself to laugh. "Come on," he said.

Nick jerked up the emergency brake and swiveled around to face Breunner in the backseat. "I'd strongly advise you not to run, Doctor," Nick said.

"Where would I go?"

"Hold that thought." Nick got out, opened the door for Breunner. "This won't take a minute," Nick said to Linda.

She watched Nick lead Breunner into the motel's front office. She had passed most of the morning fighting consuming guilt, with little success. Intellectually she knew that letting Nick into her bed while David gave them the slip was irrelevant; he had the power to escape anytime he wished, and the two events were unrelated. But emotionally she could not shake the feeling that she'd let him down.

The woman at the front desk of the hotel in Ennis had remarked David's departure, because she wondered where he could be going at such an early hour and, having seen him arrive the night before with Nick and Linda, was doubly surprised to watch him cross the highway and hitchhike the southbound lane. He was picked up by the first rig that came by, she told them.

Now Linda was pleased to see Nick returning to the rig alone; she was anxious to get back to the Rent-All, pick up the snowmobile, and start into the park. But when he got in, his face was drawn and pale. "The night clerk," Nick said. "Young woman."

"What about her?"

"A guest came down at seven for a cup of complimentary coffee and found her dead."

"Murdered?"

"Yeah, but not so anyone except you and me would know it. She opened her wrists with an Exacto knife."

"Oh Jesus." Linda massaged the bridge of her nose. "Rogan."

"Sure." Nick put the key in the ignition. "You scared?"

"Of course."

"Me too." Nick started the rig, backed out. "Scared enough I'm glad I won't be going into this alone," he said.

CHAPTER TWENTY-FIVE

Rogan tore a bite from a steak-sized sheet of jerked beef, chewed it to pulp, and swallowed; in the last hour he'd eaten a pound and a half of the dried meat and only barely managed to keep the hunger at bay. Snow whipped hard into his face, but he felt no cold. In the bottom of the backpack he found a Snickers and one Bud. He stripped off the candy wrapper and stuffed the bar in his mouth, drained the beer in one long, gulping draft, and flung the can into the snow-shrouded dimness.

Four people on snow machines had been hanging around the parking lot when he'd arrived, so he made them leave. He didn't hurt them much; he was saving it for the kid.

The beer left him thirsty. He went across the lot to one of the pools. The water was hot enough to burn, but he ignored it, cupped a handful until it cooled, and then guzzled it down. It tasted of minerals and smelled of rotten eggs, but it slaked the thirst for the moment.

The kid was near and moving closer. Rogan transmitted a quick bolt of pain, the image of a drill cutting through skull bone. Just as quickly he let it go, afraid he'd drive the kid away.

He was out of food, but that was no accident. He wanted the hunger now, and the unambiguous anger that came with it and, like a battery pack, boosted the transmission. "Come on," he said aloud, feeling good and pissed off.

Standing in the shadow of a fir, David felt the invasion of pain and pushed it aside. It wasn't difficult, and that gave him encouragement. The snow machine was down the road a ways; for the past little while, he'd been advancing on foot, his sense on full alert. Now Rogan was within his range, no more than a couple hundred yards distant—and so far Rogan had not been able to touch him in any way that counted.

David sensed his anger and knew it could work for him. Control was important, and the less Rogan had, the better. He tried not to think about having the anger focused on him.

It might be a good idea to hold back for a while longer, give it a chance to grow. But maybe that was just cold feet, and besides, Rogan could as easily come out after him—

David knew all of a sudden that the luxury of choice and timing had been taken from him. The wind carried off his muttered curse.

Linda was coming.

Nick was with her, but that didn't matter, because the moment Rogan stopped concentrating on him and sensed them, they would be dead.

David bolted out from under the tree and ran up the road, stumbled, untangled his feet, and ran on. He was weaving and trying to keep his balance while his fingertips touched at his temples through the wool mask, because as he ran, he was transmitting with all his might.

Something . . . Rogan thought, and then the notion went away, because the kid was coming. He jammed but did not transmit, felt the jam strike the kid's own transmission.

Rogan moved away from the snowmobile until

his boot soles struck the wood of the boardwalk and his hand touched the rail. Smelly steam rose around him as he backed out over the scalded earth. He put every ounce of mental strength into the jam, and the transmission began to lift like the steam.

David paused at the entrance to the parking lot, reformed the transmission, and turned it toward Linda and Nick. It was negation, pure and simple, the burning image of one word giantly written: *DON'T*.

From ahead Rogan stabbed out at him. David fell, drew his knees to his chest. Above him was a solid slab of thick metal, descending inexorably.

He could not do it, a part of his mind screamed out. He could not split his power to touch Nick and Linda without dropping his guard against Rogan. He let them go, kept his fetal position, and drew from the point in his mind a heart—Rogan's heart—pumping faster and faster, red and shiny, too fast not to burst.

The slab above him went away, but the transmission was blunted; the heart image was replaced with the slab, and David's stream of image pounded into it like a fire hose hitting a wall and washing away to either side.

"Come on, kid!"

At first David thought it was another transmission, but then he realized Rogan had suspended the image and was speaking aloud. "Let's do this like men," Rogan hollered. "You let it go, and I will too."

David did as Rogan said. The only sense still tingling was of Linda, like a whiff of her perfume.

A sign at the far end of the parking lot said this was Norris Geyser Basin, and beneath it an arrow pointed to the Self-guided Tour of Thermodynamic Phenomena, cautioning visitors to stay on the boardwalk at all times. In the arrow's direction warm, drifting vapor obscured the landscape.

Within it was Rogan. David moved forward into the mist.

The boardwalk loomed, and David stepped up onto it. To either side pools burbled hellishly. Some were watery, others thick mud. Still others were crusted over so they looked solid-surfaced. The ground near the pools was bare of snow and plants, except for a slimy-looking bright green moss, and the boardwalk's rail was moist as David slid his hand along it. He went around a corner. Inside the choking rotten-egg-flavored mist, it was warm as a spring day.

Wind gusted and blew snow that melted instantly as it touched the boardwalk's wood. The mist whipped off across the alien landscape, and ahead David saw Rogan.

He was standing where the boardwalk dead-ended in an observation platform above one of the bubbling hot-pots, his back to the U of the rail. He had changed: His mouth was twisted in an angry grimace, his skin wattled and lumpy, and his eyes tight and small and red.

"I know they're here," Rogan said. His voice grated. "If you try to touch me—" Rogan laughed. "You know what I mean."

David sensed.

Rogan laughed again. "Yeah, they're coming closer, not that it matters. Dumb, huh?"

"What do you want?" David said.

"I got no choice anymore, kid." Rogan looked at him oddly. "I'll do it quick."

Linda's sense loomed closer. "And them?" David said.

Rogan turned his hands palm up. "What do you figure?" He shook his head, as if trying to clear his mind. "Time's up, kid," he said. "Come here or else. You won't like the or-else."

David brought up the heart and made it pump insanely, the red muscle pounding and jerking arrhythmically, threatening to tear loose from the muscle mooring it, and—

White pain exploded in his head, and he pitched face forward onto the boardwalk.

Against the background of the whiteness, he saw himself where he lay on the wooden slats and knew the way to end the pain. He stood and leaned over the rail and looked down into one of the pots. It boiled furiously, and even at the distance of six feet, the heat burned at the skin of his face. He pressed his stomach against the railing. He could pitch his weight over it and descend into the caldron, and there would be other pain for a moment, but it could not possibly be worse than the white pain, and then all the pain would be gone forever.

David screamed, *"No!"*

He was still lying on the boardwalk. Rogan stood above him, his ugly face screwed in concentration. Steam haloed around him, and David heard the noise of the roiling pots. David fought the picture of himself within one of them, but it fought back, and he felt the water boiling him alive and himself embracing the release of it, but—

It was not real.

Someone else came into his mind—Linda, her powers allied with his. He coupled with her and took the image for his own, threw the seething water back at Rogan.

Rogan stumbled, steadied himself against the rail, but David was released and made it to hands and knees. Nick cried out, "David! Stay down!" and a shot rang out.

Rogan swatted at his shoulder as if shooing a fly. His boot lashed out, and David rolled away, but Rogan caught him in the ribs anyway, and pain spasmed through David's torso. Nick fired again, but he must have missed, because Rogan bent and grabbed David by the wrist, yanked David toward him. Nick fired twice more, and David thought he heard one of the bullets thump into Rogan. Rogan hugged David to his chest, and behind them Nick swore.

But Linda was still with him, and together they kept Rogan's transmission at bay. David kicked out one of his dangling feet and caught Rogan in the stomach, kicked again.

Rogan let him drop but held onto his wrist, jerked, and David slid under the railing and off the boardwalk's edge. He clawed with his free hand, but it slithered off the steam-greased planking, and he could not get purchase. His boot splashed through the hot pool's surface. He felt its heat sting through his pants.

"Like you saw, kid." Rogan's face was close to his. "Boil in hell."

His anger washed over David in ripping waves, but Rogan was no longer transmitting, could not concentrate even on the jam.

Somewhere in the recesses of his powers, David sensed the moment before Rogan let go. David lunged, got his hand around the railing, held on with all his strength, and with Linda forced the water to consume Rogan.

Above him Rogan caterwauled insanely, threw himself against the rail, and tumbled over David into the pool. Water splashed up to sear at David's legs. He held on. Rogan screamed, and a hand closed around David's ankle, dragged him down. David kicked, and Rogan let go.

Then there were other hands around David's wrists, and Nick's voice saying, "Let go of the rail." David didn't want to, but he did, and the hands drew him up, and he was standing on the boardwalk once again.

Linda said, "Oh God," and he was within her arms and pressed against her.

"Please," David got out.

She didn't understand, held him in a frantic embrace, and he had to struggle to break free. Rogan's hands were visible for a moment above the pool's surface, and then they sank, burning redly.

"He's dead, David," Nick said. He was standing beside him, his hand on David's shoulder.

"No," David said. "Linda, you can sense, he's—"

Rogan came out of the water like a geyser erupting.

David gave the white pain, and Rogan's body arced like a bow. Nick fired twice more, and David turned up the pain to a feverish, burning heat. Rogan's hand closed around the edge of the boardwalk. Nick knelt, placed the muzzle of the gun within inches of Rogan's forehead. Rogan hollered madly, and the gun went off. Rogan fell away, arms flailing. Boiling water sluiced over the wood planks, drained between the cracks. Below them the pot bubbled and then calmed.

David felt his legs buckle, arms catching at him.

Some time afterward, above the noise of the snowmobile, David heard Linda say, "Is he all right?" and Nick answer, "He's all right." A while later she said it again, got the same response. The third time David was in bed. His ribs hurt where they were taped up, and he was getting tired of hearing Linda say it over and over, so he opened his eyes and said, "I'm all right."

Linda held him. She smelled of sweat and wet wool and perfume and felt warm and alive. She was sending off so much emotion that he couldn't sort it out, didn't have the energy to try, so he said, "I'm going to sleep now," and did.

CHAPTER TWENTY-SIX

"**S**o how's school?" Linda said.

"Over." David picked up a fistful of beach sand, contemplated Linda's bare back.

Linda turned her head, recradled it on her folded arms, and gave him a look. "Don't you dare."

David let the sand dribble between his fingers. "It finished while you were out of town. How did it go?"

She'd been away for a week, returning the previous evening as Nick was leaving to do location security for a production company that was shooting in Marin County. Linda missed him, but she didn't mind the time alone with David.

"Tukai turned out to be the toughest," she said. "To get in to see, I mean. I had to stake out his house outside Tokyo. You ever try to bribe a gardener through an interpreter?"

David pretended to consider. "No," he said finally. "I don't believe I have."

"Anyway, once I explained in so many words that we had the goods on him, he saw the handwriting on the wall, just like the others." She had already made her visits to Carver, Sister Sarah, and Eshkol, and after a certain amount of persuasive threatening, each had realized that they were lucky to be rid of the Facility and its purpose. "Tukai did try to bluster," Linda said. "He wanted to know where you were."

"What'd you say?"

"That you were my properly adopted son," Linda said, "and that if he ever got within five hundred miles, you'd make him wish he hadn't."

"Thanks a lot."

"Well, it worked."

David sat up on the blanket. It was a pretty June Saturday, but Will Rogers State Beach upcoast from Santa Monica stretched for over a mile, and all the sunbathers had plenty of room to themselves. A few surfers were riding the two-foot waves that curled into the foam-frosted, hard-packed sand at water's edge. "So it's okay," David said.

"It's okay," Linda said firmly.

"I talked to Gavin Reed," David said. "He's a nice guy. Someday I'd like to be able to tell him the whole story."

"Maybe someday you can."

David pulled over the cooler, got out a Coke, and offered it to Linda. She shook her head, so he popped the top and took a swig. "I still think about Dr. Breunner sometimes. I can't really hate him."

"I think that's for the best," Linda said.

The confrontation with Rogan had taken its toll. David's bruised ribs healed quickly, but emotionally he felt emptied for the better part of a week. He slept a lot, and for a time he almost believed—in fact, hoped—that his abilities had left him. It turned out they had not—he could still sense and transmit as facilely as ever, and in the end that was a good thing. There was one more loose end to be tied off.

The Facility turned out to be located on a vast expanse of featureless desert on the Kaiparowits Plateau in Utah, not far north of the Arizona line. Breunner led them there over rutted jeep trails. The guards remained, like Japanese soldiers holed up on some Pacific island unaware the war was over.

This war was. David went in first and gave them

sleep long enough for Breunner to follow and drug them so David could concentrate on the job at hand.

Erasing the data in the Facility's computers wasn't enough; there were programs that could recover deleted files. David and Breunner unscrewed the back of each machine, slid out the chassis, and carried them outside, where Nick put a half clip from the guards' M-16s into each of the computers' innards, taking particular care to chew up the hard disk where the bulk of the data was stored.

After that they raided the Facility's motor pool for jerricans of gasoline and went from office to office, emptying filing cabinets, floppy-disk cases, and the contents of desk drawers into piles in the middle of each room. When they left, the gleam of bonfires glowed eerily from the building's windows, and glass blew out as they drove away.

They reached Flagstaff late and got tickets for the six A.M. flight to Los Angeles. The next morning Breunner rose from the table at the café where they were having breakfast and said, "Excuse me, please." David figured he was just going to the bathroom, but then Breunner looked at him strangely and said it again, more urgently.

Two minutes later David said, "Oh shit." The waitress couldn't find the spare key, so Nick had to break down the bathroom door. Breunner was on the floor, wedged behind the toilet, a prescription vial clutched in his already-stiffening fingers. The vial was empty; its label said it was "for relief of depression." Breunner carried no identification, and Nick told the police they'd picked him up hitchhiking.

On the sun-warmed beach, Linda said, "What do you say we talk about something a little more cheery?" She shifted languidly on the blanket. "Yoo-hoo," she said.

David ignored her, went on watching two high-school-age girls in bikinis as they sashayed past.

"School," Linda reminded him.

"School was good, actually," David said. "I never thought I'd say that, but live and learn. I made friends with some neat guys."

"Good for you."

David looked her over. She was lying on her stomach, the straps of her bathing-suit top undone so as not to mar her tan. "I learned this trick."

"I can't wait," Linda said.

"See, you find a girl on the beach like you are, only she's asleep," David said enthusiastically. "So you come up, and you put your foot on her suit, it's lying loose like yours is, and then you pour cold water on her back. She jumps up, and . . ."

Linda smiled. "And what?"

David looked like he wished he had not started in on this. "You see her hooters."

"*Hooters?*" Linda said.

David buried his nose in his Coke. "Well, you get the idea."

"I certainly do," Linda said.

David looked away. "You going to marry Nick?"

"Think I should?"

David shrugged. "He's a pretty good guy. I mean, he saved my life and all."

"Well then, that settles it. I'll propose as soon as he gets back."

David gave her a long look. "That'd be nice," he said with utter sincerity.

Linda reached behind her. David turned discreetly as she awkwardly did up her bathing suit. She felt an overwhelming, almost unbearable rush of affection for him. "You know something, kid?"

"What?"

"I love the hell out of you."

"I love you too," David said happily.

"Wait a minute." Linda frowned at him, contemplated the depth of her feeling. "Was that me or you?" she said skeptically.

David threw his arms around her and grinned. "That was you," he said.

Bantam Spectra Horror
because every spectrum is shadowed by the colors of the night...

☐ **The Demon by Jeffrey Sackett**
   (28596-3 * $4.50/$5.50 in Canada)
   An ex-sideshow geek moves into a small New York town, and on his heels follows a string of hideous murders.

☐ **The Horror Club by Mark Morris**
   (28933-0 * $4.95/$5.95 in Canada)
   Three young horror fans learn the true meaning of fear when they invite a new boy into their club who unleashes upon their hometown a terrifying, consuming evil.

☐ **The Amulet by A.R. Morlan**
   (28908-X * $4.95/$5.95 in Canada)
   Set in a quiet Wisconsin town, this is the chilling story of a woman's desperate struggle against the terrible power of a talisman which controls and changes the people around her.

☐ **House Haunted by Al Sarrantonio**
   (29148-7 * $4.50/$5.50 in Canada)
   Five people are seduced into a sinister web of madness, murder and supernatural confrontation by a powerful spirit who longs for a doorway into the physical world.

☐ **The Well by Michael B. Sirota**
   (28843-1 * $4.50/$5.50 in Canada)
   A man returns to his ancestral home only to reawaken the ancient blood curse that haunts his family line.

Look for these bloodcurdling new titles on sale now wherever Bantam
Spectra Books are sold, or use this page for ordering:

Bantam Books, Dept. SF103   414 East Golf Road, Des Plaines, IL 60016

Please send me the items I have checked above. I am enclosing $_____
(please add $2.50 to cover postage and handling). Send check or money order;
no cash or C.O.D.s please.

Mr./Ms._____

Address_____

City/State_____ Zip_____

Please allow four to six weeks for delivery.
Prices and availability subject to change without notice.

SF103 -- 6/91